LOOP

LOOP

KAREN AKINS

ST. MARTIN'S GRIFFIN
NEW YORK

LOOP. Copyright © 2014 by Karen Akins. All rights reserved. Printed in the United States of America. For information, address St. Martin's Press, 175 Fifth Avenue, New York, N.Y. 10010.

www.stmartins.com

The Library of Congress Cataloging-in-Publication Data is available upon request.

ISBN 978-1-250-03098-6 (hardcover)
ISBN 978-1-250-03099-3 (e-book)

St. Martin's Griffin books may be purchased for educational, business, or promotional use. For information on bulk purchases, please contact Macmillan Corporate and Premium Sales Department at 1-800-221-7945, extension 5442, or write specialmarkets@macmillan.com.

First Edition: October 2014

10 9 8 7 6 5 4 3 2 1

*To Bill, for doing everything in his power
to bring this book to life
and
to Henry and Oliver, for doing everything
in their power to prevent it.*

In Memory of Tim Berry

acknowledgments

Thank you so much to everyone at St. Martin's—I still pinch myself every time I look at the cover. A special thanks to my fabulous editor, Holly Ingraham, who seamlessly wove *Loop* into her list. Thanks also to Jeanne-Marie Hudson, Marie Estrada, Bridget Hartzler, Kerry McMahon, and the rest of the SMP team. And, of course, Terra Layton, who was *Loop*'s first champion—*xie xie*!

My agent, Victoria Marini, is the best possible combination of a firecracker and a bulldog. I'm so grateful for her vision for *Loop*—she helped make it shine before finding its home.

Word Nerds, I love you guys so much. This book wouldn't exist without you. Kristin Gray, Kim Loth, and Unicorn Sparklepants, *ahem,* I mean Mandy Silberstein, you are the best!

I have been beyond blessed with the most amazing critique partners *ever*: Elizabeth Briggs, Evelyn Ehrlich, I. W. Gregorio, Rachel Searles. You keep me on my toes and talk me off of cliffs.

Early readers and along-the-way cheerleaders, *thank you*: Abby Annis, Jenny Benson, Britain Castagna, Jessica Castagna, Rachel Cobb, Megan Daniel, Sara Ford, Anna Hagen, Erika Hagen, Melissa Hurst, Shelli Jones, Ashley Keylor, Kate Lacy, Stacey Lee, Emily Moore, Tracey Neithercott, Jonna Nixon, Eoghan O'Donnell, Amy Oliver, Cortney Pearson, Lora Scott, Morgan Shamy, Angela Story, Serra Swift, Dana Tomlin, Hannah Tomlin, Jenna Wallace, and Abigail Wen. Kelly Butterweck and Ashley Seat, thanks for loving on my kiddos. You two *never* forget to be awesome!

A big ol' thanks to: Authoress and the MSFV Sort-of-Secret Society, The Lucky 13s, SCBWI, my Woodway gals, and all the family and friends who have supported me along the way. I wish I had ten pages to thank you all by name!

Thank you to my parents, Carl and Connie Hoffman, who never made me turn off the reading lamp. To my sisters, Ellen Matkowski and Sara Hoffman, for listening to my stories long before anyone else wanted to. And to my whole family: Bill and Betty Akins, Carolyn Wagnon, Mark and Julie King, Owen and Myles, Anna and Noah, and all the Hoffmans and Wings. I love you all!

Henry and Oliver, I love you more than all the words in the world. Okay. You can go back to destroying the living room now.

Bill, *thank you* isn't strong enough. From the moment I admitted my secret dream of being a writer, you have cheered me on, read my words, and listened to every squee and whine and dream. Your support has been legen— (Wait for it.)

And to the One who whispers truth when I'm tempted to believe lies, *thank you*.

The only reason for time is so that everything doesn't happen at once.—ALBERT EINSTEIN

LOOP

chapter 1

HITTING THE GROUND is the hardest part. Nine times out of ten, it's dirt or grass. But all it takes is that one time on concrete or, worse, asphalt to send even the most experienced Shifter into a panic.

My feet slammed into cobblestone. Muskets cracked and echoed down the alley where I'd landed. Acrid gunpowder stung my nostrils, searing my throat as I fought back a cough and crouched down. The gunfire grew louder and louder, bouncing off both sides of the narrow passageway, so I couldn't tell which direction it was coming from.

Where was I? Valley Freakin' Forge?

Wyck had missed the target by well over two centuries! Good grief. How hard was a twenty-third to twenty-first Shift? And of all the Shifts, it would have to be this one. He'd pay for this when I got back. Don't get me wrong. I love a good transporter prank as much as the next girl, but plop me in the middle of Lex and Concord? I am not having that crap.

Puffs of fresh gunsmoke clouded the already-dim alley. *Get it together, Bree.* I slipped behind a barrel and pulled out my QuantCom. A Virginia address and instructions popped up: "Bree Bennis, pre-Tricentennial midterm. Deposit package contents on Muffy van Sloot's grave with following message: 'There's no time like the past.'"

I squeezed the small white box before sliding it into my pocket. I tried not to think about the *other* object, the one hidden in my shoe. Guilt burbled up in my stomach, but I squashed it down.

Hard to believe so much could ride on one trip back to the past.

Also hard to believe any person would name their child Muffy van Sloot. It almost sounded like some rich person's pet.

Boom! The gunfire sounded right outside the alley.

So help me, I thought, *if this is all for a dead cat, heads will roll.*

Dr. Quigley could flunk me for all I cared. Okay, that wasn't even a teensy bit true. I couldn't afford a single red flag on this test. Still, I wasn't taking a musket ball to the head for anyone. But at least I knew which state I was in. Unless Wyck had flubbed that, too.

What I needed was to find somewhere safe to figure out my next move. Without a sound, I pushed myself up and prepared to dash to the street for a better look at the battle. But before I could move, I heard an unexpected sound. A digital beeping. A boy and a girl, not much older than me, had slipped into the alley. The girl held up a mobile phone. "It's Rachel," she said.

"Hey, where were you?" the girl said into the phone. As she talked, the boy caressed the back of her neck. She flicked his hand.

What? I ducked back down and glanced at my Com as it analyzed the phone's ringtone. Early twenty-first century. Right where I was supposed to be. Okay, maybe Wyck wasn't a complete idiot after all.

So what the blark was going on?

"I swear we were at the pub for like twenty minutes. No, not Ye Olde Tavern. Ye Olde Pub," she said. The boy nibbled her ear. She swatted his shoulder.

"Ah, c'mon." He kissed a path of pecks down her neck to her jaw. She hesitated a moment, then turned the phone off.

The fade timer on my Com blipped down second by second. I only had five hours before being pulled back to my own time. Tight for any assignment, but even more so with today's less-than-legal extracurricular activity. With a frantic finger, I tapped the edge of the round, smooth device—perfectly masked as a pocket watch to fit into most eras. *Come on.* It was taking forever to pinpoint my location, and my destination could be hours away. There was no more time to waste. I had to do *something*.

"Hello." I stood up from behind the barrel. The boy and girl jumped apart.

"You sh-sh-should . . . Th-th-this is . . . private," stammered the girl.

"Yeah, nothing says private like a makeout session amid musket fire," I said under my breath as I pushed my way past the lovebirds and stuck my head around the corner of the alleyway.

A sea of scarlet coats, side-holstered drums, and fifes greeted me. Crowds of spectators lined the street. *Ahh, heck.* Duped by a Revolutionary reenactment parade. I checked my fade timer again. I'd lost precious minutes. Then again, I couldn't see my transporter doing something drastic like force fading me as soon as the time limit was up. Not that I would let it come to that.

I'd been rubbing the eyelash of a scar at the base of my skull without even thinking about it. *Enough. Focus.* I flipped my Com to the geolocator. Williamsburg. A good 150 miles from this Chincowhatever place on the other side of Virginia.

Contrary to public opinion, time travel is not an exact science. Whenever I need a good giggle, I'll watch an antique movie where the hero zips back twenty years, mere minutes before an explosion, to save the heroine in the nick of time. Or, for an even bigger laugh, watch one where he Shifts forward to meet his grandkids. *Snort.*

When Shift came to shove, getting me within two days and two hundred miles of my goal wasn't shabby transporting. Not shabby at all. Not that I'd admit it to Wyck's face.

I stepped into the bright street and disappeared into a mob of strollers and camera-wielding dads. I stood on my tiptoes, a necessary measure given my small stature, in search of . . .

Bingo. School buses.

It wasn't like I got extra credit for being frugal on missions. But then again, nobody handed out medals for blowing a big wad of era cash on a three-hour cab ride. A few bonus points for resourcefulness might even push me up a grade if I was teetering on the line. Up until six months ago, I never would have worried about a measly midterm. Then again, there were a lot of things I never would have considered before six months ago.

Temporal smuggling, for one.

Stop it. I had precious little time as it was. And certainly not enough to waste on a squeaky conscience. Everything had to appear completely normal on this assignment or I could get caught.

I jogged across the street, into the sea of buses. Up and down the rows, I searched. Blark, there were a lot of them.

"Come on, come on, come on." I raced down the final row and let out a sigh of relief. The last block of buses said "Accomack County School District," my destination. I staked out a hiding spot near them, behind an old oak.

A swarm of elementary kids clambered past. Too bad I couldn't hop on their bus. I was short for sixteen, but I wasn't *that* short. Rule number one of Shifting: Don't stick out.

Okay, technically, that would be Rule number two, the first one being: Don't bring anything from the past back with you. But that one's a no-brainer. Fiddle with the past all you want, fine. It's not like you can change it. Not really. (That's what I had to keep reminding myself to go through with the extra job I'd been hired to do today.)

But the future? No one wants to mess around with that.

A familiar voice drifted toward me, and I leaned deeper into the tree's shadow.

"No, *not* the tavern. The *pub.*" It was the phone girl.

"Well, you should have been in the bathroom covering that hickey," said her friend.

"Everyone knows it's not a hickey until the blood vessels break. It's a love bite."

4

"Yeah, well, guess what you can bite?"

"Jealous much?"

They stepped on one of the other buses with a group of high schoolers. Sweet relief. Their insipid banter was going to give me a headache.

Except no.

I reached for the base of my skull.

My head wasn't hurting. At all.

Most Shifters called it the Buzz—those painful twinges that scrambled your thoughts and blotched your vision. Like mosquito bites in your brain. Some Shifts were worse than others. But it was always present. Until now.

I pulled out my vial of Buzztabs. God bless the Initiative. Without their Assistance Fund I couldn't afford the pills, and they were the only thing that quashed the sensation. Of course, if today's side mission went well I'd never need their help again. I shook the tube. I wasn't sure if I should take one even though I felt fine. But *why* did I feel fine?

A soft hand brushed my shoulder before I had a chance to pop a tablet in my mouth.

"You need to give those back to the nurse, dear. We're about to leave." The chaperone, who thankfully appeared to be a frazzled mother rather than a teacher, nudged me along without making eye contact. I put the pills back in my pocket.

Chincoteague Island, here I come.

While I hadn't taken any formal classes like some of my friends, I considered myself a master of social camouflage. A pulled-down wisp of bang here, a curled-up slouch there, and I was all but invisible. As the bus filled, I fixed my eyes out the window and splayed my arms out so that I took up exactly two-thirds of the seat. Not so much that the chaperone would come and make a fuss. But enough to make it clear I liked riding solo. No one in their right mind would choose to sit by me.

Unless it was the last seat left.

A scrawny redheaded kid who was being devoured by a back-pack twice his size shuffled up the aisle. His thick, concave glasses squished the sides of his head in like an insect. Everyone else on the bus appeared the typical sixteen or seventeen years old, but I doubted the increasingly flushed kid had seen the better side of fifteen yet. He gripped the back of the padded seat two rows up in desperate search of another vacant spot. When the chaperone began calling out names, he gave up and slumped down next to me.

"Here," he responded to the name "Finn Masterson," saving me even the most basic of pleasantries. He watched me out of the corner of his eye with a look of part anticipation and part curiosity as we neared the end of the list. When the bus pulled out onto the highway, he broke down and said, "They didn't call your name."

"Nope," I said.

"Why didn't they call your name?"

"Probably because it wasn't on the list." I rubbed my thumb against some graffiti on the vinyl seat in front of us.

"What is it?"

"My name? Bree."

"Bree what?"

"Bree Bennis."

"Oh." He stared past me out the window, either deep in thought or avoiding eye contact, I couldn't tell. Or care. I wasn't even sure why I'd given him my real name, especially right now. Most of the time on Shifts, I doled out fake ones. But this kid had a sweet earnestness about him that kept the lie off my tongue.

Plus, he might prove useful when we got to our destination. A little civility never hurt anyone. On occasion, it made the difference between getting home to the twenty-third century to sleep in my own bed and standing in line at a nineteenth-century soup kitchen while I figured out an assignment.

Today it might be the difference in life and death.

Finn dove into a comic book. I pulled out my mission package. There was no point in thinking about the extra job if I didn't finish the assigned one. Nothing special with the wrapping. I shook it, and whatever was inside rattled around—probably a long-forgotten wedding ring or some other sentimental crap. It never ceased to amaze me the stuff people sent back to their ancestors. Lost love notes, baby teeth, underwear.

Oh, the undies.

And for what? Shifters saw it for what it was—pointless. It was always nonShifters who wanted to forge some imaginary connection to their past. So they could know that *they* were the ones who returned Great-Aunt Gertrude's precious applesauce muffin recipe when it mysteriously showed up tucked in her front door after she'd misplaced it all those years before.

Something bothered me now as I stared down at the box. Something amiss. Muffy van Sloot. The name oozed money. Rich people never used the Institute for deliveries, any more so than they'd walk into a barber school for their next haircut. They used professional chronocouriers. *Ehh.* Maybe this was a feeble attempt to make amends for losing the family fortune.

Or maybe it was all for a dead cat.

Finn tucked away his comic and pulled out a dinky action figure. At first I thought he was engrossed in putting it together, but without looking at me he said, "You a new student?"

"Kind of." Vagueness was usually the best policy on missions. I hated lying, and technically, I wasn't. I was a student. Just not of this school. Or century.

"You weren't on the same bus before."

I shrugged.

"Do you live on the island or inland?"

"You're just a bundle of questions, aren't you?"

Finn's cheeks flamed, and he snapped the last piece onto his toy. "I'm collecting the whole set." He held up his little treasure and examined it before unzipping the leg pocket of his cargo pants. "I've seen the movie three times already. Seen it yet?"

I looked at the action figure before he put it away. "Yeah."

And all three horrible sequels as well. Plus the franchise reboot that came out forty years after the original.

I pressed my forehead against the window and watched trees whir past in a blur of green and brown. There was something comforting about forests, sticking around from one lifetime to the next. The cool glass rattled and thrummed against my temple, sending Buzz-like vibrations all the way to my teeth. But it wasn't real. I still felt fine—better than fine. Did it mean something was wrong? A startling thought addled my mind: *Maybe Mom stopped getting the Buzz before . . .*

No.

She would have mentioned something like that. Mom wasn't reckless, no matter what people whispered.

Six months of what-ifs had seared me with a perpetual paranoia. But I needed to stay focused, especially today. Everything about this midterm had to appear absolutely normal. The sky started to peek through the foliage in a blipping Morse code, and the next thing I knew the bus began *kathunk-kathunk-kathunking* across a bridge. A long bridge.

I gripped the seat in front of me and leaned as far from the window as possible.

Finn scooted away and finally tapped my shoulder. "Welcome to my lap," he said.

"Sorry. I don't like the water." I inched back toward the window.

"And you moved to an island? Sucks to be you."

Dirt, asphalt, concrete . . . heck, I could land in a vat of Jell-O for all I cared. Just not water. Anything but water. Asphalt carried the risk of being seen. Water carried the risk of never being seen again.

After the bridge's last bump, my muscles unclenched. A sea-and-sun-cracked sign welcomed us to Chincoteague Island. The shuttered motels and deserted crab houses screamed "off-season."

It reminded me of Spring Break two years before, when Mom and I had thrown a suitcase each in the back of the old beat-up Pod Grandpa left her after he died. Right before *it* died. We took off up the coast and stopped in every brine-caked tourist trap we could find, ate so much chowder we thought we'd explode. I liked this town already, not that I intended to stay long. The faster I finished the midterm, the faster I moved on to the *other* delivery, the faster I could put this whole business behind me.

At the school parking lot, a stream of parents circled the block to pick up their children. Older students chattered a play-by-play of the trip on the way to their cars. Finn hung back and eyed me as I twisted my finger around a lock of hair. A cab ride was out. Public buses were unlikely. We really were in the middle of nowhere. *Ugh.* I was down to an hour and a half, and I had no idea how far away the cemetery was or how big it might be. I'd already made up my mind that I would finish the assignment before I dealt with the contraband item hidden in my shoe. Any red flags and school officials would swarm this place and investigate. I couldn't afford any chance of getting caught.

"Would you like a ride?" Finn dug his hands into his pockets and scraped a rock across the ground with his foot.

"That's okay." The last thing I needed was to be trapped in the back of some crusty station wagon while his mom pried me for information. I'd rather hitchhike. "I wouldn't want to put your parents out."

"I drove myself. My car's right over there."

I followed his finger to a black Porsche SUV. "*You* drive?"

He nodded.

"In *that*?"

Another nod.

"You can't be more than fourteen years old."

"I'm fifteen." He straightened up to his full height, still barely reaching the top of my head. "And I have my hardship license."

"Hardship?" I looked at the Porsche emblem again and scoffed.

"Both my parents work, and the bus leaves before I get out of soccer. I can drive myself to school and back." He pulled the keys out. "Look, do you want a ride or not?"

Given the long walk back to the highway, I didn't have any other options.

"Do you mind if I sit in the back? I need to stretch out. Umm, leg cramp."

He gave me a look that let me know my excuse was as pathetic as it sounded, but what did I care? It wasn't like I would see him after I got to my mission site. I settled in and twiddled with my QuantCom until the geolocator came up.

"Is that a pocket watch?" he asked.

"Family heirloom." Again, not a total lie. It did connect me with the past. It just had more in common with his car's GPS than his wristwatch.

"Let me know where to turn," he said.

"No problem. Take a right at the main road."

Finn tapped his foot timidly on the gas, and we snailed forward through the parking lot.

My mission timer beeped. "Umm, I'm in a bit of a hurry."

Finn shot me a *really?* look in the rearview mirror but sped up. We turned onto the main road. Right. Left. Right. Right. No, I meant left.

A few times, Finn double-checked my directions. "*This* street? How much farther?"

After fourteen excruciating minutes, we pulled into a long, brick driveway. I had expected a graveyard or a church. It was a mansion. Or at least the biggest house I'd ever seen. After all the quaint shake-shingled cottages, it seemed especially daunting. But whatever. As long as there was a dead Muffy under the sand or dirt somewhere, I didn't care. I was within spitting distance of finishing this midterm; then I could get to the real business at hand. I snapped the Com shut and opened the door.

"Thanks for the ride."

Finn flipped around to face me. "Do you realize where we are?"

"Yeah, Thirty-four Seventy-one Woodman Estates."

"I know. We're at my house."

chapter 2

CRAP. CRAP. CRIPPITY CRAPPITY. CRAP.

"What's going on?" asked Finn. His eyes darted back and forth between the rearview and side mirrors even though we were just sitting there in his driveway.

Dang if I knew. And I wasn't sticking around to find out. I fidgeted with a tube of lip gloss in my jacket pocket. The mission address must have been wrong. Yes. Yes, a logical explanation. If this Finn guy could point me to the town cemetery, I'd drop the package off at Muffy's grave and go on my merry way. I could squeeze in the drop-off afterward if I hurried. As I leaned forward to ask him where the nearest graveyard was, my gloss accidentally pressed into his rib cage.

"What do you want from me?" he said, his voice rising with each word. "Wait, is that a . . . Do you have a *gun*?"

"A gu—?" The laugh was on my lips, but then he fumbled forward, reaching for his phone. I panicked and jabbed the gloss hard into his side. "I mean, yeah. It's a gun. Don't make me use it. My gun, I mean. The one in my hand."

"Where did you get a—?"

"I'll ask the questions." I tried to make my voice as menacing as possible. "Don't move."

The color drained down Finn's neck in streaks. He looked like a chameleon that couldn't decide on a shade. "Look, you can have my wallet, the car, whatever you want," he said. "Just let me go, okay?"

Breathe, Bree. Breathe.

Before last spring, the lowest grade I'd ever gotten was a B-, in my third year. And that was after a little snafu when I accidentally asked someone to switch on the lights in a pre-Edison home. Not taking a kid *hostage*. While making a black market delivery.

Breathe.

Leto Malone had timed his proposal perfectly when he showed up in Mom's room last Tuesday. The doctor had finished his weekly *don't-lose-hope* speech. The accountant had delivered his monthly *abandon-all-hope* report.

Leto had slithered in wearing a slick suit and an oily smile. He held out a piece of junk so technologically obsolete it took a minute for me to figure out what it was—an old, paper-thin flexiphone. Then he asked if I wanted to earn an astronomical amount of money.

Umm, yes.

He placed it in my hand. Just a simple delivery to the past.

When I realized who he was—*what* he was—I practically threw the gadget back at him.

"Hear me out, kid," he said. "You know as well as I do this widget always popped up back then. Why shouldn't I give some garage hack with a few hundred quiddie the glory of becoming its inventor?"

"You want me to break the law for a few hundred dollars?" I fought back a snort.

"Are you tiffing me, kid?" He looked around like he was suddenly worried we'd been watched. "You leave this in a secure spot, call the buyer, he deposits the funds in a Swiss bank and gives you the account number. The guy thinks he's dealing with a disgruntled corporate snitch. You disappear. I collect the payment in our time. Plus interest."

Two hundred years of interest. Leto smiled as the potential amount dawned on me.

"But if I got caught—"

"You gonna get caught?" Leto scowled.

"No." What he asked of me could land me in prison. "No, I mean, I won't do it."

"These, heh, transactions happen all the time. No different from your school assignments."

It was completely different from our school assignments. Different from legitimate chronocourying. Anything delivered to the past had to pass strenuous scrutiny for era appropriateness—a fancy way of saying it had to belong in that time. Had to already exist. And it couldn't result in any personal gain on the sender's or receiver's part.

Leto was right on one account, though. The black market for illegal deliveries to the past was alive and well. Technology, medicine, and probably unsavory things that never made the news. But that didn't mean I wanted anything to do with it. I looked away.

"Suit yourself." Leto patted my mom's foot on his way out. "I thought you might be . . . motivated. But maybe you like your free options."

I shot Leto a dirty look behind his back. We both knew there was only one free option, even though I didn't see it as an option at all. I squeezed Mom's hand and willed her to squeeze back. But of course she didn't.

"Wait," I said before he reached the door. "Just this one time?"

He nodded.

"And you'd pay all my mom's bills?"

Leto nodded again, this time more slowly.

"I'll do it," I said. "But how am I supposed to—"

"Shh." He gave my cheek a not-so-gentle *thwap*. "You're a resourceful gal. Figure it out."

It actually wasn't that hard, once I realized no one would check my shoes. And if I didn't deliver this package, Leto would find someone else who would. The buyer would get his gadget one way or another. History books told us that. Leto would get his money. Whoever really invented it would go forever nameless and faceless. You can't change the past. One of those weird temporal loops that couldn't be explained. Also one of the reasons I sometimes didn't blame nonShifters for not trusting us past where they could track us.

A car drove by Finn's house—the driver craned his neck and waved as he passed. I ducked my face down. I had to get Finn and me inside the house, out of view. Then I could explain to him it was a silly misunderstanding. We'd have a chuckle, and I'd slip out the back door.

As the plan, sketchy as it was, solidified in my brain, my pit-a-patting pulse slowed its erratic pace. My training took over. I could salvage this.

"Open your door," I said. Finn obeyed, and I shimmied over the car's center console after him, careful to keep my gloss in contact with his back. "Now get out of the car . . . no, slow down . . . walk to the front door."

Again, he did as he was told. His whole body trembled, and I was thankful for it. He wouldn't detect the tremor in my own hand. Standing there, I wondered how ridiculous we'd look to a passerby. Me, a barely five-foot wisp of a thing, hijacking the silver medalist of the Nerd Olympics. Part of me wanted to reassure the poor guy that, worst-case scenario, I'd stain his expensive shirt. But that wouldn't get me in the house. The key scratched feebly against the lock, Finn was shaking so hard at that point. His fear pushed the last bit of mine away. I grabbed his hand, shoved the key in, and pressed him inside.

There were two light switches on the electrical panel next to the door. I gouged the gloss deeper into his back and reached for the closest one, flicking it to the "on" position.

A massive blown-glass chandelier exploded to life above us and bathed the foyer in golden light. I couldn't help but gawk at my surroundings. Vases, paintings, and tapestries lined the two-story entryway, floor to ceiling. The antiquities in that one room alone were worth several million dollars. A small Renoir hung next to one of the creepy Dutch Baroques, the kind that follows people around with its eyes. I wasn't sure which painter it was. Vermeer, maybe? Mom would have known in an instant and would have scolded me for not remembering. One of those infuriating *Mom* things that I sometimes missed more than the stuff I was supposed to.

I snapped back to attention and, curious to what other treasures the house held, reached for the remaining switch. At first, I thought it was a dead button when nothing turned on. Then, I noticed that the top of Finn's head had taken on an odd grass-colored tint. An eerie green light slowly filled the entire room. I looked for the source and spotted it above the doorway—three electric candles glowing like emeralds.

Holy crapoli.

"Is that a Haven Beacon?" I asked when my tongue began working again. All other thoughts slipped from my brain. The forgotten lip gloss hit the floor with a *clink*.

I'd read about Beacons, of course. I'd always found them kind of fascinating. It was an ancient tradition. Those who knew of time travelers' existence, who passed the knowledge generation to generation, placed three green-flamed candles in their window. A glowing welcome mat—*come in, warm yourself. Your secret is safe with me.* But Havens had disappeared long before Finn's time and centuries before mine.

I couldn't peel my gaze from the viridian flickering. Making contact with the Haven was forbidden. Totes verbote. Our teachers claimed it would give us an unfair edge on assignments, but that wasn't the real reason. The real reason was the threat of who we might run into at a Haven—Shifters from the past. And, more important, what information we might let slip. Most Beacons had been tracked down ages ago so our transporters could steer us away from them. How had this one managed to slip through the cracks?

Finn's eyes grew wide. I didn't see any answers in them, but I repeated my question.

"Is that a Hav—?"

"Are you insane?" Finn roared. He pointed at the tube of lip gloss at my feet. I felt a fleeting sense of shame as he touched the place on his side where he, moments ago, believed I'd held a firearm. "Get out of my house!"

I ignored him and looked around the room again, searching for a clue as to how a Beacon could have ended up in the possession of a kid who clearly had no idea what a Shifter was.

Finn grappled with the door's handle behind him, not taking his eyes off me for a moment. "Out!" he shouted as he wrenched the heavy front door open.

A short, plump woman with curly auburn hair stood on the front porch. Her arms sagged with grocery bags, but her face was taut with surprise. The house key hung from her hand limply at the lock as she took the scene in. The woman's gaze lifted to the green lights above the door, then back down to me. I glanced up at the Beacon on reflex. She narrowed her eyes in an unspoken question: *Are you what I think you are?* I looked at the wall, at the door, anything to avoid her gaze, but I could tell I hadn't fooled her. She bobbed her head in an almost imperceptible nod.

She knew. She knew who I was—what I was. And didn't appear fazed in the slightest.

The woman turned to Finn. "That's hardly what I'd call hospitality, pumpkin."

Pumpkin didn't seem to appreciate the flippant attitude at his predicament.

"Mom, I didn't . . . She isn't . . . This *nut job* could have killed me. She forced me in here at gunpoint." He gestured to the tube, which had rolled over to a nearby chair. "Okay, maybe not *gun*-point. More like—"

17

"*Gloss*point?" A gangly girl with a dark purple streak running through her hair leaned around Finn's mother on the porch and snickered. The girl looked a couple years younger than Finn but at the same time was a good half a head taller than him.

"Not helping, Georgie." Finn's mom handed the grocery bags to the girl. "Take these to the kitchen, then unload the rest from the car."

Finn opened his mouth to protest, but his mother silenced him with one arch of her eyebrow. When she turned back to me, her expression softened. She walked into the foyer, holding both hands out.

"Welcome to our home, honey," she said in a dripping southern drawl. "I'm Charlotte Masterson. Would you care to stay for dinner—I'm sorry, I didn't catch your name."

Finn looked back and forth between his mom and me with his jaw hanging open. Charlotte gave his chin a gentle tap as she passed. "Don't let the flies in."

"I'm sorry. I can't stay." I had to get out of there.

"Hush now," she said. "Nothin' fancy."

I gave the green lights a significant look and said, "I have a task to do."

I'd lost enough time as it was. I had to find that grave. Not to mention get in touch with this black market buyer. I never should have agreed to do it on this mission. Well, I mean, I never should have agreed to do it, period. I just didn't realize how blarked up this midterm would get.

Charlotte leaned around Finn and switched off the Beacon. "I'll set a plate for when you change your mind."

"Are you kidding me?" Finn said. "Hey, while we're at it, let's drop by the county jail and invite a few prisoners."

His mother rolled her eyes and tossed him her key fob. "I'm sure it was all a misunderstanding. Go pull the car around to the garage and help Sissy unload it." Finn didn't budge, so she added, "*Now,* please." More "*now*" than "please."

When the door slammed behind him, Charlotte let out one of those sighs they must teach when you become a mother.

"What was your name again?" she said.

"Bree." Might as well tell her, since her son already knew it.

"My, but you're a slight thing." She took a step back and gave me a look like she was sizing me up for a roaster pan. "Doesn't your mama feed you?"

"Actually, I go to a boarding school."

In the setting sun it might have been a trick of the light, but I could swear all the color drained from her face. "I see." Charlotte changed the subject: "When John gets back from wherever he is, I'm sure he'd like to meet you. He loves to talk . . . timey stuff with other people like him."

"John?"

"My husband."

"Is a *Shifter*?"

"Yes."

A Shifter's house. I was at a blarking *Shifter's* house. It was the rule that didn't have a number. *The* Rule: If you should see a Shifter Past, run away and very fast. Yeah, it rhymed. They said it was to help the First Years remember it, but I've never met anyone who didn't know it by heart from the cradle.

This was the red flag to end all red flags. If anyone from the Institute found out I'd had direct contact with a Shifter from the past, they'd swarm this place like fly on poo. This settled it. Forget Leto's delivery. I couldn't risk it. He said if I changed my mind I could return the package to him, no questions asked. I still had to figure out a way to pay for Mom's care, but I'd deal with that later.

"Obviously," Charlotte went on, completely oblivious to my meltdown, "we haven't told Finn and Georgie about their father's ability yet. I'd appreciate it if you didn't either."

Seriously? I mean, it wasn't my place to judge. When I was eight, my mom had picked up a bunch of pamphlets at the doctor's office (*"So You Think You Might Be Time-Traveling?"*) and laid them on my bed. *That* was her way of having the talk. Even though I knew . . . what to expect, it threw me for a loop. I was an early bloomer. At eleven, the blinkies started, little micro-Shifts a few seconds and minutes back before synching up to real time. After three days straight of me complaining of wicked déjà vu, Mom clued up and took me to get microchipped. But then again, by my time Shifters hadn't had to conceal their identities for almost half a century. Maybe keeping your kids in the dark was normal in their time.

Hard to know anything that was normal for Shifters this far back. It wasn't like we could ask them.

"When are you from?" asked Charlotte, as if she were inquiring about the weather.

"I . . . I'd rather not say."

"Oh, don't worry. John and I have been married almost twenty years. I'm the model of discretion."

I shook my head. Charlotte didn't press further.

My mission timer beeped, one hour. A fresh wave of panic crashed over me. I had one goal now. Finish this midterm and finish it fast. No red flags in my report, and I'd be in good shape to do a different delivery for Leto on my next assignment.

"Do you come to the twenty-first century often? You're always welcome here." Charlotte pointed up at the lights.

"Umm, no." I glanced at the door. I had to get out.

She must have thought I was looking at the Haven Beacon. She flicked it on and off a few times in an absentminded way. "Not even sure why we keep this thing around—more sentimental than anything. John's gotten out of a few sticky jams thanks to the Haven. But I'm surprised you even knew what it was."

"Pre-Schrödinger Elements of Shifting," I said without even thinking. Apparently, I was on track to throw out every Rule of Shifting on this trip.

All of her light flicking had started to give me a headache, which was soothing in an odd way, since my head typically throbbed by this point in a mission. The lack of Buzz still disturbed me. It was weird enough on its own but combined with all the other inexplicable elements of this mission. Of all missions.

Charlotte's voice turned wistful: "I've always wondered if—" But I didn't get to find out what she'd always wondered. A door on the other side of the house banged open. A few seconds later Finn stomped into the living room. Georgie trailed at his heels talking eighty light-years a minute.

"So when she sat down next to you on the bus, did she *gloss* over the fact that she had a weapon?" Georgie snorted in laughter. "Oh, oh. Or did she make up a bunch of lies about where she was keeping it? Did you catch that one? It was subtle. *Makeup.* Wait, wait, I have one more."

"Georgie." Charlotte shot her a warning glance. "Why don't you put away the groceries while I start dinner? And, Finn, you can help Bree with whatever it is she needs to do."

"You want me to *what*?" he said.

"Go and help Bree."

"Help her do what?" Finn asked. He, Charlotte, and Georgie stared at me, waiting.

I shook my head. No help. But then my QuantCom let out a shrill chime. I'd lost five more minutes. And it was getting dark outside. I didn't have a choice. This was their property. They'd know where it was.

"I need to lay something on top of Muffy van Sloot's grave."

It was like I'd nominated Finn to run for Governor of the Moon, the looks they all gave me.

Charlotte regained her composure. "Did you say 'Muffy'?"

Georgie lost it. "What the bleep is a Sloot?"

"I told you she was psycho," said Finn.

chapter 3

TEN MINUTES OF BRIBES, dirty looks, and death threats later, Charlotte shoved Finn out the back door behind me, flashlight in his hand.

"Let's get this over with," he said, shining the light down their deck steps leading to the small cove. Even though none of them had heard of Muffy van Sloot, Finn would help me look for her grave anyway.

Sand and wiry sea grass surrounded us on all sides. A chorus of cicadas crescendoed to a hissing roar, then dropped to a whisper. In the twilight, every shadow could have been a grave marker. A disinterested brush of Finn's flashlight beam revealed each of them to be nothing more than a large stone or piece of driftwood. The only bones I found were brittle little fish ones. If anything, my increasingly frenzied and fruitless search seemed to amuse my tour guide.

After circling the cove twice, I gave up. Dusk had descended like a curtain, and I was forced to admit it was an improbable spot for a grave, be it human or feline. I would have killed to use *my* flashlight, but somehow bathing the cove in a sun-grade spotlight didn't seem prudent.

"Satisfied? Because I'm starving." Finn started walking several feet in front of me.

There was no way that kid could be more annoying.

I turned my attention back to the task at hand, pulling the mission package out of my pocket and loosening the seal. I didn't normally look at deliverables early. Then again, nothing about this mission had been normal. Maybe the package could give me a clue about the grave's location.

"What's that?" asked Finn.

"Nothing to concern you. Can I borrow your light?"

"Yes, but wouldn't that make it concern me?"

"Fine. Just hand it over."

He tossed it to me, and I opened the box, then dumped the contents into my hand.

"Rocks," we both said at the same time.

"Wait, so we're looking for a *grave* for you to put *rocks* on?"

I leaned in for a closer look. Maybe they were gemstones or precious metal. Nope. Garden-variety colored pebbles, like the ones in my fish tank at home. This was hopeless. Nothing about this assignment made sense. And yet my future hung on it.

"I don't get it," I said.

"That makes two of us." Finn snatched the flashlight and pointed it toward the house. "Can we go get dinner now?"

I followed behind him like a forlorn lemming, still clutching the rocks in my hand, more confused than ever. With every blip of the mission timer, my chances of completing the assignment diminished, but I couldn't see anything at that point. Continuing the search was pointless. I'd run out of time to contact Leto's buyer.

Almost every light in the Mastersons' house was on. The back of their home was all glass, and from a distance it looked like a sliced-open dollhouse, its contents laid out for all to see. Georgie was up in her bedroom bouncing around with earphones on. Charlotte flitted from cupboard to oven in the kitchen.

On the bottom level of the deck, Finn stopped. He leaned against the railing and removed his shoes to shake the sand out. I did the same. A new motion in the house distracted me, and I looked up in time to see a tall man with graying dusty brown hair enter the living room from the front door.

"Oh. Good. Dad's home." The words came out of Finn's mouth, but no joy accompanied them.

I stood on my tiptoes to get a better look at John. So this was the Shifter. Finn started up the stairs, but I didn't follow. Up to this point, my actions were defensible. (Well, maybe not the gun thing.) If I went back into that house, there would be no pretense at that point. I was curious, yes, but it wasn't worth breaking The Rule. If Institute officials found out, they'd come back to question John about our interaction and he'd tell them about the hostage thing. My every mission after this would be under close scrutiny. There was no way Leto would ever hire me to do another delivery. It wasn't just my mother's bills that needed paying. There was my tuition. Our house. I could lose everything.

Then again, I'd never get another chance like this. To talk to an actual Shifter.

No! What the blark was I saying? I couldn't go in there, and that was that.

Charlotte must have heard her husband's entrance at the same time Finn and I saw it. She turned the stove off and tossed her spoon in the sink. I looked away, not wanting to witness some passionate private moment between the couple. But Finn just tilted his head to the side.

"Bing, bing, bing," he said drily. "Round one."

I looked up and could see what he meant. Far from a loving embrace, Charlotte was laying into her husband. Her words weren't audible, but the angry tone was. She pointed this way and that, toward the cove, the foyer. At one point, I swore I lip-read the words "Haven Beacon."

"I'll just stay out here and keep looking," I said. "It looks like your parents could use some space."

Finn shrugged. "They'll stop when we go in. Always do. Usually, they shut themselves off in their bedroom. Mom must be especially POed for some reason."

"They fight . . . often?"

"I think my dad's having an affair," said Finn matter-of-factly.

His frankness took me aback, to suspect his dad of something so reprehensible. My mom and I had always shot straight with each other. She never sugarcoated anything—the sad state of our teensy bank account, exactly what she thought of my bikini choice, why it was only the two of us. And I'd told her everything, too, before the accident. Sometimes, even now, I would press my lips to her unhearing ears and whisper the silly nothings that she collected like a magpie.

"What would make you think—?"

"He's always gone," Finn said. "Always brings Mom expensive gifts—all that artwork—after he's gone the longest chunks of time. He uses his surgery schedule as an excuse, but I don't buy it." He dug the toe of his sneaker into the crack between the deck's planks.

"That doesn't mean he's having an affair."

"Two months ago, I walked in on one of their arguments, and Dad was saying something about, 'We have to tell the children. They deserve to know the truth about me.' And Mom was all, 'They're too young; let them have their innocence.' Any other ideas what that could mean?" His stare dared me to refute his theory, and when I met him with silence he said, "Didn't think so."

"Maybe it's not what you think," I said. "There could be a simple explanation."

Okay, maybe not *that* simple.

Back inside the house, Charlotte planted her hands on her hips. She stamped her foot and ran her fingers through her hair.

"We can go in soon. After she gets a few good stomps in, she loses steam." He looked down at his watch, then back up at his parents. "I'd say give them another three minutes or—"

But he didn't finish his thought.

Because his father had disappeared.

Finn's mom's reaction was immediate. Charlotte clenched the air where her husband had been and stomped her foot so hard the heel broke off her pump. She grabbed the shoe and threw it across the room at the sofa. Then, with a dramatic huff, she tucked her hair behind her ears and hobbled back into the kitchen to resume cooking.

Finn's reaction was . . . delayed. His shoulders sagged. His unblinking eyes stared past me, past the house, past the world he thought he knew. Then, he staggered backward as if a great invisible hand had shoved him. A bucket of shells tripped him on the lowest step of the deck, and he landed in the sand with a thud.

"Did you see that?" His shaky finger pointed at the empty living room.

Hmmm. "That very much depends on what *you* saw."

"My dad just . . . just . . . evaporated."

"Okay, then, yes, unfortunately we did see the same thing."

I reached down to help Finn up, but rather than take my offered hand, he crab-crawled away from me across the beach. The abandoned flashlight fell at an angle that twisted his already-terror-filled face into something grotesque.

"You know something!" he yelled.

"Why don't you go back to the house and—"

"Where's my father? What aren't you telling me?" He moved farther back. "What are you, some kind of alien?"

Now this was getting ridiculous. I hadn't asked for this stupid mission. Some random person in the twenty-third century with a weird penchant for aquarium pebbles must have stuck his finger down on my name by chance, and I'd been assigned. But I hadn't signed up for *this*. Finn wasn't even the one who had anything to lose. My mother's *life* depended on this.

"Look, it's not my fault your dad's a Shift—"

Double dang. I needed to keep my big mouth shut. I fingered my QuantCom and debated triggering an emergency fade right then and there. Let Finn think I was an extraterrestrial or abducted by one or whatever his brain wanted to come up with.

"He's a what?" Finn sat up on his knees and inched toward me. "What happened to him? You know."

"This is a conversation you should be having with your parents." Like five years ago. "Not with some girl you just met." Like five minutes ago.

I turned toward the beach.

Finn jumped up and grabbed me tight around my wrist. "I'm asking *you*."

My self-defense training kicked in before I could register what was going on. I twisted my arm around his, kicked his legs out from under him, and slammed him to the ground. His Adam's apple bobbed against my fingers as they circled his throat. Finn didn't even fight; he simply lay there, stunned.

"Are you going to kill me?" he choked out.

Enough. "We're going to talk to your mother right now whether you like it or not."

I yanked him up and dragged him behind me like a limp doll. The house was dead quiet as we entered. I pushed Finn toward the kitchen. Charlotte looked up as I finally managed to shove him all the way through the swinging door.

"Did you have any luck?" Charlotte asked with artificial brightness.

"M-m-om," stammered Finn, "what . . . what happened to Dad?"

Charlotte threw the towel she held onto the counter, turning on me. "I can't believe you told him!"

"And I can't believe you haven't invested in curtains," I snapped. "Finn saw him Shift through the window. I didn't say anything."

Charlotte put her hands to her mouth. "Oh, pumpkin. We never meant you to find out this way."

"Shifting? What the he—?"

His mother held one finger up. "Language." One of the pots on the stove boiled to the top, and Charlotte ran to turn it down.

"Watch me burn dinner on top of everything. Now," she said as she turned back to Finn, "how much has Bree told you about time travel?"

Finn's knees crumpled under him, and he sank onto a chair at the kitchen table.

"Uh, nothing," I said.

Charlotte's eyes clouded with tears as she looked at her son. She waved me out of the room and shuffled toward Finn like he was an animal licking its wounds.

Relief swept through me as I scurried into the living room. It didn't last long. My mission timer let out a squeal. Less than fifteen minutes left. What was I going to do? I had turned to the door for a last-ditch attempt at finding the grave when a pudgy yellow Labrador retriever wandered into the room from upstairs. He snuffled the air and wandered to my side, shoving his muzzle under my hand. His collar said "Slug." I gave the top of his head a tentative pat, then shooed him off. He turned his nose up into the air and tottered toward the kitchen. He pushed the swinging door open with his nose.

Finn's shout rang out: "So it's *genetic*?"

"Yes, but . . . ," said Charlotte.

"When were you planning on telling me? Or were you waiting for me to wake up some morning stranded in Ancient Mesopotamia?"

Someone sure thought highly of himself. Personally, I didn't know any Institute students who'd gone back much further than the sixteenth century. Mom had been Shifting how long, almost thirty years? And she rarely ventured past the Dark Ages. But even if this upstart toot did have the Shifter gene, I highly doubted he'd go back more than seven seconds his first Shift.

I turned back to the door but paused. Everything past the edge of the deck was buried in darkness. Maybe I could find a brighter flashlight. I trotted off to their foyer. Their art collection really was amazing. Upon closer examination, it wasn't worth millions—it was priceless.

"The van Gogh's fresh out of storage."

I whipped around, clutching at my heart, to face the voice. Finn's father sat on a stool in the far corner of the room, eyeing the paintings thoughtfully. The resemblance to his son was striking. The changeable stuff, hair and glasses, was different. But the features that stuck around—a strong chin, deep-set eyes, square jaw—they shared.

"It drives Charlotte crazy that I refuse to bring them back with me. I purchase them in the past and store them. She'd rather have them in pristine condition than brittle with age, even if well preserved. I keep telling her it's time that makes them authentic. It's one of the few things I put my foot down on." His weary gaze fell on the kitchen door, which practically vibrated with muffled yelling. "Wish I'd done the same about telling the kids. I'm John, by the way." He reached out his hand.

I looked at it like it was a live snake. This was it. If I took that hand, if I spoke to him, I was officially breaking The Rule. The Rule that was in place to protect him . . . and me. And if I somehow let it slip that I'd interacted with him, I'd lose everything.

"Bree," I whispered.

"It's nice to meet you." His hand was calloused but warm. "Charlotte mentioned you're a student."

"Ummm . . ."

"I'm sorry." He took a step back. "Are my questions making you nervous? You probably don't meet too many Shifters from before your time."

"I haven't met any. Once, I thought I saw a guy fade in my peripheral vision, but when I looked over it was too late to be sure."

"Well, welcome. Let me know if there's anything I can do to help you."

"Do you know where Muffy van Sloot's grave is?" I only had a few more minutes, but it was worth a shot.

"Sorry. Don't know that name."

"Thanks anyway." I shuffled my toe along a crevice in the marble floor, and we stood there in awkward silence.

"So the future, ehh?" John finally said. "You must have some cool technology up your sleeve."

I froze. There were two directions this conversation could take. One included my involvement in a black market delivery. The other, a microchip in my skull. Either way, I could see the crack form on the thin layer of ice on which I tread.

"It didn't take you long to synch up from your Shift," I said to change the topic. That much I knew about pre-chipped Shifters. Like us, their quantum tendrils could only stretch for so long before they had to synchronize with real time.

He shook his head. "I haven't synched yet."

"What?"

"I only went back a few minutes," he said. "It happens sometimes—an emotional response when I wish I could have a do-over. I'll synch back up when things simmer down."

"So you're actually Future You?" I asked.

"Hmm." He chuckled. "I suppose you could think of it that way."

I didn't like thinking about it, period, lest it make my brain cave in. As if on cue, the back of my skull began to tingle. Ahh, finally. A little Buzz. I fumbled through my pocket for the vial of Buzztabs. I took out the box of rocks and laid them on a desk that looked like it could have belonged to Louis XIV. Heck, probably did. I started to pick the rocks back up but then thought better of it. At least I could leave them in this time, if not on Muffy's grave.

"What are you taking?" he asked.

"Oh, umm . . ." *Blark.* I could see the ice on which I tread crackle, the splinters grew even as I opened my mouth. I'd trespassed into dangerous, dangerous territory. *This* was why we had The Rule against speaking to Shifters from the past. If he knew his fate and, more important, if he knew I had the remedy for his fate buried in my skull . . . I popped a couple tabs in my mouth to give myself time to think. They dissolved on my tongue, the minty aftertaste not quite able to mask the acidic bite. The pills were a relatively recent development, only around for fifty years or so, since Shifters came out of hiding. But I could tell him part of the truth.

"They're for the Buzz."

"The what?"

"Oh, sorry, terminology's probably changed over the years." I tried to think of every slang term I'd ever heard to describe it. "Y'know, the Jolts, Electric Fuzzies, the Harsh."

He must have had a different word for it, as he met my descriptions with a blank stare. "I'm not sure what you're—"

A loud crash from the kitchen interrupted us. John sprinted across the living room and threw open the swinging door. I followed. Charlotte knelt on the ground, sweeping up a broken picture frame. She scowled at her husband at first but softened when she saw his look of panic.

"It was an accident. It fell when Finn knocked his hand against the wall."

Finn clutched the edges of the island counter, resentment radiating off him. For a moment, all I could think was, *Poor guy*.

That moment didn't last long.

Georgie walked in. She paused in the doorway.

"Hey, Dad," she said, then turned to face her brother. "What crawled up your—?"

"Georgiana Louise Masterson," screeched Charlotte, "if another child of mine utters one more word today they wouldn't say in front of the sweet Lord Baby Jesus himself, there is gonna be a reckoning."

All four Mastersons started shouting at the same time.

Even Slug barked himself hoarse, chasing his tail in circles.

My QuantCom vibrated violently, and my head started to pound in waves of rhythmic pulses. Oww. I was wrong before. This was no Buzz. My timer had expired. Whoever was on transport duty was pinging me. Hard. I'd never cut it this close before. I backed away to leave.

Charlotte noticed me exiting and said, "Oh, no, no, dear. We'll get this worked out."

My foot was halfway out the door, but I paused as Finn's voice rang out above the racket.

"How can you be more concerned about that crazy lunatic than your own son?"

"Don't you dare call me crazy!" I'd hit my snapping point.

A hush, thick as wool, draped over the room. The dog stopped barking. Every eye bore into me, then Finn. Charlotte looked like she wanted to strangle him. John turned to me, his face full of compassion and . . . something else.

I didn't want his pity. I got enough of that at home. And I had to get out of here before they questioned why I was ubersensitive about my sanity.

"I have to go." My wrist trembled as I opened my QuantCom. Relief at the prospect of going home mixed with dread. My entire body felt like a numb, stretched rubber band. One touch could snap it.

I pushed the center button and faded away.

chapter 4

"YOU DO REALIZE how close that was?" said a familiar, if somewhat disgruntled, voice.

I opened my eyes and forced them to adjust to the cool, white lights reflecting off the silver panels that lined the circular room. I hopped down off the Shift Pad and shot Charlie a charming smile.

"Nice to see you, too, Mr. Wu."

"Yeah, thanks for gracing me with your presence," he said without looking at me.

I stepped through the decontamination chamber and held my breath as jets of hot air filled with this-and-thatacide removed every trace of twenty-first century from me. Charlie's fingers slid deftly through the virtual data screens projecting in the air. He held out his free hand for my QuantCom, and when I didn't pass it over immediately he clutched his palm open and shut like a toddler begging for a cookie.

As I handed my Com to him, he dropped his voice and said, "I almost had to trigger a forced fade, you know."

"You *what*?" I swung around so fast, I almost rammed into his console. Charlie couldn't be serious. But a forced fade, that's not something you joke about.

"This wasn't some Botany romp, planting acorns," he said. "It's your History midterm."

"Why don't you let me worry about me?"

"It's *my* midterm, too, Bree," he said, then quietly added, "And Wyck's."

I swear, where I had a Shifter gene Charlie had a guilt one.

"Did you hit a snag in the mission?" he asked. "Trouble finding this van Sloot person's grave?"

"No snag. I left the package where it was supposed to be." I didn't meet his gaze. It wasn't the first time I'd failed to complete an assignment. It was, however, the first time I'd lied about it. "Drop it, okay?"

"Fine." After an awkward pause, he said, "So how about that Quantum Bio lecture on Monday?"

I just stared at him. Charlie's mental clarity checks were always as subtle as a Tectonic bomb. Transporters had to assess for any confusion in Shifters and report it. Well, he wasn't getting anything from me tonight.

"Tantalizing explication of hippocampal biorhythyms," I said. "Do you want to know who won the last World Cup, too?"

"You know I have to check." Charlie turned red, and we stood there in silence while he downloaded my QuantCom's data.

"Huh," he said after a few seconds.

"Huh what?" I couldn't afford any "huhs." Not on this mission. I tried to lean around the podium to see what he saw, but it was all wiggly floating numbers and symbols to me.

"You had some weird tendril surges toward the end of the Shift. Probably nothing. Anything unusual happen?"

"No." Everything unusual happened.

He shrugged. "I'll write it off as a data glitch."

"Does that happen?"

"Never seen it with students. Occasionally with some of the teachers." He popped my QuantCom out of its dock and handed it to me. "You should go find Mimi. She's been paging me every three minutes to find out if you're back."

"Typical Mimi." I smiled. My roommate would knit a penguin a sweater if you let her.

"When you weren't at dinner, she was—well, you know

how Mimi gets. She thought maybe you didn't come because it was . . ." He blushed again. "You know."

"Tofurky night?"

"No. It's, umm . . ."

"Oh." *Family Night.*

"I'll let Mimi know you made it back," he said. "She's in the rec room with her parents."

"Thanks. Sorry I yipped at you." It wasn't his fault. He hadn't caused this bizarre failure of a midterm. "I'm just tired. I'll grab a chomp, then call it a night."

Every inch of my body loosened while it synched up to real time. *Aah.* The tension from the fade disappeared as my internal rubber band adjusted to the slack. Now that I was back in my own time, I was safe. There was no reason I'd get caught. All I had to do was research this Muffy Whoever tonight, squidge my way through the report tomorrow, and ask Leto for a new delivery.

I walked out of the transport room, stopped at the first food dispenser I passed, and slipped a section of my hair into the scanner. I placed my order, a slice of pizza and a fizzwater. When the panel door opened, the glass of water came out but no pizza. I looked back up at the order screen. A red *X* flashed in the corner—over my limit of solo meals for the month.

"Oh, come on!" I punched a few buttons at random, but the *X* only got bigger and brighter.

"Now, now, let's not break anything," a kindly voice chimed behind me.

I looked around to see Headmaster Bergin. He was like a cross between a mustachioed Santa Claus and Theodore Roosevelt—old, portly President Roosevelt, that was. Not to be confused with young, hot Rough Rider Teddy. (*Not* that I had developed the teensiest of crushes on him during a class field trip the year before or anything.)

"Sorry, sir." I eked out a sheepish grin. "Just got back from my Pre-Tri midterm. I'm starving, but I'm over the limit."

"There's a reason for that rule, Miss Bennis. You Shifters live such solitary lives on your missions. You must embrace comradery where it seeks you, which is often around a crowded table." Bergin chortled and stepped up to the machine, allowing it to scan his silvery strands. "But believe it or not, I was once a teenager myself. Override."

Hard to believe. Bergin had been headmaster here forever, or at least since before Mom was a student. As a nonShifter, he'd been a controversial choice at the time of his selection. Shifters finally conceded when it was hire him or shut down the school. But he ended up being the right choice—a widower who threw himself headlong into his work, he'd been a better advocate for Shifters than most Shifters had been.

My face appeared on the screen as my nutritive stats adjusted. The front panel sprang back open, and a piping-hot slice of pizza popped out. True, it had a gluten-free rice crust and soy "cheez" on top, but I was famished and pizza was pizza.

"Thanks!"

"Thank *you* for all your dedicated training."

A plaster grin spread across my face. Here in the Institute, we were all special, special snowflakes wrapped in a flower. Out in the real world, we were a curiosity, our ability embraced so long as we stayed in acceptable fields and followed the Rules. *But come on.* What was I going to do? Ignore the fact that I could time-travel and become a dentist instead?

"Time-travel" is such a misnomer anyway. I mean, technically *everyone* is time-traveling—moment to moment, day to day—their quantum tendrils suctioning them to their present like tiny, invisible octopus tentacles. Some of us just have a harder time staying put. Well, *had* a harder time staying put, that is, until the invention of the microchip.

Still, it was nice of Bergin to bend the rules. He bid me good night, and I headed to my room. The smell of antiseptic over-powered me when I walked past the newbie wing. Those first few missions could be disorienting. Nauseating, really. A mopping cart ran a continuous cycle up and down the corridor. As I passed it, a scared whimper rose above the whir of the puke-mobile. I pivoted my head down the hallway and made out the form of Molly Hayashi, a first-year student who'd been in the Orientation group I'd led that summer. She was tucked in a dark alcove.

"Molly?" I called. "Are you okay?"

"Shhh!" someone else hissed from the alcove. A hand darted out and pulled the shaking girl back into the shadows.

The soles of my shoes hit the ground in a hard slap as I took off down the hall. I kicked some tru-ants, minuscule robots that monitored our school, aside. I rounded the corner just in time to see the person flick Molly on the ear.

"I mean it; you'd better do what I say," said . . . another Molly. *Oh, sigh.*

"Molly." They both turned to look at me. "What on earth are you doing?"

Bullied Molly pointed at the other one. "She appeared out of nowhere and started yelling at me."

Other Molly, who I now noticed had grown out her bangs, pointed straight back. "And *she* cost me a whole Christmas break of tutoring."

"I haven't done anything."

"Well, you certainly haven't studied enough. And you won't get to do anything—and I mean *anything*—over Christmas if you don't get your butt out of a rut and study for the Intro to Chronogeological Displacement exam." Future Molly leaned in for another ear flick, and this time Present Molly fought back.

Both girls had some scrap in them. It took all my effort to keep them apart. "Stop it! Molly." Both girls turned. "Er, Mollies, what was the first lesson on your first day of classes?"

It was everyone's first lesson. The Doctrine of Inevitability. Otherwise known as "You can't change the past." Not even if someone really wanted to. Not even if someone tried desperately hard. Not even if there was one minuscule moment in the past that sucked my whole future into a swirling black hole. And it didn't matter how hard I wished and I prayed to go back to that one moment and change it, the black hole was still there sucking me down, down, down. . . .

Stop. The past cannot be changed.

Neither girl answered my question, but they stopped scuffling when I released their arms.

Future Molly glared at her past self. "If you'd only listen to me—"

"Did *you* listen to you?" I asked, knowing Future Molly must remember this incident.

Future Molly heaved a sigh. "No."

"Then cut her, er, yourself some slack. Now off to bed, both of you." I put my hand on Future Molly's shoulder. "Wait. How did you get here?"

The question perked the girl up. "Private Shift Pad. My grandparents surprised us with one for Christmas. It even has autotransport."

Wow. Molly's family was loaded.

"Thanks for ruining the surprise." Present Molly folded her arms across her chest.

"Oh, stop whining; you'll forget about it in a week," said Future Molly.

I stepped back between the two girls. "Time to synch, Molly. Careful going back."

With a nod, the girl opened her QuantCom and faded away. Present Molly looked like a canary-filled cat.

I got in her face: "Listen to her. And study. This is important stuff, you know. People can . . . can get hurt."

The grin vanished from Molly's face like everyone's did when they remembered my mother—what I represented to all Shifters. Molly scurried backward toward her room. "I know. I'm sorry. I'll study, Bree. I promise, I will."

No, you won't, I wanted to say. But I knew there was no point.

The overhead lights in the hallways had already dimmed. I ran my hand along the cool, granite wall. The Institute had been the only constant, only solid thing in my life for six months now. There wasn't a square inch of it I didn't love. Once upon, this building had housed the U.S. Department of Education. Now it held the Division of Temporal Studies. I passed my corridor and kept walking. Lights in the computer lab were on, and I peeked through the door. Nobody there.

"Log on: Bree Bennis."

I stood in one of the raised ovals that lined the floor. Virtual envelopes appeared in the air and swirled around until they formed a big, jumbled stack in front of me. My in-box hadn't been sorted in months, but after flipping through the new messages on top I gave up and shoved them back in a folder. Even though they were only soligraphs—holographs that felt solid to the touch—the folder wouldn't shut all the way. A warning message popped up midair: "You are close to your storage limit. Please categorize and dispose of nonessential items."

"Later." I crammed the folder to the side.

Another warning appeared: "I mean it, Bree. It's time to clean out your in-box." *Sassy computers. Meh.*

A fresh message popped up in my box. It glowed a deep jade green, and when I opened it I let out an almost audible hiss. It was another brochure from Resthaven, the only free care facility available for my mother. They'd been sending me information since right after Mom's accident. My mother was going to get better, thank you very much. No one could *prove* she'd gone off the deep end. I tore the pixels into tiny bits before I hit delete.

All right, down to business. I had one shot at this midterm, and Dr. Quigley was a notorious stickler for accurate historical details and descriptions. Her mantra rang in my ears like she was there in the room with me: *I don't want to hear about our past. I want to hear about* their *present.*

I stared at the blank spaces. Even after spending a full evening with Finn's family, I knew nothing about them. Except their son was a snerkwad.

What had he called me—a lunatic? Oh, yeah, *I'm* the crazy one. I wasn't the one who had lied to him all these years. If he was going to be mad at anybody, it should be his father. Not that I blamed Shifters in the past for hiding. They were a danger to themselves and others! Hurtling through time and space at random. No, it was better now. The inconvenience of the chip and transporters was such a small price to pay for stability, for safety, for control.

And, of course, for the cure.

Ugh. Why was I allowing this family a single crevice of my brain? They'd all been dead for over a hundred years.

And I did know one thing about them: No one could ever know they existed.

So what was I supposed to say? After I took a kid hostage, I wandered aimlessly on the beach and caused a family meltdown? Oh, that would be after I recluctantly gave up on my black market delivery. No. I needed general information, stuff that would slip past Quigley in the stack of reports, that wouldn't raise any eyebrows or questions.

"Search all files: Muffy van Sloot." *Nothing. Odd.*

Chincoteague Island. More than I ever wanted to know about wild ponies, but nothing with a Muffy or van Sloot. I drummed my fingers against my thigh, then said, "Finn Masterson, Virginia," and the year I'd visited. Maybe the house could be traced back to a van Sloot.

Nada.

Neither his parents nor sister registered either.

After the second Cold War, pockets of off-the-grid communities had popped up in North America and Europe, but that was well after Finn's teenage years. Besides, I'd never heard of anyone who managed to live undetected and in the lap of luxury at the same time. I'd also never heard of anyone living in such a way without a good reason.

There couldn't be *no* trace of them.

I almost started to enter the search term "Haven Beacons" but paused.

Wait. If there really was no trace of them, it could work in my favor. As long as I kept my presentation tomorrow believable and I didn't raise any alarms, I could make some stuff up and Quigley would never know. I had reached out to close all the search results when I suddenly couldn't see them anymore. Warm, calloused hands covered my eyes.

"Guess who," a gravelly voice whispered in my ear.

"Hey, Wyck," I said as I shuffled the rest of the results away blindly.

His fingers curled away from my face. "How'd you know it was me?"

Umm, because you smell like a wad of yummy wrapped in a layer of delicious?

"Lucky guess."

"I thought you'd be in bed by now." He leaned against a stack of stools pushed up against the far wall of the lab. A lock of dusty blond hair fell across his forehead. He swept it back, but it returned to the same spot the moment his hand fell to his side. I looked down and realized I'd brought my own hand up to push it back again. I lowered it before he noticed.

"You've been moving nonstop since you left for your midterm," he said. "How'd it go by the way?"

"Fine," I said a little too fast. I smirked and added, "No thanks to you."

"Ahh, now that's just mean." Wyck slouched down farther. "Besides, who's to say I didn't land you right where I wanted you?"

"Ha! In the middle of a musket battle?"

"A musket battle?" His left eyebrow formed a perfect arch over those ice blue eyes. "In the twentieth century?"

"Twenty-first. And, okay, it may have been a reenactment." I let out a little laugh. "More like a parade, actually."

"Oh, no." He rushed over and grabbed both my hands. "Were there clowns?"

I let out a fake shudder. "They were everywhere. Ye Olde Clowns. I farce you not."

As I stood there, hanging out with Wyck, the stress from the assignment faded. He was like a Buzztab for my nerves.

"Sorry you were so far off your target," he said. "I saw the word 'island' and the thought of you landing in water . . ." His shudder was real. "Guess I erred a little too far on the safe side."

See, that's what I loved about Wyck O'Banion. Most transporters would have snipped at me for even joking they'd done their job wrong. But not Wyck. There wasn't a splinter of a chip on his shoulder.

I realized he was still holding my hands and pretended to cough so I could pull them away. "For a minute there, I thought you missed by two hundred years."

He leaned in close. "I never miss with you."

His words made me feel warm inside. I'd never felt that way before, at least around Wyck. We were just friends. I covered my cheeks, sure they were burning up.

"There you are!" My roommate, Mimi, marched into the room, hands on her hips. "Charlie said he almost had to trigger a forced fade. Are you okay?"

Wyck snapped his head up. "A forced fade?"

"No!" *No red flags.* I waved the question off and walked toward Mimi. "It was nothing. Log out! 'Night, Wyck."

I pushed Mimi out the door and down the hall before Wyck had a chance to ask me anything else. Her blond ponytail whacked me in the face as she swung her head around.

"Seriously, are you all right? Do you need any of my meal rations? That was a long mission . . . how are you on Buzztabs?"

"Bergin took pity and gave me an override," I said, "and I'm fine on Buzztabs." *Too fine.*

"Well, I'm glad you're back. Oh, I almost forgot to tell you. Pennedy and Teague broke up. Can you believe it?"

When I didn't chime in with a comment about our friends' romantic woes, Mimi waved her hand in front of my face. "Are you really okay? You usually put the rest of us to shame on mission times."

Used to. I felt a fresh wave of thankfulness that Mimi had known me long enough and was kind enough to not judge me by the last six months.

"I lost track of time," I said.

I turned away and wrinkled my nose. I'd never lied to Mimi. But something about the . . . the *weirdness* of it all held my tongue. That and the fact that if one breath of my encounter with a Shifter got out, there would be no chance of another job from Leto. No chance to pay off my mother's bills. I'd face suspension and be lucky if they stopped there.

When Mimi and I got to our room, I flopped face-first on my bed. The pillow wrapped my head in sateen silence. I tried to lift my arms, but the most I achieved was a thumb twitch. *Ehh, pajamas shmajamas.* Images from the day swirled against my eyelids—green lights and lip gloss tubes and Finn's sandy sneakers. Thinking about his shoes gave me a sunken feeling in my stomach for some reason, but I pushed it away. And then I felt a gentle tug on my own boots.

I lifted one eye off the pillow to watch as Mimi lined them up perfectly under the funky-painted chair Mom had made for me. It really was a miracle Mimi and I were as close as we were, given our opposite *everything.* Her side of the room was all white and pink and sleek. Mine was . . . me. Piles of clothes sorted into clean and not-quite-dirty-enough-for-laundry. My pet fish, Fran, who was still alive by some miracle. (Although that miracle probably went by the name of Mimi.) A bunch of movie posters. I even had a real paper one. I'd inherited Mom's obsession for anything antique, along with the inability to keep it organized.

"Mimi?" I asked. Only my face was still in the pillow, so it came out, "Mrehmreh?"

"Hmmm?" She sat down at the vanity and ran a brush through her honey silk hair.

My own chin-length bob was a windblown mess. I blew a few brown hairs out of my face as I turned to talk to her. I was one of the only girls at the Institute who kept their hair short. Most Shifters wouldn't take the risk. On a whim the year before, Mimi had cropped her hair into the cutest pixie cut, then had to trigger an emergency fade two days later burning at a stake in Salem. Needless to say, she used a wig while her hair grew out.

"I'm glad you're my roomie," I said.

I expected her to respond with a simple, *Me, too,* but instead she tossed her hairbrush on the counter mid-stroke. Before I could say anything else, she bounded across the room and flounced on my bed next to me. She smooshed me up in a lung-crushing hug.

"As you should be."

We both busted out giggling, and the tension of the day dissipated. Mimi sat up next to me and smoothed my hair down, or at least the worse-offending side.

"Seriously, though," she said, giving my hand a tiny squeeze, "I'm the lucky one."

I started to squeeze it back until she added, "Remember that weirdie that Pennedy got stuck with first year? I could've ended up with *her.*"

I slapped Mimi's wrist instead. "So I'm better than . . . what was her name?"

"Jennily? Jeffiny?"

"Jafney!" we both yelled at the same time.

"Wow, I haven't thought about her in forever," I said.

"I doubt anyone has." Mimi hopped up and moved back to the vanity. "Except maybe the poor transporter who had to do it."

"Yeah." It was the only forced fade I'd ever heard of at the Institute. Jafney had left soon after. I wasn't sure if she'd been kicked out or her family had brought her home. I'd never wondered before what had happened on that girl's mission to force them to drag her writhing and screaming back to our time.

I wondered now.

Mimi ran her thumb over the neat row of lotions and elixirs lined up on her vanity. A standing open invitation existed for me to use any that I wanted. Unfortunately, every attempt to try them out, when not under her watchful and expert eye, had resulted in me smelling like a rotten petunia or looking like a drowned water rat.

"You sure you're okay?" she said, all Mother Hennish. "That last-minute fade must be smarting. You need to rest."

My head *was* throbbing. It was like all the Buzz had built up and hit me when my feet hit the twenty-third century.

"Mimi, have you ever not gotten the Buzz on a mission?"

"You mean like a really light Buzz?" Mimi stared at me in her mirror without turning around.

"No, I mean like none at all."

"You have to report it." She spun around, her eyes agog. "Anything out of the ordinary, you know that. I mean, Bree, what if this could help them figure out what happened with your mom? She mouthed the word "mom" as if the pain of my situation could be lessened by not saying it out loud.

And she was probably right. The Buzz was one of those weird

things that Shifters found strangely comforting, like a pregnant woman yacking with morning sickness. Crapawful, yes, but reassuring at the same time. Proof that your microchip was working as it should.

Any other mission, I would have marched straight to Nurse Granderson's office and blabbed. But not this mission. Mimi meant well, but the thing that would most help my mom was paying her hospital bills. I shuddered at the thought of her ending up in Resthaven because of my failure. I needed things to smooth over, and I needed to get ahold of Leto for another delivery pronto.

"You misunderstood," I said with the lightest of laughs. "Nothing happened. Y'know what? Forget it. I'm being stupid."

"You're probably just tired and forgot how many Buzztabs you took." But she still looked worried.

"Absolutely. And I have to get up at the keister crack of dawn to finish prep for my Pre-Tri report."

"Sweet dreams."

I wish. I turned over to face the wall. The antique sterling bracelet Mom gave me when I left for the Institute clanked against the bed frame as I did so. I rubbed the heart charm and kissed it as I did every night, the "Bree" engraving almost as worn off as the shallow original etchings on the other side. As the busyness of the day ground to a halt, grief and uncertainty slithered up as usual and squeezed my throat. I pulled the soft, frayed edge of my tatter-loved quilt up to my chin.

Mimi's shoes squeaked as she tiptoed past my bed to go to the bathroom.

There it was again, that burr in my stomach when I thought about shoes. Why did I—?

I sat up straight with a gasp, heart slamming against my rib cage. My shoes! I'd dumped the sand out of them on Finn's deck earlier.

Along with Leto's delivery.

chapter 5

RULE NUMBER TWELVE OF SHIFTING: Never be late for Quigley's class. Of course, that rule went for transporters as well. And general passersby.

It was one that I almost broke as I scrambled to my seat in Pre-Tricentennial American History while a disembodied voice overhead warned me of my tardiness. *Shut up, Sassy Computer!* I slid into my desk.

"Ahh, Miss Bennis, thank you for joining us." The Quig was never in a good mood. At that moment, she looked extrahorked. Her wavy brown hair was pulled back so tight into its usual bun it lifted her prominent cheekbones even higher. Myself, I looked like a Pod wreck. If I fell asleep at all last night, it was a fitful nightmare for half an hour before my alarm went off so I could throw together whatever it was I was going to present in class today.

Every time I'd closed my eyes, all I could see was Leto's sneering face tattooed on the back of my retina. Instead of counting sheep, I counted the number of times I told myself that he wouldn't be *that* upset about the lost flexiphone. I'd lost track somewhere around five eighty-six.

I mean, it was an honest mistake. He couldn't fault me for that.

Five eighty-seven.

"For those of you waiting on anxious bits and bytes for today's quiz, I'm afraid I have to disappoint you," said Dr. Quigley.

Not surprisingly, Emmaline Walters was the only one who looked the slightest bit put out. "The time has come for you to declare your Intent of Specialization. I have been designated the caring adult to guide you through this process. So make a decision and enter it. There. You've been guided."

Quigley pushed a button on her podium and soligraph forms materialized in front of all our desks, simple check-the-box questionnaires. I picked up my stylus.

"Hey, why do we have to be here?" asked Wyck from the back. He pointed to a few transporters sitting around him.

"Mr. O'Banion, there are thirty-seven areas of Shifter specialization. Pick one."

"I'm not a—"

"Yes, but the Shifters have to get where they're going, don't they? Someone has to do it. So until we finish training the monkeys to do your job . . ." She waved her arm to mimic checking a box and mouthed the words *pick one*.

What a crapwench! Sure, I didn't blame Shifters for resenting the fact that we needed transporters. But that was uncalled for. I flipped around to look at Wyck, but he didn't meet my gaze. Every transporter in the room turned crimson. A few of them opened their mouths to say something, but she'd already turned her back on us and begun rearranging notes for the day's lecture on the wall behind her. A few Shifters in the back of the class leaned over and punched Wyck on the shoulder in a sign of solidarity, but his face had already gone blank, unreadable.

I had known this day was coming, when I had to choose a path, a future. But now that it was here, the words danced around and seemed unfamiliar. The form was straightforward enough, from the most intense, "Chronocrime Investigation," at the top, to the fluffiest down at the bottom. "Same-day chronocourier." *Phbbt.*

Grandpa used to say all Shifter jobs fell into one of two categories: curiosity or altruism. Or, as he used to phrase it, "the ones who can't help but know and the ones who can't help but help." For the most part, he was right. The majority of Shifters enter academia, studying some form of history, like my mom. And then there were expert witnesses, doggedly taking notes and measurements at the scene of an accident or crime. The rest usually went into public service—do-gooders. Activists who went back and filled out protest crowds or cleaned up the same ecosystems over and over. And medical consultants like Pennedy's older brother, who prepped the ER staff for incoming trauma patients. But being the smarty-britches I am, I always tried to stump Grandpa with exceptions.

"What about trenders? They don't do anything useful." Trenders were personal stylists who went back to the recent past and got paid by rich people to dress them in the next big thing in fashion before it was the next big thing. They held the dubious honor as the only Shifters who were legally allowed to share information from the future. Apparently, rich people have some powerful lawmaker friends.

"Ahh, but isn't there inherent goodness in beauty?" asked Grandpa.

"Do you *remember* the live-ferret coat fad?" Then I thought of one that was sure to stump him. "How about temporal smugglers?"

"That's not a calling." He kissed me on the top of my head. "That's a crying shame."

I cringed at the censure of a memory. The form in front of me flashed and brought me back to my task. I'd been thinking about the field of Temporal Ethics, but after yesterday's mission that probably wasn't a stellar idea. There was always Quantum Biology. It seemed to be the one class I wasn't in danger of failing right now. And, of course, anything in the here and now to unravel the mystery of Mom's accident in the past I wanted to do.

"Done?" Quigley didn't wait for a response. "Good."

I managed to mark the Bio box right before the form piffed away.

"Are there any questions?" she asked.

Arms shot up across the room.

"Questions that don't involve the phrases 'what should I do' or 'rest of my life'?"

Every hand went down.

Except Mimi's.

"Yes?" said Quigley.

"What would it mean if you didn't get the Buzz on a mission?" Mimi kept her attention trained forward, but her eyes slid across the aisle in my direction for a fraction of a second.

Panic sprang up in my gut. I hid my mouth with my hand and hissed, "What are you doing?" behind clenched teeth.

Quigley's lips transformed to a thin, red line. "Mild Buzzes are indicative of nothing."

"But *no* pain?"

I stared at Mimi, willing her mouth to stop moving. But at the same time, this *was* my one chance to find out.

"Likely the Shifter would have ingested some Buzztabs without remembering," said Quigley.

"But—"

"Miss Ellison, is there something you need to tell me?"

Mimi shook her head with a casual confidence only she could pull off, and our teacher let it drop.

"Today we'll cover the Chinchilla Flu Epidemic of— Oh." The Quig looked down at her screen. "First, Miss Bennis will present her midterm from yesterday."

I could feel the heat of my classmates' stares as I made my way to the front of the room. Quigley took a seat off to the side.

"My, umm, my trip—"

"Mission," interrupted Quigley. "You weren't on holiday."

"My mission was to early twenty-first-century Virginia." I looked up and realized I might as well be talking to air. Mimi and Charlie were the only ones even looking at me. Charlie always sat up front with her rather than in the back with the other transporters. At least my fellow Shifters had their eyes open. Half the transporters were falling asleep. Except Wyck, who was actually taking notes. A first.

"And?" said Quigley.

Wyck looked up from his notes and bobbed his head encouragingly.

"And everything went fine. My launching transporter landed me down a deserted alleyway in Williamsburg. There was a redcoats reenactment going on."

Quigley raised her eyebrows. I didn't want to get Wyck in trouble, so I quickly added, "Which was actually a good thing. It kept me on my toes. I had to figure out where I was based on my surroundings because it took a few minutes for my Quant-Com to quadrangulate my tendrils and register where I was. I had to use, umm, history skills."

History skills. This was going great.

"I then took a bus to the location and left the package there. At the location."

A couple transporters in the third-to-last row, Rab and Paolo, elbowed each other and started whispering.

"The location being?" said Quigley.

"The instructions sent me to a grave for a Muffy van Sloot. It was very . . . inconspicuous." So inconspicuous I couldn't find it. "Sorry. It was a routine mission. I don't know what else to say. Nothing out of the norm or dangerous. All safety protocol was followed."

"Sh'right," coughed Rab.

Quigley must not have heard him, but Wyck sure did. He landed a well-aimed kick to the back of Rab's chair.

"Umm." I'd lost my train of thought with the taunt. "As I was saying, nothing of note happened. I observed typical twenty-first-century behavior around me and then Charlie faded me home."

"Tendril tink," murmured Paolo under his breath. Several transporters around him grunted.

"You got a problem with Bree?" Charlie leaned back and growled.

"I, uhh . . ." My throat constricted.

Quigley looked down at my report. "And you rode a school bus to this Chinco"—her tongue stumbled over the name of the town the way mine first had—"uhh, Chincoteague Island. What were the other students like?"

"Very normal." I could feel a flash of color bloom across my cheeks. Finn and his family were anything but what my teacher would describe as normal. "The kid I sat next to loved movies. And action figures."

Rab and Paolo were still whispering on the other side of the room.

"And your Buzz level?" asked Quigley as if nothing were going on. In fact, she acted as if she wasn't interested in my report at all. This just might work.

"Was manageable." As it was nonexistent. I started to add something else but then paused, struck by something I'd never thought of before. The Buzz is a by-product of the genetic mutation in a Shifter's hippocampus that causes chronogeological displacement. It's a payoff. Yes, Shifters can travel through time and space because of a glitch in our brains. But the price is the Buzz. It was only after we came out of hiding that we discovered that, unchecked, the eventual price is much more costly.

My Bio teacher once described the Buzz as like the vibration on a guitar string after you strummed it. Maybe if you had your head shoved up in the guitar. Thankfully, the microchip holds back the Buzz, for the most part. Like pressing your fingers on the strings to control the pitch and tone. The chip doesn't take it away entirely, but it makes it manageable, almost unnoticeable. It also allows us to choose when and where we go. And then there was the real reason it was invented. (But there were non-Shifters in the room, so of course I couldn't mention *that*.)

After Mom's accident, when it was discovered her microchip

was no longer functional, most people thought she'd succumbed to some overpowering Buzz. But maybe it was the other way around. Her chip could have started overcompensating or something like that. My lack of Buzz might give us a hint of what went wrong on her last mission.

I was so excited by my new theory that I almost didn't notice it when Rab took out his stylus and acted like he was slicing his skull open and yanking out an imaginary microchip. I bit my cheek to keep from saying something I'd regret. The snerk. It didn't matter that there was no proof Mom had purposefully tampered with her chip. There would always be those like Rab and Paolo who claimed she did.

While I was zoning, Quigley had pulled up my QuantCom data. Translucent numbers and symbols streamed through the air in front of her. She seemed transfixed by them, but then I realized she was staring straight through them. At me.

"That's all." I scurried to my seat.

Quigley didn't say a word about my midterm. She walked to her podium and launched into the day's lesson.

When the end-of-class buzzer sounded, Quigley bellowed, "Twenty-kilobyte essay on the Chinchilla Flu Epidemic by Friday," as she walked into her office at the far end of the classroom and shut the door.

The comments from my departing classmates were to be expected. Suffice it to say, some of the spicier words would have topped Charlotte Masterson's "sweet Lord Baby Jesus" list.

As I gathered my things, Rab bumped into me and whispered, "Tink."

Mimi sputtered, "You're the . . . the . . ."

But I knew she wouldn't actually say the word.

I grabbed her hand and said, "Ignore him."

Right when we turned to leave, though, *whish,* Quigley's office door slid back open.

"Miss Bennis, Miss Ellison?"

53

The Buzz question Mimi had asked earlier. No, no, no, no, no. No red flags.

"I need to speak to you two in my office."

Blark.

Dr. Quigley sat down at her desk as we walked into the small room attached to the classroom. It was more like a closet than anything. The only things that suggested otherwise were a tiny window overlooking the street and a floor-to-ceiling wall of photographs behind her desk. Quigley sifted through the Specialization forms and didn't look at us but began talking.

"That was an odd thing to ask today, Miss Ellison. Your Buzz question." The Quig continued to look down, but a half grin hijacked her face. I felt like I'd seen that look before, but I couldn't remember one instance of her smiling in class. She finally glanced up. "Wouldn't you agree, Miss Bennis?"

I nodded.

"I'm curious as to why you would ask such a question, Miss Ellison." Quigley may have asked the question of Mimi, but she kept her eyes trained on me.

"Just a hypothetical," said Mimi.

"I see." Quigley started to wave her off, but I couldn't leave it at that. Not if there was a chance, however slight, that it could help my mother.

"If something like that did happen, hypothetically of course," I said, "do you think studying the anomaly could help advance medical research for, umm, for—"

Quigley's eyes narrowed to slits of fake pity. "For comatose patients?"

Once the words were out there—out loud—I realized how ridiculous it sounded. And how much I'd been harboring a secret hope there could be some truth to it. It *wasn't* true, of course. No progress, no leads, no hope.

Quigley pushed back in her seat. "No. As I explained during

class, the 'anomaly' would be easily explained by the distracta-
bility of human nature.

"So." The Quig looked back down at her work. "Do you feel
I've answered your question in such a way that it will never
come up again in my classroom?"

"Yes, ma'am," said Mimi.

"Then dismissed."

Mimi and I slinked toward the door, but Quigley added,
"Not you, Miss Bennis."

Mimi mouthed, *Sorry,* on her way out the door. As soon as
Mimi left, Quigley tapped the console on her desk. My midterm
materialized midair, inches from my nose. A bright red "D"
glowed in the middle.

What? No. Any assignment but this one. Please. Anything
below a C and Dr. Quigley could opt to go back to the site and
review the entire mission. She'd see the Haven Signal. And
someone in the family probably had found the black market
flexiphone gizmo I left behind.

"I'm disappointed in you," she said.

Not as disappointed as she'd be if she found out what I'd really been doing on that mission.

"I suppose I should send a review committee straight back
to this little Chincotuck place to investigate." She picked at the
edge of her square-sharp thumbnail. Squirms of dread wiggled
through my torso until Quigley spoke again. "But given your
unique circumstances, I'm not sure that's warranted."

Unique circumstances. That was one way of putting it. Six months
ago, my mom had landed on the steps of the Institute after an
otherwise routine job assignment. Her microchip wasn't working, and she was shouting incoherent gibberish. By the time help
arrived, she'd slipped into a coma. So, yeah. Some people might
go with "unique." I preferred "sucktastic." Still, thank goodness
my teacher could see reason.

"This is your final warning, though. No more mistakes, Bree. You can't afford them."

Oh, she had no idea.

Quigley turned back to the forms she was sorting. "Dismissed."

⌓

My rush of relief lasted precisely seven minutes.

I went straight to the computer lab. I knew I should let it go, but it still bugged me that my search results on Muffy van Sloot and the Mastersons had yielded zilch. As if they'd never existed. And if my assignment did come back up with Quigley, the more info I could give her the better.

Two other students were working, so I picked a station in the opposite corner. An audiovisual message from a sender I didn't recognize popped up. Curious, I opened it and immediately wished I hadn't.

"Hey, kiddo." Leto Malone's ugly mug materialized before me. His gravelly voice filled the air. "Just thought I'd—"

I slammed my hand against his soligraphic mouth and hissed, "Mute, mute, mute!"

The two students peered over at me, but I blocked their view of Leto as best I could. They turned back around to their own work.

"Shrink display. Readable Audio."

Leto shrank to the size of a chipmunk and his message scrolled above him:

Hey, kiddo. Just thought I'd check in. The boys here've been taking bets over whether you went through with it. But I got faith in ya, kid. Little reminder, though. The bank code is due now. As in now. Of course, if you didn't make the delivery, return the goods, no questions asked. But one of those things better be in my hands within forty-eight hours or I'm afraid some unpleasantness might occur.

Forty-eight hours? Every last drop of blood in my body drained to my toes as I trudged to my room. All I'd wanted to do was help my mom, pay her bills so she could get decent care. So she wouldn't end up in that madhouse Resthaven. So there might be some slim chance of her being normal again. Of us being normal again.

I had no idea what to do. I couldn't make up a pretend bank code. Leto'd check it before he let me out of his sight. But I didn't have any device to give back.

"Unpleasantness." That could mean anything. But like any good snake, Leto knew where to strike first to hit deepest. He knew my weak spots, my mom and her skyrocketing medical bills for starters. Or he could turn me in at the Institute and I'd lose the only home I had left. Of course, maybe he had even more—*gulp*—unsavory plans. He didn't become a top chrono-smuggler by passing out kittens and lollipops.

When I reached the room, I put on my everything-is-okay face. Mimi was sprawled on our couch in full mope mode.

"My life is over."

I bent over and checked her pulse. "Dang it. So close to a single room."

Mimi held up her QuantCom, lips all pouty. (And yet still magically perky. How did she do that?) "I got tomorrow's mission assignment. Botany. It's a full-dayer."

"I can see why this has compromised your very existence."

"I was supposed to go to the dance with Charlie." She chucked her Com on the seat beside her. "So much for that."

"He asked you to the dance?" *About time.*

"Yes. No. Kind of. He asked me if I was going. Does that count?" Mimi curled up in a ball and groaned. "I'm an idiot."

"You are not. He's into you; I can tell."

"You can? Really?" Mimi perked up.

I laughed. "I bet old Bergin can probably tell." When I said his name, I imagined our headmaster sitting at his desk, drawing matchy-match hearts between his pupils in the Institute roster. "Okay, maybe not Bergin."

Mimi sighed. "It's such a bumzoo. I thought maybe this was it, us finally . . . y'know." She sat up and wiped away a nonexistent tear. Oh, to have Mimi problems.

"Well, it doesn't matter now anyway," she said. "I'll be in twenty-first-century Maryland."

Whah? I scooped Mimi's Com off the couch and flipped to the top of the mission screen. The date was right around my midterm's, about three months later. As long as the Mastersons hadn't found the gadget and destroyed it, I'd be fine.

In the most nonchalant voice I could muster, I said, "Why don't I switch with you?"

"You have a mission tomorrow, too?"

"Yeah, and mine's a quickie." I slid my own Com over to her. "You'd be home in time to primp."

The glow of the mission screen made Mimi's impossibly blue eyes even bluer. "Our transporters would be in trouble, too, if we got caught. And our teachers would kill us if—"

"Why should they find out? The people who hire Institute kids to do chrono work hardly ever request a specific student. They don't care who does it as long as it gets done. Besides, if they catch us, we could feign ignorance. Oops, the roommates switched their QuantComs."

Oh, there was no way Mimi was falling for this.

"Yeah." She bit her lip. I braced for the *no,* but instead she threw her hands up in the air. "What the hoo? Let's do it!"

☉

The next morning, Mimi and I stood on adjacent Shift Pads, avoiding eye contact with both each other and our transporters. I said a silent prayer of thanks that Mimi's transporter was Charlie, who wouldn't turn her in even if it meant serving detention himself. And I was assigned to Wyck, who might not be fully awake yet.

"Ready?" Charlie winked at Mimi, and she nodded. Mimi liked the 2060s and *loved* the prospect of dancing with Charlie, so I only felt a tiny twinge of guilt as my roommate faded away.

"How 'bout you, sugar lips?" asked Wyck, looking at me.

"I, umm . . ." had an overwhelming urge to giggle and gave myself a mental slap. *Focus, Bennis.* "Push the button."

He laughed. "I didn't hear the special word in there."

I cracked a small smile. "Push. The. Blarking. Button."

"There you go. Happy landings."

And then I was hurtling through time.

I squinched up my eyes tight as I could and held my breath like usual. But the typical prickles didn't come crashing over me. Quite the opposite. It was the least painful Shift I'd ever experienced, a sensation of being pulled rather than pushed.

And then it was over.

chapter 6

OOF. The Shift may not have hurt, but the landing stung the soles of my feet like the frickens. I was in the middle of a field, far from prying eyes. My QuantCom registered a bus station half a mile up the road. I had to hand it to Wyck. The boy had good aim.

It was a nice afternoon for the walk, breezy and warm. I'd raided the cash vault before I left. I didn't want to waste any time scouting out free options, and there was more than enough for a bus ticket. The wizened counter attendant eyed the roll of bills as I peeled back a few layers.

"Where you headed?" he asked.

"Chincoteague Island."

"Going for the Pony Penning, eh?"

"Pony—? I mean, yes."

"Be crowded. You got somewhere to stay?"

I nodded, and he shot me a grin. His piano teeth had a few keys knocked loose.

"I've considered headin' up to the island one of these years and buying myself a pony. Got the land for it, but don't seem right somehow. Penning something up, what was born free like that."

I thought back to the info I'd read preparing for my midterm, about the feral ponies that had roamed nearby Assateague Island for centuries. "But if people give them a good home, isn't it a good thing?"

"I s'pose you're right." He handed my ticket over. "And it's an unforgettable sight, what I hear, watching them ponies swim the channel. You enjoy yourself."

"Thanks."

The ride took a little over an hour. I kept to myself and curled into a ball as we passed over bridges. At least I didn't have the Buzz making it worse. But the lack of Buzz only fueled my nerves. An elderly couple offered me a soda to settle my stomach, so my skin must have turned a queasy shade even if I thought I was handling the trip well.

When we arrived at the island, the same couple offered me a ride.

"Yes, please." This was getting easier and easier. Wyck might as well have dropped me in the Mastersons' backyard. I'd have Leto's gadget back in no time.

"Are you headed to the festival?" the woman asked.

"Yes. I'm staying with a family here."

"What's the address?"

Crap. What was the address? I blanked. And I had Mimi's QuantCom. It wasn't like I could check.

"Umm, the house is in the Something Estates. Wilson or . . ."

"Woodman?" A crease formed in the man's forehead.

"That's it. Woodman."

"And you *know* the owner of the house?" he asked, looking me up and down.

"Yes." Okay, so maybe I should have spent a little more time in the mirror that morning. I was wearing standard twenty-first-century clothing—stretchy T-shirt, faded jeans, scuffed boots—not exactly running with the jet set no matter which century I was in. "I'm friends with their son."

He let it drop, but the ride seemed to take twice as long as it had mere days before. If I thought I had learned more than I ever wanted to know about wild ponies before, I now knew more than I ever thought possible. The going rate for a pony at the next day's auction, the most sought-after markings, and the potential fertilizer output from three ponies.

That's right. I listened to the couple discuss horse poop for twenty minutes.

When we pulled up to the house, they looked around the property uncertainly. The windows were dark, no sign of life.

"You're positive you don't want us to stay?" asked the woman.

"I'll be fine. Thanks again for the ride." I waved as they drove away.

The doorbell played a cheery tune when I pressed it, but no one came to answer it. I backed up and stood on my tiptoes to see if the Haven Beacon was lit. It wasn't. Mostly because it *wasn't there*.

"That's weird." The mission date was three months after my midterm, and I hadn't seen any moving boxes or a FOR SALE sign last time. I went around back to the base of the deck, where I had shaken out my shoes. The sand ran through my fingers like water as I sifted the whole area. Nothing. *Dang it.*

I walked back up to the porch and leaned on the bell until it played one long note, in case someone was home and playing hard to get. A flash of movement near the window registered in the corner of my eye. The door flew open. A man's hand plunged out. It grabbed my wrist and pulled me into the foyer.

I twisted my arm to release it, but the hand held on. Tight, yet not hurting me at all. I continued to struggle against my captor, but he adjusted to my every move almost before I made it. My senses jumped to prey mode—eyes darting in the dim light— and took in every detail. Door. Fully shut but not dead-bolted. The air smelled like home-baked bread and cloves. I couldn't hear anything but the labored breaths that tickled my right ear. The rest of the room was unchanged from my last visit, except for a few new da Vinci sketches mounted high up on the wall. (Now *there* was a man sporting three green candles if ever there was one.)

As I tilted my head, the grip on my arm loosened. I turned and found myself staring into the face of, well, I had no idea who it was. But he wasn't hard on the eyes. Apparently, he'd just gotten out of the shower. He rubbed a towel slowly against his damp hair. Even with his muscles relaxed, they strained against his thin shirt.

Ba-da-bing. The Mastersons never mentioned an older son. Nephew? Live-in male model?

He let go of my wrist and took a few steps back. I fumbled to open Mimi's QuantCom and braced for an emergency fade.

"Bree. It's . . . it's you."

"How do you know my—?"

Before I had a chance to finish, the stranger closed the space between us with a single stride. He crushed me to his broad chest even as I tried to push him away. He released me long enough to catch my breath. And it was good he did, because the next thing I knew warm lips were pressed against mine, kissing them with a frantic, almost desperate energy. He clutched my hand in his, circling it around his waist. His lips calmed into a gentle rhythm. The kiss wasn't altogether unpleasant. It *was* altogether unexpected.

I reared back and slapped him. Hard.

"What was that for?" He rubbed the spot where I hit his cheek. A rosy mark lingered.

"For kissing me, what do you think?" I took another step back and held my hand against the doorknob, ready to bolt if he so much as flinched in my direction again. "Who are you?"

Confusion spread across his face. "What are you talking about, Bree?"

"How do you know my name?"

"How do I—?" His lips turned up in an uncertain smile. "It's me. Finn."

It wasn't possible. Had I undershot it by that much? I hadn't looked that closely at the date.

No, said an argumentative little voice in my mind, *Finn has carrot red hair and would get knocked sideways by a strong puff of wind. This guy has sun-kissed auburn waves and, oh my, the muscles and is a good kiss— . . . no, no, no, no, no.*

He leaned forward and rubbed my shoulder. "Are you okay?"

I couldn't turn the door handle fast enough. I sprinted up the driveway, running where exactly I'd no idea. The person who claimed to be Finn ran after me but kept a steady distance between us. When I realized I wasn't gaining any ground and he wasn't losing any, I gave up and turned to face him.

He lifted his hands in surrender. "Look, sweetie, I'm kind of confused right now, too."

Sweetie? My nostrils flared.

He stepped away and lowered his voice: "Why don't we go back in the house?"

This was insane. My thumb circled the edge of my Com, edging closer and closer to the emergency fade trigger.

"Whoa, don't do anything rash," he said.

I looked down at my Com. "How do you know what I'm about to do?"

"You have that about-to-fade look in your eye," he said.

His comment must have made my look grow worse, because he took a step back. "Just calm down. We'll talk out here."

"Okay. Talk."

He gnawed on his lower lip, and the small movement jolted a memory in me. Finn had done the same thing while we were out scouring the beach. It wasn't much, but it was enough to get me to lower the QuantCom.

"When is the last time you remember seeing me? Seeing . . . Finn?" he asked.

"A couple days ago. In your kitchen. When he . . . you called me a lunatic."

"A couple days?" His face fell.

"How long has it been for you?"

"Three years."

Dang it, Wyck. I was supposed to have arrived three months out from my original mission date. He'd missed it by *three years?* I looked Finn up and down. That would make him around eighteen years old. Looked about right. There went any chance of getting Leto's delivery back. I was in a blarkload of trouble.

"You don't remember calling me a lunatic?" I asked.

"No, I do. I'm—" He closed his eyes and took a deep breath. "I'm sorry. That was me at my lowest. I didn't know what I was saying."

"My turn," I said. "Why did you kiss me?"

"I was happy to see you."

"In the future, try this one on for size: 'Hi, Bree. So good to see you. Did you have a nice Shift?'" I held out my arm in a mock handshake.

"I'll keep that in mind."

A gust of wind knocked me off balance. It blew the front door against the house with a bang. "Where's your Haven Beacon?" I asked.

"Someone isn't waiting her turn." Finn chuckled in a way that came out almost a growl.

"*Someone* is about to disappear if she doesn't get answers."

"Fine. I took it down to keep a lower profile. For protection."

"Protection against what?"

"I . . . don't know."

"You don't know?"

"No. You wouldn't tell me."

"What are you talking about? What the blark's going on?" My confusion tripped over a fine line into fear.

"Bree, let's go inside and I'll explain everything that I can. Trust me."

"Great. Let me get this all straight. You've gone from runty toy collector to some kind of suave, paranoid recluse and you want me to traipse into your little trap and *trust* you?"

"What are you even trying to protect? A burglar could rob

you blind and your dad can go back a few hundred years and invest, like, a penny. You'd get your millions back. Who knows? Maybe you wouldn't even have to proposition unsuspecting time travelers. You could ask a girl out on a proper date and wait until the end of it to kiss her against her will."

My venting brought no relief from the unanswered questions. Instead frustration sizzled through my veins like an electric current. Still, I jutted my jaw in defiance. Finn cocked his head to the side, closed the space between us in three giant steps, and snatched away my QuantCom.

"All right. We'll do this the hard way." He hoisted me over his shoulder and marched back to the house. I could have screamed. Judging by the lack of cars in the neighboring driveway, there was no point. I spent my energy trying to grab my Com, but by the time I had almost wriggled out of his grasp we were in his living room. He dumped me unceremoniously on the couch and slouched into a love seat opposite it.

"Let's start over. Hi, Bree. So good to see you. Did you have a nice Shift?"

I crossed my arms and glared at him.

He leaned forward, and his voice took on the same intensity as when he first yanked me in the doorway. "Look, it's unfortunate that you had a recent run-in with an arrogant, ignorant prat whose world had just shattered. I was scared then." He leaned closer, perching on the edge of the couch, until I could feel the warmth of his breath on my face.

"I'm not scared anymore," he said.

I pulled my knees up to my chest. "Good for you. What changed your mind so suddenly?"

His expression darkened. "I decided what I was fighting for."

"Which is?"

"You."

chapter 7

THE ROOM WENT SILENT save for a giant grandfather clock ticking away in the corner. The minute hand clicked to the 3, and a bird shot out the front. *Cuckoo, cuckoo, cuckoo.*

Dang straight. I snorted. "Me?"

He leaned back in his seat. "You."

"Why would you fight for *me*?"

"Because you asked me to."

"What are you talking about? We spent, like, four waking hours together. Two of which you spent whining."

Finn squirmed and avoided my gaze. He pulled at a thread on the arm of his chair.

"What are you hiding?" I asked.

"Nothing."

"No, it's something. It's—" I stiffened and leaned as far from Finn as possible. The way he spoke to me. Looked at me. *Kissed me.* I forced a lump down my throat. "How many waking hours have we spent together?"

Finn kept his mouth shut and stared straight ahead.

"How many?" The words slid off my tongue like melting ice.

Finn ran his fingers through his hair and shook his head. "Obviously, I haven't spent any time with *you*. But I will. I don't know when you're coming back, though. I mean 'when' for you. I know when it was for me." With each "when," he scooted closer and closer until the tips of our knees touched.

A herd of thoughts thundered through my mind.

"Stop. Just stop." I hugged a pillow to my chest. "Start from the beginning."

"There's not much to tell until a year ago," said Finn. "That's when you—"

"Not me." We needed to get that straight right up front. "Future Me."

"That's when Future You showed up out of the blue and asked for my help."

"Help with what?" If he couldn't hand over Leto's device this trip, why on earth would I risk sneaking back again?

Finn hesitated and looked at the door. "I can't really tell you anything about the future."

"*You* can't tell *me* anything about the future? Oh, that is . . . no. No. *I* can't tell *you* anything about the future." Except apparently I already had. "Tell me what I told you."

"Maybe we should wait until my parents get home to talk about this."

"Talk now."

"You asked me to do something for you, and I agreed to do it. That's all."

"If that's all, then why did you kiss me?" I asked. "And why am I sitting here now?"

For the first time since I had arrived, Finn's cool cracked. He gazed away at the foyer, as if retracing our steps, then turned back to me. "Why *are* you sitting here now?"

Oh, yeah. I had come to him.

"That's none of your business."

"Bree." The way he said my name—a combination of Mimi's overexuberant worry and my mom's tender familiarity—it bugged me. "This is me you're talking to. What do you need?"

"Fine. You have something of mine, and I need it back."

"Something . . . futuristic?"

"Yes!"

"Something that, say, fell out of your shoe?"

"Yes, yes, yes." Now we were getting somewhere.

"Yeah, I don't have it anymore."

"What?" I clawed my hands into the chair to keep from lunging over and strangling him.

"You came and got it."

"Exactly."

"No. *You* came and got it. Future You. You left a note that said you needed it back."

"But . . . I . . ." My voice trailed off. That didn't make any sense. At all.

I needed that gadget and I needed answers.

But first, I needed my QuantCom back.

"Umm, Finn." I lowered my voice to a sultry whisper. The pillow I held fell to the floor as I edged forward. My leg brushed against his. "Could you do me a favor?"

Finn leaned in and reached to put his hands on my knees. "Anything."

Perfect.

I pounced before he had a chance to figure out what was going on. He'd had the foresight to zip the QuantCom in his cargo pants pocket, so it wasn't as easy to grab as I thought it would be. And I'd never been good with zippers. Again, Finn matched my every move before I made it. At first, he laughed, treating my attack like a playful wrestling match. It didn't take much pocket grabbing for him to figure out what was going on, though.

"Stop." He batted my hand away like I was a kitten tussling a ball of yarn. "You might hurt yourself."

Puma claws came out, and the next thing I knew I was rolling on the ground with a still-chuckling Finn. He didn't fight hard, but he also didn't fight fair. At one point, Finn clasped both my hands in one of his and tickled me. I wriggled on top of him and managed to hold down his wrist long enough to get him to stop tickling. I pinned his other hand down with my knee while I unzipped the pocket with my teeth.

Finn burst out laughing. "What are you doing?"

"I . . . trine . . . to . . . reesh . . . my . . ." But I didn't finish my thought. My mouth fell open when I noticed two people standing in the kitchen doorway staring at us, their mouths agape as well.

"Get a room," said a slightly taller, no longer gangly, definitely still-sassy Georgie.

"Get a life," answered Finn, and sat up. I scrambled off him but stayed within grabbing distance of his pocket.

Georgie stuck out her tongue at Finn; then before I could brace myself she ran over and tackled me in a hug.

"It's about time you showed up," she said. "There's this cute dress I want you to look at later, tell me how historically accurate it would be. I met this guy in the 1920s. So squeeworthy. And well, let's just say that every time I think about him . . ." She paused for dramatic effect and gave me a look like I was in on some kind of inside joke. ". . . I'm all *whoosh!*"

"I, uhh . . ."

Charlotte waved at me. "We weren't expecting you! Of course, when are we? How are things going?"

"Umm, fine. I guess." A polite lie, but I didn't really feel like explaining the vengeful smuggler who was after me.

"No. How are *things* going?" She lowered her head and did everything but say the word "wink" out loud.

"Huh?"

"Mom," Finn said, "Bree's not—"

"Did Finn not offer you anything to drink?" Charlotte looked at the coffee table and tsked. "Sun tea's steeping, but it'll be an hour or so."

"I'll take a Coke," said Georgie.

"You know where the fridge is."

"Why does Bree get special treatment?" Georgie whined. "She's practically a member of—"

Finn exploded into a massive coughing fit. Charlotte swooped down to check on her choking son, which only exacerbated Georgie's snit.

"Oh, come on, he's pretending." Georgie tossed her hair over her shoulder. "I think I'm heading out."

"Oh, no, you're not," said her mom. "Bree just got here."

"I'll see her later. Sorry. Can't help it."

"You most certainly can," said Charlotte, "Do not, I repeat, do not leave this—"

But she was talking to a patch of air.

Guess Georgie's gene had kicked in.

Charlotte plopped on the couch.

"My only consolation in life is that someday the Lord will smite her with a teenage daughter as feisty as she is. If only Dad were here. Sometimes he can go after her. You are staying for dinner, Bree." It came out more command than question. "Oh and, Finn, Aunt Lisa dropped in for the pony swim, so set two extra plates."

It was at that moment that Finn's dad popped up from the middle of nowhere next to Charlotte.

"Ah, good." Charlotte stood up and gave John a peck on the cheek. "Three plates."

"Hello, Bree," said John. His hair lay disheveled, his glasses askew. Head to toe, he was covered in a crimson coat of blood.

I choked back a scream.

Where had he been? What had he been doing? Their lives were chaos, not to mention the pain Georgie was in at this very moment from the Buzz, a fact that no one seemed to want to acknowledge. No wonder Charlotte was so worked up all the time. They might live in posh surroundings right now. But her husband could be exhibiting the first symptoms of the disease that would eventually strip them of everything—the disease that would overtake me if it weren't for my microchip—and they wouldn't even know it. For the first time, I fully grasped the ban against Shifter interaction. Even though I barely knew them, I wished I could offer them the safety I had nestled away in my own head. But the microchip wouldn't do them much good without the technology and medical expertise to support it. Knowledge that wouldn't exist for 150 years.

"Are you okay?" Charlotte asked me.

"Am I okay?" I turned to look at Finn, hoping he'd launch into an explanation. But he had fixed his gaze out the back window. He cradled my QuantCom in his open hand, like he was holding a fragile bloom. Without a single protest from him, I leaned over and took it away. "Your husband stepped out of a horror movie and you're asking if *I'm* okay. Look, I may have just met you people, but this is nutso."

Dr. Masterson had been quietly staring at me the whole time. He put his hands in his pockets and sighed. "So you're the one who started this whole mess."

I blinked. And he was gone.

chapter 8

"WHAT MESS?" I ASKED.

Charlotte looked from Finn to me as understanding dawned on her face. "Is this not our Bree?"

"She's still my Bree," said Finn in a murmur.

I ignored him. "What mess?"

"Why don't you sit down and have some tea, dear? We'll get this worked out."

"There's nothing to work out. Just tell me what—"

A chirpy noise interrupted me. Charlotte pulled her phone out and grimaced.

"I have to go pick up your aunt. One of the ponies pooped on her shoe." When Charlotte saw what must have been a look of sheer incredulity on my face, she placed her hand on my cheek. "It will take some time to explain, and I want John to be here. Why don't you guys go get some air? You can pick up the pie from Ella's. I'll call Finn when I'm back."

⚭

And *that* was how I came to be driving along a deserted beach access road in Finn's shiny Porsche SUV, a new one since the last time I'd been there, with a rhubarb pie in my lap. One of his hands rested lightly on the bottom of the steering wheel, the other draped over the back of my seat. He wasn't quite as annoying as I remembered. His stubborn streak still aggravated me, and I was pretty sure if I peeked into the glove compartment I'd

73

find a stash of action figures. But, all in all, it was a pleasant drive.

"So the blood thing. Your dad's really a surgeon?"

Finn nodded. "One of the things they never lied to me and Georgie about. They just failed to mention most of his surgeries take place before he was born."

"Why would your father say that about me causing some mess and then disappear? I mean, seriously?"

"He has a habit of doing that. The *poof*. Trust me. It's not you." Finn pushed his sunglasses up his nose, and for a fleeting moment he looked like a movie star.

It was hard not to feel flattered. But I also felt like a bug squished under a microscope, the way he glanced—no, gazed—over at me every twenty seconds. I twisted my or, rather, Mimi's mission package in my pocket. It was a packet of seeds (or, as I liked to call it, the Baggie o' fail) for Botany. Apparently some great-great-great-something relative of a woman named Agnes Wellesley of Westvale, Maryland, was dying to know if their heirloom tomato seeds were an exact genetic match to hers. It didn't matter, not really. I could go scan a packet of seeds at the Piggly Wiggly grocery store we'd passed back there and pretend they were Agnes's. She'd never know, and her great-great-great-something relative who would still find these seeds stuffed in an old box or book would still wonder if these were the genetically identical variety of seeds as this Agnes woman had, who would . . .

Chicken–egg.

No one likes a temporal loop migraine.

The fact is no one understands temporal paradoxes, not fully. NonShifters hold them in morbid fascination. Shifters simply try to pretend they don't exist. We all spout the Doctrine of Inevitability because it makes us feel better, but at the end of the day the important thing is the universe has neither exploded nor imploded. Sometimes that's the best you can hope for.

I wasn't even really sure why I was still here.

No, that wasn't true. I was buying time while I figured out how to handle the Leto situation. And that situation had gotten a lot more complicated now that I knew my future self had already come and gotten the flexiphone. Try as I might, I couldn't fathom any reason why she'd do that, I mean, why *I'd* do that.

Plus, it drove me bonkers not knowing what Finn and his parents knew about *my* future. I wasn't sure who I was angrier with—Finn for clamping his lips shut every time I asked him anything but a trivial question (and still a little bit for clamping those lips on mine), John for Shifting away, Charlotte for pretending this was all a big misunderstanding, or Future Me. For dragging me into this sinkhole of what-the-crap-is-going-on.

Finn opened his mouth like he was about to say something but then snapped it shut.

"What?" I asked, using the seed packet to fan myself.

He adjusted the air vent to blow in my direction. "I covered for you, you know."

"Huh?"

"After you first came here, when I was fifteen, that Monday when I got back to school, they called me into the office and asked me a bunch of questions about a girl who wasn't supposed to be on the bus. I didn't know how your whole school assignment thing worked, but I figured you needed people asking questions like you needed a hole in the head. So I made up a story about you being my cousin and running into you in Williamsburg and saving your parents a drive."

"Thanks." I meant it.

"Look, I'm not trying to keep anything from you, Bree." He looked over at me, and I had a sudden urge to touch his face. I sat on my hands instead. He looked back at the road. "I have a lot of unanswered questions, too. I still don't know what prompted you to come here a year ago. But I'll answer what I can."

"Okay, how many times exactly have I been back?"

He turned red. "Do you have to start with that one? I don't want to tell you about your future."

"Humor me."

"Look, don't you have a rule against that or something? Start with another one."

"Did I come back more than once?" *Oh my gosh.* Of course I had. His family knew me on sight. "Twice?" But *how?*

"Pass." His stony gaze told me arguing would be futile.

Okay. "Did you ever find out who Muffy van Sloot is?" Maybe she had something to do with my future self coming back.

"Muffy van Snoot?"

"Sloot. The grave I was looking for. There's no record of anyone by that name on this island. Ever."

"Sorry. I haven't run into anything about her. I was a bit preoccupied after you left, convinced I was going to start hopping around time and space at any moment."

"But you didn't? You're not a Shifter?"

"Alas, no. It would seem Georgie won the genetic lottery."

I scowled. Zero for two. "But there wasn't any record of you or your family either."

He shrugged.

Zero for three.

"So you not existing doesn't wig you out?" I asked.

"My family stays pretty low on the radar, what with the whole Shifting thing."

That wouldn't be enough to keep any trace of them off the database. A library card. A school sports team. Shoot, his driver's license would show up if nothing else.

"Okay, so this *thing* I asked you to do, did it have to do with school? Or someone named Leto?" Maybe I confided my plans to Finn for some . . . unfathomable . . . reason.

"I really can't talk about it. And frankly, you didn't tell me much about the future," he said. "We, uhh, we spent a lot of time *not* talking, if you are picking up what I am throwing down."

"Consider it picked up. Or better yet, why don't we leave it where it is? On the ground."

I turned and stared out the window. He really wasn't going to tell me anything. *Erg.* I might not be able to do anything to change whatever my future self told him, but I had a right to know what it was. I *needed* to know what it was. Leto Malone didn't mess around. Finn simply needed a little encouragement.

I slipped my QuantCom out of my pocket and pretended to check some settings. Finn was too busy singing along to the blaring radio to notice the small metal doohickey pop out of the top, where the winder would be on a real pocket watch. With a cursory glance at the screen, I adjusted the intensity down to the lowest setting. Just a teensy warning zap to get his attention. A nifty feature, the stunner.

"One last chance. What did Future Me tell you?" I asked.

"One last—?" The ocean reflected in his sunglasses, all pearly and swirly, as he turned to face me and switched off the radio. "Bree, we've been over this. We can discuss this with my parents. Later."

"Well, I say there's no time like the present." I reached over and tapped the end of the QuantCom against his shoulder. "Now how about those answers?"

When he didn't respond, I repeated the question. When he still didn't respond, I nudged him on the arm.

"Finn?"

The muscles under his shirt tightened. His legs stretched and stiffened. His teeth gritted into an angry grimace.

Why was he—? I looked down at my Com. *Buh-lark.* I meant to set it on "mild," to give him a little jolt and scare him into shooting straight with me. It was on "max." *Crap, crap, crap.* I hadn't meant to immobilize the poor guy.

We lurched forward in a burst of uneven acceleration, and the

state of Finn's neuromuscular system became the least of my
worries. The SUV careened toward the side of the road. Its tires
caught the mixture of sand and loose gravel on the shoulder and
fishtailed. I grabbed the steering wheel and wrenched it around,
a difficult task with Finn's death grip on it. The road hairpinned
a hundred yards ahead. No way I could steer through that curve
with Finn seizing like a landlocked fish in the driver's seat. *Crap!*
We were going to die!

Stay calm. Maybe I could off-road it. A grove of trees grew to
our left. The beach stretched out to our right. *Nope.* I'd have to
take my chances on the road.

A light flashed in the distance and blinded me for a second.
The sun was glinting off something. The square frame of a moving truck came into focus as it rounded the sharp curve ahead.

Oh. No.

Finn's mouth was clenched, but I could tell he was trying to
say something. All that came out was a guttural grunt.

"Brrrrr . . ."

He couldn't even get my full name out.

"Hang on," I said, unbuckling myself and leaning down to
pull his foot from the pedal. Our speed dropped a little, but the
foot wouldn't budge far. "I can't get it loose!"

The oncoming truck's horn blasted again as we veered into its
lane.

"Okay, beach it is." The wheel protested as I tugged it around.
We spun through the gravel onto the sand.

"Brrrrr!"

"Kind of busy now, Finn." The sand slowed us further, but
not enough. Ocean filled the whole windshield, and I froze. We
were headed for the water.

"F-f-f-inn." I clutched his hand so tight, it was as if I'd been
the one hit with the stun gun.

"Brrrr . . ."

This was it. I was going to die in an overpriced status symbol with a crazy chronostalker whose father was convinced I was some Jezebel who had caused . . . well, I didn't know what, but it couldn't be good. And none of it mattered, because I was about to drown.

It was all my fault.

No. Future Me's fault.

And that was all it took. It was like her voice filled my brain: *This isn't how you die. Get out!*

No time to think. I unbuckled Finn's seat belt, reached over him to unlatch his door handle, swiveled my leg over, and kicked the door open. Prying Finn's fingers off the wheel, I wrapped my arms around his torso. The sound of my own heart thundered through my ears. Against my chest, the *kathump* of Finn's, each beat matching my own racing rhythm.

"Unhh." I shoved off from the middle console like a coiled spring as the front tires hit the waterline.

Our tangled bodies scraped a shallow trench through the wet, hard-packed sand and skidded to a halt. The car decelerated rapidly with Finn's foot off the pedal, but it was too late. With a *shoosh,* it rolled up to its roof into the water. Each wave sucked it deeper and deeper.

The left side of my body felt like it had lost a grudge match with a loofah. Blood seeped into the corner of my eye. A gash on my foreheard stung like the devil. Finn didn't seem to have any major injuries. I rubbed his hands and feet, trying to return sensation to them. He lay next to me like a clump of kelp.

"Brrrr . . ."

"It's okay. We're safe. I got us out."

"Brrrrr . . ." Finn started to wiggle his fingers and bent his knees to the side. A cough rasped its way up his chest and out his loosening jaw. "Brrr-ake."

A moan escaped as I collapsed onto the sand next to him. I could have stepped on the brake. We lay there side by side staring at the clouds overhead as his arm and leg twitches subsided.

"I've never driven before," I said after a few minutes of silence.

Finn lifted himself up on his elbows and grimaced as he touched a raw spot on his cheek. "And you never will again." He sounded like he'd inhaled as much sand as I had lodged down my bra.

"I'm so sorry. For your car. For . . . zapping you."

"Why again did you do that?" He rubbed the back of his skull, feeling for bumps, his movements still stiff.

"All your answers to my questions have been so cryptic. I was trying to get your attention." *By stunning him?* the little voice shouted in my head. I had just violated every rule of Shifting *ever.* Including the ones that hadn't been written yet. I suddenly found myself fall-on-my-face grateful that he didn't exist in any of our data systems. Because this little stunt was beyond review board. Beyond expulsion.

Finn stared at the bubbling spot where his car had been. "You wanted my attention? I'd say you got it."

"I didn't mean to turn the stunner up that high. It was supposed to sting you, to make you listen. I can't believe I wrecked your car. I'm so, so, so, so sorry." I buried my face in the sand, a bad idea given my wound. "Oww!"

Finn reached over and drew me close.

"Shhh," he said. "It's my fault. I shouldn't have provoked you earlier."

"What? Stop it!" I pushed him away. "I drove your blarking car into the blarking ocean. I could have killed us both. Yell at me. *Blame* me."

An infuriating laugh filled the space between us.

"How is this funny?" I asked.

"It's not, but you know that thing you said earlier about investing the penny?" He shook sand out of his hair and pulled his shoulders into a sheepish shrug. "It's kind of true. We're not hurting."

One final bubble glugged to the surface where his Porsche had been.

"I guess I could pay you back in stock tips," I said. A hint of a laugh, more shock than anything, came out. The sun melted toward the horizon. I took off my shoes to shake the sand out.

"You don't owe me anything." His hand inched its way toward mine. A wave lapped high on the shore and reached my toes, an excuse to hop up.

"So back to my questions."

His shoulders shook in a silent chuckle.

"You still won't answer me?"

"Not won't, Bree. Can't."

"You can't remember what I said or did a year ago that apparently changed your entire outlook on life?"

"No." He stood up and brushed sand away. "I *can't* talk about it, at least not right now."

"Sounds kind of paranoid," I said.

"This coming from the girl who attacked me with a freeze ray gun?"

"It's not a ray gun," I mumbled. "More a . . . nerve disrupter."

"And yet that doesn't make me feel better."

"Look, just tell me. Obviously, I'm going to find out soon enough." So there.

"I can't."

"You mean 'won't.' "

He tossed his hands in the air. "What I mean is you made me promise I wouldn't tell you!"

Finn took off walking up the beach toward the road without a syllable of explanation.

"What do you mean by that?" I scrambled after him, stumbling over the tire track mounds. My legs were so much shorter than his, I had to take two steps for every one of his long strides.

"What do you think I mean?" He turned around and looked

at me like I was somehow the crazy one. "Future You must know about this trip. She didn't want me to tell you what she asked me to do."

"That does *not* sound like me."

"Y'know what?" he said as he took off again. "I don't think *you* sound like you."

"And what's that supposed to mean?"

"Look, I'm trying stay positive, but you're making it really hard."

"Oh, thank you for reminding me! Everything is Bree's fault . . . I almost forgot for all of two minutes."

"That's not what I'm saying." His pace slowed, but he didn't turn to look at me.

"Then what are you saying?" I jogged forward to catch up with him and put my hand on his shoulder.

He flinched away from my touch.

"What I'm saying is, for the life of me, I can't figure out what could possibly happen in the next however many months or years of your life that sucks some of the shrew out of you."

My breath turned to cotton in my throat. Snappy comebacks raced to the end of my tongue. Most involved his lack of kissing skills and love of action figures. But they all dissolved on the tip before I could blurt them out. Angry tears brimmed my eyes.

Finn put his fist to his mouth. "I didn't mean that."

He reached out to me, and I bristled away.

"I get it." I'd had enough. I wiped my face with my shirt and strode past him.

"No, you don't."

"Yes." Finality pounded in my voice. "I do."

⬭

Finn knew a shortcut back, and he kept his yap shut on the walk home. The silence, awkward as it was, gave me a chance to mentally sift through the bizarre situation I'd somehow gotten myself into. What I knew: Apparently, at some point in the future I would return to visit the Masterson family. I would, umm, become friendly with Finn for some reason that would surely make sense at the time. It certainly didn't now. I'd take Leto's delivery with me. And I would ask for Finn's help with something. What I didn't know: everything else.

As we neared Finn's house, a headache started pounding across my temples. It wasn't the usual spot as the Buzz. Probably a result of the crash mixed with wanting to cry.

I rubbed at my silver locket bracelet, wishing, wanting, needing my mom in that moment. The last sliver of sun glinted off the topmost windows of the Masterson home as we reached their driveway. A lace of clouds melted from orange to red to pink. The view would have been magnificent if I were able to focus on anything but the increasing pain that pummeled my head. It was a strange sensation, like a gnawing from the inside out.

"See? Not far at all." Finn turned to look at me. A paper-thin smile strained his lips.

Charlotte was pacing on the porch with her cell phone. As we crunched down the gravel driveway, Finn waved to get his mom's attention. I caught the tail end of the phone conversation.

"Never mind. He's here." She ran down the front steps and called, "Where's your car?"

"Bay," said Finn.

"What?"

"In the bay."

"You mean the *water*? Why is your car in the—?" She stopped when Finn coughed and shook his head from side to side, pausing on my side with an extra cough.

"Was Bree driving?"

"No. It's a long story, Mom."

"Are you two all right?"

Finn nodded. I started to, but a new wave of agony seized the base of my skull. Jagged shards sealed my eyes shut. I couldn't escape it. This was no Buzz.

I reached out and grabbed Finn's shoulder. "Hurts . . . hurts." The words came out in a choke and seemed distant, like someone else had spoken them. Even my tongue wasn't immune to the pain.

"Is Dad back?" asked Finn. He cradled me against his shoulder. My limbs went stiff, then limp.

"He's in the house."

"Get him!"

Finn's dad came running out the door a few moments later. But it was too late. I was being pulled inside out. Pulled with a ferocity I'd never experienced before in Shifting.

The tips of my fingers tingled. I reached for my QuantCom but couldn't make out the screen. The world around me darkened by the second. In the distance, John shouted something. I couldn't understand him.

I was dying. Was already dead. This must have been what had happened to my mom.

Wait.

No.

It hit me. I wasn't dying, though in that moment I wished I were. This was a forced fade.

I was in so much trouble when I got back.

But then I became aware of another sensation, that of being held. Finn lowered me to the ground. Warm, strong arms wrapped around my cold and lifeless ones. He held me against his chest slowly rising and falling, so different from my own panicked panting.

"No!" I pushed Finn as hard as I could, but he only held tighter. I had to get him off me. He'd never survive the Shift.

"Trust me," he said quietly.

Trust him?

"Let go of me." I tried in vain to get away from him. "Get him off of me!" I shouted to Finn's parents.

Charlotte struggled to reach out to Finn a few yards away, sobbing. "Not like this. John, can't you—?"

"Not yet, Char." John held her back. "It has to happen."

I thrashed like a salmon who thought it could escape the bear. It was no good. Finn was a persistent bear.

I rolled over. I would squirm off of him, push him away from a death sentence. As the pressure became unbearable, I gave up and let myself fade. My last coherent thought was, *This must have been the mess Finn's father was referring to.*

Killing his son.

chapter 9

THE FIRST TIME I ever witnessed my mother Shift, I was six. Our neighbor Mrs. Jacobs had to back out of babysitting at the last minute, so Mom lugged me along to her lab at the National Gallery of Art. She'd discovered a potential ink discrepancy in one of the early Impressionists' signatures—or something like that—and she needed to run back to 1864 and check it. Settled into a corner of the room with a bag full of be-good-or-else bribes and the other Art Historians fawning over me, I was in heaven. Until my mom stepped onto the Shift Pad and disappeared. Just like that. Gone. She'd told me it would happen that way, but to see it—to see *her* vanish—was too much for my six-year-old brain.

Mom's transporter, Jex, was one of the old-old-old-timers. He had fuzzy white tufts growing out of his ears, and when I asked him about the hair he said it was to filter out the whiners. Mom had told me to give him a wide berth when I visited her in the lab. She needn't have bothered. He smelled like pickles and cheap cologne.

As soon as my mother Shifted, I started whimpering. Then crying. Then wailing. Jex was not what one would call sympathetic.

"She's only gone back a few hundred years. Stop yer belly-aching."

"But . . . but . . . but . . ." Each sob turned to a painful burr in my throat.

"Do you want me to force her fade?"

The way he said it, even at that age, I knew there was only one answer to that question. But still, I couldn't stop the tears. Mom's assistant Amelia had to scoop me up and rush me out of the room until I calmed down.

"Did I get Mommy in trouble?"

"With Jex?" Amelia planted me on a bench in front of a portrait of a girl sitting quietly with stockinged feet hanging off the edge of a bed. Maybe Amelia hoped to inspire me. "You don't need to worry about him. He snarls, but he doesn't have any teeth."

"He doesn't have any—?"

Amelia sighed. "I mean, he would never follow through on that threat, a forced fade."

"Is a forced fade bad?"

"Very."

"Does it hurt?"

"You'll never need to worry about something like that."

"But does it?"

Another sigh, this one without looking at me. "Yes."

I thought she'd elaborate, but she didn't.

∞

Amelia had told the truth.

"Hurt" didn't cover it. I gasped for breath. My lungs had been crushed into a tiny ball. *Everything* had been crushed into a tiny ball. My head had somehow simultaneously caved in and cracked open. And my stomach . . .

Oh, blark.

I turned my head and heaved, but nothing came up. I forced my eyelids open.

White stone loomed overhead. I curled my fingers into the ground, and they met grass, but not the cool, soft green I'd tromped through in Chincoteague. It prickled, scratching against my

87

wrists. I blinked and willed my eyes to focus. The Jefferson Memorial stretched out above me, fuzzy, then sharp, fuzzy, then sharp.

There was no denying the "forced" in the forced fade. So different from the normal synch sensation, that of a taut rubber band slackening. My band had snapped. I brushed my trembling palm across my face, and when I pulled it away a streak of red stained it. I pressed my fingers to my nose. Blood. Gushing out. Oozing down my wrist. This couldn't be happening. I pinched my nostrils shut and fought back another dry heave.

When I reached my arms out to push myself up, my right hand brushed against something soft. I looked over to see what it was, and vomit crawled back up my throat.

Finn.

No. This couldn't be real. He was a hallucination. But when I touched his cheek it was solid.

"Finn." My voice was hoarse and hysterical. It built to a scream. "Finn!" I shook his shoulders. He didn't move.

Panicked, I pressed my lips to his. Still warm. Soft. But motionless.

I buried my ear in his chest, listening for breath, but I couldn't hear anything over the roaring in my own head. What had I done? Future Me knew about this. *Knew* about this! I should have found a way to stop him.

"Don't be dead, don't be dead, don't be dead." I rocked back and forth.

Help. I had to go for help. I stood, like a marionette pulled upright. But I had no one I could turn to. Not for this.

My QuantCom vibrated and started beeping. I threw it as far away as I could with a roar. Given how worn-out I was, it wasn't far. Fury spread to my core, but there was nothing to pummel, no one to scream at. I alone had caused this.

I gulped a mouthful of air but couldn't draw it down my throat. *This.* This was what drowning felt like. Finn's hair had fallen into his eyes. I knelt down next to him and brushed it away. And then the sobs started, plump tears splashing across his chest, his arm. *No,* I thought bitterly. *His corpse.*

The corpse sat up and rubbed its head.

"Aiggh!" I flung myself backward against the cold stone of the memorial.

"That hurt like a—" muttered Finn before he spotted me. "How long have I been out?"

"You're alive."

"Barely."

"You. Are. Alive." I dug my thumb into a crack in the marble beneath me. Something real, something solid.

Finn looked at me as if he was walking into a trap. "Yes . . ."

"How are you alive? People can't Shift into the future."

"We didn't." He propped himself up on one elbow and pointed to the Washington Monument in the distance. His mouth split into a cocky grin. "I kept us in my time."

I bent over, grabbed his finger, and moved it a few inches to the left, toward the western side of the Tidal Basin. When I removed my hand, his arm dropped. As did his jaw.

"What is that?" he asked.

"The Barack Obama Memorial fountain."

"The *what?*"

"Obama was our nation's first black president. He served in office from 2008 until—"

"I know who President Obama is . . . was . . . is." Finn felt around in the grass for his sunglasses. He shoved them on and blinked at the shimmering fountain.

"Yep. It's still there," I said.

His head swayed from side to side. "How could it not have worked?"

"How could what not have worked?"

"I was supposed to keep you in the twenty-first century with me. Safe."

"Is that what Future Me told you to do? Cling to me to keep me in your time?"

"No. I mean, yes." Finn closed his eyes. "I don't know."

I grabbed him by the shoulders. "What *exactly* did I instruct you to do?"

"Protect you."

"Protect me from what?"

"You didn't say."

I let go of him. "That's it?"

Way to be specific, Future Me.

He hedged a moment, then nodded. "Yes. That's it."

"And this is your way of protecting me? Breaking every law of quantum mechanics to hang out with me in the twenty-third century."

"Whenever Dad Shifts, he makes sure not to touch Mom or me. He says touching a nonShifter would stop him from going anywhere. I thought . . . I thought I was keeping you safe."

"You're lucky we didn't land in the Institute. That's where I'd be if this had been a normal fade. That's where I'm supposed to be. A forced fade messes with your tendrils—wrenches them through the space-time continuum." My vision was still fuzzy around the edges, and I fought back another wave of nausea.

"Where you're supposed to be? Maybe you're *supposed* to be back in Chincoteague with my family. Safe."

"Safe." I snorted. "You're the reason I'm in danger."

As if on cue, my Com vibrated again. I didn't need to open it to know something was wrong. *Good grief.* Of course, something was wrong. Everything was wrong.

The face of it flashed red when I picked it up. I tossed it back to the ground like a steaming potato.

"They know."

"They know what?" asked Finn.

"The value of pi. What do you think? They know I brought something back with me."

It happened occasionally. A bottle cap stuck in the shoe, gum in the mouth, a forgotten wrapper in the pocket. They all shared the same fate.

Straight into the incinerator.

"Another one of your Shifter rules?" He smirked.

"Nope. Not a Shifter rule. One of our country's laws, Finn. *Laws.*"

"So what . . . you just changed the future by bringing me here?"

"I didn't bring you here! You *clung* to me. And it's not that simple."

"Explain it to me."

"Do you realize the bacteria and germs and . . . general filth you have on you right at this very moment?"

Finn smirked. "The worst I have is a cold coming on."

"From a virus that was likely eradicated forever ago. No one would have any immunity to it now. That cold could cause an epidemic. And the earth's atmosphere is different now. What if it mutated into a new strain?"

"You don't get sick every time you go back in time, do you?"

"Shifters are vaccinated. Then decontaminated when they synch. But there aren't enough vaccines to protect the entire population against every disease throughout time."

"So it's bad that I'm here."

"You think?"

"What you're saying is you need *protection.*"

"Because of *you*! Oh my gosh." I grabbed my head. It still felt like it was going to explode from the forced fade. At least my nosebleed had stopped. "A human being. From the past. I'll go to prison for this."

Finn's gaze wandered off to the distance. He picked a blade of grass from the lawn and twisted it around his thumb. Technically, I could have made a citizen's arrest of him for committing a misdemeanor, but I let it slide given the circumstances.

"They know it's me?" he asked. "The object you brought back?"

"No." I laughed.

"But they know it's a person?"

"Trust me, if anyone in their right mind believed I somehow managed to bring a human back from the past you'd be in a lab already and I'd be in jail."

An impish grin spread across Finn's face. "Take off your shirt."

"What? No." Seriously, was there a single guy out there who had the ability to think with anything other than his hormones?

"Did you forget?" Finn took his own shirt off and threw it to me. "You fell in a mud puddle on your assignment and borrowed a random stranger's shirt. Very nice guy. You'll have to remember to thank him someday."

I'd heard worse.

"What will you wear?" I pointed at my own formfitting T-shirt. It would fit around one of his biceps if we were lucky.

"A smile." He waggled his eyebrows at me as I started to lift my shirt.

"Turn around." I looked around to make sure no one else was looking our way.

For once, he didn't argue with me as he swiveled his body away. "I was going to."

"Yeah, right. After that kiss earlier?"

The tips of his ears reddened. "No, I was."

The time for squabbling had passed. I pulled his shirt on. "Okay, you can look."

He turned around slowly, and I made every effort not to look at his bare chest.

Okay, maybe not *every* effort.

"All right." He clapped his hands together. "Where to now? Your school?"

He couldn't be serious.

"*I'm* going to my school," I said. "You're going . . ."

Yikes. Where *was* he going?

A siren wailed in the distance. Even if it wasn't for me, it made my next decision easy. I snapped the QuantCom shut and grabbed Finn's hand. We scurried across the autumn-faded lawn and down the wide white steps of the memorial. At first, Finn lagged behind. I didn't know if he felt sick from the forced fade or nervous to be in the twenty-third century. And I didn't give a mouse's left butt cheek either way.

"Hurry up," I said, clawing my nails into the palm of his hand.

Whatever misgivings he had, he put them aside. Soon his footsteps fell in with mine. We raced down to the edge of the Tidal Basin. I stole one final glance at my QuantCom and plunked it into the water.

"Whoa!" Finn jumped back from the splash. "Isn't that, like, your security blanket?"

"It's not providing me much security, is it?" Still, I couldn't pull my eyes away as it sunk into the murkiness of the basin.

"They can't track you now?"

"Of course they can. They'll use my chip." I dipped my hands in the water and wiped the blood from my face.

"Then why did you—?"

"To buy us some time. It'll slow them down." QuantComs weren't waterproof. One of those weird quirks that came in handy sometimes. My friend Pennedy once panicked after a botched Chemistry final and shoved the whole thing in her mouth.

"Where are we going?" Finn asked.

To the only place I could think of. "My house."

"You don't think they'll look for you at your own house?"

"They will. But they won't be looking for you." The plan had formed in my mind without much direct thought on my part. Step 1: Hide Finn. Step 2 . . . well, that part of the plan was still fuzzy. "It's the perfect hiding spot."

Finn's hand slipped out of mine when he stopped moving. "Hiding?"

A breeze flapped my hair across my face when I turned to face him. I stuck out my lower lip and puffed it away. "What did you think you'd be doing?"

"I thought *we'd* be running, searching, fighting."

"There's no *we*. And there's nothing to run from or search for or fight against."

Another siren in the distance, louder this time, didn't help my case.

"Make you a deal," I said. "If something comes up that I need protection from, you will be my official go-to guy."

My promise appeased him enough for him to start following me again.

"Are we near your house?" he asked.

"Not too far. We can take the Metro."

"They still have that?" asked Finn.

I smiled my first real smile since I'd gotten back. "Oh, yes."

chapter 10

IT WAS AS ENTERTAINING as I'd always imagined it would be, watching someone from the past ride the Metro for the first time. Like a frontier woman stepping into a stratoscraper or a Roman soldier wielding a stunner.

"Hold on tight," I said. The cylindrical cabin was half-empty, its eggshell smooth walls visible where people normally stood shoulder to shoulder, but I still kept my voice low.

"I've ridden the Metro before," said Finn. "I don't think I really need to—"

"*Hold. On.*"

The other passengers were already staring at Finn's bare chest. The last thing I needed was him plastered against the back wall. He laid his hand loosely on the strap.

"Loop it through."

His mouth turned down into a skeptical frown, but he obeyed. The strap clamped down on his wrist and tightened. And just in time.

The other few passengers, who had sensibly brought their MootBoots, swayed slightly as the train bullet-blasted out of the station. Like rogue pendulums caught in an upswing, Finn's and my feet shot up behind us and smacked against the top of the coach. Finn let out a yelp, and I poked him in the chest. A man with an ample Afro at the front of the cabin looked up from his reading and shook his head, laughing. *Those crazy daredevil kids,* I could almost hear his thoughts. But then he did a double take when he noticed my face. He averted his eyes. To the ceiling. To the solographic ads bobbing along, bumping into riders' shoulders. Recognition was smeared all over his face, though.

Her.

Like everyone else, he had seen the news stories. The theories. The accusations. My mom's injuries were still a mystery. She'd gone on a last-minute Shift for work that morning, not out of the ordinary. Poppy Bennis was always chasing forgery leads. But she synched before she was scheduled, and she landed on the steps of the Institute of all places. Her chip had simply stopped working.

Everyone had a hypothesis. Most Shifters believed it was a spontaneous malfunction or inexplicable injury. They knew that no Shifter, or at least no sane one, would purposefully disable her chip. "Unless, of course," they whispered, "she . . . but no, surely someone would have noticed the symptoms before now." Most nons claimed she had tampered with it, another logical conclusion. I, who should have had the best guess of anyone, didn't know what to believe. Nor did I care. All I wanted was to disprove the Shifters' worries and the nons' theories before I lost her forever.

I spared the guy any further discomfort and looked away, thankful none of the other riders had recognized me yet. Finn didn't notice. He was too busy palming the smooth, clear top of the train, looking for another handhold. I considered hooking my toe on one of the foot latches on the ceiling but didn't bother. It was a short ride. We'd be there any—

Moment.

With the sudden decrease in velocity, our feet swung in the opposite direction. I pulled my knees into my chest and dangled until the wrist strap loosened. Finn came precariously close to kicking a priest in the face with his lanky, flailing legs. When his strap came undone, he plummeted to the ground. Probably should have warned him about the stopping.

The other passengers swayed again, and a few reached down to deflate their leg stabilizers. Even though none of the other travelers were from the Institute, I was anxious to get out of the cabin and onto the open space of the platform.

The moment the doors opened, I took off toward the stairs. Three steps down, I realized Finn wasn't behind me. Wearing a nasty pale pallor, he had staggered over to the railing on the platform and retched over the side.

"Nice." I walked over to him and patted his back. "Y'know, for someone who took his first time-travel experience like a man, I'm surprised a little train ride did you in."

"That," said Finn, coughing and pointing at the quickly filling coach behind him, "is no train."

Finn wobbled over to a bench and sat down with his head between his knees. I itched to get moving.

"Come on." I reached over and tugged on Finn's hand.

He squinted through bleary eyes. "Could you give me a minute? I'm in the future."

"Yeah, I know. The question is *how*." I counted to seven. "We have to go."

Finn clutched his stomach but nodded. We emerged in the refurbished section of Old Georgetown, not to be confused with the slightly sketchy section where my house was. Out on the road, a police officer hovered on a dasher near the corner of the busy intersection, greeting the arriving Metro passengers with a friendly wave and monitoring Pod traffic. I walked as far as I could around the officer and turned my face away from her.

At the end of the block, I spotted a vacant double Publi-pod floating over its docking station. Under normal circumstances, I wouldn't smack one of those nasty red orbs with a twelve-foot pole. They always smelled like urine or stale beer. At best.

But it was free, and anything was better than the increasingly curious stares of passersby. Finn was oblivious. Or maybe he just liked walking around without his shirt on.

"Come on." I hurried over to the unoccupied Pod before someone else claimed it.

"We're riding to your house?"

I nodded.

"In *that?*" One of Finn's eyebrows drifted up his forehead.

The Pod bloomed open like a flowering bud when I waved my hand in front of the door sensor. One petal on each side bent into a stair-like ramp. "Sorry if it doesn't meet your usual standard of luxur—"

"Sweet!" He ran around to the far side of it. "It's like the Jetsons."

"The Whatsons?"

"Never mind. *This* is how I pictured the future."

"Shhh!"

Public-sanctioned time travel, spectral holo-imaging, the elimination of carbon pollution. And the guy went gaga over a glorified golf cart.

I climbed in opposite Finn and screwed up my nose as the petals closed around us, sealing in the odor. "Ugh."

Undaunted, Finn's face lit up. "Do you think I could drive it?"

"Umm . . . sure."

I leaned forward, close to the mouthpiece. Publi-pods were notorious for being finicky and temperamental. The console reeked, triggering my gag reflex. My companion didn't notice, too busy turning the front-view window on and off with a look of wonderment on his face.

"Destination: Four-Twelve Piccadilly Avenue." I turned to Finn and lowered my voice. "Okay, say 'go.'"

"Go!" he shouted with glee. The Pod took off. Finn grabbed the handle in front of him. *Double ugh.* If he had any clue of the filth, the years of grit and grime, the disgusting . . . Actually, he was a boy. He probably would have grabbed it anyway.

"No wonder you've been so hissy about spending time in the twenty-first century," he said. "This thing is great."

I didn't know about "great," but it was efficient. Dodging other Pods and hopping curbs, we sped along without stopping once.

"I'm surprised these don't have seat belts," said Finn, trying without success to hide the nervous edge in his voice as we swerved past a light post at the end of my street.

"Foam."

"Huh?"

"Foam. If they sense an impact, they fill with a breathable, biodegradable—never mind." Apparently, Future Me really hadn't told him much about the present. Well, I certainly wasn't going to. "We're here."

The Publi-pod had halted in front of a crumbling brownstone town house, built a hundred years before Finn was born. The shutters were drawn, and weeds poked through the gaps in the front walkway. Mrs. Jacobs from next door had laid out a few small pots of mums on our home's otherwise empty front stoop to make it look a little more lived-in.

It wasn't until Finn and I stood in front of the scanner next to the door that I felt a wave of misgiving about the plan (or lack thereof). Finn would wait at my house and then what? Sneaking him into the Institute would prove nearly impossible, but there was no way I could afford a private Shift Pad or even a rental. And this was all assuming it was even *possible* to Shift him back. I still had no inkling how he'd made it to the twenty-third century in the first place, much less alive and well . . . and petting my cat on the porch swing.

It didn't help that the one person I could trust with my questions, who should have been on the other side of that door with a batch of fresh-baked lemon bars and a bear hug, was lying in a hospital bed in a coma. There would be no more lemon bars. No old-movie marathons or picking a new paint color for my bedroom every summer. I'd be lucky if the spiders hadn't barricaded themselves into the hall bathroom.

But there were no other options. Finn couldn't run around unchecked. I swept my hair through the scanner and tucked it resolutely behind my ears. I pushed the door open, and we stepped inside. A net of scents swung over me, trapping in all the memories of the years, good and bad. Linseed oil, dried eucalyptus, furniture polish for all my mom's antiques, that funky stench we could never get rid of after the curry incident. Even though it was a husk of the home it used to be, my soul filled with longing for what the house represented, for what it could be again if my mother ever recovered.

No. Not if. *When.*

All she needed was the right care—the *best* care—and that meant staying where she was. I had to convince Leto to give me another chance. I could prove myself with another delivery, a freebie. And then maybe he'd pay me for the next few.

Listen to me. The next few.

"You'll want to hide before they get here," I said quietly. "I doubt they'll poke around too much, but you should stay in my closet until they're gone. My bedroom's on the second floor, first door to your right."

I looked over at Finn, who was surveying the room with a frown, unable to hide his disappointment. I turned my head to follow his gaze and realized I couldn't blame him. The place had been pretty much abandoned for six months. Not that it was much to be impressed with before.

"I'm sorry it's not as nice as you're used to," I said.

The center of Finn's eyebrows knit together to form an unspoken question, but before he could ask it I added, "My mom doesn't make that much," then corrected myself, "*didn't* make that much."

"No." He reached over and touched my shoulder. "It's not that at all. I just thought it would be more, umm, futuristic."

"Oh." I looked around the room again, trying to see it through his eyes. Through past eyes. It *was* old, even to Finn. But that was the way Mom liked it. We could have bought a bigger place out in the suburbs, but my mother was too attached to this place for some reason.

"The kitchen's been redone over the years. And the circuitry's new. But, yeah, I can see what you mean."

When I took a step forward, the hardwood floors squeaked as if to agree with Finn's assessment of the place. Even if our house were thoroughly modernized, though, I doubted he would have been impressed. People during his time were so obsessed with faster, smaller, sleeker. That doesn't always make things better. Sometimes simple is best—cotton and curtains and shoelaces.

I gave my head a little shake to clear it. Company would arrive at any moment. Finn needed the basics. I gestured to the left.

"There are some insta-meals in the pantry. Ten seconds in the reconstituter and they'll be . . . edible."

I pointed out the entrance to the bathroom and was scanning my hair to open it when I realized, shoot, Finn needed access. I rummaged under the sink for a pair of pincers and clamped them down on a couple strands of my hair.

"Hold these." I handed the pincers to Finn. "Tight."

"What? Why am I—?"

I yanked my head away from him and let out a yowl. But the hair came out.

"Aighhh!" He dropped the pincers. And the hair.

"Dang it, Finn. Help me find it. We don't have much time."

"Find what?"

"My hair! It acts like a key for all the locks."

"Why didn't you pluck it out like a normal person?" He bent down to help me look. "Or, better yet, *not* pluck it out like a normal person. You could have cut it."

"No. The follicle has to be attached for the DNA to register."

"So nobody sheds in the future? You're born with the hair you have your whole life?"

"Don't be silly." I pictured a baby with a pompadour. "Our hair comes out when we wash it with a special solvent. In the shower."

"Of course it does." He lifted up the strands from a crack in the tile. "How silly of me."

"Don't lose those," I said.

He started to push himself up when my smoosh-nosed fluffy white cat, Tufty, jumped into his arms.

I looked frantically at Finn's hands for the hair.

"Got it." He motioned to his fist. "By the way, this is by far the ugliest cat I've ever seen."

"Shh." I covered Tufty's ears. "He'll hear you."

"At least he's not deaf as well," said Finn with a chuckle.

I laughed, too. Finn wrapped his free hand around the back of my head, and before I had a chance to back away he leaned down and kissed me on the forehead.

"That's not, umm . . ." I jerked away, my cheeks burning.

"Sorry. I forgot for a second that you're not you. I mean, you're not her."

"Looks like you have everything you need," I said a little too loudly. "Food, shelter, and"—Tufty nuzzled against Finn's bare chest—"oh."

Clothes.

"There are some unisex shirts in the back of my closet." Which was where Finn needed to be. "Any questions?"

Finn leaned against the banister. "Yeah. How am I supposed to protect you from here?"

I blinked. "By laying low and not bringing attention to yourself until I figure all this out. Oh, and if my future self shows up here, tell her to get Leto's delivery to me. But you stay put."

"What if I'm supposed to protect you from something at your school?"

"If there were evil minions stalking the hallways, I would have noticed them. Now go upstairs." Even I was taken aback by the clipped, military cadence of my voice. Finn was right. I really was a shrew from the bowels of Hades around him. Okay, maybe he hadn't said the "Hades" part. But he was probably thinking it.

"Aye, aye, Captain." He lifted his hand in a mock salute.

Any remorse I felt for how I'd treated him vanished. As he started up the stairs, I grabbed his arm. "This isn't some game, you know. This is my life. I'm going to be in a lot of trouble when I get back. I'll be lucky if they don't expel me." And I'd be lucky if Leto didn't break my thumbs.

Finn's voice softened: "I know. Just be careful. Remember, I'm here to help. You don't have to worry about me. Or Tufty."

The cat swooned as Finn scratched his ears. Tufty wiggled free and hit the ground in a rapturous stretch. Finn trudged up the steps, Tufty close at his heels.

At the top step, he turned around. "So you're going to sit here and wait for them to come snatch you?"

"Don't be a drama queen," I said, "and, yes, I'm going home."

"I thought *this* was your home."

My finger snaked its way through a layer of dust. For a flash, I saw my mother's hand along its path. *Why dust, sugar booger? It's God's doodling pad.* A faint grin splintered my lips, but with it I felt a crack form in the wall that had grown around my heart. A wall I *needed*. I wiped the smile away and put a fresh layer of plaster over the crack before Finn could see me waver.

"There's nothing for me here."

chapter 11

I STOOD AT THE HALL MIRROR on the far side of the living room and practiced my best dazed and disoriented look. Hmm, perhaps dazed with a touch of contrition would be the better bet. Except with contrition came culpability. I mussed up my hair and smudged my eye makeup but only succeeded in making myself look like a boozy raccoon.

They'd send the school nurse. Oh, and, good gravy, our guidance counselor. Counselor Salloway would fret and fuss over me, especially since the first place I went was my abandoned house. *Was all this because of your mother's accident? Do you want me to find you a support group? Would you like to talk about it?*

No, no, and *heck* to the *no.* But I'd play along. I had to.

Footsteps shuffled on the porch. Distinct words escaped a cloud of muffled whispers on the other side of the thick door. "Forced. Hurt. Locked." At least I hadn't heard the word "expelled." Yet. The handle jiggled and rattled, and something metal scraped along the edge of the frame. I crossed my arms across my chest. There was no way this could end well.

The voices on the porch quieted, and a lone pair of feet clunked up the rickety old steps. A familiar, booming voice said, "Emergency override," and the door swung open without the expected *bang.* I still jumped.

A new lump of fear strangled my tonsils as my rescuers entered the room. Leading the way was Headmaster Bergin himself. He twiddled the ends of his snowy mustache and squinted into the hazy, dust-moted air. Trailing behind him was Dr. Quigley, looking thoroughly furious, and then the nurse and counselor as I'd expected. There were even a couple medics in red scrubs standing in back of everyone. They seemed familiar, but before I could place them Headmaster Bergin spotted me standing in the corner and rushed to my side. He threw a comforting arm around me, and my shoulders stiffened at his touch. The smell of menthol and mustache wax overwhelmed me as he opened his mouth to speak.

"There you are, child. We've been worried sick about you."

"Have you?" I asked in a flat tone. *Dang it.* I was going for mild concussion. It came out bored zombie.

"Oh, my dear, you're not yourself. She'll need to be evaluated for trauma." Bergin motioned to the medics in the back, but instead Nurse Granderson pushed his way through the gathered throng.

"I'll check Bree out. It sounds like she might be concussed. And of course, there are the aftereffects of the forced fade."

He pointed some sort of laser into my eyes and rolled a scanner from the crease of my elbow to the tip of my middle finger. A perplexed look crossed his face. He rubbed his goatee. "Heart's racing. But, otherwise, her vitals are all normal."

Stupid vitals.

He examined the scrape across my forehead. I winced, and he pulled his fingers away. "But she's clearly been in some form of altercation." He moved the scanner this way and that around my face. I sucked in a sharp breath at the coldness of the metal probe. Nurse Granderson made a goofy face that only I could see, and I relaxed a little. He was used to treating upset tummies for homesick First Years. He probably enjoyed a nice gash once in a while.

"There's sand present in the wound," he said. "I'll clean it out and close it up when we get back to the Institute, but the spot may be a bit tender for a day or two, kiddo."

Counselor Salloway bustled to the front, her unruly hair flouncing to the sides. She grabbed my hand with a showy flourish and patted it. "She might be a little emotionally tender right now, too."

Bleh. That was me fighting the urge to throw up in my own mouth.

"We were surprised you came here instead of the Institute."

I needn't have looked up to know who was speaking. Dr. Quigley rubbed the polish on her nails without even glancing at me.

"I . . . I must have been disoriented," I said. "Went home without thinking."

"Of course, of course. Understandable given the circumstances." Headmaster Bergin pinched his chin and looked at the door. "You don't happen to remember what those circumstances were, do you?"

"I was on a bus. Wyck had landed me in a perfect spot, near a bus station. When I was getting off, my foot caught in the strap of someone's bag. And that's the last thing I remember." The wound stung as I patted it for good measure. Surely a steep fall could have caused that kind of damage.

"I wish I could remember more," I said. "When I got back, my QuantCom started blinking red, and I tried to figure out what I could have accidentally brought back with me before I remembered that I got mud all over my top when I landed in the field. A guy on the bus offered his shirt to me, so I had that on. Must have dropped my QuantCom somewhere along the way. Then, I ended up here."

Every face in the room had settled into a stunned mask during my story. Several of them looked at Finn's shirt like it was a rabid animal. I couldn't imagine what they'd do if they knew I'd stashed the owner upstairs. I drew a deep breath and prepared myself for an onslaught of questions, but Bergin raised his hand to hold them back.

"Well, it's fortuitous—just short of miraculous, really—that Miss Ellison returned so early from her mission. Or should I say *your* mission, Miss Bennis?" Bergin gave me a stern look, but the corners of his lips twitched up. He let out a jovial chuckle. "When I told you I remembered what it's like to be a teenager, I was not handing you carte blanche to break every rule in the book."

Oh, sweet shades of poo, he actually believed my story. I might make it out of this. "I know," I said. "I'm so sorry. I promise I'll never—"

"Hush now. I know you won't. And now that you've experienced some of the repercussions, hopefully you've seen the reason for our many rules." The hint of smile vanished. "But you will need to serve a detention to reinforce those very rules. There will be no dance for you tonight, Miss Bennis."

Aww, shucks.

"Or your roommate," he added.

"Please don't punish Mimi. It was my idea. So she could go to the dance in the first place."

I imagined Mimi's crushed expression when she found out she couldn't go. There was no way I could make this up to her. I was such a liar. But the lie had served its purpose.

"And I'm afraid," said Bergin, "that you will also be Anchored."

"Anchored?" He couldn't be serious. I'd never heard of a student being Anchored. Ever. I mean, we cracked jokes about it. But we were never serious. There was no point in staying at the Institute—in being a Shifter—if I was locked down in time. If you thought of your tendrils as rubber bands, Anchorment turned them to chains.

A quiet but collective gasp went up around the room. All except for Quigley, who looked downright pleased.

"A temporary measure, I assure you," said Bergin. "But we simply can't ignore a forced fade. You do understand?"

I had no choice but to nod. While I was Anchored, there was

no way I could do another delivery for Leto to make up for my botched one. I paled as it sank in what that meant.

Bergin turned to Quigley. "You'll see to their punishments, Lisette?" In addition to occupying the position of the Institute's most loathed teacher, Dr. Quigley was also the dean of discipline. On second thought, the two were probably related.

"Oh, yesss." Quigley dragged the *s* out in a pleased hiss.

I stared at the Quig. It was hard to figure her out. First she almost flunked me. Then she gave me a second chance. Now, at the prospect of doling out my detention and tethering me down in time, she sounded like Bergin had handed her Santa Claus wrapped in an Easter Bunny.

"Nothing too harsh." Bergin must have noticed my pallor.

My feet clung to the floor as our group shuffled across the living room to the front door. Bergin led us and spoke in a low voice to Nurse Granderson by his side. The red-scrubbed guys, who I realized hadn't said a word the whole time, trailed behind him. Counselor Salloway followed in their wake, muttering to herself and swatting dust out of the air like a cat stalking a housefly.

Quigley stayed at the back of the line with me.

Just as Bergin was halfway out the door, an unmistakable *thump* sounded above us. I swallowed hard and ignored it. Thankful I was at the rear of the line and that the Quig appeared not to have heard, I hurried forward. *Thump.*

Ms. Salloway stopped mid-step in front of us. She spun around. "Did you hear that?"

"I . . . Hear what?"

Quigley eyed me like she didn't believe me for a millisecond.

Headmaster Bergin turned around and held his hand up. "We should check it out. This home is unoccupied. I wouldn't want anything to happen to the Benniss's possessions."

"Of course not," said Dr. Quigley drily. "I'll run upstairs and look around."

I held my breath as she ascended the stairwell. Right as Quigley was about to reach the stairway landing, Tufty flew out on the top step, hissing and spitting.

Almost as if he'd been tossed.

Dr. Quigley's splayed fingers flew to her chest. In a fluid motion, she reached them up to smooth down her hair. "Well."

Tufty pranced down the stairs and nuzzled Dr. Quigley's shins, which earned him a not-so-gentle nudge onto the next step.

A frown formed on Headmaster Bergin's face. "Who's been caring for your cat, Bree?"

"My neighbor feeds him. We have a cat port and perimashield, so it's not a big deal."

"Looks like we have our culprit," said Nurse Granderson, and scratched Tufty under the chin. "I'd like to hurry back for Bree's full medical eval, if you don't mind."

Bergin nodded but threw another long look up the stairs before turning back to the front door.

Eyes on my feet, eyes on my feet, I repeated to myself as we walked out to the Institute's Quad-pods parked on the street. I didn't so much as glance at the Publi-pod parked right behind us, the one in which Finn and I had arrived. Headmaster Bergin rode in the first Pod. At first I thought the men in the red scrubs would get in with him, but instead they turned and walked in the direction of the Metro station.

Nurse Granderson and Counselor Salloway settled into the front of the second Pod as I took my seat with Dr. Quigley in the back. They took turns adjusting the aromatherapy controls between *revive* and *soothe* and shooting worried looks backward at me.

As we pulled away, the Quig leaned over so that her lips were even with my ear. In a hot blast of breath no one else could hear, she whispered, "*So* glad you managed to find a Publi-pod in your mental state. And a double even. Imagine that."

I pulled my hands under my legs so she wouldn't notice how hard they were shaking.

chapter 12

"CLEAN IT . . . BY HAND?" Mimi chewed on her thumbnail and leaned away from the bucket. "You mean, by *hand* hand?"

Quigley laid the cleaning supplies at our feet. "If there's another appendage you'd care to use, Miss Ellison, by all means be my guest."

"But this will be so *hard,*" Mimi whined, and stomped her foot.

"That is the general idea of a detention. Don't forget to wipe each individual item in my office, ladies. Except leave the frames alone. I'm particular about their alignment." With that, Quigley clicked her stilettos together and marched out.

I could tell it was taking every scrap of my roommate's emotional energy to keep from crying. Her thumb was always a little shabby on an otherwise perfectly manicured hand. Tonight it was a bloody nub.

"Hey, Meems, you've got a little something on your, uhh—" I touched a spot near my hairline.

She rubbed her forehead. "Here?"

"Nope."

"Here?"

"On your tiara."

She threw a rag at me. "You're evil."

At least I got her to laugh.

Mimi had actually taken news of the detention better than I expected. It didn't hurt that in a show of solidarity Charlie had refused to attend the dance and asked if Mimi wanted to hang out after the punishment was over. And when she heard that I'd been Anchored, it put a measly detention into perspective.

The cleaning in and of itself didn't bother me. We'd never owned a Cleanoo in my life. Even selling the occasional painting on top of her meager Temporal Art Historian's salary, my mom never had three nickels to her name. Saving money required a plan. And planning wasn't exactly Poppy Bennis's strong suit. *Oh.* Shame bubbled up in my stomach as it did every time I had a negative thought about my mother. Besides, there were worse things than knowing my way around a sponge and mop rather than how to turn on an expensive machine.

Mimi spritzed cleaner into the air and gagged as she sucked in a deep whiff.

I took the bottle from her and handed over the dust rag. "I'll get the office. You wipe down the desks."

I started by polishing the large window that overlooked the classroom. I rubbed a speck in the corner, but it was just a scratch. When I looked up, I spotted Mimi walking toward the office door. Then she shook her head as if arguing with herself and went back to the desk she was cleaning. A few seconds later, she did the same thing. After the third time, I stuck my head out.

"All right, out with it."

"Out with what?"

"Whatever it is you're dying to say." I leaned against the doorway.

Mimi scraped at the fingernail she'd been chewing. "Did it hurt?"

"Did what hurt?"

"The forced fade."

"Oh." We hadn't talked about it since I'd returned that afternoon. The subject had hung in the air like a defunct Publi-pod as we got ready for the detention. In my defense, I'd been a little preoccupied trying to figure out how to return a temporal fugitive to a previous century. Oh, and track down my future self to steal back an illicit item she'd stolen to return it to the rightful stealer. So, yeah. Not exactly seeking Mimi out for a heart-to-heart.

"It hurt." The worst of the pain hadn't even been physical. I felt a new level of shame as I walked the halls, knowing the students had one more *Bree* thing to gossip about. I'd been thinking about that girl Jafney who left after a forced fade our first year, about how people still talked about her as a pariah. No one knew the truth about what happened to her. Most likely, we never would. And the ugly part was, it wouldn't matter if we did. She'd done something bad, or at least something the school defined as bad, and she'd paid the price. That was the truth.

"A lot?" Mimi asked.

"A lot."

"I'm so sorry," Mimi whispered.

"For what?" I looked up.

"If I hadn't been so fixated on the dance—"

"It was my idea to switch missions." I so did not need her guilt on my conscience. I had enough of my own.

"But I should have laid low when I got back so early. It was a simple litter pickup for an environmental group. I didn't realize when we switched that a genetic check on seeds would be so complicated or . . . dangerous." She pointed at the still-raw spot on my head, and a tear popped over the edge of her eye. "I thought you'd be back right after I was. I never should have put you in that position."

Hi there, guilt, my name is Bree. Come in and get comfortable. Looks like you'll be staying awhile.

I twisted the corner of the cleaning rag around my pinky and mumbled, "Don't worry about it."

"No." Mimi brushed the tear away and tossed her hair over her shoulder. "The last thing you need is another splotch on your record. I *will* make this up to you. It is my solemn vow."

Oh, no. Mimi's solemn vows usually ended in her either causing a dramatic scene in the cafeteria or making some craptastic heart-shaped craft representing our friendship that I'd have to wear everywhere for three weeks.

Mimi returned to her cleaning with a new fervor. She marched from desk to desk like a soldier, pausing a little longer than necessary over Charlie's usual one.

She was right, though. The splotch on my record was bad. A forced fade *and* an Anchorment. That was one heck of a splotch. But the splotch on my conscience felt even worse. There was nothing I could do about either right now except clean. I turned to finish the rest of the office. *Oy.* Quigley's photo collection was the stuff of legends. And not in a good way. I was thankful I didn't have to tackle it. Pictures were arranged puzzle-style floor to ceiling across the entire back wall. Most were fairly recent shots from history, but some were quite old. A few iconic moments intermingled with scads of clandestine snapshots no doubt taken by some kiss-up shutterbug trying to get on Quigley's good side. (Assuming the woman had one.)

The wall had the same dizzying effect as the entryway to Finn's house, only with photographs instead of art. Finn. My guilt got another little dagger swipe in. There was so little time to settle him at my house. He had to be bored out of his bazinga. And completely freaked out. The important thing was that he stayed hidden.

I turned my attention back to the task at hand. Running the dust cloth over my teacher's possessions felt like spying somehow. That is, if spying was tedious, mundane work.

Still, several of the pictures held surprises. Whoever painted that famous portrait of the signers of the Declaration of Independence was delusional. John Adams was shorter and squattier in real life. Queen Victoria at her coronation was prettier. The Treaty of Fiji was signed on a dreary-skied day, not bright and sunshiny as I had always pictured it.

There was one snapshot of Quigley herself posing with

Leonardo daVinci as he sketched the *Mona Lisa*. So he was definitely a Haven member. Well, not much of a shocker there. I dusted the snapshot quickly and moved on. Of all the pictures on the wall, that one felt the most like I was prying. Something about their smiles or the way the two of them had their heads together, like they'd been sharing an inside joke. Quigley almost looked . . . happy.

The remainder of the wall was filled with the usual suspects, pictures that no History teacher's office would be complete without. Moments that started wars and ended them. I dusted her lamp and walked out to the classroom to help Mimi finish.

"So when's Casanova picking you up?" I asked.

Mimi's cheeks crimsoned. "It's not like that. At least, I don't think it is for him. He offered to show me how to beat level twenty-nine in Bocce Blaster is all."

"He didn't ask *me* to come."

"That's true." Mimi brightened. "Maybe I should suggest we all go on a double date some time. That's no pressure, right?"

"Are you serious?" I choked on a mouthful of air. The thought of Finn in a modern restaurant ordering who knows what was ludicrous. And he'd pee his man-panties if he stepped foot in a modern cinemaplex. He was probably used to stationary seats and only three- or four-story screens. Not to mention how awkward it would be when we said "good night" at the—

"Sure. He's always flirting with you," Mimi said.

"Who?"

"Wyck. Who are *you* thinking of?"

"Oh. Wyck. Of course."

"Charlie even said he took his name off the duty roster from next week on. I bet he's waiting to see when you get de-Anchored so he can make sure he's your transporter."

"I . . . I doubt it." Huh. Nice, normal Wyck O'Banion who didn't run around breaking the laws of physics or harassing my cat. Something in my chest fluttered. "I've never really thought about it."

"Well, let me know."

"Hey, Mimi. You ready to go?" Charlie appeared in the doorway looking equal parts nervous and excited.

Mimi pursed her lips and turned to me. She pointed at Charlie. "Do you mind if I—?"

"Go." I pushed her toward him.

The desks gleamed as I walked down the aisles. I went back and double-checked the office to make sure I hadn't missed a spot. The picture of Dr. Quigley with da Vinci was a tiny bit crooked. Surely Quigley wouldn't mind if I straightened it. The frame was secured tightly to the wall. As I adjusted it, bits of plaster fell all over the floor and the other pictures.

"Crap." I tried to brush it off, but I only succeeded in knocking several other photos wonky.

Out in the classroom, a pair of footsteps approached. *Blark.* Quigley would kill me for disobeying her orders. I got down on my hands and knees and tried to blow the dusty plaster away, but it got in my eyes and mouth. *Phbbt.* The steps came closer. And closer.

I scooted around on my heinie trying to dust up as much of the plaster as I could on my pants.

A peal of laughter rang in the doorway. I let out a sigh of relief. *Wyck.*

"I thought you were the Quig," I said.

"I get that a lot." He shot me a lopsided grin that brought the flutter back.

"What are you doing?" he asked.

"Detention."

"Quigley assigned you to dust with your butt?"

"I knocked a picture loose cleaning it, and the rest is history. Lots and lots of history." I laughed at my own joke.

"Here, I'll help." He bent down and wiped the plaster up
with a cloth. Guess Wyck didn't grow up with a Cleanoo either.

"Why are you here?" I asked.

"Looking for you. I passed Charlie in the hall. He said you
were still being detained."

"Why were you looking for me?"

"I need to apologize."

"Apologize? What do you have to apologize for?"

His eyebrows knit together.

"The forced fade," I said. "It was you."

"I thought you already knew. Dr. Raikes decided to check up
on Mimi, and he discovered she was already back. He put it together. I tried pinging you first."

"I was preoccupied." With a crashed Porsche.

"Well, I hoped you'd come back easily."

"So I have you to thank for this headache?" It had been
pounding like a nonstop Buzz since I'd left my house.

"I think that fall you took is the more likely culprit."

"Oh . . . yes." It was hard keeping up with the lies at this point.
"Well, maybe if you'd aimed better I wouldn't have gotten in that
mess in the first place."

I looked away. I was being unfair and I knew it.

Wyck called me on it. "What are you talking about?"

"You undershot it by almost three years." If I'd arrived only
three months later as planned, none of this with Finn would have
happened. I'd have picked up Leto's delivery and left, no fuss.

"I was going to ask *you* about that. Your tendrils fought the
Shift the whole way. And you had some seriously crazy surges
once you got there. What was going on?"

The surges again.

"N-n-nothing." Except that was a lie. Something was different. It had actually felt better than normal. Painless. "What do
you mean my tendrils were fighting it?"

"It was like they had a mind of their own. I tried to force your tendrils toward the right year, but they kept, I don't know, latching on to a different time. And then there were those surges. No idea what that was about."

"Did you report it?" Panic.

"No. Why? Do you know what caused it?"

I had a pretty good theory. First the surges on my midterm and then again this time. My QuantCom must have registered John's and Georgie's Shifts somehow. Wyck wrinkled his forehead, deep in thought. It wasn't something I wanted him thinking too much about.

"Maybe the surges had to do with my concussion."

"Well, at least clumsiness is one thing you can't blame on a transporter." He scowled. "Not that most of you Shifters won't try."

"*You* Shifters? What's that supposed to mean? I don't deserve that. Not from you."

"*From you,* as in a transporter?"

"From you, as in my friend." Or at least I thought he was.

"Yeah, some friend." He pushed himself up and backed away. "You swapped your mission with Mimi without even telling me. I covered for you as long as I could. You should be thanking me."

"Oh, yes, thank you. You pushed some buttons, and it ended so well." As soon as the words had come out, I wished I could gobble them back up. I hadn't meant for it to come out like an accusation of his skills. "Wyck, I'm sorry."

I reached out to him, but he'd balled his hand into a fist at his side. He was already halfway out the door by the time I stood up.

"Wyck!" I started to follow him, but I had to finish tidying up Dr. Quigley's office or risk dragging Mimi down with me again. Great. Apparently Future Me's idea of protection involved me alienating the only people left in my life I could still call friends. I straightened the frames and gave each one a final swipe, extracareful on her da Vinci photo.

"Lights off."

In that moment, my mind was made up. Lies, lies, lies. Enough. First Mimi, now Wyck. I was sick of lying to the only people I had left who cared about me. It felt like my lies created a bigger gap than the seven hundred years between the Quig and Leonardo. The faster I shipped Finn home, the better.

chapter 13

"BREE, YOU CAN'T!" Mimi threw her body across our doorway, blocking it.

Shouldn't have told her.

"You were force faded *yesterday* and you're Anchored. If you get caught cutting class, you're finished. What could be so important?"

"I just need some space." I tried to push past her, but she grabbed hold of me and went limp. By the time I made it into the hall, I was dragging her along on the floor behind me like a lethargic snake.

"Mimi, no one's going to—*oof*—catch me unless there's a big—*oof*—scene." I bent down and lifted her chin. "I promise to be careful. I won't get caught."

"You're going to need to do better than that."

"Fine." Only one thing would appease her. "I give you my solemn vow."

I could already see the glitterfied friendship barrette or whatever in my mind. I wouldn't say Mimi looked happy, but she unclamped my leg and sat up.

"Stay away from the greenhouses," she said. "Raikes has been in and out all week planting seedlings."

"Thanks, Meems." I gave her a kiss on the top of the head. She didn't know it, but she'd given me a helpful bit of information in my quest to figure out a way to sneak Finn in, the real reason I was skipping. The greenhouse skylight was out.

And it was too bad. I didn't have many options. I started by checking all the common-area windows. Locked. There was the ancient ductwork system but no exterior access. One of the school custodians rounded the corner with a heaping bin of dirty towels. I ducked behind a recycling bin.

The laundry chute! I waited for the custodian to head into the guys' locker room and took off running toward the basement. It was perfect. I took the old, abandoned stairs two at a time and pushed open the utility room door. Perfect, perfect, perfect. It didn't even require hair access. I'd figure out a way to deliver a message to Finn detailing the plan. All he'd need to do was meet me at the base of the chute outside the building. I opened the metal door.

My heart sank. The hole was minuscule. A two-year-old wouldn't fit in that thing.

There went the perfect plan. I trudged up the steps. It was hopeless. Even when I figured out a way to get Finn *in* the Institute, I still had to get him *out* of this time. For that I'd need a transporter, and I had driven away the only one who might have helped me without asking questions.

At the top of the stairwell, I stood as still as possible as a Cleanoo whirred past on the opposite side of the door. This was all Finn's fault. The more I thought about him, the angrier I got. Whatever Finn was supposed to "protect" me from was of his own making. Well, his and Future Bree's. It was like they were colluding against me. He hadn't told me everything she'd said. I knew it.

I stuck my head out in the hallway to make sure it was empty, then edged out, my back flat against the wall.

Clickety-clickety-click-clickety-click-clickety.

I heard them before I saw them. A fleet of tru-ants skittered down the hall past me, tiny robotic tattletales that they were. I raced after them, stomping and squashing their beady little eyes before the sensors could pick me up. But all it would take was one and I'd be—

Beep-beep-beep. My speak-eazy sounded in my pocket.

Busted.

It beeped again, and the droning voice of Dolores, the head-master's assistant, came out of it in a nasal whine: "Bree Bennis, report to Dr. Bergin's office immediately."

Blark! I thought I'd caught all the ants. I'd be lucky to avoid a stint mucking the puke carts. Or worse. It was odd that they'd called me to Bergin's office instead of Quigley's, oh-she-of-little-mercy. But I'd take it.

His door was open, and I walked in. His office, which I'd only been in once before, emitted an aura of reverence. The last time, there were more people in the room than I could count, but it was Bergin himself who had broken the news to me that Mom had been found on the steps of the Institute half-dead and talking gibberish. Today it was just me and him. The air smelled like furniture polish and wool socks.

He waved me in and slid behind his massive desk with a heavy sigh. It reminded me of a walrus claiming a rock. He adjusted a frame on his desk, which rotated through pictures of his wife. I perched on the stiff-backed chair in front of him. After Mom's accident, I'd felt a strange kinship with Bergin. If there was any-one else at the Institute who truly had reason to wish the Doc-trine of Inevitability out of existence, it was him. His wife had died in one of those unthinkable tragedies, an allergic reaction to the safety foam during a Pod accident. The kind of rare thing that had made people shake their heads and say, "In this day and age, how is it possible?"

Bergin turned off the frame and looked up. He didn't *look* angry. Maybe I wasn't in trouble after all. It might be he wanted to check and make sure I was feeling okay after my injury. No detention. No more splotches on my record. If anything, he looked distracted. He pulled a thin metal object out of his pocket, an old-fashioned writing pen, and began twirling it between his fingers, clicking the end in and out between twirls.

"That's in great shape," I said, hoping to keep him distracted. As if he'd called me here to discuss antiques. It actually *was* beautiful. I'd never seen one up close like that. Mom worked with ink tools all the time at the Gallery. She specialized in forgery detection. But I'd never been allowed to touch one of hers. I craned my neck to look for paper but didn't see any.

"Hmm?" he said, as if he'd just noticed I was there. Then he looked down at the pen. "Ahh, you know what this is?"

"A writing pen from the . . . twentieth century?"

His jowls puffed in disappointment. I must have gotten the date wrong.

"Close enough," he said, and tucked it in his pocket, but I knew it was one more mark against me. A Shifter who didn't know history. A Shifter who didn't follow the Rules. Then his head tilted to *that* angle, and I knew what we were here to discuss.

A Shifter who might turn out like her mother.

And that's when I remembered where I'd seen the men in red scrubs from earlier. They had helped Bergin explain my mother's condition to me that day. Bergin opened his mouth to speak, then shut it. He licked his lips a few times as if he was trying to taste the words before he spit them out. I slumped into a defensive little ball like I did whenever Counselor Salloway called me to her office for this exact same purpose, to discuss my mom. Along the way, I'd learned that nobody could *make* you talk.

"Miss Bennis, a most disturbing matter has come to our attention," said Bergin.

"Huh?" There was no way his news could be worse than my imagination. It certainly couldn't be worse than the last time he had brought me in here.

"We've become aware of the situation regarding your mother's hospital bill."

My heart lurched to a stop. He knew about Leto. He knew about the botched black market delivery. He knew everything.

"I can explain." No, I couldn't.

"No explanation is necessary."

"What . . . what are you going to do to me?"

"*To* you?" Bergin frowned. "I want to do something *for* you. Or, rather, to connect you to people who can help you with your mother's medical costs. The Initiative for Chronogeological Equality."

My heart resumed thumping, but it was a hollow thud. He didn't know about Leto. Then I got angry. Why couldn't they have come to me before Leto had? None of this would have happened. Chicken–egg. It had happened. There was nothing I could do to change it.

And I desperately needed help, whoever these benefactors were, now more than ever.

"Why do they want to help me?" I mean, I hadn't exactly been the poster child for Shifter Excellence lately.

"Well, to be honest, they think you might be able to help them in return."

Bergin chuckled when he noticed what must have been a suspicious look on my face.

"Nothing unsavory, I assure you. Are you familiar with ICE?"

"They're the ones that pay for Buzztabs if someone can't afford them."

"And microchips. One of their functions, yes. I'm on their advisory board. They've been following your mother's case with great interest. There are many within ICE who feel that your mother is the victim of a horrible crime."

"*What?*" I'd heard more theories than I could count about what had happened to my mother, but never that she'd been attacked.

"The crime of ignorance. And Shifting regulations that weren't serving her best interests. I know we don't fully know what happened to your mother that awful day, but we do know one thing: The system failed."

"But what does this have to do with me?"

"Like it or not, Miss Bennis, you've become a sympathetic figure to those who want reform in the world of Shifting."

"I have?"

He nodded.

"Well, I don't believe my mom tampered with her chip, if that's what you're getting at. And Mom was a stickler for protocol on missions." Well, except for the one glaring exception, the reason so many nonShifters thought she'd tampered with her chip. "If I signed up to be the poster child for some kind of anti-chip movement, she'd flip over in her—"

My breath caught in my throat, and I curled up tighter.

"Nothing like that." His voice turned gentle: "ICE simply wants the regulations placed on Shifting to be more balanced. It will benefit everyone. Shifter and non alike."

"So what exactly do they want from me?"

"For now, just your assurance of support." He smiled. "Don't worry. When the time comes, they'll have some easy public relations task that you'll be happy to help with."

"And in return, they'll pay all my mom's hospital bills?"

"Yes, now I know you have free options available, but—"

I snorted. He was talking about Resthaven. I would do *any-thing* to keep my mom out of that place.

"Where do I sign?" I interrupted.

Bergin smiled and handed me a form and a stylus.

"I hate to have to even mention this," he said, "after all you've been through, but some of your recent activities have been, shall we say, less than commendable. Switching missions, a forced fade. These are the kinds of actions that could corrode relations between Shifters and nonShifters. *Some might even say they reflect negatively on your mental state.*"

My breath snagged in my throat. Bergin's words packed a hidden warning, and we both knew it.

"ICE is investing a lot into your mother," he said. "Please don't make them regret their decision."

"Absolutely." *Flaming piles of blarking turds.* I had to get rid of Finn. Now.

"Excellent. And I think that . . ." Bergin's voice faded away, and with a startled expression he turned his gaze to the doorway. "Yes?"

I flipped around to see what he was looking at. Dr. Quigley had stepped into the room. She glued her eyes first on me, then on Headmaster Bergin.

"We had a meeting," she said.

"We did? Oh, of course. Come in." He turned back to me, his demeanor suddenly brisk. "That will be all, Miss Bennis."

"Can we talk more later?" I asked.

"I'll keep you updated."

"But—"

He looked up at Quigley again with a strained smile, then back at me. "I said that will be all, Miss Bennis. Tut-tut, don't want to keep you from any more of your classes."

I glared at the dean on my way out of the room. Who did Quigley think she was, barging in like that? An anger-fueled pressure built behind my ears as I stomped toward the gymnasium. I gulped down a couple of Buzztabs without bothering to stop for a glass of water, my second dose of the day.

No. My third.

My Buzz had been so wonky since that midterm. It felt like my tendrils were being pulled ten different directions at once, but there was no way I was going to report it. Gym was the last class I felt like going to, but Bergin wouldn't file skipping class under "commendable." There were only twenty minutes left when I arrived.

Coach Black tossed a gravbelt at me and grunted, "Aerial day."

Tall heights. Loved them about as much as water.

I cinched the belt up and buoyed a few feet off the ground, did a little jazz-hands thing, and kind of kicked my feet around. Maybe it would appease him and he wouldn't make me go any higher.

"Nope," said Coach. "All the way up to the top mark, three flips, then you can free float."

"But—"

"You got a problem with that, Bennis?" He pulled out his whistle and gave a tiny *tweet* to Patrice Wallingham and another transporter who were bobbing along the ceiling chatting. I expected him to reprimand them, but he just smiled and waved them on. Coach Black was one of the few nonShifter teachers at the school, and he always played favorites with the transporters. I scowled and had started to say something I'd regret when a strong hand wrapped around mine and gently tugged me upward.

"She's good, Coach." Wyck flashed me one of his infamous come-hither grins and only let go when we reached the mark. I panicked, grasping the air for something to hold on to, but there was nothing. He slipped his hand around my waist to steady me. "Easy there."

Tweet-tweet.

Coach pulled his whistle out of his mouth and made a V at me with his stubby fingers in the universal *I'm watching you* sign. Then he rolled his arms over each other.

The flips.

"We'll do it together," said Wyck. He placed his hand at the small of my back and guided me forward. The world tumbled around me. I had no idea how long I'd been spinning when he grabbed me by the shoulders. "Whoa there."

It took me a moment to recover my equilibrium.

"So you're not still mad at me?" I asked.

"About that, I'm sorry I stormed off last night."

"No, I shouldn't have blamed you for how the mission went." I kept my eyes glued to his. If I didn't, I'd go back to panic mode. "Transporters always get the crap end of the stick. I'm the one who needs to apologize."

"Don't. You're one of the good ones, Bree. And I really do feel horrible about the forced fade. Promise you'll let me make it up to you."

I started to argue with him, but then it occurred to me that I'd just found Finn's transporter. I bit my cheek to keep from smiling too widely.

TWEET.

"Less chatty, more twirly!" yelled Coach Black.

Above me, Patrice snickered and whispered to her friend. If Bergin thought I'd have an iota of sway with any of the non-Shifters at the Institute, he was going to be sorely disappointed.

"You wanna hang out later?" asked Wyck, ignoring them all.

"I can't," I said. "Homework." If sitting on my bed figuring out a way to sneak Finn into the Institute without raising suspicions qualified as homework.

Wyck mimed a knife stabbing into his chest. "You're killing me here, Bennis. You know that, don't you?"

"Another time," I said, meaning it. I clutched his elbow one last time to steady myself.

A few minutes later, Coach blasted his whistle and tapped each student's name on his clipboard to indicate he'd tortured us all a sufficient amount. We hit the showers, and as I passed Patrice Wallingham's locker she murmured, "Tink."

That was it.

"Do you want to say that to my face?" I asked.

Out of nowhere, a tru-ant crawled onto my toe and stung it. "Oww." A warning. Literally. I needed to toe the line.

Fine. If ICE wanted a poster child, they would get one. I dressed in a hurry.

Mom's bills were a thing of the past. I'd be rid of Finn soon. And surely my future self was just keeping Leto's delivery safe for me—she'd give it back in no time. Nothing could shake me. Then I walked out into the hall and saw the welcome banner.

Family Night.

⊙

Mimi had her feet tucked under her legs on the sofa like a nesting bird. A gleaming smile matched her shiny, fresh-brushed hair. When she saw me walk in, her face fell, not in *a don't-rain-on-my-parade* way. In an *I-wish-I-could-get-you-your-own-float* kind of way. The first few Family Nights since my mom's accident, Mimi had told her parents to stay home and had spent the evenings with me instead. But after a while, it seemed silly. Besides, I loved seeing the Ellisons.

I pulled up my messages and tossed a few new pieces of junk mail away. One envelope glowed a dull orange. In the spot where a real envelope would have a seal, this soligraphic one had a countdown clock, ticking away, only a couple minutes left. I turned it over and over but couldn't get it open.

Feet skittered past in the hall as more and more names were called. Mostly the younger students, but a few of my friends.

"Molly Hayashi." That First Year who I'd caught coming back to berate herself. She should try to get in good with her parents while she still could.

I pried my nail under the seal of the envelope, but it stuck tight.

"Wyck O'Banion." Probably his brother, Den, sneaking contraband junk food in.

Why couldn't I get this thing open?

"Charlie Wu." He'd play it cool but was always secretly giddy when his grandma visited.

The envelope timer hit zero and sprang open.

Dolores cleared her cactus throat over the P.A., and Mimi

scooted to the edge of the couch, waiting for her name to be called next.

I pulled out the note. It read:

Hey, kiddo.

Deadline's up. [*Leto.* The name came out like a swear in my mind.] *You disappoint me. I hate being disappointed. Which got me thinking about disappointments in general: What sort of things get a resourceful gal like Bree Bennis down? Nothing came to mind, but in a stroke of luck, I'm headed to the hospital soon. I'll be sure to drop by your mom's room to ask her. No one knows you better than her, right?*

P.S. Tough break on that forced fade. My sources tell me you have a new friend to help you through it. Glad to hear it.

My skin went frigid as I tried to rip the note up. Even as I tore and tore, the pixels knit themselves back together, yet another reminder that I couldn't escape Leto. He knew about Finn. Which meant Leto must be having me followed. This was bad. This was very, very bad. And that threat against my mother. He wouldn't. He couldn't.

Of course he can! a voice shrieked in my head. *He's a blarking chronosmuggler. What were you thinking?*

And Bergin had *just* warned me to be on my best behavior. If I got caught . . . But then, paying for my mother's bills was the least of my worries if Leto got to her first. I whimpered.

"Bree Bennis."

I jerked my head up. Dolores had said my name. This couldn't be happening. Leto. *Here.*

Wait. My brain caught up with my racing pulse. Leto operated in shadows, not school cafeterias. There was no way he'd come here. But I had no one else, or at least no one who cared enough about me to . . .

Oh. No. Finn. Didn't.

chapter 14

UNDER NORMAL CIRCUMSTANCES, one more set of footsteps would have added to the din in the steel and glass portico. Today the sound of my feet silenced the rest.

I could hear everyone's thoughts. "What's she doing at Family Night? Bree never comes to Family Night. Who does she have other than her mom?"

Yes. Who?

My long-lost—what would Finn have gone with?—cousin, probably, stood there at the welcome desk, his arms spread wide like he was expecting a hug. Hug, my arse. He'd be lucky if I didn't give him a giant slap upside the noggin. With the prying eyes that surrounded us, a quick neck squeeze it was. It wasn't my fault I hadn't had time to file my fingernails in a week.

"Ow." Finn grabbed the spot on his skin where I'd left a claw mark. "Nice to see you, too."

My cement smile fractured. "What are you doing here for Family Night, dearest . . ."

"Distant cousin Finn."

"Yes, as you can see, so many of the other students have their *distant cousins* visiting them."

Finn's lip brushed my ear as he bent down to whisper, "I'm not here to see the other students."

Heat radiated from the base of my neck and tingled down my spine. Nerves. And anger. Too bad sending Finn away would only draw more attention.

"All right." I rumpled my fingers through his hair so the style didn't look so ridiculously out-of-date. "I'll handle the introductions. Follow my lead and keep your blabber shut. You're my withdrawn and dim-witted relative who happens to be both nonverbal and—"

Ow. I stumbled into Finn. Mimi's mom had stepped on my foot as she plowed past me with her husband, their hands outstretched. Mimi had inherited the supermodel gene from her mom. Her dad? Kind of looked like a peeled potato with dead caterpillars for eyebrows.

"Mimi didn't tell us Bree had any family in the area!" Mrs. Ellison grabbed my hand, only to release it a second later to grab Finn's.

"It's so good to meet you. How are you two related?" asked Mr. Ellison.

"You'll sit with us at dinner, won't you?" His wife interrupted him before I had a chance to make something up.

"And we'd love you to join us in the weekly Ellison Yahtzoid game later on."

"How could Mimi never have mentioned you?" Mrs. Ellison looked at her daughter with a hint of reproach.

"Yes, Mimi, how could you never have mentioned him?" Her husband joined her.

Mimi's mouth burbled open and closed like a fish. I couldn't tell if she was shocked by Finn's sudden appearance or by the parental admonishment. They were both firsts, for sure. I squeezed Finn's (oh my, rather firm) biceps to warn him into silence. Too late.

"I'm Bree's cousin. Only in town for a short visit."

"You have a cousin?" Mimi looked at me as if this omission had been a personal slight. I could see the hurt build up behind her eyes. I was the worst person ever.

Finn waved off Mimi's question. "Like fifth or sixth, twice removed . . . by marriage. Something like that."

Mimi's chin started to quiver.

Don't you do it, Mimi. Don't do it, I pleaded to her silently.

It was too late.

"Ellison team hug!" Mimi and her parents swooped down on Finn and me and swallowed us up in a giant grizzly hug that knocked all the air out of my lungs. *Phhpt.* I blew away a mouthful of either Mimi or Mrs. Ellison's gold-spun hair and staggered back. Thankfully, Finn looked more amused than annoyed.

Not that I cared one nano what Finn Masterson thought.

Mimi stepped away. Her voice went all squeaky like it does right before she starts crying. "It's just so good to have you here because . . . because . . . ."

Her squeaks trailed off, and she looked away.

A serious expression clouded Finn's face. "Because it's always good to have family around." He turned to face me. "I was so sorry to hear about your mom's accident."

My first reaction was to toss on my Teflon smile as usual, but then I realized there was only one way he could have known about my mom's accident, since apparently Future Bree hadn't told him. He'd gone through my drawers, and he didn't even have the decency to look sorry.

Mrs. Ellison reached out and took my hands in hers. "You know we keep your mother in our thoughts and prayers."

"Thank you."

"I probably would have done the same thing if I were in your mother's situation," Mrs. Ellison added, giving her husband a meaningful look.

"Mom!" hissed Mimi. "There's no proof she tampered with her chip."

"Oh, I'm so sorry, Bree. I didn't mean . . . I only meant that if she *did* tamper with her chip . . . I mean, I wouldn't blame her what with the situation with . . . I mean . . . oh, sweetie, I'm so, so—"

"Don't worry about it, Mrs. E."

Sometimes, the well-meaning comments of the few nonShifters who weren't up in arms about my mother hurt worse than the jabs of those who were. Of course, Mrs. Ellison was sympathetic to Shifters since she was married to one and had a Shifter for a daughter, but she still believed that Mom had purposefully tampered with her chip. Not that I blamed Mrs. E. Once the story broke and reporters latched on to the details about my father, it seemed like the obvious conclusion. But Mom's chip wasn't damaged at all. No scars. No signs of trauma. It had just stopped working.

And then her body stopped working.

I glanced back over at Finn. He was staring at me. I'd grown used to stares. Total strangers stretched their necks to see the girl from the news. People needed to believe my mother had done something reckless or ridiculous or romantic. Shifters needed something preventable. NonShifters needed something stoppable.

Finn's stare held none of those things. And it threw me.

Counselor Salloway flitted into the room and announced dinner was served. The crowd surged and thinned as students with no family visiting filtered in to eat. The Ellisons moved forward. Finn paused by the welcome desk to fill out a name tag along with a handful of other people.

He waved the compubadge in the air. "Is there a pin or something to attach it to my shirt?"

At least he was wearing one.

I grabbed the tag away from him and slapped it against his chest. Finn's face lit up like he'd witnessed a magic trick. Here I'd been feeling sorry for him cooped up in my house. He'd probably kept himself entertained watching the dishwasher. That and rifling through my stuff and plotting how to invade my school.

When I didn't move for the stylus, he picked it back up. "Do you want me to fill yours out?"

"People know who I am." I lowered my voice: "And people *don't* need to know who you are."

"It'll make me stick out less if you're wearing one, too."

He had a point. I nodded my consent. Finn took extra care in forming the letters so they weren't the same messy chicken scratch as his own. It was kind of sweet. Kind of.

He held the tag up. "So what makes it stick?"

"Body heat."

"Oh." With the tip of his finger and the lightest of pressure, he touched the center of the tag to my chest, right under the collarbone. I smoothed it the rest of the way down. I looked over my shoulder to make sure no one was listening to our conversation.

Because there was about to be a smackdown.

"How did you even know tonight was Family Night?"

"Your, umm, fridge told me this morning."

I'd been back to the house only a handful of times in over six months. It had never occurred to me to reset the reminders. It had never occurred to me that Mom would have remembered to set the reminders in the first place. I imagined them going off every week, reminding nothing and no one just how alone I was in this world. And the single time someone *was* there to hear them, it was the one person I wanted to stay away.

"You took a Publi-pod to get here?" I asked.

"Publi-potty is more like it."

Ha. The initial charm must have worn off.

"What if you'd been seen?"

"I was seen."

"I mean by people who could tell you're from . . ."

"What? The past? I thought you said no one would believe it, that it isn't possible."

"It's not."

"Then how am I—?"

I shoved my hand over his mouth. "Not the place."

He licked my hand. Licked it. I jerked it away.

"I can't believe you—"

"Yeah, I know. Bugs the crap out of you when I do that."

I got up in his face. "How many times have I had to tell you to stop?"

"Not you," he said. "Remember? Future You."

Wow. What were the chances of breaking every law of quantum dynamics and *locating the universe's most annoying person in one fell swoop?*

"Are you hungry?" I asked.

"Starving. Those instant meals are technically edible, but . . ."

"I know." I'd felt a little guilty about that, too. "I'll try to figure out a way to get you some fresh groceries before you go back tonight."

Finn stopped. "Go back?"

"Until next Family Night." This was actually the perfect way to sneak him in. "I haven't had time to recruit a transporter to solve the last piece of our problem."

He moved forward until the tips of his boots touched the toes of mine. My name tag strained against my shirt, toward the competing warmth.

"What problem is that exactly?" he whispered.

"How to—" I took a step back to concentrate. "How to get you back where you belong."

"Wherever you are. That's where I belong."

"Yeah, yeah, I get it. You want to finish your Captain Protector gig." I narrowed my eyes. "Aren't you the least bit concerned with how you're going to get home?"

And there it was. A flash, before Finn wiped his face of emotion. Worry. Homesickness. Something. He turned away before I could call him on it.

"How 'bout that dinner?" he said with a smile.

①

Family Night meals are always the best. Fruits and veggies come down fresh from Hydroponics. Trays stacked with plates and bowls fly to the tables the second we touch the order button on the menu. Even the lighting's better. A million little twinkle lights floating in the air rather than the usual harsh solar tubes.

Finn ogled it all. This must have been what he expected of the future. I kicked him under the table when he became so mesmerized by the sauce dispenser he missed the punch line of one of Mr. Ellison's corny jokes.

Toward the end of dinner, Mimi's parents became more and more insistent about me joining them for a game of Yahtzoids. I shot Mimi a desperate look. She picked up on it at once.

"Let's give Bree and Finn some time alone." There may have been some Ellison under-table kicking, because both her parents got the hint at the exact same time.

"Of course," said Mrs. Ellison.

"We'll run up to the rec room now." Mr. Ellison pushed his chair away from the table. "See you later."

"Or . . . not," added Mrs. Ellison.

"Thanks for understanding," I said. "If I don't catch up with you, have a good week."

The dining hall had emptied out for the most part. I stretched out in my seat and cupped my chin in my hands. Finn entertained himself zipping the dishes away on the conveyor that ran down the center of the table. Dinner had actually been relatively pleasant. I forgot how nice Family Night could be when you weren't by yourself. Maybe by next week I could figure out a way to talk Wyck into helping me without divulging who Finn really was or why he needed to go to the twenty-first century. This was all assuming Finn would Shift when I stuck him on a Pad. If he didn't, we were yoinked.

I didn't notice at first when Rab and Patrice stalked up behind me. When I saw them, I dipped my head low and concentrated on the last bite of my vegan flan.

"Have a good dinner, Tink?" said Patrice.

"Heard you were handing out safety tips. How to survive a forced fade." Rab let out a guffaw, and they kept walking.

Finn looked up from the conveyor belt. "Did they just call you Tink?"

I nodded, keeping my head down.

"Is that your nickname—short for Tinker Bell?"

"Uhh, no."

"So why did they call you that?"

I looked up, expecting curiosity or amusement. Instead, Finn looked frustrated.

"It's hard to explain." Plus, I flat-out didn't want to. "Are you okay?"

"There's so much she didn't tell me."

"Good. She wasn't supposed to tell you anything."

A movement over on the transporter side of the cafeteria distracted me.

Wyck and his brother, Den, sat in the corner sifting through a bag, likely full of items high in fat, sugar, and/or some other forbidden substance I craved on a regular basis. Not tonight, though. Tonight I wanted nothing more than to hightail it out of there without any uncomfortable introductions. I whipped my head around hoping Wyck hadn't noticed me.

No such luck. Wyck swaggered over.

"For you, madame." Wyck reached into the bag Den was holding and pulled out a chocolate bar. "Told you I'd make it up to you."

I tucked it away before a teacher could confiscate it, although Quigley was the only one who would be so evil as to take away a single piece of candy. "We're not quite even yet."

"Oh, don't worry." He leaned against the chair next to Finn and handed over another morsel. "You've only gotten your first taste from me."

Finn stiffened. The fork he had clenched in his hand screeched across the conveyor belt. Everyone within earshot winced.

"We'll just leave it at 'you owe me one.'" I yanked the fork away.

Finn hadn't said a word, but when Wyck laid a hand on Finn's shoulder he pushed his chair back and stood up.

"Care to introduce me to your company, Bree?" said Wyck.

"This is Finn Ma—" *Crap.* "Uhh, my cousin . . . my distant cousin."

"Nice to meet you." Wyck stuck out his hand and Finn took it.

"I think we've already met," said Finn, squeezing Wyck's hand so hard the tips of both their fingers went white.

"Sorry." Wyck looked Finn up and down, bemused. "You must be thinking of someone else."

"I never forget a face."

"Guess I have a look-alike." Wyck wrenched his hand away and shook it out. I shot Finn a dirty look when Wyck turned away, but Finn ignored me. His gaze was fixed on some random spot on the opposite side of the dining hall like he was trying to work out a Trig problem in his head. Then he seemed to shake it off and come back to his senses. He glanced at the name compu-badge adhered to Wyck's chest.

"Well, it's nice to meet you, too. Wike, is it?"

"It's pronounced 'wick.' Like dynamite."

"Except wouldn't that be 'fuse'? You're thinking of a candle." Finn held his finger up like an imaginary flame. A puff of air escaped his cheeks.

Wyck guffawed and slapped Finn on the back. "Bree never told me she has such a clever cousin. Come to think of it, she never mentioned she had a cousin at all."

Heh. I let out a halfhearted laugh, but my shoulders tightened when Finn put his arm around them.

"*Distant* cousin," I said.

"We're regular Einsteins," said Finn.

Wyck's lips broke into an uncertain smile. "Umm, yeah." He

brushed his thumb against my chin and winked. "Catch you in class tomorrow, Your Hotness."

With that, the brothers left to make their rounds with the verboten loot. When they were out of earshot, I grabbed Finn by the wrist and jerked him toward me.

"*What* was that?"

He shrugged in that maddening way. "I was making conversation."

"Candles? Einstein? Why not make a general announcement? 'Hi, I'm Finn. I'm from the past. Care to show me how a simple compubadge works?'" I thumped his badge with my palm, and it stuck tight to my hand. A game of tug-of-war between me and his shirt ensued.

Rip.

The shirt lost.

"If you're done taking my clothes off—"

"I'm *not* taking your—"

"Calm down." The order came out firm but not harsh. He put his hand on my trembling knee under the table and held it still. "I thought you said nobody realized it was possible for me to travel into the future."

"That's true." The thumping in my rib cage subsided a little. It *was* Family Night. Nothing could be more natural than a visit from my cousin. Albeit one I had never mentioned. To anybody.

"Do you go on many missions with him?" Finn asked.

"Who are you talking about?"

"That Wyck guy."

"Wyck?" I snorted. "Why would you think I'd been on a mission with Wyck?"

"Well, you go to Shifter school with him."

"He's a transporter."

"What does that mean?"

"Transporters can't Shift. That was a nice touch pretending you'd met him before, by the way."

"But I wasn't—"

"And for whatever reason, your name doesn't come up in searches, so I guess we're safe there." *Wait.* "Why *are* you here? Did my future self bring back the flexiphone?"

He shook his head. *Dang it.*

It wasn't until that moment I realized Finn still had his hand on my knee. My heart sped back up. He squeezed my leg, and his eyes lit up like green fireflies in July.

He looked all around and lowered his voice an octave: "I think I found something."

"When you were going through my . . . stuff?" I hadn't forgotten his comment earlier about Mom's accident. I kept the data disk with the news story about it in the back of my underwear drawer.

At least he had the decency to turn a nice remorseful shade of red. "I'm sorry about that. Really, I am. I was searching for a clean pair of socks, and as soon as I realized the stuff in your drawer was your . . . things, I pulled my hand out, but before I did I brushed against this little button-looking thing and then a newspaper shot out of it. It looked like real paper, but it wasn't really there. It was like a holograph thingy. Is any of this ringing a bell?"

Still a Nosy McNoserson. But yes. I nodded.

"Right then." He looked pleased at first, but then the Trig look came back. "Bree, I think our moms are friends with each other."

chapter 15

"UMM, YEAH." I stared at his mouth waiting for something that wasn't nonsense to emerge, but it didn't. "I'm going to need you to leave."

"What? Now?"

"Yes."

"Okay." He looked kind of stunned. *Welcome to the club.* "I guess we can talk about it later."

"No, no. Not my school. I need you to leave my century." *And my life.*

It was like the night a bunch of friends and I watched this movie where every time the main character touched another person they switched brains. In the final showdown, the good guy was fighting a slew of bad guys on the deck of a hovercraft speeding over a lake. No one could keep track of whose brain was whose. The good guy tumbled over the side, but he caught a rope and pulled himself up to barefoot water-ski. That was the point where Wyck laughed so hard he spit popcorn all over the seat in front of him and yelled, "Yeah, right, like *that* could happen!"

The hero had been *switching brains* with people the whole movie, but barefoot waterskiing? That was the part that blew Wyck's mind. Still, I sort of understood his reaction. That was the moment Wyck's plausible-o-meter had been pushed over the line.

Finn had snapped the needle off mine.

Our *mothers* were *friends*? There weren't even words to describe the absurdity of that idea. I should make one up. "Preposterdiculous." No. No, it didn't even deserve its own made-up word.

"Yep. You're going to need to go," I said.

"Didn't you hear what I—?"

"Now."

"Bree, I'm not going anywhere until we have a chance to—owwww!"

There's a teensy nerve right where the neck meets the shoulder that, if squeezed just so, can turn a, say, six-foot man into putty. If you know where it is. (I know where it is.)

Finn wrenched his body around, trying to wriggle out of my grasp. I held on tight and frog-marched him to the place where I should have frog-marched him the moment he showed up at the Institute. Thankfully, there weren't many people milling around in the halls. The few who were, were busy with goodbyes. The hallway to the Launch Room was deserted. As Finn and I approached the door, I pinched extra hard as I bent to brush my hair against the scanner. The door opened. The room was empty.

We slipped in, or perhaps I should say *I* slipped in and dragged the now-writhing Finn along with me. He was going back to his time. And I was going back to pretending that none of this had ever happened.

"What the heck, Bree? I'm trying to tell you something important and you're—owwwww!"

"I don't want to hear it." Okay, truthfully, part of me desperately wanted to hear what he had to say, but the panicked, frustrated, exhausted, overwhelmed side of me had my brain in a hammerhold of a nerve pinch. "Finn, I want you to leave."

"Well, too bad. I'm here to help you."

"I want you to leave."

"Bree, you need me."

"I want you to leave."

Each time I said it, my words came out more cold, more pointy.

From the look on Finn's face, I could tell they'd finally pierced him. His lips curled in on themselves into a defeated line.

"If that's what you really want," he said.

The kicker was that there was this part of me, however small, that wanted—no—needed him to stay. I told that little part to shut up.

"That's what I really want."

I centered him on the Shift Pad. He stood there on the circular metal, the fight sucked out of him, all stoic like he was a fricking Spartan headed to war or something. I turned on the controls and looked at him as little as possible. With no Shifter gene and no chip to control it, I had no idea how this would work. But it had brought him here. Surely it would work in reverse.

"Ready?" I asked.

He didn't say anything.

"Right. I guess this is good-bye then," I said.

Still didn't say anything.

The console felt warm to the touch as I slid my index finger down the gauge. *Wow.* There were a lot more buttons and dials and whatnot than I had realized. Still, I'd seen transporters do this more times than I could count. The familiar beeps and bips sounded throughout the room as I powered the Pad up. I couldn't help but take one long, final look at what was probably the most sincere, albeit incredibly annoying and misguided, guy I'd ever meet. I touched the final launch button.

Nothing happened.

Actually, not true. Finn didn't move one blessed millimeter or millisecond, but something did happen. As I was poking at the controls trying to figure out why he was still there, the door to the Launch Room slid open. Wyck and Den O'Banion walked in.

Wyck's face contorted into confusion. As he saw it was only me and Finn, he relaxed a bit.

"Whatcha doing, Bree?" he asked, a tiny edge to his voice that wasn't there earlier.

"Grand tour," I said. Because whose cousin doesn't want to visit a sterile, climate-controlled room full of circuitry and metal? "What are *you* doing here?"

I asked the question simply to change the subject, but the edge was back in his voice when he said, "Grand tour."

Den fidgeted at Wyck's side, and I noticed him shift their junk food bag behind his back. They must have been getting ready to sort through it. Did they think I'd narc on them? It was only candy and stuff we couldn't buy in the school store.

"Wyck, it's fine. I'm not going to tell anyone." I pointed to their bag and swished my finger across my lip.

Wyck looked down at the bag, and any strain he was feeling visibly melted away. "You're a real plinker, Bree. You know that."

I couldn't hold off the smile. "Stop it. You're making me blush."

I should have taken the opportunity to ask him for his help, to transport Finn then and there, but something held me back. And just as quickly, the moment was gone.

"Heh-hem." Finn cleared his throat, and as Wyck and Den turned to look at him I silently powered down the console. "How about the rest of that tour, Bree?"

"It's getting so late," said Wyck. "Why don't I walk Finn out for you?"

"No. I'll show him out." I didn't need Finn sharing any more insights from the past.

Finn wrapped his arm around my shoulder as we walked out the door. I didn't smack his hand until we had made it through the exit, when I let out an audible *phew*.

And I could have sworn I heard one from the Launch Room as well.

◯◯

After loading Finn into a Publi-pod headed to my house, I trotted straight to bed. As I lay there staring at the ceiling, the weight of what had happened (or, rather, what *hadn't* happened)

in the Launch Room pressed against me. Finn had Shifted here.
I should have been able to send him back. Maybe the problem
was my lackluster transporting skills. Or maybe it was Finn. I
needed to ask Wyck but had no idea how I could explain it without raising his supicions.

A restless, dreamy sleep eventually overtook me. In it, I fought
off an army of glowing green cats, all wearing red scrubs and
wielding writing pens as tiny swords.

○○

"Shh."

I woke to Finn's shadow hovering over me. A warm hand that
smelled vaguely of cinnamon covered my mouth, holding any
scream in. Not that I was the screaming type. The hand did,
however, scare the peewilligers out of me, so I bit it.

"Oww."

Finn Masterson could swear to protect me all he wanted, but
if I died of a coronary it would be all his fault.

"You deserve it," I hissed. The sheets rustled as I pulled them
up to my chin and looked over to Mimi's bed, but my roommate had put her privacy canopy up. The Metro could barrel
through our room and Mimi wouldn't hear. To be safe, I grabbed
the belt around Finn's waist and pulled him onto the mattress.
With the push of a button, my own privacy canopy shimmered
down from the ceiling.

Oh my gosh. Future Bree knew about this! That this creeper
would sneak into the school somehow, into my *room,* and she still
went back in time and asked him to protect her. I mean, me. Us?

I may have just bit Finn's hand, but I would bite her *head* off
if our paths ever crossed. Well, after she gave me Leto's delivery
back.

I grabbed Finn's shirt and pulled him close. "Why are you
here?"

"I told you. Because our mothers—"

145

"No. Not the preposterdiculous reason you gave me earlier."

"That's not a real word."

"You forced me to make it up! How'd you get back in?"

Finn held up his pinky. My chestnut strands snaked around it, turning it a garish shade of purple.

"What part of 'go home and wait quietly' is so difficult for you to comprehend?"

"And what part of 'our moms used to hang out' is so uninteresting?"

His words crashed against me. I backed away. There was no rational response. Of course it was interesting. Paralyzingly so. It was also impossible. And I'd had enough impossible to last me the rest of my life. Once I shipped Finn back home, I could pretend he never existed. I could bargain with Leto somehow, maybe agree to do as many deliveries as he wanted free-of-charge once I was de-Anchored. And Bergin and ICE never had to know about any of this. My lips curved in to form the word "out," but before I could say it Finn had his cinnamon hand back on top of them.

"The Truth lies behind the enigmatic grin," he whispered.

My heart sped up. I grabbed the corner of my quilt to keep myself from shaking.

"What are you playing at?" That gibberish about the Truth was the last thing my mother had said before she slipped into a coma, when she was found splayed out on the steps in front of the Institute. All the news articles reported what she said with a public plea for anyone who knew what it meant to come forward to help solve the mystery of what had happened to her.

"That saying, about truth," he said, "does it mean anything to you?"

"I don't know. My mom believed in seeking wisdom in unexpected places?" That usually shut the reporters up.

"You really think that's what that means?"

"No. It means . . . it means my mom was talking nonsense at that point," I finally said.

As I spoke, I watched Finn's reaction out of the corner of my vision. I expected the typical fear from a fellow Shifter, or from a nonShifter, the *poor-thing* head tilt. But his neck didn't bend an inch. If anything, he looked almost excited.

"What if it's not nonsense?" he said.

"And maybe my mom's not really in a coma. Maybe she's just faking it." I clamped my mouth shut so hard, my teeth sliced into my tongue. I was being horrible. That accusation he'd flung at me after I crashed his Porsche, it was true. I was *worse* than a shrew around him, and I didn't want to be that person. It wasn't his fault he'd been dragged into the twenty-third century. Okay, it kind of was. But he'd had decent intentions.

"I'm sorry," I said. "I don't mean to snap at you. You bring something out in me. It's the fact that you shouldn't be here. That you don't seem to care that you're here, stuck in the wrong century. That you—"

"—heard that same 'Truth' saying more times than I can count growing up from my own mom?"

I scrambled to the edge of the bed where Finn sat. "You *what?*"

"My mom used to say it all the time—to herself, to Dad, to Georgie and me."

My mom wasn't crazy. All that rambling, it meant something. Finn didn't even realize what he had just given me. Hope. If I could prove that she wasn't exhibiting signs of mental instability when she went into her coma, sending her to Resthaven would no longer be a threat. Other free options would open up for us.

"What does it mean?"

"I think it means our moms must have known each other at some point."

"No, what does the saying mean?"

"Which part? 'Truth' or 'the enigmatic grin'?"

147

"Either."

Finn scooted back against the wall. "No clue."

"Argh!" I clutched my pillow and flomped it down next to him. "Then why are you even telling me this?"

"Don't you want to know how they both know that saying?"

"It's a saying."

"Is it? I've never heard anyone else use it. Ever. Have you?"

"No." It was like two completely unrelated topics had been smacked together. A stitch in time saves radishes. Curiosity killed the waffles.

"Doesn't it bug you not knowing?" he asked.

"The only thing I want to know is how to get you back where you belong." Whatever the saying meant, it wouldn't do me any good if Finn got caught. There was no way that ICE would fund so much as a pedicure for my mom if they found out about him.

Mimi flipped over and whacked her butt against the canopy, temporarily breaking the soundproof barrier. She snored and smacked her lips, saying something about Charlie before she rolled back over. I grabbed my covers and pulled them over Finn and me.

"What are the chances you have a Shifter gene that will kick in and your tendrils will synch you back to the twenty-first century without a fuss?" I asked.

"Your lips are so cute when you say things that mean nothing to me."

"Quantum tendrils. They're the invisible bits and bobbles in your brain that root you to a time period."

"So Shifters have these tendrils?"

"Everyone has them."

"Then why can't everyone time-travel?"

"Everyone does time-travel. Most people just do so in a linear fashion, one moment to the next. With the occasional slipup."

Finn raised his eyebrows.

"Déjà vu."

"Gotcha. So these tendrils are on your, what, skin?"

"They're rooted in your hippocampus. That's a part of your brain," I added when he still looked confused.

"I know what the hippocampus is. Sort of."

"In your time, all scientists knew was that the hippocampus played a function in memory and spatial orientation. And it does do those things. They're just more closely related than the scientists realized. I guess you could think of Shifting as tendrils stretching. But they can only stretch for so long and so far before they have to join back up with the time they're genetically most drawn to. That's called synching. So if a Shifter is gone to another time period for, say, five hours, then he'll come back five hours after he initially left."

"Okay, I know what synching is. Dad's told me that much. But what is it that draws tendrils to a certain time period?"

"We don't know for sure." And I wish I did. It might answer how Finn was even here and give me a clue as to how to get him home.

"So"—I patted his knee—"feeling stretchy?"

"I'm not going anywhere," he said flatly.

"Could your dad have been born in this time and somehow spends large chunks of time in yours?" It was a long shot but worth asking.

Finn shook his head. "My grandparents live in Boston. My granddad's a Shifter."

"Maybe there's some freakish genetic mutation that runs in your family that allows you to Shift to the future." I looked at Finn hopefully. "Has your dad said anything about that? That he's been to the future. He could come . . . fetch you."

"Nope. He's never mentioned it. But even if he could do it, I doubt he would. He's a little busy saving the world."

"To save his own son?"

Finn shrugged, but even knowing him for the short time I had, I could tell the thought bothered him.

"It's not like he has that much control over where he's called."
Finn's voice rang hollow, a dim echo of the hurting kid in his
kitchen.

"Called? What do you mean?"

"I don't know. He goes where a surgeon's needed most, I
guess."

"So your dad gets pulled willy-nilly through time and space
to wherever someone needs their appendix out?"

Finn frowned. "He's a trauma surgeon. And I don't know that
he'd say 'pulled willy-nilly.' Partly because it seems to be more
purposeful than that and partly because . . . who on earth says
'willy-nilly'?"

I brushed his question off. I collected words in the past like
his parents collected art, but I wanted to stay on topic.

Finn continued. "Dad goes back to battlefields mostly. 'Fix
'em under fire.' Calls it his specialty." Finn pointed around the
dorm room. "But isn't that why you're here? To learn how to go
where you're most needed?"

"Something like that," I murmured.

Finn wouldn't let the subject drop. "What about your mom?
Did she feel like she'd found her calling?"

"Yes." That one I could answer with conviction. "My mom
loves forgery detection. She would have gone into it whether she
was a Shifter or not. But Shifting made it easier."

"Exactly," he said. "So she went where she was supposed to
go. I think that's what it's like for my dad. He may not know
exactly where he's going, but he knows it's exactly where he's
meant to be."

Something about the way Finn phrased his comment bothered
me. "Where he's meant to be." An old, crumbling photograph,
real photo paper, flashed in my mind. In it, a young and laughing
Poppy Bennis nuzzled into the arms of a geeky but handsome
bespectacled man a few years older than she was. From the look

on her face, you'd never know she'd ever heard of the Buzz. If it had been a painting, I would have named it *Adoration*.

Not that I'd ever met him in person. I tried to peel the image out of my mind, but it clung there like a stubborn compubadge.

Where she was meant to be . . .

I pushed the covers off of us. I needed some air. I'd always thought of my microchip as a life preserver, keeping me afloat in time and space. Right now, it felt like a sinkweight.

"Finn," I said softly, "did Future Me ever talk to you about my chip?"

"Why? Do you think it might have something to do with the saying?"

"No. I'm just curious."

"Not really. I mean, I know you have one. But you never wanted to talk about the future. You changed the subject if it ever came up."

I nodded again. Sensible.

And yet I wanted to cry.

chapter 16

FOOD WOULD BE OUR DOWNFALL.

In order to successfully harbor a secret souvenir from the past in one's closet, it turns out one has to feed him. With all my solo meals for the month used up, I managed to sneak out a total of one apple and two slices of toast after breakfast the next morning. Lunch netted a dollop of hummus wrapped in a basil leaf and more toast. Nothing at dinner fit in my pockets.

Finn's stomach grumbled even as he stayed his chipper self, sitting in his corner of the closet in my dorm room. The whole day.

And night.

Breakfast the next day yielded another apple. When I dropped by my room to give it to him before class, Finn was sitting on his pile of pillows, scouring the article about my mother's accident again.

"It says she seemed weak even before she repeated the thing about the enigmatic grin over and over. Did anyone look into that?"

"Yes."

"And?"

"And nothing. She wasn't sick. Wasn't injured."

"Then she just slipped into this coma?"

"On the way to the hospital. Look, I don't understand why you feel the need to dwell on it."

"Why I—? Bree, I'm locked in your closet. You have no idea how frustrating this is for me. How am I supposed to keep you safe from here?" He closed the holo-paper with a snap, and it disappeared. "If Future You had just given me a little more information. *Finn, protect me from . . .*"

Well, the possibilities to *that* fill-in-the-blank were endless.

My mind immediately flew to Leto, but it didn't make sense that my future self would ask Finn for help with that fiasco. She'd already gotten the delivery back from Finn.

"Who knows?" I tossed him the apple. "Maybe I'll make up the whole 'protect me' thing to lure you here to my closet paradise." I tapped my fingers together like a nefarious villain.

"Yeah, maybe." He tried to smile, but only one side of his mouth put forth any real effort. It made me think of the words we'd both been obsessing over the last day. "The truth lies behind the enigmatic grin." I still needed to find out how both our mothers knew that same odd phrase. It could be the key to proving my mother wasn't going insane when she'd said it.

Finn chomped the apple. "Am I making you want to lure?"

"Not particularly, but keep trying my clothes on. That should do it."

"I'm not . . ." He threw a dirty sock at me. "Trying . . ." And a tank top. "Anything . . ." He picked up a bra and blushed before tossing it to the other corner of the closet. "On."

I gathered the sock and tank top and dumped them on top of him. "Maybe you're supposed to protect me from an avalanche of my own junk."

"I swear, if you summoned me two hundred years into the future to be your personal maid . . ."

I laughed again as I swished the closet door shut on him.

Ⓞ

Yep, food would be our downfall.

When I returned to my room after my next class, I found Finn sprawled out on my bed surrounded by plates.

"What the—?" But before I'd maneuvered all the way through

the door, I caught sight of Mimi and Charlie sitting on the edge of the couch watching Finn like he was on display at a museum.

Mimi sprang up. "Don't be mad at Finn! I opened your closet to borrow your pink tank top, you know, the one with the sparkly neckline, and he was just sitting there." Mimi's lower lip slid into a pout. "Like a lost puppy."

The puppy polished off a giant falafel and started in on a pile of yam crisps.

Charlie slid his arm around the back of the couch. His fingertips grazed Mimi's shoulder. "Don't worry. He told us everything."

"Everything?" Even I could hear the panic in my voice.

"Everything." Finn tossed me a crisp with a wink. "All about how I'm homeless because my parents kicked me out."

Homeless. Fabulous. Because *that* social ill hadn't been eradicated a century ago or anything.

"Even about . . . ?"

"Yes." Finn balled his hand into a fist and held it against his heart. "Even about our secret, forbidden love."

I was going to kill him. And when I did, I would bring along a set of reviv-a-paddles, so when he was good and dead I could resuscitate him. And kill him again.

And maybe once more for good measure.

"You told them I was in *love* with my *cousin*?" "Glare" was not a strong enough word for the look that had taken over my face.

"Of course not, sweetie. I told them the truth. The whole truth. About meeting you for the first time a year ago when my family was here on vacation and our falling madly in love with each other. And fighting—" He held his fist up in the air. "Fighting for that love when my parents disapproved of me pledging my heart to a Shifter."

Mimi wiped a tear from her eye. "Which is so crazy to me, since all my mom's parents did was make sure my dad's chip was functioning correctly."

Even Charlie looked a little misty.

I turned to face Mimi. "You're not freaked out that I was stashing a human being in my closet? A live human being."

"It's a little creepy," conceded Mimi, "but you put up with my snoring."

Good grief.

"I still can't wrap my mind around it, man." Charlie ran his fingers through his hair. "Coming all this way to be with Bree."

"You have no idea," I said under my breath.

Finn nodded and popped a mint into his mouth. "Yep, all the way from New Mexico."

Oh, this was too much.

"New Mexico," I said, "which is nonexistent, since it was annexed by Texas over ninety years ago."

"The one and the same. Old New Mexico." He stood up and reached for my hand, which I shoved in my pocket leaving his dangling in the air like a strung-up fish. "Where small, hidden pockets of traditionalists cling to the old ways and despise what they do not understand. Like Shifting."

"Because if there's anything your parents are clueless about, it's time travel."

"We'll make them understand someday, pookie." Finn squinched up his nose at me. "Someday."

Killing him at this point would be justifiable homicide. A slap on the wrist at most. Maybe even a medal for doing society a favor.

Charlie and Mimi must have misinterpreted the intensity of my bloodlust as regularlust. They both stood up at the same time and nearly ran over each other as they prattled off weak excuses to leave the room.

Mimi turned back around after she already had one foot out the door. "It's just so romantic and exciting. You're like Romeo and Juliet . . . only without the dying part."

I forced myself to nod along with Finn. But Mimi didn't move. She stood there like she was expecting something.

Oh. Yes. My secret, forbidden love.

I leaned over and gave Finn a peck on the cheek. Mimi's face fell in disappointment. She flashed me a scathing look and jerked her head toward the rather pleased-looking Finn. Okay. I could do this. I needed her to buy whatever crazy story Finn had spun. I exhaled a little puff of air and adorned myself with my most charming grin. On my tippiest of toes, I leaned in to meet Finn's lips in the chastest of kisses.

But Finn was having none of that.

He clasped his hand across the small of my back and drew me in close, so close the thump of his heart hammered against my shoulder. My lips held their ground, shriveled into a pucker he couldn't penetrate. His peppermint breath tickled my nose. It took me back to the bus ride when I first met him. He had offered me a breath mint while he was playing with that silly toy. The memory cracked my mouth into the tiniest of smiles. Finn took my parted lips as an invitation and kissed me more deeply. My own heart started to pound. I could feel each rush of blood *everywhere,* right down to the tips of my fingers, which had unwittingly found their way to his shoulders. I tried to call my soldier lips to attention, but they had dropped their weapons.

Traitors.

Charlie leaned back in the room and coughed. The sound knocked me and Finn apart. It felt like thunder in my ears. Charlie caught Mimi's hand in his and tugged her out the door.

She fanned her face and mouthed, *Hot,* at me like Finn wasn't standing right there.

"Go," I hissed, then added, "You can't tell *anyone.*"

The door sealed shut behind them. There I was with my new pseudoboyfriend. The sunlight glinted off the auburn lowlights in his hair. He flopped down on my bed, laced his fingers behind his head, waggled his eyebrows at me.

I walked up next to him and pinned my hands down over his. His earlobe tickled my lips as I whispered in it.

"Not a chance."

chapter 17

"SO I'M YOUR SECRET GIRLFRIEND?" I plopped down at my vanity and took off the bracelet Mom had given me, so I could rub lotion on my hands. "Was this your plan all along?"

Finn didn't answer, and when I turned around to look at him he was propped up, staring at my wrist.

"What?" I asked.

"Your bracelet."

"What about it?"

"Sorry." He shook his head like he was coming out of a daydream. "I'm finally getting to the point where I can separate you from Future You in my mind. But now you're wearing her bracelet."

"It was mine first."

"I know. It's just something I associate so strongly with her. She always had it on. And there you are. Wearing it."

"My mom gave it to me. Of course, you already knew that."

"I didn't." He flomped back down on the bed. "Anytime I asked you about it, you avoided my question. I thought it was some big secret."

"Why would I keep that from you? It's a bracelet." I clasped it back on. "So can we talk about what just happened? Did you think you'd walk into my life, declare your undying devotion in front of my friends, and I would melt into your arms—your insta-girlfriend?"

"The only thing I was thinking was, 'Oh, crap. How am I

going to explain this closet situation?' " Finn sat up and fluffed the pillow, but it returned to my pre-programmed setting when he laid it on the bed. After two tries, he gave up and slammed his head back into it. "Plus, I was starving and Charlie had a candy bar. An honest-to-goodness candy bar. Not those twigs and seeds you've been bringing me."

"Those twigs and seeds provide optimal nutritional balance for the physical and cognitive demands of an active Shifting lifestyle."

Finn stared at me like I'd sprouted a third eyeball. He waited until I was done before he sat up and clapped his hands together. Again. And again.

"Bravo! Did they serve a helping of brainwashing with the twigs this morning or was it beamed directly into your brain via your microchip?"

"You don't know anything," I said. "You don't know anything about me or this school . . . or my mom."

"I know you can wolf down a big ol' greasy order of fries in three minutes flat when you don't think anyone's watching. Without breaking a sweat about whether or not your nutrition is optimized. I know you chew on that little section of hair tucked behind your ear when you're bored. And you have this weird fear of squirrels that defies all reason."

"They have creepy eyes."

He kept talking like he hadn't heard me. "I know you're addicted to movies like most people are addicted to crack cocaine. And"—he pursed his hand in the universal sign for "shut your mouth" before I had a chance to interrupt him again—"I know you have no idea what crack cocaine is. You have no problem defying this school's authority as long as it's on *your* terms. And even though you don't want to accept it, I know you well enough to know it's driving you as crazy as it's driving me that we don't know what an enigmatic grin is, much less how or why both of our mothers have mentioned it."

Toward the end of his speech, Finn's voice had settled into a heavy whisper. His eyes latched on to mine and held me there, as tightly as if he were embracing me with his arms rather than with a stare. His chest was heaving, and I couldn't seem to draw a full breath either.

I looked away and broke the connection.

I . . . I didn't have time for this.

Still, as much as I wanted to Shift him out of my life and pretend none of this had ever happened, that wasn't reality. Reality was I had no idea how to get rid of him. Reality was ICE was scrutinizing my every move right now. Reality was if we got caught, if people found out what he really was, then hospital bills and Leto Malone would no longer matter.

Reality was I had no idea what to do next.

"So what now, Nancy Drew?" I asked.

"For someone who was born after my great-great-great-grandchildren, you sure make a lot of anachronistic references."

I shrugged. "My mom had a thing for the twentieth century."

Finn made a low rumbling noise and punched one of my pillows. Up to this afternoon, I would have described his behavior as go-with-the-flow. To the point of obnoxious, really. *Crash my Porsche? No problem. Suck me through time against all laws of physics? Just say when.*

He wasn't going with anyone's flow now.

"What shimmied up your shorts?" I asked.

"You're trying to tell me this trail of bread crumbs isn't driving you berserk? Your mom loved the twentieth century. My parents were born in the twentieth century. Does that seem like coincidence?"

"It was a *century*, Finn. Do you realize how many people were born in those hundred years? Billions. More than any century before. Or since."

He picked the pillow up and twisted it, ignoring me. "If only there was a way to track any overlap when they could have met. Maybe your mom went on a mission to my mom's time."

I chewed the edge of my lip. If I did find a connection, it could forever dissipate any doubts about my mother's sanity. And any talk of her ending up in Resthaven. But if Finn and I got caught, ICE would yank their offer. She'd definitely end up in Resthaven.

Blark. I wasn't kidding anyone. Nothing gambled, nothing gotten.

"There is a way," I said.

He dropped the pillow. "How?"

"The chip." I pointed to the nape of my neck. "Every Shift is registered. It's public record."

One of the first concessions we made once we came out of hiding.

"So not only do they track you across space and time; they record everywhere you've been? Isn't that invasive?" he asked.

"Better invasive than the alternative."

"The alternative being . . . ?"

I opened my mouth to answer but then snapped it shut. I couldn't discuss this with him. It didn't matter that he was in my time. He was still the son of a Shifter.

"Nothing. Look, just trust me. Chips are a good thing. For everyone." I fed him the usual rhetoric. "They keep Shifters safe and allow us to control when and where we go. And they give nonShifters peace of mind that we're not taking advantage of our ability."

"Taking advantage? In what way?"

"Well, look at your family and your money and your art collection. I know your dad doesn't bring the paintings back with him, but it's still cheating."

Some might even say stealing.

Finn shrugged. "He can't hold down a steady job. There's no way he could explain the absences. He doesn't do anything illegal. He only invests in companies in the past if he believes in what they're doing and sees positive results."

"I know. But now that Shifters are out in the open, we can't do stuff like that anymore." The exact kind of stuff I'd agreed to do for Leto. Well, no. Leto was worse. He wasn't investing in entrepreneurship or creativity. He was destroying them.

"So we can track all your mom's trips?" Finn clasped his hands together. "Good. Let's go."

"*We're* not going anywhere."

"You're right. You should go. I'll write down the dates to look for."

He pulled a journal and pen out of his pocket and started writing.

Clueless.

"The information is only available at the Central Infobank," I said.

My words didn't produce their intended shock-and-awe. He didn't look up from his scribbles.

"Okay. How soon can you get over there?"

"Let me blink and teleport there." I closed my eyes. "Oh, wait. I forgot. I can't."

"Actually, you kind of can. But I see your point." He put down his pen.

The location wasn't even the problem. Even if I *could* teleport to the Central Infobank, I couldn't access any records as a minor. And it was a secured database. I'd need valid ID.

Finn sat back down and pulled me next to him. I was so spent, I didn't even fight him. Neither of us spoke.

Time was not on our side. Time to think. Time to discuss. Time to plan. It was an odd feeling. I had long thought of time as an ally of sorts. As of late, it was more like a snake waiting to strike or strangle. Or slither away.

"I need you gone." I knew it sounded cruel, but it was true. It would solve so much. I wouldn't have to worry anymore about ICE discovering his presence.

"I'm not going anywhere until we follow up on this. You don't even know how to get rid of me. That Pad thing didn't work. And I'm not going near another one until we've figured out this clue."

"Clue." I snorted. More likely, a pointless Pod chase.

"I'll make you a deal," he said. "I realize the longer I'm here, the riskier things get for you. And the last thing I want is to put you in danger. I'll leave . . ."

My face split into a triumphant grin.

". . . *after* we find out what that saying means."

I did still need to figure out how to even Shift him home. This way, I'd be doing something productive in the meantime.

"Deal." I stuck out my hand. "I'll try to figure out what an enigmatic grin is."

"*We'll* try to figure it out."

"Fine. And, yes, the logical starting point would be researching my mother's missions."

"So it's simply a problem of getting to the Central Interbase?"

"Infobank. And, no, that part should be fairly simple." I ran my fingers over my head. "It's a problem of hair."

⦾

Oh my gosh, I was *not* doing this.

I closed my eyes and dipped my fingers a few inches closer on the second try, but no dice. It was too gross. Just. Too. Gross.

The door opened over on the student side of the locker room. My classmates' chatter reverberated off the frosted-glass wall that separated the students' side from the faculty's—where I was currently crouched in the farthest shower stall peering down a filthy drainpipe. A single strand of hair clung to the side. I'd seen it once in a Mergie Hendrix movie. She had to impersonate a Canadian spy, so she snatched a hair the only place she could, in the shower—right before it would have gone down the drain, never to be seen again.

It wasn't this icky when she did it.

It was now or never. Not only because of the threat of discovery posed by the students on the other side of the thick glass wall or a teacher walking in. The greater threat would soon be misted out of the inconspicuous spray nozzles that lined the edge of the pipe, leaving it as sparkling clean and hair-free as all the other ones. It was a miracle I had found this one.

Yep, now or never.

I gave the pipe one last inspection. *Blech. Never.* I pushed up on my hands to walk away. There had to be another way. The railing was slippery when I grabbed it. My hand smacked back down on the shower floor. The silver bracelet from my mother clanked against the tiles. The sound steeled me.

"Now."

I plunged my hand as far as it would reach down the murky drainpipe, nearly up to my armpit. The tip of my middle finger grazed the edge and found the hair. Inch by inch, I pulled it up the side of the drain. The trail of sludge left in my finger's wake grew thicker and thicker, but I didn't dare move or reposition my hand lest the strand slip away. The lip of the drain posed a special challenge, how to get the hair all the way out without leaving a noticeable pile of pilge.

There was also the small matter of not heaving up the twigs and seeds I'd eaten for lunch. Keeping one finger firmly glued to the precious hair, I pushed the heap of glop down with the other hand. It was just in time, too. The sprayers released their cleaning concoction. All signs that the drain had ever been used evaporated before my eyes.

But I had the hair. Of course, if I was *caught* with the hair . . . Nope. Couldn't think about that now. I was scared Shiftless as it was.

I got up to leave, then stopped with a jolt. Coach Black's voice boomed over the speaker. It took me a second to realize it was over on the student side. "Break's over, ladies. You've got three minutes to get back out here before I send in the tru-ants. With their stingers *on*."

"They can sting my—" One of the girls on the other side of the wall must have enjoyed Gym about as much as I did.

"Speaker's turned on two-way, Silvey," Coach's voice boomed again.

I was glad I hadn't said it. I'd thought it. When I'd left after the first round of bruiseball, Coach Black had been under the impression I was headed straight to Nurse Granderson's office with an aching shoulder. Coach might not take kindly to my detour into the faculty locker room. I wouldn't last long with a bunch of tru-ants on the loose, though.

BZZZZZZZZZ!

Aiggh. I threw my hands over my ears. I could only imagine how bad it was on the other side of the glass wall with those things chasing the girls around like the student-seeking missiles of annoyance that they are.

Coach Black's voice over the speaker was a blessed relief from the high-pitched, droning screech: "That was a warning, ladies."

Some warning. But it must have gotten through, because the next sound I heard was their feet running toward the door. Then silence. Except for the whir of the ants hovering around in the girls' locker room, clanging into lockers and bumping into bath-room stalls.

I took a tentative few steps toward the exit. Most of the ants had never had a reason to go on the staff side. It was unlikely they'd go on a manhunt for me here. Almost as if reading my mind, though, one of them zeroed in on my silhouette on the glass wall and began bumping against it like a bruiseball on the rampage. The tru-ant whined and whimpered, only a mild nui-sance for the moment. But I needed to get out of there.

The exit was only a few feet away, but before I could reach the button the door slid open a few inches. Murmurs of a hushed argument drifted into the room. I bolted for the farthest toilet stall and pulled my feet up as the arguers entered the locker room.

"Do you think she's put the pieces together yet or not?" asked the first person in a low voice. I could tell it was a man. It sounded like he was facing away, then toward me, then away again. It took me a moment to realize his voice was coming out of a speak-eazy. That voice. It was familiar, but I couldn't place it.

"Shh! Let me check if I'm alone." The second person's whisper was barely audible. I couldn't even tell if it was a man or a woman. I would guess woman based on the location, but it was pretty clear whoever it was had ducked into the locker room for the sole purpose of getting out of the hall.

"We're running out of time," said the man over the speak-eazy.

"No such thing," said the other person. There was a strange pitch to their voice now, like it was coming from an odd direction, below me, and I realized they must be checking under the shower and bathroom stalls. I pulled my feet up higher.

"But what if she—?" asked the man.

"This isn't the time to discuss it. But, believe me, she will. Don't underestimate her. I've made that mistake." Even in hushed tones, the speaker cut the man off with authority. The person moved back toward the door, but before it opened they added, "And we need to be ready when she does. It certainly didn't take her mom very long to figure things out. The last thing we need right now is to clean up another mess like that. But don't worry. If it becomes a problem, I'll take care of her."

chapter 18

MOM'S CHIP HAD MALFUNCTIONED. That was all.

An accident.

So why couldn't I breathe?

The sound of gushing blood roared through my ears with each heartbeat as I felt my way blindly down the hall. I'd say the trip back to my room was a long one, but that would imply I remembered a single step of it. Somehow, I had the presence of mind to wrap the precious, precious hair around my pinky.

I reached my dorm room and leaned my forehead against the wall outside. These walls that had been my only home for the last six months were suddenly caving in. Every night I'd spent crying, praying, screaming—someone had done this to me. To her.

I could take the jabs, the insults and insinuations. But not this. Please not this.

I bent my head toward the scanner but paused. I had no clue how to handle this with Finn. With all that protection talk from my future self, he already acted like I was walking around with one foot in the crematorium. If he knew what I now knew— that someone actually was a threat—I wouldn't be able to pry him out of this century with a crowbar.

I opened the door slowly in case Mimi had beaten me back and freed Finn from his closet exile already. But Mimi wasn't there. As I moved toward the closet's sensor, I heard his voice coming out of it and hesitated, pressing my ear to the door.

"She'll come around . . . no, she won't. Come on, yes, she will. She doesn't realize yet how she feels about you, but it's in there. Oh, who are you kidding? You *clung* to her like a spider monkey. I mean, seriously? That was your plan? *Georgie* could have done a better job protecting her." Finn laughed at his own joke. "Okay, maybe not Georgie. But the monkey might give you a run for your money."

I jerked away. There was no way I would let Finn know I'd overheard *that*. I backed up to the doorway and coughed.

Finn's personal pep talk came to a halt.

I counted to three as slowly as I could and walked back to the closet. When it slid open, Finn met me with a smile so forced I wondered if he had sprained his cheek muscles.

"Hey. I didn't hear you come in." He pushed himself up from his makeshift bed composed of a pile of clothes and blankets and brushed some nonexistent dust from his hands. He folded that same journal he'd pulled out earlier closed, tucked a pen in the back. "I was writing. Well, doodling. Mom made me start journaling after I found out about Dad. Couldn't exactly go to a shrink, could I?"

Oh, but he should have. First I caught him babbling to himself. Now he was flat-out lying to save face. Must. Stop. His. Mouth. *I can think of one way to stop it.* My mind drifted back to our kiss the day before. *Get ahold of yourself, brain.*

"Have you been out there, uhh, long?" He bent down and massaged his calf.

"No," I said a tad too quickly, and flashed Finn a reassuring *I-don't-think-you're-an-idiot* look. It must have worked, because a relieved smile replaced his overexuberant one. I'd been so caught up in my own fears the last few days, I'd ignored the fact that Finn had his own. He winced as he tried to stretch his leg out. It really was cramped in that closet.

"I got the hair." It uncoiled from my finger, and I placed it in an empty Buzztab vial on the desk, picked it up, put it back down again. I couldn't stop replaying what had happened in the locker room in my mind. Over and over. I was feeling claustrophobic again. I needed to go somewhere to think.

Finn's joints crackled as he stretched his shoulders.

"Hey, would you like to get out of here for a little bit?" I asked.

"Are you serious?" He looked at the door. "Is that smart?"

"Not that way." I pointed to the abandoned air grate at the top of my closet. "Through there. It's a vent that leads to the greenhouses. Our Botany teacher's leading a field trip all day with the younger students, so no one will be in there."

"I'd like that."

I shoved the vial containing the hair into my pocket. There was no way I was letting it out of my sight. Finn hoisted me through the grate, then scrambled up behind. The smell of lemongrass and rosebuds enveloped me as we approached the greenhouse opening. I peeked out to make sure it was empty. Finn helped me down before dropping beside me.

"You come here often?"

"Not as often as I'd like. It's so peaceful. So green."

"It's not easy being green," said Finn, only in this garbled singsongy voice.

"I . . . suppose."

"Really? You know who Ron Weasley is, but you don't know Kermit."

"How'd you know that?"

"Oh, please. You have Potterphile written all over you."

Hmmph. "*She* told you?"

"Yep."

"You have no idea how much I wish I could smack her right about now."

"You have no idea how much I wish I could hold her." He looked away. "I'm sorry. I shouldn't have said that."

"Doesn't matter. Neither of us gets our wish." I twisted a waxy hoya leaf between my fingers. "It appears I'm good at starting messes. Not at clearing them up."

Before he could defend her, I said, "So who's this Kermit guy?"

"A singing frog puppet."

"That's bizarre."

"Hey. I saw a tiny cow fly by your window this morning. A cow."

"They're called pegamoos. It was someone's pet. They're notorious little escape artists."

"I want a pegamoo."

"You don't."

"I do."

"You can't house-train them."

"They fly."

"They bite."

"They fly."

"What if I told you they breathed fire?"

"They. Fly. Plus, I don't believe you."

"Why not?" I tried to look cross, but really I was curious.

"Your tell."

"I have a tell?"

"Your right eyelid twitches when you're lying."

"It does not!" It twitched. *Dang tell.* "Did I lie to you often?"

"Only once."

I waited for him to elaborate, but he didn't. We sat in silence for a minute, until, in a quiet voice, he said, "This is what I miss. Not some dramatic moment that you seem to think defines your future self. I miss the Kermits and the Harry Potters. This is when it's hard to remember that you're not you."

I squeezed his knee. "You're still not getting a pegamoo."

"You don't know that."

"Yes, I do. Doctrine of Inevitability. People would have noticed a mini flying cow in the twenty-first century."

"But—"

"No but. Doctrine of Inevitability. You can't change the past."

"Can't or shouldn't?"

"Can't."

"Have Shifters ever tried?"

Have Shifters ever tried? "Name an atrocity. Any atrocity."

"The Holocaust."

"2167. A group of fifteen freedom fighters Shifted back to assassinate Hitler."

"What happened?"

"You know what happened. They failed. They emergency faded out of a gas chamber in Auschwitz. You can't change the past. Those Shifters' tendrils had always taken them to that spot in time. They'd always failed and always faded back."

"But—"

"You can't change the past!" My stomach clenched, and my voice broke.

"You've thought about it." Something about Finn's voice soothed and rankled me at the same time. "With your mother."

It wasn't a question, but I nodded anyway.

I'd swum an ocean of if-onlies for the last six months. But all my if-onlies had floated around one of two things: preventing some sort of accident and talking my mom out of something rash. Never had I imagined staring her attacker in the face.

An attacker who was still after me.

"All right. Let's do this." A spark blazed in my voice, a fire that even I didn't recognize. The sooner we figured out this Truth saying, the sooner I was rid of Finn. Then ICE would pay for Mom's treatment and I could beg Leto for mercy (which I'd already started in reply to his note).

"Oh-kay." Finn drummed his fingers against a terra-cotta pot and studied me. "Mind telling me where this enthusiasm came from?"

"You don't like it?" I asked.

"No, that's not it. It reminds me of . . . you."

Good. At least I didn't turn completely helpless. Still, fear soaked the flame that was growing in me. With each passing minute, I drew nearer and nearer to the Future Bree who asked Finn for help. I hadn't stopped to consider the things that had to happen in the intervening time to prompt me to do that. Bad things. Would it be my mom's attacker? Or Leto? Or some other threat I hadn't even considered?

"So when are we going to the Infobank?" Finn hopped up and plucked a pear off a tree.

"Tomorrow." I traced my initials in the dirt, then, for some ridiculous reason, Finn's beneath. I wiped it away before he saw. "There's a student trip to the Pentagon, and we should be able to sneak away for a few hours."

He gagged on the pear. Mush sprayed across the surrounding flowers. "Excuse me. Did you say 'Pentagon'?"

"Yeah."

"As in *the* Pentagon? Across the river, that giant building shaped like a . . . pentagon?"

"Yes."

"So they're going to let us waltz right into *the Pentagon?*"

"Yeah. Well, no." *What a silly question.* "We'll have to pay the admission."

Finn blinked. "What are you talking about?"

"What are *you* talking about?"

We stood there blinking at each other until . . . "Oh, yeah." I smacked my forehead. "It used to be a military thing."

"*The* military thing." His eyes widened. "Is there world peace now?"

"As a general rule, I don't like to discuss current events with pastlings."

"Pastlings?" He swallowed hard and closed his eyes like the word tasted bitter to him. "I saw a flying cow today. Humor me."

"You have a point." I curled up and tapped on the end of the vial, trying to figure out what color the strand was. Dirty blond?

Light brown? Gray? Hard to tell with one strand. "But sorry to disappoint you. Human beings are still human beings. They built a bigger Defense Building."

"And I'm sure the other guys built bigger ones, too."

I shrugged. "Some before us."

He leaned against the pear tree, his head swaying slowly. "And we've got forty-nine states now."

"Forty-three."

He held up his hands. "I don't want to know. I only want to know how we're going to access your mom's file."

"Like I said, tomorrow we'll go to the Pentagon. You can slip out early from the Institute and take a Publi-pod. Once we're there, we'll ditch the group and use this"—I held up the vial—"to access her records. Then, we'll sneak back in and rejoin the group before the end of the day."

Easy.

⟲

"Watch out for the—" *Eww.* Someone hadn't cleaned up after their flying cow.

I was sitting on my window ledge, watching Finn as he shimmied down the drainpipe and looked for a Publi-pod on the street below. Finn scraped his shoe along the sidewalk. He looked bizarre standing two feet away from a machine that could clean it.

"Who are you talking to?"

I whirled around from the window. Wyck stood in the doorway, waiting for my answer. *Dang it.* Mimi had left our door open when she ran down to breakfast a few minutes ago.

"No one. Just . . . people watching. What are you doing here?"

"Came to see if you wanted to split a Pod."

"Sure!" If I snagged us a double, it would be the perfect time to ask him for his help with Finn. I'd do it now, but anyone could walk by. I was feeling paranoid after the locker room yesterday. Of course, I wasn't sure if it classified as paranoia when someone was really after you. "I actually have something I wanted to ask you about."

He stepped into our room and sat on my bed. I plopped down next to him and nudged him on the shoulder.

He nudged back. "There's something I've been meaning to ask you, too. I thought maybe sometime we could—"

He was interrupted when Mimi dodged back into the room, snatching something off her vanity. "Forgot my speak-eaz . . ." Her voice trailed off when she noticed Wyck. She suddenly looked confused, bordering on disturbed.

Crap. She thought I was "cheating" on Finn.

"Wyck was asking me about splitting a Pod to the Pentagon," I said.

"Charlie and I will ride with you guys," she said.

"You don't have to do that. You'll want some alone time."

"I don't mind at all," she said, not taking her eyes off of Wyck.

⟲

I was a chatterbomb the whole way to the Pentagon, worried Mimi might attempt to steer the conversation to my forbidden true love. But she was unusually quiet. When we reached the Pentagon, Wyck climbed out of the Pod and rushed over to my side to help me out. His hand disappeared before I had a chance to take it, though. Another one, which I recognized as Finn's, reached inside the Pod. I took it with a sigh and stood up. He must have been waiting here for half an hour. He and Wyck stared each other down with thinly masked sneers on both their faces.

Mimi finally perked up when she saw Finn.

"Wow, Bree." She sounded like she might pop at any moment. "What are the odds of meeting your distant cousin on an outing like this?"

Mimi's face exploded in a melodramatic wink when the boys were busy finishing their impromptu handshake/wrestling match.

The upside of Mimi's pathetic acting skills was that I never had to worry about being lied to. The downside? Mimi, along with Charlie, would be providing the necessary diversion for Finn's and my getaway. Of course, Mimi was under the impression we were headed to a cozy kissing spot rather than a secured database. But how much acting skill would it take to pretend to faint anyway?

Oh, sweet plaid knickerbockers of Zeus. We were doomed.

The chaperones started walking around, applying our admission tattoos. I shooed Finn off so he wouldn't arouse any of their suspicions. Wyck threw his arm around my shoulder as we waited. My heart sped up. My first inclination was to flirt back, say something coy, lean into him. But something held me back. It felt weird all of a sudden.

An agitated look crossed Mimi's face, and she kept fidgeting like she wanted to lunge forward and rip Wyck's arm off me. Charlie clasped Mimi's hand and tried to act as casual as possible, but I could see his arm muscles strain to hold Mimi in place.

"Sooo . . ." The word dribbled off Wyck's tongue like honey. "What was that favor you were asking about earlier, Bree? Because I could probably snag us some alone time today."

Charlie gave up all pretense of casualness. He circled his arms around Mimi's waist and forcibly held her back. I lifted Wyck's hand from my shoulder to calm my roommate down, but she was still agitated.

"We'll talk later," I said to Wyck.

I walked over and wrapped my arm around Mimi. Maybe she was nervous about the diversion later. Charlie moved over by Wyck, and they started talking about sports.

"Are you okay?" I asked Mimi. "You seem on edge."

"I'm fine." She was lying.

"You know I have to keep up appearances with the whole Finn thing. It has to be a secret . . . because of his parents."

"It's not that. I saw something back at the Institute that

seemed—" She looked up and snapped her lips together. When I followed her gaze, I could see why.

Dr. Quigley was standing in between Wyck and Charlie, affixing their admission tattoos. But she was staring straight at us. I squeezed Mimi's shoulder. It trembled. What had Mimi seen the Quig doing?

Quigley walked over and secured the tattoos on our arms, her voice chilly. "This is your assigned meeting place. Four o'clock." She started to walk away but paused. "I'll be keeping my eyes open today."

That sounded like a warning. I shot Mimi a worried look, which she returned. Wyck and Charlie, however, broke out laughing as soon as Quigley was out of earshot.

Charlie took Mimi's hand and tugged her toward the entrance. He always turned into such a kid when we came here.

Wyck sauntered over and leaned down so his heady scent filled my nostrils. "What was it you needed help with?"

"It's actually a transporting issue."

He raised his eyebrows. He must not have expected that one.

"You see, I have this friend who was trying to Shift the other day—"

"Private Pad or public?"

"Umm . . . public. Anyway, he—"

"It was a guy?"

"Yeah." Did that matter?

"I thought you were maybe talking about yourself, those crazy tendril surges you had on your last mission."

"Oh, I didn't—"

"Because I have a theory."

"You do?" *Uh-oh.*

"Another Shifter."

I froze. Panic erupted within me like a volcano, and I had to tamp it down before I said or did something I'd regret.

"What would make you say that?"

175

"I knew I'd seen spikes like that before, but I couldn't remember where until the other day when the First Years took their class trip to the Early Years. All their Coms registered those surges. When they got back, this little guy said one of the pre-chipped Shifters they were visiting disappeared mid-sentence."

"Wow."

"What's even wilder is you must have been in really close proximity to a Shifter on your mission. And not known it, of course."

I'd been right in my suspicions earlier. John. My QuantCom picked up his tendrils somehow. I kept my face as neutral as I could. No one knew I'd spoken to another Shifter. People would assume what Wyck assumed, that I was oblivious to his presence.

"That's, umm . . ."

"Y'know what," he said, backing away. "We'll have to finish this later. Your chaperone is here."

"My what?"

But Wyck was already cutting in front of some Third Years to get to the entrance. Finn walked up behind me and slipped his hand around my waist. *Arg.*

"Thanks a lot." I pushed it away. "I was this close to getting Wyck to help us."

"I don't want his help," said Finn.

"Excuse me?"

"I don't trust that guy."

"You don't *know* that guy."

"I know enough."

"Oh, what do you know?"

But he didn't have the chance to answer. We'd reached the front of the line at the admissions booth. I still needed to buy Finn's ticket. I'd actually had to borrow some money from Mimi to afford it, but I didn't want him to know that.

Without saying a word, he began to scratch my back, starting up between my shoulder blades and working his way down to my lower back. Just the way I liked . . .

I edged away from him. He had no business knowing the way I liked it.

chapter 19

THE SMELL OF SPUN SUGAR and all-things-fried assaulted my nose the moment we stepped inside the Pentagon. All that junk food. It was a free-for-all with the younger students who rarely got to go on outings from the Institute.

Like twinkling fireflies high above, acrobats in glowing bodysuits of every color dangled and twisted from the cavernous ceiling. A man on ten-foot-high pogo stilts bounced into my path, sending me stumbling into Finn for support. Three bobble-racers zoomed overhead, and I ducked as one of the racers sliced the air where my left ear had been. When I looked up, Finn's eyes were glazed over.

"I know," I said. "Hokey, isn't it?" The place was so dated.

But he didn't answer. He was still all *nyeh* about Wyck, I guess.

"I need to be seen by as many Institute staff as possible before we dart. For an alibi." I took Finn's arm and stepped onto a nearby disk-dasher, hovering a few inches off the ground. He was still giving me the silent treatment as I tapped off with my foot. "Keep your eyes open for anyone who looks like an authority figure. And keep your distance," I added, scooching away from him on the disk.

After we had made our way around one full wing of the Pentagon, Finn opened his mouth for the first time. "It's an amusement park."

"You're just now figuring that out?" I asked. "Real quick there, MacGyver."

"Okay, how do you keep doing that?" He turned to face me and the floating disk wobbled to the side. "*I've* never even seen an episode of *MacGyver.*"

"I told you. My mom went bonks for anything twentieth century."

"Did her job take her there a lot? To study twentieth-century art?"

I looked down and picked at my fingernail. "Only one trip that I know of. A Picasso."

"Hmm," said Finn. "So I wonder why she was so obsessed with—?"

"She went all over." I interrupted him before he could go too far down that particular path. That was the last thing I wanted to talk about with Finn. "A lot of her job was fact-checking, making sure the right artists got credit for their work."

"Did she catch any fakes?"

"A couple early twenty-second-century sculptors." I shrugged. "Oh, and she once caught an accidental switch-up on a painting in the Renaissance period."

"That sounds exciting," he said with sincerity.

"Not really. It was a family switch-up. The dad got credit for the son's work. Or maybe it was the other way around. And, of course, her findings have an asterisk by them. *As reported by a Shifter.*"

"Why?"

"Nons still don't entirely trust us. It's not like they can go back themselves and double-check."

We skimmed through two more sides of the building. Finn couldn't keep the stunned expression off his face every time we passed another area. I tried to see the aging amusement park with fresh eyes. New eyes. But all I saw was the garish colors, the same old rides that had been there since I was a little girl. Probably the same ones that had been there since my mom was a little girl. The waterless swim tank, bubble tram, even the old "Guess

Your Molecular Density" guy was still there. Mimi and Charlie both thought it was cheesy fun. I refused to ride anything that took me more than four feet off the ground, kitschy or not.

When we were almost back where we started, the disk-dasher wobbled. Finn caught me around the waist and pulled me close to his chest. Closer than necessary. I inched to the side. We reached the entrance to the Pentagon, and he almost fell off the disk-dasher when it jolted to a stop. I hopped down. The ground always felt shaky after so long on an uneven surface. I kicked the floating disk into the corral with the other waiting ones and headed for the center courtyard.

"We should do a quick pass through the middle. There'll be a couple teachers out there for sure. Then we'll wait for Mimi to pretend to faint and we're out of here."

Only a handful of people strolled around in the expansive open space at the center of the Pentagon. Storm clouds had loomed on the horizon since early this morning. They pressed closer and closer. But I was right. Nurse Granderson and Mrs. Perez, my Biology teacher, meandered around the lawn on their dashers, poking students who were sitting too close to each other on the benches. I gave a little wave to make sure they both saw me. Finn and I headed back inside right as Charlie rushed past with a look of terror on his face.

I elbowed Finn in the rib cage. "Now *that's* acting."

"Nurse Granderson, you have to help! It's Mimi." The two staff members raced after Charlie across the courtyard without giving Finn or me a second glance. That was our cue. I smiled and grabbed Finn's hand. There wasn't a soul in sight.

We slipped out the exit, and the first raindrop fell.

The sprinkle turned into a deluge as we raced toward the street. There was a long line for the Publi-pods. As we waited, Finn lifted the edge of his jacket up and sheltered me from the worst of it.

"So they don't control the weather yet? Disappointing."

"Just because you *can* do something doesn't mean you should."

"You're right. And I like the rain. I guess the more things change, they more they stay the same."

"Except that's not true," I said as we moved one step forward in the line. "The saying should be, 'The more things change, the more people try to keep them the same.'"

"You've got a point. But people *can* change. Here, I'll show you; let's take the Metro." A big, fake grin spread across his face, and I couldn't help but laugh.

"You've convinced me. Change is possible."

The nearest Metro station was a short walk. Finn entertained me with songs in the frog voice, but he broke off mid-verse when we stepped onto the platform.

"Hey, don't freak out and don't act weird, but I think some-one might be following us."

"What? Where?" I whirled my head around.

"Oh, that's . . . good. That's very good." Finn grabbed me by the waist and pulled me forward. The express lights flashed to sig-nal the passing train approaching in a couple minutes. But I wasn't going anywhere until I knew who was following me. It could be my mom's attacker. Or someone from ICE checking up on me.

Then I saw him. Standing in the shadows about twenty feet behind us.

Leto. He was with a burly woman whose hair was slicked back. She looked like she could bench-press more than a few Finns.

"Fancy meeting you here," he called.

"It's okay," I said to Finn, squeezing his hand. "I know him." I turned to Leto. "I can explain what happened."

But when Leto pulled out a stun-popper and the woman opened her coat and ran her hand along a barbed club I realized they weren't there to talk. Or at least to hear what I had to say.

"Oh, please do." He started to walk toward me, the thugette a few steps behind him. "The way I see it, there're only two options. Either A., you sold my doohickey to a higher bidder, or Two, you thought you'd get in the game yourself. So which is it, ya little brat? You a fink or a thief?"

"Neither. I mean, option three, umm, C. I have it. Just not with me." I tried to give him my truthiest look, which wasn't hard since I wasn't actually lying. I had it. Not in this particular time, but I did have it.

Oh, I was going to slap my future self senseless.

At least my revelation had its intended effect. Leto stopped moving. "Well, why don'tcha give it back, kiddo?"

"I will. I'm going to. But I have to go get it."

"Where is it?" The express lights flashed faster now, reflecting off Leto's beady pupils like pinpricks of evil were squeezing their way out.

"A safe place."

From the look on Leto's face, the only location he considered safe was his own front pocket. "So go get it."

"I need more time."

Leto guffawed. "A Shifter who needs more time."

"No . . . I . . . I . . . Give me one day." Because, y'know, a day would solve everything.

"Twenty-four hours."

Which some lovingly refer to as *one day*. I kept my commentary to myelf.

"How 'bout you make a down payment and I'll give you an extra hour or two?" From the lascivious look in his eye, I knew he didn't mean money. *Eww.*

Finn picked up on Leto's meaning at the same time. A protective growl rumbled from his chest. He took a step toward Leto, but the thugette moved between them and unholstered her weapon of torture as she stalked forward. The express lights reflected off the spikes, turning them crimson, like a boding of my blood to come. Finn and I were trapped, the five-foot platform drop-off behind us.

Before I could stop him, Finn jumped down onto the tracks. "What are you—?"

"Come on!" He held out his hands. The express lights glinted like a strobe now, and I could see a speck approach in the distance. But Leto was closing in, too. I hopped down, and Finn and I raced to the other side. He pushed himself up and lowered his arm to lift me.

As my feet scrambled against the ledge, Leto reached the other side.

"Twenty-four hours!" yelled Leto as Finn hoisted me up the rest of the way. "Not a minute more!"

"And then what?" I was feeling a little more bold and a lot more angry with those tracks between us. "You'd really attack me with that thing over something that cost you practically nothing?"

I wasn't sure if I was referring to the woman or the weapon, not that it mattered.

"Nah, of course not," he hollered over the roar of the approaching train. "I'm going after your mother."

The express bulleted through the station, but the sound was nothing more than a hollow ringing in my ears. I caught glimpses of Leto through the passing train cars, that sick smile stuck to his face. Terror rooted me to the spot, and I would have stayed there all day if Finn hadn't pulled me along with him as he sprinted down the stairs.

At the bottom of the far exit, we jumped in an empty Pod and he said, "Central Infobank: Go."

"Stop," I said. The Pod lurched to a halt. "Saint Raphael's Research Hospital: Go."

"Stop." *Screech.*

"Go." *Squeal.*

"Stop!" Finn stared at me for a few moments as we sat there at a standstill. I couldn't tell if that last command was aimed at the Pod or me. "What are you doing?"

"I have to get to my mom." And do what exactly? I was no protection against Leto. And while a tryst to the Infobank might slip ICE's notice, there was no way I could skip school and walk into the hospital without getting caught.

"Bree, I don't know what's going on, but we don't have much time. This is our one chance to access your mom's records. You said so yourself."

"I know." I clutched my head. He was right. I had to approach this rationally. Leto didn't have anything to gain by attacking my mother today. His best-case scenario involved trapping me to become his little time puppet. Still, I didn't want him anywhere near her. I tapped my speak-eazy.

"Connect me to my mother's nurse at Saint Raphael's." I waited for him to answer. "Yes, this is Bree Bennis. The last time I visited, my mom seemed a little worn-out. No visitors until further notice."

He changed her status, and after we disconnected I calmed down enough to say, "Central Infobank: Go."

"You wanna tell me what that was about?" Finn asked once we'd started moving.

"Not really." I yanked a wig out from my bag, the one Mimi had used after the witch-burning incident. I figured a little disguise wouldn't hurt. Although now I wished I'd thought of it earlier. Plus, it would be easier to separate out the stolen strand from the fake ones than from my real hair.

"That man was chasing us, Bree. Chasing us. With weapons. Still want to convince me you're not in danger?"

"His name's Leto. And the situation's under control." *Liar.* "I have something he wants. I just need to figure out a way to get it back to him." I tried to straighten my wig, but my hair slipped out the back.

"It's that phone thingy, isn't it? The one you left in Chincoteague."

"It's junk. But, yeah, it belongs to him. Look, let's get to the

Infobank, figure out how our moms knew each other, and then you're going on your merry way. You won't need to worry about me anymore."

"Ha!" Finn adjusted the wig and tucked away stray strands. "You think I'm going anywhere now? Fat chance."

"But you promised."

"I made that promise before I knew about this Leto guy." Finn swiveled my shoulders so he could fix the back of the wig. He pulled something sticky from my back. "What's this?"

It was a compubadge that said: "Tink."

"It's—"

"Don't say 'nothing.' I'm tired of *nothing*. I already know it's not your nickname."

"It's short for 'Tinkerer.'"

"What does that mean?"

"Tendril Tinkerer. Someone who tries to modify their chip or turn it off."

"Why would someone do that?"

"People have their reasons."

"Why would someone think *you'd* do that?"

"Not me, my mom." The tattered photograph floated to the surface of my mind. "Well, maybe me. It's complicated."

"Bree"—he gripped me by my shoulders—"talk to me. *Please*."

"I . . . I can't."

"I don't understand this whole chip thing. It's so intrusive. Controlling where you go and appeasing nonShifters aren't good enough reasons to have a microchip implanted in your head. I mean, Shifting can't have changed that much in two hundred yea—"

"We go insane, Finn!" I lowered my head and my voice even though there was no one around to hear. "The mutation in Shifters' genes that allows us to travel through time eventually mutates further and causes a Madness. The chip prevents it. That's the real reason for the chip."

"Since when?" Finn backed away as if the insanity was contagious.

"It's one of those time conundrums. Right after we went public in the Early Years, about a half century ago, some of the Shifters from the future—from past this time, I mean, from *my* future—showed up talking crazy. Claiming events from the past were wrong. It wasn't even big stuff, just things that didn't add up, things that didn't make sense." I leaned back in the Podseat and started to chew on a piece of my hair until I remembered it was a wig. "So Quantum Biologists *quietly* investigated the phenomenon and discovered that there was one thing that separated the normal Shifters from those crazy ones."

I tapped the base of my skull.

"Your chip." He traced his finger along my scar.

"Somehow by allowing us to control where and when we Shift it prevents the Madness. It was so soon after Shifters had come out of hiding, they weren't sure what the difference was exactly. One hypothesis is that the Buzz eventually leads to psychosis, so by stopping the Buzz they stopped the Madness."

"Well, when did this Buzz thing start?" he asked.

"What do you mean? You had it back in your time."

"No, we don't. Shifting doesn't cause my dad pain." He shrugged. "Or Georgie."

"Of course it does. Maybe they just suffer in silence."

"Georgie made Mom take her to Urgent Care last week after she got a paper cut."

"Well, maybe . . ." But I didn't have an explanation. What he said didn't make any sense. Of course they had the Buzz. That's why we were forbidden to speak with Past Shifters. I waved it aside. Finn didn't know what he was talking about. "That's all beside the point. The Buzz is only one hypothesis of what causes the Madness."

"You should have told me already. Why is it some big secret?"

"Shifters knew it would be catastrophic if word got out." I

shook my head. How could I make him understand? "When Shifters came out of hiding, it wasn't an easy transition. Most nonShifters didn't trust us, and really, they didn't have reason to. We'd been lying and hiding to that point. The rest saw opportunity—wanted us to do their temporal bidding. Imagine how those same nons would have reacted if they found out that these people they already feared were going to go cat-poop crazy? Hysteria.

"So they offered the microchip to any Shifter who wanted it. The thing is, we discovered the Madness right after Shifters came out of hiding. No one really knew what was normal for Shifters. They probably all eventually developed the Madness but just kept it hidden along with their existence. We decided to do the same. We told the nons the chips are for safety and control, things that are good anyway."

"The chips aren't required then?"

"No. But of course everyone scrambled for them the moment they were available. Only a few Shifters have refused chips. The cracked ones."

"Cracked for wanting to be free?"

"No, literally insane. It's already started, Finn, the first signs of mental incapacitation. There's a special convalescence home for them, and that's where . . . that's where they'll send my mom if I can't pay her hospital bill. That's why today is so important. Shifters already think she was showing the first signs of the Madness with all that Truth gibberish. But if I can prove she was in her right mind, then I might be able to find another option for her."

"Why didn't you tell me all this before?

"I couldn't. The Rules we have, they exist to protect all Shifters, present and future . . . and past. If your dad knew about this disease—if any Shifter from the past knew—what do you think he'd do? He'd freak out. When we found out about the Madness, Finn, I can't even tell you how bad things got. Shifters refused to have children, afraid they'd pass on the gene and doom future generations. Some attempted experimental surgery to have their hippocampus removed. It was horrifying. We weren't just facing the Madness. We were facing extinction."

"So only Shifters know about this?"

"And a few select nonShifters. People in authority like Bergin—my headmaster—and transporters to a certain point. They know to report any symptoms of confusion or dementia."

"Wow." Finn dug his fingers through his hair. "But how does all this fit in with your mom? Why would people think she tampered with her microchip if they knew what she was risking?"

"I can't talk about it. Not right now." Not with Finn. "Will you trust me?"

Finn nodded, but from the look on his face it took something strong within him.

The Pod stopped at the Central Infobank. I'd never actually been there. It wasn't what I expected at all. I double-checked the address. We were in the right spot. The building itself was small and unobtrusive, two-story red brick with vines crawling up the sides, off Lincoln Park. A single sign marked the entrance, clear words against an etched-glass door. I opened it, an old-fashioned push one like mine at home. Mom would have loved everything about this place. Except the reason Finn and I were here.

When we stepped inside, it was like stepping into a different world, a modern one. The interior had been gutted and was all glass, floor to ceiling. One room. There was a single worker manning the operation. He looked to be around Mom's age. He sat on a clear stool behind the clutterless counter, also clear, flipping through a holo-paper. His hair was shaped into such a precise buzz that I wondered if he programmed his clippers to go one strand at a time. Two tufts of hair turned up at his temples. He gave the distinct impression of an owl on a perch.

The wall behind him shimmered and sparkled like a million-faceted diamond. A bell tinkled as Finn and I made our way into the room, but the man didn't glance up from his reading.

"Hello?" I said.

Again, he didn't look at us or say a word but held out one bony-fingered hand. When I didn't move toward it, he said, "ID," in a reedy, disinterested voice.

"Of course." I unwrapped the stolen strand of hair from around my thumb and held it against my scalp. This was my last chance to back out. He tapped a round, upraised portion of the countertop.

"Scan," he said.

"Thanks." I leaned my head down and carefully held the wig back as I brushed the hair on top of the scanner.

A soligraphic screen shot out of his desk at an angle so that only he could read it. I turned away so he couldn't get a good look at my face in case a picture of whichever staff member's hair it was came up. But he barely looked at the screen or me.

"Welcome back," he said in an absent tone.

"Thanks," I said uncertainly. "I'd like the Shift record for, umm, Poppy Bennis."

He touched a seemingly random spot on the desk and repeated my mother's name. Behind him, a pinprick lit up. The light zig-zagged across the wall and grew larger and larger until it stopped in the exact middle, where I recognized it as a data button, only bigger than any data button I'd ever seen before. An inch wide, but almost a quarter inch thick.

Mr. Personality touched another spot on the desk, and a hole formed in the wall directly in front of the data button. He pulled the button out, walked back to the counter, tapped yet another spot, and punched a few boxes on the info screen. That's when it hit me: The sparkling wall behind the attendant was the actual file archive. Each sparkle, a separate disk, buried layers and layers deep. The glass wall to his left was composed of three separate booths, all with opaque glass doors. The attendant laid the button in the center of the counter and turned back to his holo-paper.

"I hope you find what you're looking for in the file this time, Miss Quigley."

chapter 20

SHARDS OF GLASS SLID DOWN my throat as I tried to draw a mouthful of air. *I can't breathe. I can't breathe.*

I'd never hyperventilated before but was pretty sure this was it. *Quigley had accessed my mom's file.* Owlie might as well have reached over the counter and slapped me. It would have jarred me less. I mean, yes, there was all that *I'm-watching-you* stuff at the Pentagon earlier. She'd given me the willies in class the other day. And the faceless whisperer in the locker room might have been Quigley.

No. It *must* have been Quigley.

"It certainly didn't take her mom very long to figure things out. The last thing we need right now is to clean up another mess like that."

My mom must have discovered something, something she wasn't supposed to. Quigley had attacked her to shut her up, had put her in a coma somehow. And now Quigley thought *I* was after the same information. I looked up at the huge shimmering wall. Maybe I was. But I didn't even know what I was looking for.

A high-pitched squeal filled my ears. I looked around before realizing it was my own wheezing breath. Finn snatched the button off the desk and heaved me up by my armpits. He half-carried me over to one of the booths before the attendant had a chance to question us. Or remember what Dr. Quigley looked like; namely, not a sixteen-year-old schoolgirl.

Once we were safe inside the soundproof room, Finn and I started in on a hissing match.

"Who's Quigley?"

"The Institute's dean of discipline, and she teaches one of my History classes. She has to be the person who attacked my mother."

"Attacked? What are you talking about?

"The other day, when I came back to the room so fired up, I'd overhead a conversation in the faculty locker room. My mom's accident was no accident."

"What? Why didn't you say something?"

"Because I . . ." *Didn't want you to freak out.* "Forgot."

"Forgot?" Finn's cheeks blanched. "Look, are you positive of what you heard? I mean, don't you think there could be another possible explanation?"

"I'm sure." I had spent the past twenty-four hours thinking of nothing *but* other possible explanations. Logically, not a single one made sense. I'd heard it with my own two ears.

"Why didn't you say something earlier? This is exactly what I've been talking about, Bree. We need to go to the police."

"We can't. They'd find out about Leto and you—I'm breaking the law, Finn. And even if they didn't prosecute, ICE would refuse to pay my mom's bills and she'd end up in Resthaven and . . ." Thick tears clung to my lashes. "Besides, what would I even say? 'Hey, I don't know who, how, or why . . . but my mom was attacked'? *I'd* be the one shipped off to Resthaven. Welcome to Crazytown, population: Bree."

"You're not losing your mind. And no one is going to hurt you, not if I can help it. I just don't understand why Future Bree didn't tell me all this."

"How could she not tell *you*? I'm the one she should have warned about all this." I gripped my hair, forgetting it was a wig, and it fell off. My real hair was a mess beneath. "What kind of loser can't even earn the trust of her future self?"

"Don't say that."

"Why not? It's true."

Finn shook his head again. "Everything she did she did for a reason."

"How can you defend her? She's caused this whole mess. Even your dad said it."

"That's not what he meant."

"How do you know what he meant? Are you still keeping information from me?"

"I'm not keeping anything from you, Bree. I want to help you."

"I . . . I don't need . . ." The tears splashed down my face in silent streaks.

He wiped my tears away without a word.

"Okay, you can help," I said.

He handed the data button over with a laugh. "So very kind of you. Only one thing: Could you pretend for two seconds that you don't hate me?"

"I don't hate you." My words still had a little bite that I hadn't intended.

He raised one eyebrow.

"I don't hate you," I repeated. It was true. I'd pushed him away out of fear at first. But now I was more afraid at the thought of facing all this by myself. "I need you . . . your help."

"You have me . . . it." He let out a low chuckle. "Let's be honest. Where else am I gonna go?"

We exchanged an unspoken truce with our eyes, and I laid the data button flat out on the palm of my hand. As I ran my finger around the edge of it, a neat stack of soligraphic files flew out of the center. They hovered in the air in front of us. Hoo boy. This wasn't going to be easy. It was a massive number of files, hundreds of Shifts over hundreds and hundreds of years.

"Organize by destination date." A trip to the early 1300s shuffled to the front. I tossed the first half of the files to the side without even looking at them, then pulled them out one by one, barking out dates.

"1948."

"Not unless you're looking for my grandparents."

"1961."

"I won't tell my mother you said that."

"A few from the 1970s."

"Maybe they met as little kids?"

Nah. "1998."

Finn reached out and grabbed the file. "I bet this is it."

He opened it, and his face fell.

"What does it say?" I tried to snatch it out of his hands.

"'Class Field Trip to Australia.'" He handed it to me. "Sydney Opera House when your mom was fourteen."

"So? Maybe they met there."

"My parents have never been to Australia."

"How do you know that?"

"My mom's always talking about how much she wants to visit Australia and New Zealand someday. It's her dream vacation, but she hates traveling with Dad because she ends up flying home alone."

"Okay, next trip was"—my hope plummeted—"2054." There was no overlap.

"There has to be another trip in there." He pulled the small stack of files that were still organized in his direction and rifled through each one. "Maybe some are stuck together."

I pulled them back. "That's not the way it works."

"Or maybe my dad met your mom in the past at some point." He grabbed a handful of the first files that I had pushed aside.

It was possible, I guess. "Do you know specific dates he's Shifted to?"

Finn thumbed through the first few before pushing them away in disgust. "No. And it's doubtful your mom went to many battlefields."

"This whole thing is doubtful." I threw the soligraphic files I was holding. They scattered through the air. There were so many floating around, I had to brush a few aside to even see Finn.

"There has to be some way to know for sure if our mothers met at some point," said Finn.

There was. "I could go back and talk to my mom."

"Is that a good idea?" The way he said it answered his own question.

"No. But I don't have any others." What I was considering was true insanity. "Any decent transporter should be able to get me back really close to . . . to the right time. It's only been six months."

"But aren't you still on, like, time detention?"

"Anchored. Yes, but I could get around that with a teacher override." I held up Quigley's hair.

Shifting Rule number (wait . . . it didn't have a number because no one would do something so scrape-your-heart-out-with-a-spoon stupid): Don't go back in time to talk to your now-comatose mother right before she's almost killed.

"Are you sure you can handle that?" he asked as if he could read my mind.

"Any other ideas?" It didn't come out mean or sarcastic. I welcomed an alternative, but we both knew there weren't any.

He didn't respond.

"Cache files," I said. The strewn soligraphs flew through the air and lined up in front of me like a glowing accordion. The data button sucked them up when I touched it to the corner of the files. I was about to close the button when I realized one file was smooshed under my foot.

Finn bent down to pick it up. "Is this one an extra?" he asked. "No label."

"No. That's not how data buttons work. Everything has to be categorized." I took the folder to show him how to open it. But it stuck tight. "That's weird."

The letters on the label were a digital smear, like someone had erased them in a rush. I held it up to the light but still couldn't read it. Changing a public record would take some high clearance. Or some serious know-how.

"Can you make this out?" I handed it back to Finn.

He squinted at the folder. "That might be a *J*. Or a 'nine.'"

Or nothing.

"I wish I could get a better look at it," I said. I took the file back from Finn and slid it into the data button. "But we need to go soon."

Finn stared at the button in my palm and bent his neck in a resolute nod. "Right then."

He unbuttoned his fly and pulled down his pants.

"What are you doing?" I squealed as he shook the first leg out.

"It's okay. I have boxers on." Superhero ones. But that didn't explain his deranged behavior. He pointed to my hand. "You need that data disk, don't you?'

"Why is stripping your answer to everything?"

He hopped around on one foot while he slid the other leg out. "You'll need to hand that guy something the same size and shape so we have time to get away with the real disk. Hence, my button."

"Oh." This could actually work. "Let me help."

With me tugging on his pant legs and Finn wrenching the button, *pop!,* it came off in his hand.

"Voilà." He held it up in triumph.

"You seriously have to stop doing that." I shielded my eyes from all the half nudity going on across from me.

Finn pulled up his jeans and tied the top together with a strip of fabric he tore from his shirt. Both buttons glinted in the brilliant light of the room, but Finn's wouldn't fool the attendant for long.

I plopped the wig back on and reached to open the door. Finn put his arm out to stop me. "Wait. What if this is what causes the danger you need protection from? Stealing this button. Sneaking back to see your mom."

"What if doing nothing does?" I patted him on the cheek. "I can play that game, too."

I moseyed up to the counter and plunked the pant button down without a word. I received none in return, which was exactly what I wanted. We walked calmly to the door, pushed it open, then started sprinting the moment our feet touched pavement. It had stopped raining. Steam rose from the sidewalk in the late morning sun. I figured it would be about thirty seconds before the attendant realized the switch.

It was five.

Finn and I hadn't made it to the corner when Mr. Personality stepped out from the Infobank. "Hey, you left the wrong button!"

But we didn't turn around. Didn't pause.

"Get back here! You left the wrong—" It was at that point it must have hit him that this was no innocent mistake, that it wasn't even a data disk he was holding. Heavy footfalls sloshed behind us, gaining ground. He was surprisingly fast for someone who hadn't moved more than three inches the whole time Finn and I were in the building.

"There!" I yelled. A Publi-pod hovered on the opposite side of the street. I ran toward it, dodging two street-vacs. Finn nailed a third with his thigh. I waved my hand in front of the Pod's access sensor. "Open, dang it."

The Pod split open.

It was a single.

Mr. Personality bumped against one of the vacs in his hurry across the street. I shoved Finn in the Pod and jumped in behind him. The moment the Pod closed, I shouted, "Destination: Pentagon. Go!"

Mr. Personality stood in the middle of the road, kicking the ground with his hands up in the air. That was one horked-off Owl. I let out a sigh of relief and sank back into the seat.

"That was actually kind of fun. Where to next?" Finn leaned back and I fell into the crook of his arm.

"You thought that was *what*?" I tried to move away, but there was nowhere to go. My head bumped against the side of the

Pod. I scooted forward and my knee jabbed into the console. Begrudgingly I moved back to his lap. My Buzz had finally subsided the last few days. I didn't want to tempt its return. I searched for a place to put my hands, but between his ripped shirt and unbuttoned pants I couldn't get situated without touching his bare skin. I felt a fresh wave of heat rush to my face. He must have read it as anger. Which, there was some of that, too.

"I shouldn't have used the word 'fun,'" he said. "That's not what I meant. I meant—"

"You do realize how much trouble I'll be in if—who am I kidding?—*when* they figure out I stole this?" I held up the data button. "I'll be expelled. Which I'm sure I'll be distracted from that fact as I'll be *in prison*. No one will pay for my mom's bills. No one. She'll end up in a mental institution."

Which was where I was beginning to feel I belonged.

"I'm sorry." He took a deep breath and rearranged his body to look out the window, which sent me tumbling to the other side of his lap. "See? This is exactly what I was worried about. It's putting you in too much danger. I think we should cancel the trip to talk to your mom. There has to be some other way to find out what an enigmatic grin is and how our mothers knew each other."

"Y'know what?" I found myself yelling, and I wasn't even sure why. "I don't care what you think. Whatever oath or promise you made Future Me, you are officially released from it."

"What are you talking about?"

"I'm letting you off the hook. I can take care of myself. Future Me must not have realized or, I guess, *remembered* how annoying this whole Protector act is."

"I'm afraid it's not up for debate." His jaw set into a hard line.

"So now you and Future Me get to decide everything?"

For a moment he looked stumped, but then he said, "It's also not up for a vote."

"I don't think you get it. I don't want your pity, and I don't need your help."

"Well, maybe you should have thought of that earlier . . . I mean, later." Finn reached out to the smooth panel in front of him. He clenched his hands around an imaginary steering wheel, then sprang them open with a scowl. "Here's an idea, Bree: Take a memo. Dear Future Self, if you don't want Finn's help, then don't go back in time two hundred years to a scared sixteen-year-old and beg him for it. Don't tell him he's the only one who can save you. Also, don't wear your hair like that and laugh at all his cheesy jokes and smell like cherry blossoms in the spring. And don't—" Finn stopped and turned his face back to the window.

"Don't what?"

He shook his head and continued to stare away.

"Don't *what*?" I grabbed his face to force him to look at me. Softened my voice and smoothed away the prickles.

Finn pulled my hands away from his face and clasped them to his chest.

"Don't make me promise to break your heart."

chapter 21

"WHAT?" I JERKED MY HANDS AWAY from Finn's chest, squished them under my legs, until I remembered I was still perched on his knee. I pressed my palm back against Finn's chest. I needed him at least an arm's length away. "What are you talking about? Break my heart?"

"I lied to you before." Finn's thumbnail dug into the seat cushion. The rush of his pulse ebbed under my fingers. "When I told you earlier what Future You had asked of me, I wasn't telling the whole truth."

"I told you to protect me *and* to break my heart?" I leaned my head against the side of the Pod. To heck with Buzz prevention. It felt fine right now anyway. "That's what I said, verbatim?"

Finn nodded. "You made me promise to do both. You said, 'When all else fails, you have to break my heart,' and I told you I would." He gritted his teeth. "So I guess that means I've lied to you twice now. Well, once to you, once to Future You. Because I can't do it. I can't break your heart."

It didn't make sense. One of the things that had bothered me the most about the whole "Protect me" thing was how selfish it was. But "break my heart"? I might not be a martyr, but I wasn't a masochist. Neither sounded like me at all.

"To be honest," said Finn, "I thought Future You was a little crazy when she said that. Crazy hot." He let out a nervous laugh. "But still crazy. Sorry. I guess I shouldn't be making sanity jokes."

It comforted me somehow to hear Finn refer to my future self in the third person. Dang straight. I wasn't *her*.

"Did I—did she tell you why she wanted you to break my heart?"

He shook his head.

I wasn't her. But I needed to widen the gap. Me from her. So we'd never touch.

"Ask me something you don't know about me," I said.

"Apparently, there's a lot I don't—"

"Anything."

"Really? Okay. Umm, what's your favorite flavor of ice cream?"

"I don't have one. No dairy. My diet is optimized to provide nutritional balance for—"

"Yeah, yeah, active synergy for blah, blah, blah." His face contorted with mock disgust. "No favorite ice cream. Sad. Umm, what's your favorite time period?"

"I don't have one of those either. Some I like more than others. Anything before the invention of deodorant is iffy." The Pod hit a puddle and wobbled. A spray of muddy water clouded the front-view window. The backs of my legs ached from balancing on Finn's knees. I scooched back and settled into the crook of his shoulder. In this tiny space, I couldn't avoid his body. Or the flutters that went through mine being so near him.

"Don't tell me they restrict that, too. You have to have a favorite. Your mom had a favorite."

"Yeah, but that's because my—" I shut my mouth and watched the raindrops race one another down the window. Maybe I could go back to the ice-cream question.

"That's because your . . . ?" Finn prompted.

He might as well know. Given how he claimed to feel about me, he deserved to know. "When my mom first started working for the National Gallery of Art—it would have been, well, seventeen years ago now—her first assignment was assisting on this high-profile Picasso counterfeit. It was an extended mission. Weeks at a time for several months." I drew a deep breath. "And that's when she . . . met my dad."

"Your dad was on her research team?" Furrows formed along Finn's forehead.

"No, my dad was—"

"Pablo Picasso is your *father*?" Finn tried to stand up, but instead he whacked his head on the ceiling and sent me sprawling to the floor.

"No." My elbow smeared against something sticky, and I used Finn's shirt to wipe it off. "My mom never even met Picasso. My dad was a Brit Lit professor at Georgetown in the 1910s where her team was doing some of its research. My parents fell in love. She knew she was breaking all the Rules to be with someone from the past, but she thought if she married him they'd let her go back and visit him."

"And?"

"They didn't."

My mother's heart would forever be tied to the twentieth century. As would my quantum tendrils. Genetically, I was just as much a child of my father's present as my mother's. Sometimes, it felt like my tendrils clung to every moment in between them—a bridge—trying to pull my parents together.

The sprinkle of rain had stopped. The windows clouded. Our Pod suddenly felt like a humid tomb.

"So you've never met your father?" Finn finally said. "That's so wrong. They shouldn't be allowed to do that."

"The authorities have their reasons. Security. NonShifter relations."

"But it's so senseless. If two people are in love, they shouldn't be held apart over a little thing like time. I mean, if she didn't have her chip, she could go back and see him whenev—oh."

"Exactly. Now you see why people think she tinkered with her chip."

"And why people might suspect you of wanting to do the same thing. You must miss him a lot."

I shrugged. "It's hard to miss someone you've never known. I mean, he died before I was born. By about two hundred and fifty years. I guess you could say I miss the *idea* of a father."

Yet here was Finn, dead for . . . well, I had no idea how long he'd been dead, since we still hadn't figured out why he wasn't in any databases. I had a new appreciation for what it must have been like for my mom, walking away from the love of her life. Not that I was in love with Finn. Or anything like that. At all.

"I'm so sorry," he said. "Did you believe them? The people who thought your mom tampered with her chip? I mean, before you found out she was attacked."

"No. She loved my dad, but she also loves me. She never would have risked it. She knew I'd have no one if . . ." I choked up. "And she knew it would have been too risky for my dad, too. She obviously never told him she was a Shifter. It would have put him in danger, having that knowledge."

"Why? My mom knew about my father while they were still dating. And the Haven's existed for millennia."

"In secret. In hiding. Would you want that for someone you loved?"

"I guess not."

"Things are so much better now that Shifters are able to live out in the open."

Finn didn't look like he believed me.

"What?" I said. "It's the truth."

"Truth." He chuckled and faced the window.

We fell into a solemn silence until we rounded the corner to the Pentagon. My shoulders started to unclench. But even from a distance, I could tell something was wrong. The Publi-pod slowed at the entrance, but I barked, "Passenger request: Circle the building," before it had a chance to stop. As the Pod window cleared, I could see a cluster of people on the lawn. Three Institute staff members stood among a crowd of Pentagon workers, pointing back to the ticket gate. She had her back to us, but I recognized one of them instantly as Quigley. A few red-scrubbed medics, like the ones at my house the other day, were also wandering around, holding speak-eazies up to their mouths.

"They're definitely searching for something," said Finn, peering out the back-view hole, "but it might not be us."

As soon as the words were out of his mouth, one of the workers lifted something from his pocket. He tapped it; a ten-foot soligraphic version of me appeared on the Pentagon lawn. *Eep.*

"Okay, scratch that," said Finn. "Maybe the Infobank already notified this Quigmire person that someone was impersonating her."

"Quigley. And maybe." I wasn't convinced. "Why would she jump so quickly to the conclusion that it was me?"

"Video surveillance?"

"Impossible. There are strict privacy laws. Image capture is illegal on public property."

Finn grabbed the data button and held it up. "So we'll get rid of the proof. They can't fingerprint it if they can't find it."

"Fingerprint?" A snort escaped me. "Are you kidding?"

"Are you telling me they've lost the ability to check for fingerprints?"

"I think you'd have to miss something to say it's been lost. Fingerprints are über-easy to alter, destroy, steal . . ."

"I don't know. Your brilliant hair system seems a bit flawed. I managed to pretend to be you. And you stole Quigley's hair."

"Yeah, well, I don't think there are many people who are willing to risk the consequences of getting caught."

"Death?" His voice slipped to a hushed horror.

"No. They laser your hair off. Permanently." Eyebrows, eyelashes, body hair. Everything.

Finn laughed as if I'd told the one about the priest, the rabbi, and the Martian.

"Laugh all you want. Shavies are social pariahs. You can't get a job. You can't use public transportation. I doubt you'd be able to find someone to sell you a used Pod."

His smile faded. "Bree, I had no idea. Why did you risk it?"

The obvious answer was to get rid of him, but if I was being honest with myself, the other reasons had outweighed that. It wasn't like sneaking into the Infobank had triggered the answer-pocalypse, but I'd hoped for at least a little insight into what was going on—who attacked my mom, proof that she hadn't tampered with her chip, proof that she wasn't a victim of the Madness. If anything, I had more questions than before.

I scratched my fingernail across the dashboard. "I guess after so much numbness of not knowing, I thought truth—any truth—would hurt less."

"We'll tell them I did it," he said.

"Finn, you don't even exist."

"Even more reason they'll believe me. They'll think I'm some lunatic who held you hostage for your identity."

I dug my nail farther into the Pod, prepared to argue. After a few more seconds of scratching, though, the Publi-pod must have decided it wouldn't stand for the abuse. It stopped in the middle of the street and popped open. We were three hundred yards or so from the entrance, far enough that we wouldn't be immediately noticed. Close enough to see we'd need another way back in. All the entrances would be monitored. There was only one direction left.

Up.

"We'll have to sneak back in through the roof." The building was five stories high. I was all of five feet high. Finn was a sturdy six, but something told me those extra twelve inches wouldn't prove all that useful in this situation.

"We could run," said Finn.

"No, I don't want to give them any reason to track my movements today." I was scared enough that they already had.

No matter what, we couldn't sit there in the stalled Pod any longer. I motioned to Finn to follow me toward the edge of the building, around the corner from the entrance. I kept one eye peeled for tru-ants, but they must have all been swarming inside the amusement park. As Finn and I neared the exterior wall, I grasped for the first time why the fortress of fun represented military might for so long.

Finn mistook my silence for deliberation. He flew into solve-it mode. "We could jimmy one of the windows open. Or I could hop ledge to ledge. Or we could—"

"Or we could use my grappling hook." I pulled a metal tube, four inches long, from my pocket.

"Who carries a grappling hook?"

"Standard issue. A girl has to be prepared."

I heard shouts in the distance and pulled us flat against the building.

"What *don't* you have in that pocket?" asked Finn.

"Patience."

Finn rolled his eyes.

"You know you love me." I chuckled. As soon as the words flew out, I felt my cheeks flame. I puffed them full of air and blew it out as slowly as I could.

Finn had the good sense to pretend not to hear. A crack in the wall was suddenly the most interesting thing he'd ever seen, and he only looked up when I stepped away from the building. I aimed the end of the tube at a spot under the roof's overhang. It would be like the training exercises in Gym class. Only four stories higher. With people chasing me.

A pea-sized target shot out the end when I pressed the trigger switch. *Ping.* It found its mark. I pushed a second button on the tube, and it telescoped in length, soft-grip handles poofing out of the ends. I peered around the corner of the building. The searchers had turned in the other direction for now. Hoping they wouldn't look up, I grasped one end and held out the other to Finn. "You ready?"

"It's broken." He pointed at the place where the target had landed. "There's no wire."

"It uses electromagnetic pulses."

"You're telling me I'm supposed to trust a pellet gun and a broken car antenna with my life?"

"It's perfectly safe." There was nothing like arguing the contraption's merits with Finn to attempt to convince myself as well. Skepticism marred his usually calm features.

"Look, I'm terrified of heights," I said. "If I can do this, you sure as heck can."

"I thought it was water you were afraid of."

"I'm not exactly president of the Altitude Fan Club either." The target was so far up I couldn't even see the blink of its operational light. What I wouldn't give for a gravbelt right now. I drew a deep, steadying breath. "You with me or not?"

He laid his hand on the handle in silent acceptance. I pushed the center switch again. Immediately the muscles in my hand clenched the handle tight in an involuntary grasp, frozen in place. I looked up into Finn's wary green eyes and he bobbed his head to indicate his hand was locked as well. When I pushed the center button once more, we lifted a couple feet off the ground before a red light began blinking. We thudded back down.

"Are we too heavy?" Finn asked.

"No. It can hold up to six hundred pounds." *Think, think, think.* In training, we'd only done a few duet ascensions. Coach Black always paired us together by weight. "I think we're off balance. We need to get, umm, close."

The daggers in my eyes dared Finn to make a wrong move.

He blinked. "Okay, so I'll slip my . . . arm around your . . ."

"Shoulder," I said.

"Waist," he said at the same time.

At least he hadn't said "butt."

"Shoulder," I repeated.

We stepped together. Finn circled my upper body in the crook of his arm. His skin was dry and warm where it met the back of my neck, still moist from my rain-soaked hair. He opened his hand and cupped the back of my head, then seemed to think better of it and balled his hand into a fist. He closed his eyes for a second, and I wondered what he was thinking. Or praying.

I pressed the center button one last time.

chapter 22

I'M GOING TO DIE. I'm going to die. I'm going to die. I'm going to die.
Any qualms about propriety or personal space whistled away with the wind whipping past my ears. The world rushed down. I rushed up. Green. Gray. Blue. Nothing was solid. I hugged Finn as tight as I could and dug my face into his chest.

"Woo-hoo!" Finn pumped his free hand in the air.

That snapped me back to my senses. I nudged him with my shoulder. "You're going to get us caught."

The jerking motion threw our balance off. A red warning light blinked on. Finn clutched me closer. The flight couldn't have taken more than five seconds. It felt like five minutes. When we reached the target my eyes were closed again, but I knew it was bad. The street sounds below were nothing but a muffled murmur.

"Wow." Finn gave my shoulder a little squeeze. "You can see everything from up here."

"Can you see a way to get us onto the roof?" My voice was a whimper, eyes still shut.

"Oh, yeah, sorry." He began swinging his torso in an attempt to get a leg up over the edge. Every time he did so, my body swung right along with him, a limp rag doll. His fear of heights certainly didn't seem very feary to me.

"Man, that broken car antenna has a death grip on my hand," he said.

"That is a *good* thing." I hadn't intended my voice to screech so much, but at least it got him to stop swinging.

208

"If I were a few inches closer . . ." The whole apparatus shuddered as he strained upward and heaved his leg over the edge of the building. Using the rod for support, he pushed himself all the way onto the roof. The red light blinked back on as the handle jerked and swayed. I reached my free hand up and grabbed a pipe that ran along the edge of the building.

"Okay," said Finn, swiveling his body so it lay flat against the roof. "I think I have a pretty good grip here."

"Think?" I adjusted my hand so I had a firm grasp on the pipe. *"Pretty good?"* I chin-upped over the rod to see how secure Finn really was. Wrong move. The red light on the center of the rod came back on, this time unblinking. A shrill beep accompanied it, louder and faster as I leaned forward to inspect it. My fingers wriggled. They were no longer glued to the handle.

"Uh-oh." I flung my newly released hand up to the pipe next to the other one. The grappling rod gave one final *bleep* and plummeted to the ground.

"Bree!" Finn plunged his torso over the edge and reached for me, but I was too far under the overhang of the roof. "Hold on. I'll figure out a way to get to you."

"Stay on the roof." It wouldn't help matters if both of us were stuck.

The color drained from my knuckles as I struggled to keep my grip. My legs flailed wildly beneath me. I kicked one of my feet up and managed to hitch it over the pipe. Then the other foot, which at least took some of the pressure off my arms. From the ground I probably looked like one of those extinct tree sloths that scientists were constantly cloning into existence, only to have them die off again.

Eep. Dying. Not the best line of thought.

"My leg's hooked around a vent up here now." Finn stretched down and thrust his hand as far toward me as he could. "I can reach you if you hold out one of your hands."

"Or. I could *not* let go of the pipe."

But as I looked around, I realized there were no other options. The effort scorched my muscles as it was. By the time Finn found help, it would be too late.

"Okay." *Crapcakes. Had I just agreed to this plan? Yes. No other way.* "Tell me when."

He wiped his hand on his shirt and stuck it back down. "Now."

I closed my eyes and threw my hand out into nothingness. The pain that had branded my arm disappeared; a firm pressure took its place. The next thing I knew, my wrist was locked with Finn's. I sailed through the air, cracking my eyes to see if I needed to grab on to the overhang. But all I could see was the gray of stone. Wall? Sky? *Thud.* My body slammed against something solid. I puckered my lips and kissed it. Solid. I loved solid. Finn had flung me all the way to the roof in one swoop of an arc.

He flopped down next to me and grinned. "That's going to be the best sprained shoulder ever."

"New goal in life," I said once I had crawled a safe distance from the edge. "Never be that far off the ground again. Ever."

"Solution," said Finn. "Move to Chincoteague Island. Nothing's over two stories high."

I couldn't help but let out a little laugh. I leaned against one of the solar bubbles that dotted the white roof like igloos scattered across a frozen tundra. "Yeah, but after two hundred years I wonder if those ponies have taken over the place."

"Oh." He smiled, but there was a hint of sadness in his voice. "I was thinking of my time. Probably all skyscrapers and laser hotels now."

"What's a laser hotel?" My laugh was in earnest this time.

"I don't know. It sounded futuristic and cool. Of course, you can pretty much put the word 'laser' in front of anything and it sounds cool."

"Laser pencils," I said in a robotic voice.

"Laser chairs." His robot was better.

I snorted as I thought of another one. I slid down the panel until my heinie hit roof. Finn joined me.

"Laser . . . bracelet." My face fell.

"How could you have a—?"

"No." *No . . . no . . . no.* Where was it? I grabbed my wrist and searched the ground where we sat. "My bracelet. It's gone."

How could I have lost it? I jumped up and ran over to the spot where I'd landed. It had to be there. It had to.

"Help me look for it. It's sterling silver with a heart-shaped locket on it." My hand stayed clasped over my wrist, as if I could magically make the bracelet reappear if I left it there long enough. On the white roof, the silver should have been easily visible. The bracelet must have fallen off when Finn had grabbed my wrist.

It was gone.

I had failed. I could never get it back.

I could never get her back.

I traced our steps back to the solar bubble and sank down. My hands fell limp. Imprints remained where the links had pressed against my wrist. I traced them with my finger.

"I always rub the heart when I need to feel close to my mom. Stupid, I know."

He followed the path of my finger with his own. "Nothing you do could ever be called stupid."

"Even sneaking back to your time and dragging you into all this?"

"Especially that." He had that look in his eyes I was learning to recognize, but I didn't know how I felt about it. It was like when he stared at me he saw past me, through me, in me.

"Finn, I need to—"

There was a *bang* in the distance. I peered around the corner of the solar bubble. Coach Black had lumbered onto the roof through one of the emergency hatch doors. He wasn't more than fifty yards away.

"So much for sneaking back in undetected," whispered Finn.

"I'm in trouble no matter what. But we could still get you out unnoticed. Wait here at least an hour before you go back in."

He peeked around the edge of the bubble and punched the air in frustration, but then his shoulders fell. "Yeah, I don't see any other way."

"Go ahead and give me the data disk. I'll try to figure out a way to crack into that file." I held out my hand. "And if I asked you to wait until next week's Family Night to come back to the Institute, you would . . . ?"

"Show up at your bedroom tonight anyway."

It was worth a shot. "You still have my hair?"

He nodded.

Coach Black had begun to lumber in our direction in his search.

I started to stand up, then paused. "Be, umm, careful."

"*You* be careful."

"I'm not the one who has to keep hiding."

"Shouldn't be too bad. Though if you told me this morning I'd be doing this I'd have sworn you were nuts."

"Which part? Stealing government property, running from smugglers, or hiding out at the Pentagon amusement park?"

"None of the above." Finn took my wrist and unapologetically kissed the tips of my fingers. "Leaving you behind."

And with that I had to walk away. Each step harder than I expected. But I wanted . . . no, *needed* to put some space between me and Finn's hiding spot before Black found me. I jogged off in the other direction, toward the hatch, careful not to glance back at Finn.

"Bennis!" The arteries on Coach Black's sweaty neck flared in and out like angry gills when he saw me. "Whaddya think you're doing up here?"

Subterfuge, identity theft, and some light espionage work.

"Nothing. I needed some air."

"Some air?"

LOOP

"Yes, sir." With the lie off my lips, it didn't sound so absurd after all.

He pointed toward the center of the Pentagon. "Was the five acres of green space not good enough for you for some reason?"

Hrmm. I started to stammer an answer, but he cut me off.

"Aren't you even going to ask why I'm looking for you? Why *everyone* is looking for you."

"Of course." I'd play this as naïve as possible.

"It's your roommate Mimi."

"Oh, yes. Before I came up here, someone mentioned she'd fainted on one of the rides. Nurse Granderson was fixing her up."

"Fainted? I don't know anything about that. But she fell down a flight of stairs a few hours ago."

His words dangled in the air. Sharp as knives, dull as a hammer.

"What?" I gasped. My entire body went numb.

"The other students are back at the Institute. A handful of teachers are still here to look for *you*." It came out like an accusation, like I had shoved Mimi down the stairs or something.

"Where is she? Is she all right? Can I see her?" Without waiting for an answer, I turned to run for the hatch Coach Black had emerged from.

He caught me by the shoulder. "She's at the hospital. We're waiting for news."

"Can you take me to her?"

"No." He pressed his hand on the top of my head as I descended the ladder like he alone was the gravity that held me to the earth. "Someone else is keen on having a word with you."

Coach Black offered no further information about Mimi's condition the whole way back to the Institute. It was torture. *Chase me. Dangle me. Slam me. But talk to me.*

An hour later—still no word on Mimi. The only slight positive was that I was waiting outside Headmaster Bergin's office rather than Quigley's. He was the lesser evil by a long shot.

My relief was short-lived.

chapter 23

BERGIN WASN'T IN HIS OFFICE yet when Dolores ushered me in. The entire top of his desk was aglow with compufilm. At first I assumed it was paperwork, until I leaned forward and saw that it was news clippings about his wife's accident, mostly editorials debating how such a tragedy could and should have been prevented. At first I wondered why he was obsessing over it now, but then I noticed the date in one of the articles and realized tomorrow was the anniversary of the accident.

I snapped back against my chair and turned around as two shadows widened across the desk until they merged into one. Quigley loomed behind Bergin with a look on her face that conveyed new heights of annoyance. At first I felt panicked to be caught in her eager clutches, but then a resolute anger took its place.

Headmaster Bergin slipped his colleague a wary sidelong glance before walking around the desk and sinking into his overstuffed armchair. He pulled out a data disk and tapped the edge, sucking the news clippings into it. His eyelids had a new set of bags under them since the last time I had visited his office. Guilt prickled my gut. What with this anniversary and Mimi's accident, my recklessness was the last thing Bergin needed to deal with right now.

"Miss Bennis," he began. His mustache ruffled as he blew a mouthful of air through it and backed up. "Bree. Let me start by saying you're not in trouble."

"I'm not?"

"No. I'm not angry. I'm . . ." He looked up at Quigley, who was staring out the window, lips pursed tight. "*We're* concerned. All of your teachers and the whole staff. You haven't been acting like yourself lately. Perhaps you haven't had adequate support following recent events."

"I'm fine."

"I owe you an apology." He kept on speaking like I hadn't. "I believed, or perhaps convinced myself, that you were coping without difficulty. But even aside from your recent accident—"

"My accident?"

"Falling off the bus on your last mission," Quigley said without lifting her gaze from the window one inch. The glass reflected the dean of discipline's smug expression. Her breath clouded the glass, but from the chill I felt it could have been frost.

Bergin's brow furrowed. "Hmm. Nurse Granderson seemed positive you didn't experience serious head trauma, but—"

"No, no," I said. "It's been a long day. I've been worried about Mimi."

"Didn't Coach Black tell you how she was? I'm so sorry. This must have been so vexing for you. Your roommate had a few broken ribs and bruises, a minor concussion, but she should mend quickly. However, I do want to speak with you about what happened."

Relief rushed through me. Mimi was going to be okay.

"I don't know much," I said. "I was up on the roof when she had her accident."

"Yes. Accident." The headmaster opened a drawer in his desk and pulled out a stack of compufilm. "We have reason to believe it may not have been one."

I leaned forward to the edge of my chair. "You think she was *pushed?*"

Bergin's chair wobbled and he looked up in a startle. "I didn't say 'pushed.' Why would you think she was pushed?"

Quigley remained motionless on the other side of the room. I ventured a peek out of the periphery of my vision. Only *one* person had eavesdropped on Mimi and me at the Pentagon that morning. And only *one* person had told us straight out she'd be watching us all day. Only *one* person had last accessed Poppy Bennis's Shift record, which had been erased. And now that *one person* was standing across from me while my mom and roommate were lying in hospital beds.

I held the back of Quigley's head in a captive glare before returning my full gaze to Bergin. I might not know *why* my mom was attacked, but I was certain of the *who.*

"No reason," I said smoothly. I needed to wait until I was alone with Bergin to tell him what I'd heard in the locker room.

"I understand Miss Ellison and a student transporter, Mr., umm"—Headmaster Bergin shuffled the compufilm around on his desk and pulled up a sheet with notes scribbled on it—"Mr. Charles Wu, they're close?"

"Yes." *Wait.* Where was he going with this?

"Did she seem upset about the relationship in any way?"

"I don't know that you could call it a relationship, per se. She and Charlie like each other. A lot. They've gone out a couple times. Kind of."

"So Miss Ellison wasn't angry at him for any reason?"

"No," I said with half a shrug.

"Or"—Bergin took a deep breath and looked at his hands—"carrying his child?"

"What?" The chair I'd been sitting in clattered over as I jumped up. *What on earth? "Who* said that? That's beyond laughable!"

Bergin motioned me to right the chair and sit back down. "Another student seemed to think . . . Oh, it doesn't matter. It was clearly false. You know how rumors can fly."

The room had taken on a red tinge in the corners of my vision. Mimi had overheard Quigley say something that raised a red flag. Quigley must have found out and come up with this student story to slander Mimi and cover her tail.

"So, what?" I asked. "You're suggesting *Charlie* pushed her?"

"No one is suggesting anyone pushed Miss Ellison."

"Then you think Mimi threw herself down the stairs? Because she was *pregnant*? Mimi's never even kissed a guy, much less . . . Good grief. And with Charlie? They're, like, the patron saints of handholding."

Bergin shook his head with a heavy sigh. "We were simply hoping you could provide some insight into this incident, given your close friendship with Miss Ellison."

"Yes, we are close." I looked over at Quigley. "I would do anything to protect her. Anything."

This could be my only chance to trap the Quig into talking. I needed to put out some tasty cheese to get my teacher to bite, though.

"There *was* one thing." I tapped my finger against my chin. "Probably nothing. But when we were waiting for our Pentagon ticket tattoos this morning, Mimi mentioned she'd seen something odd earlier."

"Odd? Did she tell you what it was?"

"No." I hesitated. "She didn't get the chance."

"Sir!" Quigley traversed the room in three swift steps and stood in front of his desk, blocking my view. "I hardly think this is the time to sit and idly speculate about all the possible gossipy teenage angst that could have prompted Miss Ellison to toss herself down the stairs. We don't even know for certain that it's the case."

And that's how to trap a rat.

"True." Bergin strained forward like he wanted to question me further, but then he looked up at Quigley and leaned back in his chair.

"The important thing is that we expect Mimi to have a full recovery," he said. Quigley had moved to the side, and I saw her flash the headmaster a meaningful look. He lowered his head in a defeated nod.

"But that brings us back to the other reason I wanted to speak to you," he said. "Certain staff members feel that you would benefit from a recovery time of your own."

Quigley fluttered her eyelids. I could have sworn I detected another smirk before Bergin went on. "A time of rest and relaxation away from the rigors of the Institute."

"But the Institute's my home." The only home I had left. For a split second, everything disappeared. The enigmatic grin, the stolen file, Mimi's accident—everything. Suddenly I felt like my wide-eyed twelve-year-old self, crossing the school's threshold for the first time, falling in love with every corner and cranny. Going on my first solo mission, my thumb glued to the panic button on my QuantCom the whole five minutes as I walked across that empty field that would become First Time Forest and planted an acorn in the middle. Home.

"And the Institute will continue to be your home," soothed Bergin, "*after* you've had a chance to restore yourself to top form in a more accommodating environment."

"Is *she* putting you up to this?" I couldn't help but ask. Though I didn't give Quigley the satisfaction of so much as a sideways glance.

"I assure you, no one is putting anyone up to anything," said Bergin. He looked up at my teacher guardedly. "But as the dean, yes, Dr. Quigley does have the final say on student discipline procedures."

"I thought you said I wasn't in trouble."

"Bree, please—"

"Do you see what the strain is doing to her?" Quigley cocked her head to the side and put on a brilliant display of mock pity. "I think the sooner Miss Bennis leaves for Resthaven, the better."

Resthaven? What? No! She couldn't do this.

I pulled myself together. "No thank you," I said as if declining Tea with the King of England.

The headmaster's cheeks flushed. "I'm afraid it's not an invitation. More of a firm request."

"And I'm afraid I'll need to decline either way." Who cared about classes and missions and sleeping in my own bed? If they shipped me off to Resthaven, I could kiss any payments for my mother good-bye. ICE wouldn't want a deranged girl for a spokes-anything.

And I still needed to get Finn home. And prove my mother hadn't messed with her chip. And work things out with Leto. *No!*

"It won't be permanent." Bergin had apparently not prepared for my dissent. He was sputtering like a half-empty teakettle.

"But I—"

"You're leaving tomorrow morning." Quigley cut me off. "Stay out of trouble until then." Her voice was distant and matter-of-fact. Like she hadn't, in one fell swoop, stripped away everything I had left to care about.

They couldn't make me go. I'd . . . I'd run away. Of course, I wouldn't get far with a microchip in my skull.

The sun had burned its way through a layer of clouds outside. Its light filtered into the office. Ironic. Dark rainstorms earlier when the day was so full of hope. Sunshine now that it was all gone.

Bergin looked miserable as well. For the first time since I had come to the Institute, he seemed *small*. I couldn't imagine how many strings Quigley had pulled to force this move to Resthaven. I beseeched Bergin with my eyes: *Do something.* But he hung his head.

The headmaster's hand tremored up to his pocket, the one where he kept his antique pen. His thumb twitched in an anxious tic like he was clicking the end of the pen in and out in his nervous habit, but then he looked up at the dean and seemed to think better of showing even that much weakness. He formed his hand into a fist instead and dropped it to his lap.

"I believe that's all, Lisette," he said quietly to Quigley. "I have one additional matter to discuss with Bree."

"I'd be happy to stay," she said.

"No, no. It doesn't concern you."

Ha! I shot the Quig a scathing look.

"Very well." With that, Quigley turned on her heel and strode out of the room, but she didn't look happy about it.

Headmaster Bergin reached out to squeeze my hand, which was lying on the desk in a lifeless heap. "There's no reason to believe this will be a long stay at Resthaven. We'll have you back as soon as possible, right as rain. I will see to that."

Yeah, right.

"However"—Bergin pulled his hand back—"there is one thing I wanted to discuss with you before you left. It's about your mother."

"Has ICE changed their minds?" I shook my head. I'd failed. She was headed to Resthaven, too. At least we'd be together.

"Bree, there have been some . . . some setbacks in her condition."

"What?"

"I received a call this morning. She's destabilizing. The doctors are doing everything they can, but—"

Leto. Leto had gotten to her. *Wait. Bergin said "this morning."*

"I spoke with her nurse this afternoon," I said. "She was fine."

"You did?" Bergin looked genuinely startled. "Perhaps . . . perhaps they didn't want to worry you before they had a chance to speak to you in person."

But that meant it couldn't have been Leto.

"I'm sorry, Bree," said Bergin. "ICE will still pay for her hospital bills for as long as it's . . . necessary."

I choked on a sob.

If it wasn't Leto, there was only one other person who could have gotten to her. *Quigley!* She had done this. I wouldn't let her get away with it.

"There's something else I need to tell you," I said. "It's about my moth—"

Bergin's intercom sounded and his assistant's voice filled the room: "Headmaster Bergin?"

"Yes, Dolores?"

"There's an urgent call for you on your speak-eazy, channel one. Private communication requested."

"Please excuse me, Miss Bennis." He picked up the receiver and said, "Bergin speaking . . . Yes. . . . Oh, no." His hand drifted to his mouth and he blew out a deep breath. "I see. Yes, I understand. I'll notify the necessary people immediately."

When the call ended, he stood up and wandered to the window. His head bobbled from side to side. After a few moments, he turned to face me. The rims of his eyes were bloodshot.

"I'm so sorry to tell you this, Bree, but your roommate, Mimi, has taken a turn for the worse. Her concussion must have been more serious than they realized at first. I . . . I don't have any easy way to say this. She's slipped into a coma."

chapter 24

SLEEP MAY HAVE COME. Maybe not. I couldn't tell. Nor did I care. Salty tears had glued my eyes shut.

My Buzz had returned full force over the last few hours. If it even was the Buzz at this point. Since my forced fade, there was no rhyme or reason to it. Pain during class and meals. Fine when I was in my room. No telling how many Buzztabs I'd downed. Dozens.

Plink. Plink plink.

And apparently, I was experiencing auditory hallucinations as well. I smooshed my pillow around my ears and squinched up against the wall. Maybe I was going insane after all.

Plink plink.

Plunk.

I put my pillow down and sat up. There was no way I had imagined *that.*

The window whined as I pushed the button to open it. Two stories below, Finn stood in the bushes squinting up and chucking pieces of—

"Ow." Whatever it was hit my cheek. "What are you throwing?"

"Sorry," Finn whisper-shouted. "Rocks."

A smattering of stones already littered the windowsill. I picked one up. Purple. "Where did you find a purple . . . ?" *Oh my gosh.* "Please tell me you haven't kept those stupid Muffy van Sloot rocks on you this whole time."

"You never know when pebbles will come in handy."

"When on earth would *pebbles* come in—ow!" Another rock stung my cheek.

"Sorry. Couldn't help myself."

I brushed the rest of the colored rocks into my palm and leaned over to my desk to dump them into my fishbowl. "Sorry, Fran."

When I turned back to the window, the telltale *ping* of the grappling hook sounded outside. I rushed to the sill.

"You can't come up yet."

"What? Why not?"

"I, umm, I need to—" The embarrassing answer was I didn't want him to see me like this. But I couldn't say that, so I said, "I need to turn off my laser fish."

Finn chuckled. In the amount of time it took for him to turn his attention back to the task at hand, I made a mad dash to my closet for a sweater to cover my flimsy camisole, grabbed Mimi's brush off her vacant vanity, and popped a tooth-cleaning tablet in my mouth. With a whir and a thump, Finn hopped into the room like he'd been magno-grappling for years.

I stumbled backward in surprise. The haphazard, half-packed suitcase in the center of the room stubbed my toe, and I let out a yelp.

Finn reached out to steady me and looked over at Mimi's empty bed. "What's with the suitcase? Where's your roomie?"

With those two well-meaning questions, the weight of the entire day slammed against my heart once again. I crumpled onto the bed.

Finn sat next to me and tilted my chin up tenderly. "What happened?"

For the first time, I welcomed Finn's comfort. His still eye in the middle of my raging storm. Somehow, he managed to keep up as everything about the day gushed out of me in spurts: My mom's deterioration. Mimi's so-called accident. The move to Resthaven. Quigley had won. I didn't even understand what game she was playing, but she'd won.

"There's no point going back to see my mom now. I'm going to confess to chronosmuggling for Leto. That way they can put up guards around her." I brushed away a final, clinging tear. "I need to figure out a way to Shift you back to your time. Tonight."

"Bree, you need answers now more than ever."

"No," I said with more conviction than I felt. "I think this is it, what I need protection from—Resthaven. And Quigley. She wants to lock me away with a bunch of nutcases so no one will believe me when I claim she attacked my mom. But I was wrong, Finn. I mean I will be wrong. I should never have asked you to come here to help me. We need to get you home."

He was the one person left in my life *I* could still protect.

"You're probably right," he conceded. "Too bad I don't care. We're going to see your mom. Now."

There was nothing I wanted more than to see my mother, to be held and told everything would be all right. To breathe in that sweet scent of hyacinth perfume mixed with the musty smell of old canvas one more time. But in that moment, it was selfish and wrong. It seemed like something Future Bree would do. Me, me, me above everyone else. If I agreed to the Shift, I alone knew my true motives. And they were anything but pure.

Finn still thought the enigmatic grin was important. I just wanted to hug my mom.

"There's no point," I said. "Even if Mom knows what that Truth saying means, it won't help her."

"How do you know that?" asked Finn. "Maybe it will explain her condition."

"Finn, I—"

"We're going," he said. "Do you think Charlie could transport us?"

"Us?"

"I was going to try to cling to you again."

"No." The word jumped out of my mouth like a harsh bark.

"To me going with you or to Charlie transporting us?"

224

"Both. I can't risk you getting caught. And I can't risk him getting in trouble. Quigley will be watching him as it is."

"I'm going with you." The way Finn said it told me there was no point in arguing. Likely he wouldn't be able to Shift anyway like before, so I didn't bother correcting him.

"There's no way to set it on autopilot?" he asked.

I shook my head. "Not at the Institute." There was only one option. "I could ask W—"

"No." Finn didn't even let me get the—yck out.

"Why? Are you jealous?"

"No. But I'm telling you, I don't trust that guy."

"He's the best student transporter at the Institute. Give me one good reason not to trust him."

Finn opened his mouth as if he was about to say something but closed it again. "I can't."

"Then let's go." I hopped off the bed and grabbed my shoes.

"Wait." He caught hold of my wrist and pulled me back toward him. The tips of his fingers hovered inches from my cheek as if he was trying to memorize each curve of my face.

"I've been thinking about it. It's not too late to go back to my time, to my parents," he said. "Maybe they could help. My dad has picked up a lot of knowledge from Future Shifters. Some of them might be from beyond this time. What if one of them could figure out a way to keep you there with me?"

It was tempting. I reached up and squeezed his hand before moving it back down to his side.

"The margin of error on a two-century Shift is so wide. We could end up five hundred miles from Chincoteague. By the time we got to your parents, they'd force fade me back. Besides, my mom is here. I can't leave her. Or Mimi." I bent down to put on my shoes.

A puke cart whizzed past the doorway and filled the room with the sickeningly sweet scent of cleanser. The carts had been on a warpath since the students had returned from our Pentagon outing. My Buzz had actually subsided since Finn had gotten there, but the smell, combined with crying all evening, made me reach for my glass vial of tabs out of habit. I shook it, but it was empty. Mimi had a spare container on the vanity. I snatched it up with greedy fingers and downed a few without counting.

"How many of those are you taking?" Finn asked with a frown.

"A few." I didn't look at him.

A few too many.

Finn picked up my empty vial. "How long have you needed these?"

"Since I first started Shifting." No, that wasn't entirely true. "After my chip was implanted, I mean. But I didn't have any real Shifts before that, so it's essentially the same thing."

"Could that be what makes Shifting hurt now?" Finn asked.

"My chip?" My thumb drifted to the nape of my neck and traced the numb eyelash of a scar. "No. The chip helps control the pain of Shifting. I told you that."

Finn's frown grew deeper. "So it hurt *before* they put the chip in?"

"No." His question flustered me for some reason, and I pressed against the scar. "I mean, yes. I mean . . . it prevents the pain. The tabs are for the Buzz that breaks through."

Finn placed his hand over mine and felt along the scar's path. My skin prickled and hummed under his touch, almost like I was building up for a Shift.

"I'm so sorry you have to live like this," he said.

"Live like what?" I pulled away. Whatever connection I felt splintered. "Free from pain and misery? Free from insanity? Oh, poor me."

"Pain and misery? My dad's been Shifting for decades without any problems. Georgie took to it without a hitch. I just think it's a little suspicious that I've never witnessed this so-called Buzz before I got here. Dad's never shown any symptoms of mental instability. And there's this convenient rule that you're not allowed to talk to any Shifter who could tell you any different."

"This is ridiculous," I said a little louder than I meant to. I glanced over at Mimi's bed out of pure reflex, and my heart did a flip-flop. I lowered my voice back down. "I explained why we can't talk to Shifters from the past. And even if they're not in pain, it's not like your father and sister have it perfect. They don't even have any control over where they go."

"Do you?"

I ignored his question. "The Rule is in place for *your* protection. And for mine."

"Again, says who?"

"Says everyone."

"Everyone who has a chip in their brain already."

A puke cart paused outside my door. They usually didn't snitch, but I couldn't take any chances of them reporting Finn's presence. Quigley would ship me off to Resthaven tonight and he'd end up in a lab. I grabbed him by the shirt collar and dragged him onto my bed, lowering the privacy canopy around us.

"We discovered the Madness right after Shifters came out of hiding, Finn. And everything was so secretive before then. For all we know, the Madness eventually did overtake all Shifters in the past. It's possible that your dad and Georgie *will* go bonks eventually. Do you really want to tell them their fate if so?"

"No, but surely there has to be some alternative to having your every move monitored and controlled."

"I don't mind it, Finn. The control is a *good* thing."

"And would the father you've never met agree with that?"

I jerked away, forgetting I still held the glass vial of Buzztabs. They flew out of my palm and shattered against the wall. Pills and bits of broken glass rained down across the bed. I shook as I tried to pick them up one by one.

Finn knelt next to me. "I'm sorry. I crossed a line. I shouldn't have said that."

"Why not?" I asked, my voice shaking as hard as my hands. "It's true."

He steepled his steady hands over my trembling ones. "I trust you. If you say you need your microchip, you do."

"I do." *He trusts me.*

I just wasn't sure I trusted myself.

Finn deftly plucked the rest of the Buzztabs from the glass and brushed the remaining shards into his hand. He leaned around me to dump them down the recycling bin.

"Guess sometimes the truth is just hard." He was quiet for a moment, then squinched up his nose. "*The Truth lies behind the enigmatic grin.* What if it has something to do with your chip?"

"Then why would *your* mom know that saying?"

"I don't know."

"We need to get going." I retracted the privacy canopy and grabbed my QuantCom off its docking station. "Wyck's room is on the way."

Finn slid the door open. "Why don't you let *me* wake him up?"

⚭

"Yes, I know it's asking a lot." I stood in the middle of the Launch Room doling out feeble answers to Wyck's questions for what seemed like the twenty-seventh time. "It's just that Finn was out of the country and never got a chance to see Mom before the accident. I realize it's breaking some rules—"

"More like each and every rule we have, Bree. You're *Anchored.*" Wyck's hair stuck out in five different directions and he sounded groggy, for which I was grateful. Maybe once Finn and I left, he would chalk it up to sleepwalking and a bizarre dream after too many chili dogs at the Pentagon. Mom could get us to a Shift Pad to synch me back up and figure out how to send Finn home from there.

"I'm not stupid. I won't try to change anything." I handed him my QuantCom.

Wyck shrugged and yawned as he uploaded the destination

data into my Com. "Doctrine of Inevitability. Wouldn't matter if you did."

I knew that, of course. But hearing it out loud crushed a little something within me.

"Besides," Wyck said with a mischievous grin as he handed back my QuantCom and took Quigley's hair, "I never said I mind breaking a few rules. But if you get caught—"

"I won't. Just promise you won't tell anyone, okay?"

Wyck crossed his finger over his heart.

"Of course not. Wild ponies couldn't drag it from me."

I relaxed with his reassurance and was surprised to feel the tension in Finn's hand when I took it to lead him to the Shift Pad. His eyes were fixed on Wyck. The control board flickered on.

"If anything happens to her," said Finn, "I hold you personally responsible."

Wyck didn't bother to look up from his task. "And if anything happens to *you,* I will personally pat myself on the back."

"Watch yourself," said Finn.

"I prefer watching Bree, thank you very much."

"I'm standing right here." I clamped down on Finn's hand. I could feel him pulling away from me . . . to what? Fight Wyck for helping us?

"Bree . . ." Finn turned to face me. "Let's do this some other way. I'll explain later."

"Oh, don't get your undies in a bunch. I'll get you there," said Wyck.

Finn made a chuffing noise, but he followed my tugs to the Pad.

Before Finn had a chance to protest further, Wyck looked up from his console. "You ready, sugar lips?"

I nodded.

Finn wrapped his arms tight around me. Wyck brought his fingers up into a lazy salute in Finn's direction. As we faded away, three of Wyck's fingers went down.

chapter 25

MEMORIES DANCED across my retinas as I jostled through time. It was the first Shift in months I'd kept my eyes open, and the sensation dizzied me. But I couldn't shut them. Even though I knew full well the trip was foolhardy, excitement welled within me.

We landed with a metallic thud on the Metro platform closest to my house. I whipped out the QuantCom to confirm the date and nodded in an appraising manner. It was the morning of my mom's accident. A Saturday. Puffy clouds drifted across an otherwise blue sky. A train zipped by, and Finn toppled over from his crouch.

Finn.

"Well, I'll be laserspanked. It worked. You Shifted again." Must have been my sad transporting skills earlier after all.

When he didn't answer, I said, "Say what you want about Wyck, the boy can transport." I brushed some dirt off my hands and reached over to give Finn a hand up.

He didn't take it.

"Did you hear what he said?" Finn asked in a soft voice.

"What who said?"

"Wyck. Right before we left."

"What? The 'sugar lips' thing? That's just how he talks."

I grabbed Finn's hand and pulled him forward, whether he wanted to move or not. It was the middle of the night my time. I had to get back before anyone woke up, so we only had a couple hours. We'd only get one shot at this.

Finn shuffled forward like he was sleepwalking.

"Wild ponies," he murmured.

"What?"

"He said 'wild ponies.' "

"So?" I asked. "It's only a saying."

Except it wasn't. The real saying would be "wild *horses* couldn't drag it from me." But he was half-asleep when he'd said it. I couldn't see why Finn was getting all worked up over it.

"You'll think I'm a lunatic," he said. A train flew into the station behind him and mussed his hair. "That's why I let it drop before."

"I already know you're a lunatic. But what are you talking about? Tell me what?"

"I saw him."

"Saw who?" I took the first few steps down the platform stairs.

"Wyck."

"Wyck? Where?" I looked around.

"In town. In Chincoteague. Near the school parking lot a few months after Future You first came back. I don't know if he saw me, but I saw him."

"You didn't see him." I shook my head.

"I did."

"You didn't. I already told you. He *can't Shift*. It is physically impossible for a nonShifter to Shift." I scuffled forward and looked down at the QuantCom. We really needed to get on the move. There weren't any Publi-pods out that I could see.

"Maybe he hasn't discovered his ability yet," said Finn. "He could be a late bloomer."

"Blooming from what? It's genetic. Neither of his parents are Shifters." My arms formed a big X across my chest. "No genes equals no time travel."

"I know what I saw."

"You saw one of his ancestors or somebody who looked kind

of like him, that's all." I started walking again to close the conversation.

Finn jogged after me. "But how do you explain the wildponies comment?"

I stopped and whirled around to face him. "I don't. Because there's nothing to explain. It was a simple, middle-of-the-night, barely awake mistake." But the more I thought about it, it really was odd. It was an old-fashioned saying—out of character for Wyck. Shifters picked up stuff like that all the time, but not transporters. Still, the thought was preposterdiculous. For him to have inherited the gene, it would have to have been directly. Like me from my mom. Like Georgie from her dad. Neither of Wyck's parents could Shift.

I expected Finn to argue more, but he didn't. If anything, he'd gone quieter than usual.

"Let's get going," I said.

He quickened his pace to meet mine, and we settled into a steady run. The closer we got to my house, though, the heavier my feet felt. The reality of seeing my mother—not just dreaming it, imagining it, conjuring little mental dioramas—clenched my muscles in an already-tense situation. Turning the corner onto our block, my legs gave one final leaden protest and locked up.

Finn was fifteen feet ahead before he realized he'd left me behind.

"What's the matter? Is your Buzz back?"

"No, my head's fine. But I don't know if I can do this."

Finn turned to look at the house, then back to me. "Do you want me to go talk to her by myself?"

I swallowed the lump in my throat. "I need to do this."

I had to clear her name. And maybe she could give me some hint as to why Quigley would attack her. It could bring insight into her condition. There might still be hope for her to improve.

When we reached the door, I lifted my hand to open it, then wavered again. Barging in felt like an intrusion, but if I rang the doorbell to my own house it would wig my mother out. The light was on in Mom's top-floor studio. My hand trembled as I brushed my hair over the scanner and pushed the front door open. Finn reached out and steadied it. He was getting pretty good at that.

"You can do this."

I had to.

The stairs creaked as I made my way up the first flight. Tufty appeared out of nowhere and gave me the stink eye before running love circles around Finn's ankles.

"Hey, Tuft," said Finn, and picked him up. The footsteps above us in the studio stopped.

"Shh. She'll hear us," I said.

"Were we trying to sneak up on her?"

"Good point. I guess I've gotten used to the secret agent act lately. But I wouldn't want to give her a heart attack before she slips into a coma." A sad attempt at humor.

"Bree, you know you can't tell her—"

"I know. I—"

"What are you doing here?" My mom's lilting voice rang down from the landing above. There was no accusation or anger in it. Only delight and surprise.

Tears pricked and moistened the corners of my eyes. Mom wiped her paint-splattered hands on an old rag.

"I wasn't expecting you until dinner. I thought you and Mimi were going shopping today."

Shopping. Yes, that's what I'd been doing before the world imploded. Shopping. So normal. So . . . nothing.

Mom motioned to Finn. "And you brought a friend."

"I . . . I . . ." *Here we go.*

"Hi, I'm Finn." He jumped up a few steps and gave her a small wave. "And this actually isn't your Bree."

Mom looked back and forth between us like she was waiting for the punch line.

"Okay, whose Bree is she?"

"No, what I mean is—"

"What he means is I'm on a Shift from the future." I licked my lips and waited for her response.

"Oh." She tossed the rag she was holding onto a laundry basket in the hall and ushered the two of us down the stairs to the living room. "Why didn't you say so, sweetie? Did you two drop by for a snack?"

"No." I sank into the sofa, and Finn joined me. My eyes refused to budge from my mom for even a millisecond. I didn't want to imagine what must happen in the next twelve hours to land my mother babbling and broken on the steps of my school. But the more I knew, the more I could help her.

"Mom, we need to ask you some questions. Just answer honestly even if you have no idea why I'm asking or think I can't handle it."

My mother's demeanor darkened, and she glanced at Finn with a new wariness.

"What's going on?" She sat down opposite us.

"Nothing. I'm fine, Mom, but I—"

"Who is he?" She pointed to Finn who shrank back.

"Don't worry about him. He's a—" I looked at Finn and for the first time realized what I truly thought of him. "He's a good guy. A really good guy."

I turned back to my mom and mustered my most reassuring smile.

"I need to know what the saying 'The Truth lies behind the enigmatic grin' means."

Mom bobbed her head a few times as I was speaking, then said, "I have no idea what you're talking about."

"No, you . . . you have to."

"I'm sorry, sugar booger. No clue what that means."

"Okay, let's try it from another angle," said Finn. "How do you know my parents, John and Charlotte Masterson?"

"Your parents?" She looked bewildered. "I don't know any Mastersons."

"Maybe you knew my mom by her maiden name. Langston."

"Charlotte Langston? Now that does ring a bell."

Finn and I both sat up straight. I reached for his hand and squeezed it in excitement. He entwined his fingers with mine, and when I looked down I couldn't tell which belonged to him and which belonged to me.

Mom snapped her fingers. "No. You know who I'm thinking of? Sharla Lanksbury. You remember her, don't you, Bree? I worked with her years ago when I first started at the Gallery."

No, no, no. I brushed aside my mother's rambling and tried to bring the conversation back into focus.

"Mom, this is important. I want you to think really hard. You have to have heard that saying before. 'The Truth lies behind the enigmatic grin.' Can you think of anything it might be referring to?"

"What is this about?" Mom's expression turned from confused back to concerned. "Is this for a school assignment?"

"Sort of," I said at the same time that Finn said, "No."

I shot him an exasperated look. *Work with me here, Finn.*

Mom stood up and moved toward the kitchen. "I think I should give the Institute a call."

"No!" we both cried in unison, and lunged forward to pull her back to the chair.

"Bree, *what* is going on? You two have exactly"—she looked up at the clock on the wall—"three minutes to explain. Then I'm getting the Institute on the speak-eazy."

"Okay." I took a deep breath and grabbed my mother's hand. "Finn is a friend of mine, and we realized a few days ago that you and his mom have both said that thing about Truth and the enigmatic grin. You, umm, you say it in the future, and it stuck out to me. So we need to figure out how you two know each other and what it means."

"You need to go further back," said Finn.

I shook my head, but he pointed up at the wall clock that Mom was still checking every few seconds.

"Further back," I said with a sharp exhale. "All right. I met Finn for the first time on this weird mission a couple weeks ago, only it was a few years ago for him. And I couldn't find a grave for someone named Muffy van Sloot, so I—"

"Too far," whispered Finn. "And too confusing."

"Well, why don't *you* take a stab at it?"

"Bree Evelyn Bennis, that is no way to talk to a guest." Mom shot me the *you'd-better-apologize-and-I-mean-it* look.

I muttered, "I'm sorry," to appease my mom, but Finn wasn't even listening.

"I was born over two hundred years ago." He blurted it out, then stared at my mom.

Silence.

Then a sound came out of her mouth that sounded like a cross between a tru-ant and Tufty's yowl. It took me a moment to realize it was a laugh.

"No, really, what's going on?" She looked back and forth between the two of us.

I wanted nothing more than to pat my mother's shoulder and say, *Ha, ha, he's kidding. Now can you make me an avocado sandwich on rye?*

What came out was, "It's true. I don't understand it either, but I need your help."

Mom went back to a moment of silence and then flew off her chair chattering. "So is this all to figure out a way to get him home? Or is the Institute already working on that? What am I saying? Of course they're working on it. Well, no. What am I saying? This is beyond the Institute. Are you in trouble? Has he been decontaminated? How did he get here in the first place?"

I waved my arms, speechless, to get my mother to stop. But she ranted on and on.

"Mom," I said when she paused to take a breath, "I don't have any answers right now. And I don't have much time. But I am in trouble. You *can't* tell the Institute I was here. If you want to help, I need you to think really hard about what it could mean, the phrase I told you earlier. 'The Truth lies behind the enigmatic grin.' It could be something from when you were a student or from work or—"

"It could have something to do with your microchip," said Finn.

Oh, blark. I buried my face in my hands.

Mom's head snapped up. "*What* did he say? Has anyone tried to tamper with your chip, Bree?"

"Nobody's tampering with anything, Mom."

"Because if someone tries to mess with your chip, you could end up—"

"It's okay." I was the last person she needed to remind about the dangers of chip tinkering. I reached over and rubbed her arm. "Really. Nothing's wrong with my chip."

She sank back into her chair. "You're *sure* you've heard me say this thing about Truth and a grin? I'm racking my brain, but . . . nothing. Maybe it's something I pick up in the future."

What future? "No, Mom. It has to be something you know about now. It has to be."

Tufty hopped off Finn's lap where he'd been lounging and leapt to the mantel. One of Mom's unfinished paintings was propped on the ledge, just a gray background with a few pale smudges. I had left the canvas there after the accident as a shrine to my mother, a testament to who Poppy Bennis was, to who I dared to hope she might be again. I had never thought much about the ragged, shredded edges until Tufty sank his claws into the frame and began kneading.

"Tufty," Mom and I scolded at the same time.

A stunned expression took over my mother's face.

"I think I know what it means." She clutched the arm of the chair, her nails white with excitement.

"You know what the saying means?"

"Yes. Well, not the whole thing. The enigmatic-grin part. It has to be—" Mom squinched up her nose and started arguing with herself. "No, that doesn't make sense. If there was something *behind* it, we would have found it ages ago."

Both Finn and I jumped up.

"Behind what, Mom? Behind what?"

"Behind the—"

But she didn't get a chance to finish her sentence, not that I would have heard a word she said anyway.

There was no warning, like there had been last time.

No headache, not so much as a twinge.

A bomb simply exploded in my head.

I crumpled to the ground, shrieking and writhing in pain. In some dim corner of my mind, I was aware that Finn and my mother were at my side. I attempted to speak, to listen to what they were saying. Or, rather, screaming. But it was nothing but a muffled garble.

Whoever wanted me back at the Institute wasn't messing around. And they didn't seem to care whether they brought me in alive or dead.

chapter 26

ALIVE. BUT BARELY.

A solitary, dim lamp illuminated the small room where I lay heaped in the corner. My head pounded in throbbing pulses. I dragged myself upright and let out a hoarse cough. Blood flecks splattered the lamp in some kind of grotesque Rorschach, and another ribbon of red drizzled to the floor from my nose. I gagged back a rush of vomit. My body couldn't take another one of these.

I pinched my nostrils to stop the flow and looked around the room. When I recognized where I was, I wondered if arriving dead might have been the preferable option. A heavy weight pressed against my chest, constricting my breath. It took a moment to realize it was Finn still clinging to me, unconscious but breathing. But that wasn't what scared the blark out of me.

A wall of hodgepodge photographs came into sharp focus as my vision cleared. We had landed in Quigley's office. I had to get us out of here, but the Institute would be crawling with staff and tru-ants looking for me. Air entered my lungs harder and harder with each breath. And it had nothing to do with the 170 pounds of lean muscle now nuzzling into my camisole.

"Finn?" I poked his shoulder.

"Whah?" He opened his eyes and looked around, then let out a muffled groan. "We're inside your school, aren't we?"

"It was a six-month Shift and local. We're lucky we didn't end up in the Launch Room."

Not that Quigley's office was any better. Probably worse. The sole, minuscule bright spot was that Quigley was currently not in said office. I wriggled out from under Finn and lifted my head to peek out the window into the darkened classroom. A shadow passed by in the hall outside.

"Should we sneak out and try it again?" Finn asked.

I sagged against the wall. Even that small exertion left me gasping for breath through my blood-caked lips. "This place will be on lockdown."

And when I thought about asking Wyck for more help, I got a blarky feeling in my gut.

"Are you okay?" Finn steadied me and wiped my face clean.

"I will be." This room was the last place I wanted to be, but I didn't think my legs would hold me yet.

"Your mom was on to something," said Finn, again seemingly unfazed by the forced fade. "I could tell."

My mom. I reached my hand out in front of me. Minutes ago it could have brushed my mother's cheek. Now Poppy Bennis was back in a hospital bed. I closed my eyes and summoned those last few coherent moments with her.

"Something about the grin," I said.

"And the 'behind' part, too," said Finn. "She said, 'If there was something *behind* it, we would have found it by now.' What did she mean by that? Who's 'we'? And behind *what*?"

"She said it out of nowhere. One minute, she had no idea what we were talking about. The next, it was like some light switched on in her brain and she started jabbering to herself about the grin and . . ." My eyes slid out of focus. Something *had* triggered my mom's epiphany. "Tufty."

"Where?" Finn jumped up on his hands and knees. He felt around beneath him and peered under Quigley's desk. "Did we accidentally bring him back?"

"No, no, no." I fidgeted and smoothed my hands on the floor in front of me. I had to think. All the pieces were there. I knew it. But the puzzle wasn't fitting together. "His claws. The canvas. That was when Mom realized what the enigmatic grin is."

Finn pumped his pointed finger. "You're right. What was on that painting?"

"Nothing." Just a plain background. A few splotches.

The office had started to feel claustrophobic. I couldn't *think*. All Quigley's photos seemed to be staring straight at us. Or maybe laughing. That one with her and Leonardo da Vinci, especially. I was thankful I'd dropped my QuantCom at the house. It would be harder to track me. But still only a matter of time before they locked my location. Finn and I had to get out of here. I needed to put the "enigmatic grin" out of my mind and concentrate on finding another hiding place for Finn.

Hiding place.

"That's it!" I squealed, and sat bolt upright like someone had zapped me with a stunner.

Finn tumbled backward and almost brought the lamp in the corner down with him.

"Don't you see?" Oh, it was perfect. "He was in the Haven. The painting. He must have hidden something on the back of it. A code or a map or something. He's the key. We have to get back to him. Leonardo's the key!"

While I was thinking out loud, I had stood up and begun pacing the office.

Finn pulled me down next to him. "What are you talking about? Someone hid something on the back of one of your mom's canvases?"

"Huh? No, when my mom saw Tufty scratching that canvas on our mantel, she realized the saying had to do with a painting. Leonardo's. He was a member of the Haven. There's a picture of him and Quigley over there on the wall. Don't you see? He has the answer to everything."

"Leonardo . . . DiCaprio?" he asked.

"Who?" *No.* I had to stay focused. "Da Vinci."

Understanding dawned slowly across Finn's face. He nodded.

"The *Mona Lisa*," we said in unison.

"Of course," Finn said, "the enigmatic grin. It all fits. She's known for her mysterious smile." He clapped his hands together. "There must be a hidden message on the back of it or under the paint. Something about Truth."

"Exactly. Wait. No." Disappointment flooded in as quickly as my elation had. "You heard what my mom said. Art Historians have scoured that portrait for centuries. Examined it. X-rayed it. Used scans that don't even exist in your time. If something was there, they would have found it by now. That's what confused Mom."

And me.

Finn shrugged. "So we go back and ask da Vinci ourselves."

I skipped the *too far, too dangerous, too impossible* argument.

"Parlez-vous Italiano?" There was no telling what mishmash of languages I'd used, but it got my point across. Finn gulped and shook his head.

"It was a good thought," I added.

Then I looked up at the wall of photos and realized it wouldn't matter if Finn and I were both fluent in sixteenth-century Italian. If we sneaked back and landed in da Vinci's kitchen. If we arrived the exact minute he put the final stroke on the portrait. We were too late before we'd even begun. Quigley had gotten to him first, when he had sketched the blarking painting.

The arm-in-arm photo of them mocked me from its place of honor right above Quigley's chair. Any attempt to Shift to his time would be pointless. They were in league with each other. He'd already told her any secrets in the painting. There wasn't anything behind the enigmatic grin anymore.

All that my mother had gone through was for nothing. I scowled. A sudden desire seized me to smash Quigley's face. First her eyes. Then her nose. Then that stupid, smug smile.

I stood and marched over to the wall, grabbing a stylus off her desk as I went. My legs found a new strength.

"Bree?" Finn stood as well and looked nervously out the classroom window. "What are you doing?"

"What I should have done a long time ago."

Pop. I jammed the stylus through one of her eyes.

"Bree," Finn hissed.

Pop. Pop. The other eye and the nose.

Finn rushed over and held back my hand, which had started to shake anyway. I stared at Quigley's mouth. The lips curled into a knowing sneer. Leonardo and Quigley weren't friends. They were accomplices.

My free hand formed a fist. I'd punch the whole thing in. Show Quigley what I thought of her. It wouldn't solve anything, but it would feel—

"Amazing." My hand dropped to my side. The last piece of the puzzle slipped into place before my eyes. Quigley had been so adamant that I not touch her frames when I was cleaning. But the da Vinci one had been crooked already, like someone had hung it in a hurry. The plaster had flaked off when I had tried to straighten it.

I ran my fingers around the curves of the frame, prying the edges from the wall. It had been there the whole time. Inches from my grasp. Literally.

"The Truth lies"—I gave the frame a good yank and it popped right off the wall—"*behind* the enigmatic grin."

There was nothing there.

That wasn't entirely true.

There was a hole.

Plaster flaked to the ground like snow as I stuck frantic fingers in the hollowed-out section of the wall. It was shallow, eight inches long by two inches high. And empty.

"No, no, no. It was so perfect. I mean, it didn't explain how both our moms had heard the saying . . . clue . . . whatever it is. Or what the Truth was. *But it was sooo perfect.*"

243

My mix of elation and disappointment was short-lived. A soft clapping sound filled the air behind us. Finn and I whirled around. Terror.

Dr. Quigley stood in the doorway, applauding.

"Not bad," she said with an appraising nod. "I knew you'd figure it out. It's a shame you're too late."

My knees went weak and I leaned against Finn for support.

But I didn't collapse until he took a step toward Quigley and said, *"Aunt Lisa?"*

chapter 27

APPARENTLY, I HAD SLEPT through the "What to do when you find out your traitorous pseudoboyfriend is in league with your evil History teacher" lesson in Risk Assessment 101. But, like all lessons in Risk Assessment 101, it would have gone something like this: *Push-the-Blarkin'-Emergency-Fade-Button-Already.* Which wasn't very helpful in the present situation. I did the next best thing. I darted to the corner of the office, grabbed the floor lamp, and swung it around like a weapon. There was nowhere to run. I was trapped.

"I can explain, Bree," whispered Quigley, edging her way across the room with her hands up. "But you need to bend down below the window. Everything needs to look very, very normal if anyone looks in my classroom door."

Finn, who was inching my way from the opposite side, obeyed and slid down the wall. Of course he did. She was his aunt.

"What's going on?" he asked Quigley. "Are you a *teacher* here?"

And with that, it became official. I had never been more confused in my life. One minute, I was finally about to get the answer to the question—well, one of the questions—that had been driving me bonkers since I'd first heard the name Muffy van Sloot. The next thing I knew, I was trapped in the gnarled branches of the world's most twisted family tree.

As if she could read my mind, Quigley said, "I realize you have no reason to trust me. And you're probably questioning everything you know about Finn here as well. But I need you to believe me; he's as confused as you are right now."

Either Finn was a fabulous actor or Quigley was telling the truth. All the color had drained from his cheeks. Quigley continued to move toward me. Finn's eyes flitted back and forth between the two of us.

"Take one more step, Quigley, and I'll scream my head off," I said. "I may not know everything, but I know enough."

"Wait. Aunt Lisa is . . . Quigley?" Finn froze for the briefest of moments, then lunged at me. He was so fast, I didn't have a chance to brace my body for the impact. But he didn't hit me. Or knock me down. Didn't even jostle me. Instead, he crouched in front of me facing Quigley. He squared his shoulders in a defensive posture.

"What's going on here?" he all but snarled.

Rather than look miffed or even surprised, Quigley maintained a serene expression as she walked to her desk and sat down.

"My, my, Finnigan. Is that all it takes to turn on poor Aunt Lisa? A threat against your precious Bree?"

"Yep." Finn twitched as Quigley folded her hands across her desk.

"Good." She leaned back in her chair and smiled.

I slid down the wall, not out of obedience, but out of sheer shock. The lamp tumbled from my grasp and smashed on the floor. Quigley winced at the sound, glancing out the door, and adjusted the overhead lights to compensate.

"What are you talking about?" Finn asked, but I held up my hand to interrupt him.

"I'm going to fire off some questions," I said. "I don't care who the answers come from. But, so help me, they'd better come."

My protector (or possibly traitor) and enemy (or possibly ally) both nodded their heads.

"What did you do to my mom?"

"Nothing," replied Quigley without skipping a beat.

Okay, perhaps best to take a different route.

"What *happened* to my mom?"

"That requires a bit of speculation, as she's in a coma and can't tell us, but I believe she was attacked."

"Yeah, I believe that, too." I grabbed a shard of glass from the broken lamp and wielded it in a threatening way.

"Not by *me*." Quigley sounded genuinely shocked at the suggestion.

"Who then?"

"I . . . I don't know exactly. From the times I've been able to sneak Nurse Granderson in to check on her, it appears her coma is medically induced."

"Meaning?" said Finn.

"Someone's drugging her. It's true that her chip isn't functioning, but that seems to be unrelated to the coma."

"Okay. Are you really Finn's aunt?"

"No." Both Finn and Quigley answered at the same time, Finn with more vehemence.

"She's a friend of my parents," said Finn. "I thought."

"Actually, I'm not yet. I've only met you once when you were much younger. I wouldn't have recognized you if you weren't the spitting image of your father. It doesn't surprise me that I'll befriend them at some point, though. I found them to be . . . admirable."

Sounded like she had some future self issues, too.

Quigley turned to me, and her voice took on an almost pleading tone. "Will you let me explain? At least as much as I'm able."

There was something in the Quig's eyes that had never been there before. Dare I dream, humility? Or *friendliness*? Whatever it was, I found myself saying a reluctant "Yes."

"About a year ago—"

"You've known about this for a *year* and couldn't save my mom?"

"Let me finish." Quigley went back to her usual clipped

commands. "About a year ago, an object came into my possession. It's a device—from the future—and I was tasked with hiding it. To keep it safe at all costs."

"What does it do?" I asked. "The device?"

"I don't know. I wasn't told that. I know a lot of people are after it, and I know it's the only one of its kind."

"But what *is* it?"

"It's . . . well, it's *Truth*. But unfortunately, I—"

"What did you just say?" Finn beat me to the question but had to hold me back from scrambling over to Quigley's desk.

"Were you the one who told my mother that saying? About Truth and the enigmatic grin?" I strained against Finn's grasp. "Were you?"

"No." Quigley leveled me in her gaze. "I believe *you* were."

"Me?" I stopped struggling. I may have inadvertently also stopped breathing.

"Unless I'm mistaken, you've just returned from a little heart-to-heart with your mother. I've never actually met the woman." Quigley threw her hands up in a halfhearted shrug. "Well, conscious, I mean."

Oh, she would pay for that. Finn couldn't hold me back. In a blink, I launched myself at her. Quigley didn't flinch. As calmly as if she were applying a fresh coat of crimson lipstick, she pulled a QuantCom out of a drawer and zapped me at the lowest stun setting. My heart fibbed a beat from the jolt. I backed off.

"Get. Down. You will be seen," said Quigley.

I rubbed the numb spot on my arm where I'd been stung as I slouched back to the corner. "But I heard it from *her*."

"*Everyone* heard it from her." Quigley made no attempt to disguise her annoyance.

Finn was too quick for me. He pinned my arms against my sides and held me tight. "Let's hear her out. She obviously knows more than we do."

"As I said," Quigley went on, "while your mother was busy announcing my clue to the whole world—"

"*Your* clue?"

"Yes, *my* clue. I told you I was the one that hid the device. Do you think I'd do that and not tell someone where I left it in case something happened to me?"

"Tell who?"

"Isn't that obvious?" she said.

I swear, this conversation was like some never-ending game of Russian roulette with no bullets.

"Nope," I said. "Not obvious."

"Finn."

"Yeah?" He looked up in surprise.

"Finn. That's who I told," said Quigley.

"What are you talking about? You said you don't know my family yet. You've only met me once when I was little."

"*That* was why I went back in time to meet your parents when you were a baby. To make sure they told you the clue."

"And that was the clue you came up with? 'The Truth lies behind the enigmatic grin'? From *that* I was supposed to gather you'd hidden some device behind a photo of Leonardo da Vinci painting the *Mona Lisa*? In the freaking twenty-third century?"

"I was in a crunch. I wanted to take it back to Leo to stash away. He owes me a favor. But, in the end, I decided he couldn't be trusted. That man would trade his own mother for a cool enough gadget." She looked at the photo and frowned as she noticed the poked-out eyes and nose. "I assumed one of your descendants was destined to find it, especially after Bree's mid-term assignment to Chincoteague Island popped up. I never dreamed you'd come here posing as Bree's long-lost cousin. Which, by the way, was beyond reckless."

Amen.

"But that clue is so convoluted," said Finn. "How the heck

was I supposed to realize that an 'enigmatic grin' referred to the *Mona Lisa?*"

"I'm sorry. Did I not choose a famous enough painting for you, Finnigan?"

"Why Finn?" I asked, my eyes drifting up to meet Quigley's. She stared at me, her mouth ajar.

I stated the question again, thinking she didn't understand. "Why did it have to be—?"

"You mean you don't know?" she said. "I thought it was . . . obvious."

"No. *Not* obvious." Opposite of obvious.

"Because *you* told me to, Bree. When you brought me the device."

I hadn't—*dang it.* Future Bree.

There's one Rule of Shifting most of us never stop to ponder. It goes without saying. Or at least it should: Never piddle in your own past.

As I sat there, trying to assimilate this new scrap of information, I had a new appreciation for that rule.

The not-ha-ha-funny part was that I wasn't all that surprised. I should have been shocked. Flabbergasted. But somehow, in my mind, Future Bree had taken on a separate identity. Persona non exista.

And yet she had held back information—important information. Kept it to herself. We were missing something. It didn't add up.

"Why did you fail my midterm? And Anchor me?"

"You told me to do that, too. Although your initial report truly was a pathetic excuse for a—"

"Hey. I had my reasons." I gestured at Finn.

"As did I," said Quigley. "You have no idea how much scrambling I've had to do behind the scenes to buy you time for whatever it is your future self wants you to do. I've been deleting tru-ant readings left and right. Oh, and I had to alter the Quant-Com data from your last two missions. That was a treat."

"Why did you alter my QuantCom data?" I asked.

"Those surges. Your Com was picking up on another Shifter's tendrils as they Shifted."

My theory was right.

"I assume that Shifter was your father," she said to Finn.

"Or my sister." Finn nodded. "But how did you find me in the first place? Bree couldn't."

"He's not in any of the databases," I said. "I searched down to the tertiary level."

"Yeah," said Finn. "What she said."

"He's not in the system because I erased every trace of him when the device went missing. As a precautionary measure."

"Missing?" I said. "You mean you *lost* it?" I might not like the chick, but Future Bree must have risked a lot to bring it here, whatever it was.

I could hear Pods moving around on the street below, and I looked at the clock. Four a.m. We needed to hurry.

"When did you realize it was missing?" I asked.

"You're not going to like the answer," said Quigley glumly.

"Why not?" But even as I said the words, I knew why.

"Your mother. As soon as she announced the clue, I ran to my hiding spot, but it was already gone."

Finn's eyes widened. "How did whoever stole it figure it out that fast?"

They didn't.

"They Shifted there from the future," I said.

"Precisely," said Quigley. "There's no way of knowing how long it took them to figure it out. Months, I suspect. Maybe years given the havoc they've wreaked throughout history to examine the *Mona*'s panel."

Quigley picked the photo up and traced the edges of the frame with a sad smile.

"Have you never wondered why the *Mona Lisa* has been vandalized so often? The 2130 gashing attempt. The 1911 theft. Oh, and don't forget that madman who doused it with acid in the 1950s. All trying to decipher the Truth clue. I just don't understand how a fellow Shifter could be so reckless with our treasures from the past." Quigley was really getting worked up.

"But why?" I asked. "I mean, with the Doctrine of Inevitability, surely they knew that it was a moot point, that they wouldn't succeed."

"I don't know," she said, "but still, someone figured it out eventually. They took the device before I had a chance to realize the threat. I've tried to go back and recover it so I could put it in another spot, but my timing is always off. I'm either too early or too late to catch them. They must have taken it immediately after I hid it."

The office darkened as a hazy shadow moved across the room. Someone had passed through the light in the hallway outside the classroom. The shadow came back in the opposite direction and paused. Quigley sucked a hiss of air through her teeth.

"Keep low." The words escaped without a twitch of her lips.

chapter 28

QUIGLEY SHUFFLED a pile of soligraphic files around her desk, all trace of emotion wiped away. The shadow loomed larger, and Quigley looked up and pretended to see it for the first time. *Whoosh.* My hair fluttered as the office door slid open. Quigley glided forward to lean against the entrance, blocking the path.

"Any luck finding her?" she asked.

"Nope. Shouldn't be much longer, though." I recognized Coach Black's husky baritone. "Already got a preliminary fix. Definitely in the building. They're pinpointing now. See, this is why chips need to be mandatory. Situations like these. Already knew she was a risk, what with her mom being a tink and all. Wouldn't want to be her in about fifteen minutes."

"Or right now," I whispered under my breath. Finn tapped my knee and held his finger to my mouth.

"I'll keep my eyes open, but I think we both know this is the last place she'd come," said Quigley with a lighthearted laugh.

"I'm gonna go grab some spare ants from the locker rooms. Wanna help?"

"I would, but I'm combing through the proximity sensors."

"Good idea. Don't work too hard."

"Is there such a thing?" Quigley let out a . . . was that supposed to be a girlish giggle?

Oh, for the blarking love—was the woman attempting to *flirt* her way out of this?

"Tell you what, Chuck, I'll hunt you down for coffee in the morning after we get her shipped off to Resthaven."

"You're on. Let me know if you find anything on the sensors."

She wiggled her fingers at him. The moment the door closed, she shook her hand like something nasty clung to it. Quigley walked back to her desk and collapsed into the chair.

"It's getting worse," she said with a sigh.

"What is?" asked Finn.

"Don't tell me you haven't noticed?" She directed the question at me. "You of all people. I see the way transporters look at you in the halls. I hear the whispers in class. Anti-Shifter sentiment is reaching a new high."

"Not my problem right now," I said.

Quigley gave me a strange look, like she was measuring something within me that no one else could see.

"We should hurry." She reached into her desk and began grabbing data buttons, compufilm, and her speak-eazy. "I'll let them know we're on our way."

"Let who know? Where are we going?"

"Resthaven."

And with that, I was officially back to not trusting the crapwench.

"Like blark you are!" I stiffened and was thankful that Finn, who had only heard of the place from my earlier rant but seemed to remember the vile nutso bin it is, pulled me protectively to his chest. He pushed his shoulder next to mine. I felt taller for it.

Quigley stopped her hurried packing and stared up in surprise. "Where else would we go?"

"Anywhere," I snapped. "Anywhere else."

She leaned back in her chair and pressed her fingers to her eyes. I was about to grab Finn's hand and make a run for it when she said the opposite of what I was expecting.

"Bree, what do you know about the Haven Society?"

"You mean green lights and hot meals? That Haven?" It was

Finn who answered. I knew he was thinking about the candles above his own front door at home. As was I. And, for the first time, I was also thinking about the same green glow that came from the Resthaven brochure I'd been constantly barraged with since my mother's accident.

"Yes, that Haven," said Quigley.

"They're extinct," I said. "The Haven was founded hundreds of years ago, maybe thousands. But they're extinct."

"Not extinct," said Quigley. "And *not* founded thousands of years ago. Or even hundreds. They were founded in our future, Bree. Or, rather, they will be. They aren't an ancient society that simply helps Shifters. They're a futuristic society entrusted with safeguarding our secrets."

I tried to wrap my head around what she was saying but couldn't. "But they're all mad at Resthaven. Everyone knows that."

"That's what I thought as well," said Quigley. "I wrote them all off as unhinged. Until I received a visit a few months ago from someone I couldn't ignore."

"Who?" asked Finn.

"Myself," said Quigley.

"Your future self?" So I definitely wasn't the only one with future self issues.

"She'd disabled her microchip," said Quigley.

"What?" I gasped. "Was she—?"

"Aunt Lisa's not crazy." It was Finn who said it, and he addressed Quigley. "You may not know me, but I know you. You don't turn into some raving lunatic."

"Exactly. I was surprisingly coherent. Articulate, even." She snapped her satchel shut and swallowed deeply. "But the Madness had still begun. I was confused on facts I should know. Simple things. Recent events."

"Then why trust anyone based on her recommendation?" I asked.

"I told you that the Haven exists to safeguard secrets, but that's

not entirely true. She said that they exist to guard one thing."
Quigley pushed herself up from her seat. "Truth."

The Truth lies behind the enigmatic grin.

"It has to be related to the device," I said. "But what does it
mean? What Truth?"

Quigley blinked.

"You don't . . . know? I thought that was—"

"*Don't* say 'obvious'," I said.

"I wasn't going to. I was going to say, I thought that was why
you're here. To tell me. Future You didn't. She just gave it to me
and told me it held the Truth. She instructed me to hide it and
give Finn the clue. I assumed she would tell you what it was for.
I thought that was why you and Finn sneaked off from the Pentagon, something to do with the device."

"We were stealing my mom's Shift record." I pried the data
button out of my pocket. "The one *you* destroyed."

Quigley shook her head. "Again, not me. I went after your
mom's accident to check to see where her last mission was. The
file was already erased."

I sat there and glared at her, unsure if I should believe a word
that had come out of her mouth. She'd just admitted she was going to lose her grip on reality. Well, sort of.

Almost as if he could hear my hesitance, Finn pulled his journal and pen from his pocket and wrote: "Everything she's said
has lined up with what we know so far. I don't think we have a
choice but to trust her for now." He tilted the page so I could
read it, then underlined "for now."

He was, unfortunately, right.

So basically, the woman I thought was my enemy had been
protecting me this whole time. Which meant some *other* nameless,
faceless nemesis was waiting in the wings. Homing in on our location at this very moment. Plus, I had to wrap my head around
the fact that Future Me was aware of everything that would hap-

pen. Clearly this device was important. But it made no sense that she would give it to Quigley to hide if she knew somebody would steal it.

When I caught up with Future Bree, there was going to be a serious arse kicking.

"What does the device look like?" I asked.

"It's a simple design. A metal cylinder about this long." Dr. Quigley moved her hands a few inches apart. "And thin. Maybe only a quarter inch wide. It could be anywhere."

Finn twirled his pen over his knuckles. With each pass, he clicked the end in and out. In and out. "Do you think Future Bree just came back and got it?"

Like the flexi-phone.

Quigley shook her head. "I thought of that, but no. She specifically told me to keep the device safe until she needed it. Plus, it had to be someone on staff at the Institute to gain access to my office."

Finn's brow furrowed and he continued his nervous pen twirling and clicking. *Twirl, click. Twirl, click.* It was starting to annoy me. I opened my mouth to tell him to stop it when—

Nervous habit.

"Oh my gosh." I grabbed his hand. "You're brilliant."

"I am?" He lifted his thumb off the pen mid-click.

"I know where the device is," I said.

"You do?" Quigley rushed forward. "You've seen it?"

"Yep." My thumb ticked up and down like I was clicking a pen in and out. In and out.

I'd been within arm's reach of it in Bergin's office when he'd brought me in to offer to pay for my mom's bills. His pen. But he hadn't actually used it. I'd never seen him with any paper. Paper was a rarity, sure. But no one would carry a pen around everywhere with him without anything to write on. Ballpoint pen, my heinie.

"And precisely how do you intend to force me onto the Thinga-ma-pad?" Finn stroked the bruise that bloomed across his upper arm. "Ow."

Quigley's death grip on me was fake.

On Finn, not so much.

"Ease up." I grabbed Quigley's clenched fingers, but right when I did so one of the dorm room doors flew open in the First Year wing as we passed. A bleary-eyed Molly Hayashi—the girl I'd caught Shifting back to literally beat herself up over her grades—wandered into the hallway rubbing her eyelids. She looked around for the source of noise that had woken her. When she saw that it was the *click-clack* of Quigley's four-inch stilettos, Molly flew back into her room with an *eep*.

I kind of wished I could join Molly.

All this for a ballpoint pen. Sure, the device wasn't *really* a pen. But it had better do something worthwhile. I quickened the pace.

My sudden burst of bravery had shocked even me, although I knew what it stemmed from—the fact that I had a future self. That knowledge made me feel almost invincible. But I didn't have those same reassurances for Finn. Sending him home had been my stipulation, and Quigley had readily agreed.

"Finn, you're a greater liability than asset right now," she said. "This might be our one chance to send you home."

We had to try. He'd been able to Shift when Wyck transported him. I just hoped Quigley's transporting skills were better than mine. The crazy thing was, now that we had a decent shot of getting Finn home I kind of wanted him to . . . stay. I was going to miss him and his stripping ways.

"But I haven't done anything to protect Bree yet," said Finn. "Why would Future Bree ask me to protect her if she knew I was going to go straight home?"

"Oh, why does Future Bree do anything?" I asked.

"Shh." Quigley came to a dead halt as we reached an intersection of corridors.

A tru-ant poked its beady little eyes around the corner. Quigley and I tried to stomp it, but it was too fast. It zipped off, beeping away as if cackling at a hysterical joke. Quigley cursed and clenched my arm tighter.

"We have to hurry."

But it was too late. Within moments, footsteps reverberated through the hall. Coach Black rounded a corner farther down the corridor, his arms full of tru-ants. His face lit up. Quigley sped up, dragging me along and pushing Finn forward.

"Look what I found," she called to him, giving my arm a few reassuring squeezes. "You aren't going to believe it. Hiding in my storage closet."

"Huh ho. Well done, Lise. Two for the price of one. I'll take 'em from here."

"Nice try," she said with a too-cheerful laugh. "These two are mine."

Quigley tried to navigate around him toward the Launch Room.

He took a step to block her path. "Bergin's office is thataway." Coach Black's expression didn't hold enough surprise for my taste.

"Of course. It's . . . it's late." Quigley steered us to the opposite side of the hall.

"Sure you don't want me to go with you? Make sure you don't get lost?"

"No need." She clicked past him as fast as she could without a backward glance. When Coach Black was out of earshot, she pried her nails out of my arm. "It looks like we'll need to adjust the plan."

Hmm, yeah. The plan.

So far, the plan consisted of sending Finn home (which didn't work out so hot), marching me down to Bergin's office, waiting for Quigley to distract the headmaster, turning the office upside down (neatly) in search of the device thingy, and . . . running like hellfire was nipping our heels.

Needless to say, the plan was not without its share of wrinkles. Fine. Our current strategy made my data disk theft look like a masterminded, high-security art heist. But it was the best one we had.

It was the *only* one we had.

When we reached Bergin's office door, Finn took a deep breath, reached his hand out to mine, and said, "No matter what, I stick with you."

"You seem to be good at that," I said.

"Shh." Quigley leaned forward and brushed her hair against the scanner. As the door slid open, her QuantCom clattered to the ground.

I leaned down to pick it up. But then the room came into full view. And the Com slipped out of my hold.

"Mom?"

chapter 29

"MOM?" I REPEATED.

So much for the plan.

It took a few moments for me to notice Headmaster Bergin sitting at his desk, his hands clasped under his chin. It took a few moments to notice anything, really, except my mom. In the room. Awake.

Well, kind of awake.

A ribbon of drool dripped down the corner of her chapped lower lip. It pooled in a crease of her hospital gown, paper-thin like her skin. Her head pivoted in slow motion to the sound of my voice. Half-closed eyes focused on empty space above us, and her mouth drifted open and closed a few times before her jaw fell slack. To my relief, her head swiveled back to Bergin. A peaceful coma was one thing. Zombie Poppy made me ill.

"Welcome, welcome. Look who's awake."

I couldn't tell if Bergin was talking about me or my mom. Either way, the sick feeling in my stomach spread. He had told me earlier she was getting worse. That was before I knew her coma was medically induced.

"Could any of us have foreseen this joyous turn of events?" He clapped his hands together. "Imagine my surprise, Miss Bennis, at finding an empty bed when I went to your room to tell you the wonderful news. Tsk, tsk. You sent us on quite the little ant chase."

"I'll see to her punishment immediately, Headmaster," said

Quigley. "This is a disciplinary matter. No reason for you to get involved. Besides, she's headed to Resthaven in a few hours."

"Oh, I think we both know she's not going to Resthaven anytime soon."

A foreboding feeling lashed me to my core. Bergin knew about Resthaven. There was no telling what else he knew. Or suspected.

"I'm perfectly capable of handling this little infraction." He chided Quigley like a disobedient puppy, and there was a slicing edge to his voice that had never been there before. "But not tonight. Tonight is cause for celebration."

I looked over at my mother. Celebration. Not quite the way I envisioned it.

"Before you know it," he went on, "things will be back the way they should be."

I looked between Bergin and Quigley, unsure of how to respond. This was the moment I'd dreamt of. My mom awake. Promises of normal. But then I looked over at Finn and realized normal was no longer an option. Or maybe just that my normal would never be the same. I might not know what Truth that device held, but I knew I had to find out.

"Actually, I haven't decided yet if I'm going to replace Mom's chip." I glanced at Quigley again for backup. "And I'm transferring Mom to Resthaven for her recovery."

Bergin's grin faltered for a blip.

And that's when I saw them, skulking in the shadows of the draperies behind Bergin's desk. Two men in bright red scrubs. I couldn't tell if they were the same men who had been in my house when I dropped Finn off. Heck, I couldn't even tell the two guys standing in front of me apart, except one of them was bald. A Shavie. I didn't want to think about how he'd gotten his job. It certainly didn't look like he was there for his bedside manner. For the first time, I noticed the initials *ICE* were emblazoned across both their lapels.

"A new chip wouldn't fix everything, Bree," said Bergin. "The Initiative for Chronogeological Equality wants to put *everything* aright."

"By doing what? Repairing her current chip?" I rolled my eyes. Six months of memories, of laughter, of love, of *life*. That's what she lost—what we both lost. "You want to fix things? Put things right? Give us back the last six months."

"Okay," said Bergin quietly.

"Okay?" I snorted. "And how do you plan to do that? Go back and change the past?"

"Precisely."

His calm inflection struck me mute for a moment, but then I laughed in earnest. "Umm, you can't change the past."

"*You* can't." Bergin's mouth fought its way into a straight line, but a snicker escaped out the side. The Red Scrubs behind him chortled along to whatever the inside joke was.

I stopped laughing.

"No one can," I said. "Shifters have tried over and over. It's impossible."

"Exactly," said Bergin. "Shifters have tried. And Shifters have failed. Because Shifters' tendrils have always stretched to that spot in that moment. The past isn't their past. It's their present."

I looked up at Quigley to see if she had some insight into his rambling, but she appeared as lost as I was.

Bergin pulled open his top desk drawer and pressed a series of buttons, revealing a hidden panel in the bottom. He removed two objects and laid them next to each other on his desktop. The first I recognized as the shiny silver object he'd told me was a writing pen. The second looked identical until I noticed a slight difference. The first device, the one I remembered from earlier that had been taken from Quigley's office, had a jagged end, like someone had carved a triangle-shaped notch out of it. This second one ended in a clear bulb filled with swirly blue fluid.

He picked up the first and clicked the end in and out. In and out. I glanced at Quigley and she nodded to confirm it was the stolen device.

"I'm sure you know what we want of you," he said. *Click.* In and out.

"I . . . I don't," I answered truthfully.

"Don't play coy, Miss Bennis. Your mother already announced that convoluted clue to the device's location." He picked up a Com off his desk and walked over to my mom. The stunner jutted out from the end. I didn't know what a zap from one would do to her already-fragile nervous system. I couldn't risk finding out.

"I have no idea what you're talking about," I said, "but whatever it is you want, I'm sure we can figure something out so no one gets hurt."

"Exactly." Bergin clapped his hand against my mom's back in a hearty slap, and Finn and I both winced at how close the stunner came to her exposed neck. "No one needs to get hurt."

He reached down in an almost involuntary movement and brushed his hand against his dead wife's picture.

"No more hurt," he said again quietly. "Ever again."

Okay, this was getting creepy. I had to get us all out of here. Forget the device. Whatever it did, the world wouldn't end if I left it and ran.

While Bergin was still staring at the picture of his wife, I motioned to Finn and Quigley that we should bolt. They both nodded and Finn looped his hand under my mom's arm. For a moment, I had forgotten about the Red Scrubs' presence, but they hadn't forgotten us. They strode around opposite sides of the desk and glared at Finn until he let go of Mom.

Bergin snapped back to attention.

"Now, now," he said to the Scrubs. "I'm handling this."

They returned to their post, but the menacing scowls didn't disappear.

"Look, I just want to leave and pretend none of this happened," I said.

"What if you didn't have to pretend?" asked Bergin.

"Are we back to the absurd changing-the-past talk?"

"It's not absurd."

"But the Doctrine of Inevitability—"

"Applies to Shifters."

"Precisely," I said, "and Shifters are the only ones who can travel to the past."

"Again, Shifters aren't traveling to the past. They're traveling in their present."

Ugh. Not the best time for a chicken–egg headache.

"Okay then," I said. "Shifters can't change anything in their present, which happens to be in everyone else's past. Better?"

Bergin chuckled and picked up the second device. "That answer would get you a passable grade in Introduction to Chrono-geological Displacement. I should give Dr. Raswell a raise." He paused, twirling the device thoughtfully. The pearlescent blue liquid sloshed against the sides. "Have you ever been in love, Miss Bennis?"

The question made me startle, and I side-eyed Finn as I stammered out a nonanswer.

Bergin kept talking as if I weren't in the room. "My wife was beautiful. After she died, I remembered thinking, 'If I could just see her face *one more time,* that would be enough.' If I could count those freckles that she complained about but never went to have removed. Or I'd memorize the exact shade of her hair— the color of wheat the day before harvest. And her eyes, so blue and so deep, you could drown in them."

I squirmed. Those were the exact thoughts I'd had about my mom not twelve hours ago. *Just one more time.* Of course, I was a Shifter. I'd been able to go back and do what he was describing.

"But it wouldn't be enough, Bree, would it?" he said as if he had read my mind.

"What does this have to do with changing the past?" I asked.

"I want you to understand the possibilities, the potential for good, in what I'm about to tell you. This"—Bergin held up the blue fluid-filled device—"is the Initiative for Chronogeological Equality's Portable InterChronogeological Stabilizer. We've nicknamed them IcePicks for short. It acts a bit like your microchip, only it bypasses the need for hippocampal mutation. After genetic calibration, it allows unmutated tendrils to adhere to different time periods."

"Could you, umm, translate for those of us who skipped that class?" Finn said.

"In short, this device allows nonShifters to Shift."

"Excuse me?" My ears must have been malfunctioning. That or my brain.

"It's true. ICE has been developing it for quite some time."

"That doesn't make sense. ICE exists to help Shifters, to help us pay for chips and research better Buzz control."

"And that very research has . . . aided them in developing the Pick."

"What, like guinea pigs?" asked Finn.

"How exactly does it work?" Quigley beat me to the question.

"How?" Bergin didn't look any of us in the eye. He took his time smoothing down the panel that concealed the IcePick's hiding spot.

"Yes. How?" I stared at Bergin.

"I . . . I don't really . . ."

Oh my blark. This was getting better and better.

"Are you trying to tell me you don't know how it works?"

"I . . . umm."

"You'd trust that thing to screw around in someone's brain without fully understanding how it even works?" With an uncomfortable jolt, I realized the same accusation could be flung at Shifters with our chips. I stuffed the thought away. Our chips were necessary to prevent the Madness. What Bergin was describing was a madness all its own.

"The Pick was developed to improve relations between Shifters and nons." He sounded like he was quoting a brochure. "To eliminate inherent jealousy over your abilities."

"So *anyone* who wants to travel to the past can?"

"That was the original plan, yes. But during initial test runs, we discovered an unexpected side effect. We've had to modify the plan accordingly, be more selective."

"Meaning?" asked Finn.

"We can change the past."

"No, you can't," I said. This was beyond preposterdiculous. Bergin was crazier than those unchipped Shifters at Resthaven.

"I assure you, we can."

"So somebody can *finally* go back and kill Hitler?" said Finn.

"No," said Bergin. "If I were to travel to 1939 Berlin, I would only be able to observe and participate, much like any Shifter does now."

"But you just said—"

"I should clarify," said Bergin. "NonShifters are able to change their own pasts. A nonShifter is able to interact with his or her past self to . . . correct course, if you will."

"You claim people have already done it," I said. "Then why has no one noticed these supposed changes?"

"The alterations only have a *significant* impact on the changer's life. They create a new, improved time line. Everyone's quantum tendrils—"

"Is he talking about the brain tentacles?" Finn whispered to me. "Shhh."

"Ahem, everyone's quantum tendrils adjust seamlessly to this new time line—leaving everyone, including the changer, blissfully unaware that any alteration has taken place."

"Everyone?" The question came from Quigley. She'd gone unusually pale during the conversation.

"Of course *everyone*." Bergin's billion-watt smile didn't diminish the creepiness factor of it all. In fact, it added to it.

"Fine," I said. "Say any of this is true—heck, say all of it is—what does it have to do with my mom?"

"As I said, we want to use the IcePick to restore things to good. With your cooperation, we can prevent two tragedies from ever having occurred."

"Two?" I asked.

"My wife's untimely death and your mother's unfortunate coma."

"I don't follow how they're related."

"Directly, they're not."

"Then—"

"Bree, my wife's accident never should have happened. If she'd left home one minute later . . . if the Pod had corrected course one second earlier . . . one inch to the left . . . it *wouldn't* have happened. And then for her to have had an allergic reaction to the collision foam? It was a statistical anomaly. Implausible! It *shouldn't* have happened." Bergin slammed his fist down on the desk. "For decades, I've been hounded and hunted by that thought."

"Everyone thinks that way after a tragedy." I should know. "It feels like your life has been blown to smithereens."

"Exactly." He tapped the drawer where he'd stowed the Pick thing. "This will put those pieces back together. My wife is supposed to be alive. I can change that."

For a smattering of a moment, I felt sorry for Bergin. He wasn't some monster who wanted to control the world. He was a man who had never healed. And yet, somehow, that made him all the more dangerous.

"So do it," I said. "What's stopping you? Go back and prevent your wife's death. If what you're saying is true, I'd be none the wiser."

Given that his appointment to headmaster was a sympathy vote, I would probably never have even heard of him.

"Yes, well, that brings us to the dilemma. We've encountered a . . . problem." He lifted the stolen device from his desk. *Click.* In and out. "A problem only you can remedy."

"Why would I help you?"

"In return for your help, we'll alter the past so that your mother never falls into her coma."

"You just said that as a Shifter I can't change my past."

"You wouldn't be the one doing the altering."

"But you also said a nonShifter can only change events in their own past."

"Yes. I did."

"So how could *you* stop *my mother* from going into a—?" I gulped and looked over at Finn. He was already shooting me a *get-there-faster* look.

"You did this to her," I said. "You attacked my mom and in-duced her coma." I had been so blind. Bergin was the first one on the scene when my mother had landed at the Institute.

But that also meant he could take her out of it in a blink. He could go back in time and stop his past self. He said it himself . . . I would never know it had even happened.

"What is it you want me to do?" I asked. I could see that blank canvas in my mind, the one propped on the fireplace. Only now it was a completed painting, full of my mother's vibrant colors and bold strokes.

"Simple," said Bergin, holding the stolen device out toward me. "Destroy this."

"Fine." I whacked it across the corner of his desk. It dented the oak, but otherwise nothing.

"Stop this dangerous nonsense." He snatched it back. "You know what I meant. Destroy it safely. *All* the components."

"I don't even know what it is." Other than what my future self had told us, that it was the Truth. The Truth about what? It looked almost exactly like that ICE contraption, but the IcePick was the very opposite of the Truth. The Truth was that life is painful and messy and complicated. By changing the past Bergin wanted to rid himself of those things, but it was all a lie. Because in the middle of the pain and the mess and the complications, life is also full of beauty.

I loved my mom more than breath, but even if I could blink and have her back it would still be a lie. She'd been attacked as she'd tried to warn me, to tell me the clue that led us to this device. The Truth mattered to her. It mattered to me.

That's when it hit me. What the device did. Maybe it reversed the changes the nonShifters had caused. Restored the true time line, the Truth. The fact resonated deep in my soul, as if I'd always known it. Almost like a memory from my future self.

But I still didn't know why he needed *me* of all people to destroy it. Even if I wanted to, I didn't know how.

"I see you've put it together." Bergin slipped the device into his lapel.

"I think so. It's a . . . reverter, isn't it?"

Bergin nodded.

"When this device is used to reverse the changes, it creates an echo of sorts in the IcePick user's brain. A faint memory of the way things should be."

"You mean the way you manipulate them to be," I shot back.

"Semantics. These echos are causing unnecessary pain and confusion. We want to *stop* people's suffering, not add to it."

"To those who can afford it, I'm sure," Finn pointed out.

I nodded. It was like those billionaire astronauts from Finn's time who bought their way onto space shuttles. Only *they* weren't screwing up the space-time continuum. I didn't care what Bergin claimed. Even the tiniest change in the past could have staggering consequences in the present and future. And stopping someone from dying wasn't a small thing. But now I understood why he needed the device gone before he went back to prevent his wife's death. He didn't want any chance of *that* change being reversed. And to then be plagued by the memory of what he'd attempted to do would be torture.

"You're messing with things you don't understand," I said. "You said so yourself. You don't even know how the Pick works."

"But it does. That's all that matters. Your choice is quite simple, Miss Bennis. Destroy this reverter, and I will go back and prevent your mother's coma."

"I don't want any part of this," I said. If my mom's coma was medically induced, it could be medically uninduced. Yes, I could never get the last six months back, but if that was the price for the Truth, so be it.

"What if that Pick thing fell into the wrong hands?" I pointed out. There would be no way to undo the damage without the reverter.

"I *wanted* to offer you a positive incentive, in aiding your mother," said Bergin. "But there are other ways to motivate you as well. Your mother's recovery tonight may be miraculous, but it's by no means permanent. In fact, last I remembered, her condition was worsening. It would be such a tragedy if further loss were to befall your family."

My blood boiled in my veins. "You haven't even told me why you think I, of all people, can destroy it!"

"My. Your personal time line is in a tangle, isn't it?" Bergin looked downright amused. "Because, Miss Bennis, you're its creator."

The news shouldn't have surprised me one bit. I mean, I already knew Future Bree was up to her belly button in this mayhem. But for the first time, I wasn't furious at her, wasn't angry at all.

I was proud.

Looked like that Biology Specialization would come in handy after all.

I had no idea when or how I'd come into possession of one of their IcePicks in order to modify it, but I made up my mind then and there. I would. I would create that reverter so Bergin and his rich cronies couldn't turn the space-time continuum into their personal playground.

"Bree"—Bergin slid into his grandfatherly façade with ease—"it's unfortunate what happened to your mother, but—"

"Liar!" I screamed. "You did this to her. You and your insane desire for control. You drugged her and are holding her hostage until I do your bidding. "

A purple rage spread over Bergin's face, but he didn't deny my accusations. His hands shook as he grabbed his stunner and dialed it to the maximum. He thrust his hand at my mom's neck, but I dove in between them and pushed it away. It missed her skin by a millimeter. Bergin let out an animalistic roar and unleashed his anger at me instead. He lunged at me, and I ducked at the last moment.

"Wait." Finn stepped forward and blew out a slow, sure mouthful of air. "I'll tell you how to destroy it."

What are you doing? I mouthed. Had he held more information back from me?

Bergin's face filled with relief. His lips split in triumph. "I knew someone would see reason."

The men in red smiled at each other and stepped back next to the poster. Bergin held out the reverter to Finn.

Finn took it gingerly and clicked the end a few more times. "The trick is to—"

A splintering *crunch* cracked the quiet. Flecks of red dotted the collar of my headmaster's starched white dress shirt.

Finn had slammed his fist into Bergin's nose.

chapter 30

I ONLY HAD TIME for a quick, *what-the-heck-did-you-just-do?* glance at Finn before Bergin threw himself at me. I grabbed the QuantCom out of Bergin's hand and shoved him backward. The Com's stunner was still turned up to max. He made another move toward me. *Zaap!* I got him on the arm.

Bergin lurched forward, his muscles stiffening. It left him in a bizarre sprinter's pose as he crashed to the ground. Red flashed in my peripheral vision. The two ICE guys ran around Bergin's desk. I kicked the QuantCom out of the bald one's hands and ducked as a meaty fist slammed into the spot where my face would have been. Finn tried to hit the other guy but only grazed his chin. The guy elbowed Finn in the head, and I landed a jab to his solar plexus. He doubled over, and I zapped his neck. He tumbled behind Mom's chair.

The bald guy had backed up. He slipped his hand into his pocket and pulled out a metal cylinder, turning it around and around in his hand. It looked like my grappling handle until—

Berrzzzz

A foot-long laser blade shot out the end.

Finn almost sounded excited when he said, "It's a flippin' lightsaber!" The blade sizzled through the air and sliced the corner off Bergin's oak desk. "And, holy crap, it works."

I diverted Baldy to the right while Finn kicked him in the side. The smell of burnt cloth filled the air as the blade swiped a swath off Finn's jeans. I seized Baldy's blade arm and twisted it backward. Finn grabbed the corner of the desk from the floor and smashed it against Baldy's shiny head. The guy's hands flew open in surprise. The laser blade swung through the air toward my mother, missing her chest by inches as I caught the handle.

Baldy regained his senses and clutched my arm, lowering the blade toward my mom's heart. Finn snatched the QuantCom from my other hand. He zapped the guy between the eyes. There was a blur of red as Finn shoved him over the desk.

I stuck my head between my knees and tried to breathe. It was kind of hard, as all the air had been sucked out of the room from it spinning so hard. Bergin's rigid fingers dug trenches into the plush Persian rug that lined his office.

"So much for the plan," said Quigley. She was frozen in the corner in shock.

I'd completely forgotten she was there. *Thanks for the help, Quigley.* She tucked the single strand that had worked its way out of her bun back into place and rushed over to the windows.

As she tugged at the curtains, she said, "We have to hurry. Finnigan, bring that blade over here."

He smiled. "For the laser curtains?" he said in a robotic voice.

I let out a reflexive laugh but then looked over at my mom, her pupils drops of ink in pools of bloodshot pink. I wouldn't let them touch her again.

Quigley and Finn went to work slicing the window treatments into silky strips of fabric to fashion a makeshift rope.

"Tie them up and gag them," Quigley said. "Tight."

While I triple-knotted the two ICE goons and Bergin to opposing corners of his desk, Finn gently picked up my mother. By the time I finished tying my headmaster up, his hands had already begun to twitch. Thankfully, the two men in red were out cold. I grabbed the reverter off the desk and tried to break into the drawer to get the IcePick, but it was locked down.

"What now?" I asked.

"Let's stun them again," offered Finn.

"No. Another shock could permanently damage their nervous systems," said Quigley.

Finn and I both shot each other a *so?* look, but neither of us had the nerve to say it out loud.

"Let's move," said Quigley. She wrenched a hair from Bergin's head, shut the door behind us, and entered a code to lock it. Finn adjusted my mom's weight farther up on his shoulder when we reached the hall.

A muffled thumping started up behind us. Apparently, Bergin had already regained the use of his legs.

"I need to get your mother to Nurse Granderson."

Quigley pulled a speak-eazy out of her pocket as we made our way through the halls. "Connect: Granderson."

A few moments later, a tired male voice said, "Do you have any idea what time it is?" It was our nurse, but I recognized it from somewhere else, too.

"You were in the locker room," I said, but she shushed me. I was right, though. It was Quigley and Granderson talking that day. I pieced the conversation together in my memory. They must have actually been discussing how they *hoped* I would figure it out. So when she had said to not underestimate me, she really meant "don't underestimate me." And when she talked about taking care of me, it was probably the plan to send me to Resthaven.

"Poppy's awake." Quigley took a deep breath and added, "Bree and Finn are with me. We have the device back. But the situation's worse than we realized."

Granderson said a word that I was sure would only squeak past Charlotte Masterson given the circumstances, then said, "How soon can you get Poppy over here?"

"How can they protect her? They're all insane." I tugged on Quigley's sleeve like I was a toddler.

And she ignored me like I was a toddler.

"Dev, ICE developed a contraption that allows nonShifters to change their pasts. It looks like this particular device has been modified to reverse the changes." She pressed the speak-eazy up against her ear so I could barely tell what he was saying. Quigley let out a little groan. "That's what I was thinking, too. And Bergin's involved. I bet Black is, too. You were right about your suspicions. They're the ones who have been drugging Bree's mom. To control Bree."

Granderson yelled a word that wouldn't get past Charlotte no matter what.

"I'm sending Bree and Finn to hide the reverter," said Quigley. "I'll be there as soon as I can with Poppy." She ended the conversation with Nurse Granderson right as we reached the main entrance.

"Right then. Let's go." She reached toward the door button, but I slammed my hand against the panel.

"What makes you think Resthaven can protect my mom? They can't even protect themselves from the Madness."

"Don't you see, Bree?" She pointed to the reverter Finn still clutched in his free hand. "There is no Madness. Bergin said everyone's tendrils adjust seamlessly to the changes they've brought about, but what if that's not true? What if unchipped Shifters' tendrils are clinging to the correct time line? They'd be aware of all these small changes. And it would come off as appearing—"

"Crazy," I whispered. "And the timing makes sense. The Madness didn't begin until Shifters came into the open, so non-Shifters wouldn't have changed anything before then. The worst cases of the Madness are from Future Shifters."

"Who would have experienced the most changes," said Finn.

Quigley curled my fingers around the reverter.

"This is our only hope to spare Future Shifters from the Madness. To return the time line to how it should truly be."

"The Truth."

"You have to hide it. I don't want to know where. I'll do everything in my power to keep your mother safe."

I lowered my hand from the panel, and Quigley brushed Bergin's hair against it to open the door. There was a nip in the moist, pre-dawn air. Finn handed me his sweater, and I wrapped it around my mother's flimsy gown. I wiped a spindle of drool from her cheek. We scurried down the Institute steps toward a docked Publi-pod.

"Where should Finn and I hide the—?"

"I told you I don't want to know," Quigley almost shouted, but then brought her voice back down. "As soon as we get to Resthaven, we part ways. Get it out of this time if possible."

She turned to Finn. "Whatever happens, keep Bree safe."

I leaned over to give my mom a kiss. She lifted her head an inch as my lips met her warm cheek. Her eyes shone in a way that I could only describe as Mom-ish.

In a voice of mere breath, she said one word: "Safe."

"Soon, Mom. Soon."

As Finn situated my mother in the Pod (it was a double and would be a tight squeeze with all of us), I turned to Quigley.

"I don't know how to thank you."

Quigley's face relaxed into an actual smile, be it small, and that was when I saw the resemblance. With her lipstick smudged off and her hair pulled loose next to her heavyset eyelids.

"*You're* Mona Lisa." I couldn't help but laugh. Their secret.

"Told you he owed me one."

I shook my head in disbelief.

Quigley stepped into the Pod and scooted over. There would be just enough room for Finn, and I could squeeze onto his lap. He had a foot in the Pod and was pulling me toward it when the tinkle of shattering glass destroyed the last shreds of daybreak quiet. A blast of whirs, buzzes, and beeps, exploded behind it.

A swarm of tru-ants had blasted through the front doors. They pulsated in one giant blob. Coach Black stood in the middle of the metallic cloud, sneering. Bergin was hunched over behind him.

"Oh, blark." We all three said it.

I had to get my mom away from them. I stuck my head in the Pod and whispered, "Destination: Resthaven. Go."

"Keep it safe!" I could barely make out Quigley's muffled shout as the Pod sealed up. Finn and I jumped out of its path, and it shot down the street. It disappeared into a dot as it turned the corner past the Capitol.

"Two on two," said Finn. "We can take them."

Spoken by someone who'd never been stung by a tru-ant.

I grabbed his hand and ran.

chapter 31

"NOT THAT I'M TRYING to pee all over this parade," said Finn, "but you do realize I'm going to be no help with hiding places."

His cheeks had turned all splotchy, and he drew a deep breath when we slowed our sprint to a jog. Nice thing about tru-ants, the longer they're at it, the more apathetic they get about the chase. After three blocks, most were like "meh." After five, I started stomping the few remaining motivated ones. But as soon as Bergin locked my position through my microchip, we'd have a lot worse than ants after us.

I desperately needed that position to be a few centuries away.

Where the heck was I going to find a Shift Pad to use? There was one at Mom's work, yes, across the National Mall, but if I tried to break into the National Gallery of Art . . . Might as well head back to the Institute.

The PayPads wouldn't open for a few more hours. Not that I had any money. Or even knew where the nearest one was. I'd have to access a database to find out. That would give away our location, sure as a strand of hair.

We needed to find a private Pad. It was the only solution.

Easier said than done. Their cost was astronomical—more than our house, Mom's hospital bills, and my Institute tuition combined.

I'd never even heard of anyone who had their own Pad. Well, except for . . . "Molly!"

Finn looked at me like I'd yelled something in Bulgarian.

"Molly Hayashi," I said. "She's a First-Year student, and she likes me." This could work; this could actually work. "Her family owns a Shift Pad."

I ran harder. I had no idea where Molly's family lived. Guess I could talk a stranger into using their hair to search for her address. That way our location wouldn't pop up automatically. Okay, maybe *I* couldn't talk someone into it, but Finn could. That boy could needle a nudist into a nightgown.

We'd reached the edge of the Mall, halfway between the Smithsonian Castle and Freedom Orb. As I dashed past the floating sphere, the irony didn't escape me. I'd never felt more ensnared in my life. The sun crested the horizon and turned the many monuments along the wide-open expanse a fiery orange. It was normally my favorite time of day. Sometimes, when I returned home from a mission near dawn, I would go sit in the greenhouse and watch the city glow. Today, running on much confusion and zero sleep, it had a disorienting effect.

A few hundred yards to the west, the Washington Monument rose above everything, its long, thin finger set ablaze. The compass of the city. That great bastion of democracy.

I always thought it looked like it was flipping off the politicians.

But, more important, it was out in the open. Soon, joggers and early morning commuters would descend on the area. It would be harder for the ICE goons to attack us here. I clutched Finn's shoulder and steered him across the street toward the lawn.

"I think Molly lives nearby. She must be in the city or not too far, because her parents come every Family Night. There's a database search station up by the Lincoln Memorial."

We raced along the edge of the Reflecting Pool. The excitement of getting to the Hayashis' private Pad sped me along and I didn't even shudder at the water a few feet to my right. Luck had finally turned to my side when I remembered that the Hayashis had their own private Shift Pad.

I halted mid-step. My big toe jammed against a crack as I

stomped the sidewalk. All my pain and frustration funneled out my mouth in a muted howl.

A private LaunchPad that Molly wouldn't receive until Christmas.

I sank to my knees and pounded my fists against the ground. Tears blurred their way out. After the night I'd had, it was a shock I had any left.

"We can't cut a break. It won't work," I said. "She doesn't have it yet. I don't know what else to do."

And why should I? Who appointed me She Who Must Fix Everything? Oh, wait. I knew exactly who: Future Bree.

"I could really use some help here!" I yelled to the sky. "Come on. Tell me what I'm supposed to do! What? You'll talk to Finn? Confide in him but not me? *I'm* the one who needs you. *I'm* the one whose life you're screwing with."

Finn knelt beside me. "She can't hear you."

"Yes, she can. She remembered this moment, Finn. She . . . she left all these half clues and nothing hints. She knew, Finn. She knew what she was doing. She knew you had no future with her. It's impossible, don't you understand that? We're an impossibility. And yet she went back and she toyed with you. She convinced you she cared about you to get you to do what she wanted."

"She isn't a liar," he said. "You don't become that."

"Then how do you know my tell?"

"One time." His jaw stiffened. "She lied once, the last time I saw her."

"What did she say?"

"That we would never see each other again." He nudged me gently with his foot. "It's pretty clear she was wrong."

"Oh, Finn." I couldn't bring myself to point out the obvious. Nothing was clear anymore. ICE could change the past. Which meant ICE could strip us of our future. Future Bree knew that.

Fog rose above the surface of the water and licked the edges of the sidewalk. We were alone except for two joggers on the far side of the pool. Finn sat down beside me and put his arm around my shoulder.

"It *is* going to be okay," he said. It wasn't. But that was still the right thing to say.

It was chilly out. I rubbed my hands together to warm them. The heat of Finn's body softened my shivers. He wrapped his hands around mine and lifted them up to his mouth to blow on them.

I leaned my head against his shoulder. If it weren't for the whole being-chased-by-an-evil-organization-bent-on-warping-the-time-line thing, it would have been a nice moment.

The two male joggers across the way stopped running and began to argue with each other. I glanced up at them. That must have been what Finn and I had looked like so many times. What a waste. Pointless bickering. I would have been lost these last twenty-four hours without him. Kind of hard now to remember why I'd pushed him away for so long. Might as well throw him a scrap.

"You're not bad, you know," I said in a tiny voice.

"Hmm?"

"As a kisser," I blurted, "you're . . . not that bad."

Finn tightened his arm around me. " 'Not that bad.' High praise."

"Okay. Fine. Quite skilled."

"Well, I learned from the best."

"Who have you—?" Jealousy flared before I realized who he was talking about. Warmth flooded my cheeks. "Oh. You're being nice. I've never even kissed anyone."

"You're, uhh, you're good at it, all right. But maybe you need to practice between now and our first kiss."

Our first kiss.

The warmth moved down my neck and chest. I *would* survive this somehow. I would see Finn again. Well, not my Finn, but *a* Finn. We might not have a future, but at least we would have a past.

If I could stop ICE in time.

"I'm sorry for all this," I said. "I never meant to drag you into it."

"Don't apologize. You didn't force me here against my will. And I realize I haven't exactly been the most cooperative of accidental time travelers."

"But I'm still the one who—"

"Bree," Finn said reproachfully, and took his arm off my shoulder, scooted away from me.

The warmth vanished. It left a cold hollow where my heart should have been. After all we'd been through, he was rejecting me. Not that I blamed him. I'd been so horrible at times. But it still stung. I shrank from him, but then he pulled me close against his chest.

He brushed my bangs away from my face. "Anything you want. Anything."

The glow worked its way back to my heart. A fleeting moment of perfection in chaos. Anything I wanted. *Anything.*

"I . . . I want you to—"

My breath cut off. Across the Reflecting Pool, one of the joggers turned to face us.

Wyck.

He must have followed us here. To warn us. Or . . . something.

"Finn." I poked him in the rib and jerked my head in Wyck's direction.

Finn swore under his breath. "How did he find us?"

I started to defend him, but somehow I couldn't. I had a bad feeling. Then a horrible realization slammed me.

"He's the only one who could have told Bergin about our Shift earlier. And—" *Oh, crap. Ohcrapohcrapohcrap.* When I had still suspected Dr. Quigley of something heinous, it was because I thought she was the only person who had overheard my conversation with Mimi at the Pentagon. But there *was* another person who had heard it. Mimi must have seen something odd with *Wyck,* not Quigley. He'd been standing right by her at the time.

"Hand me the reverter," I whispered.

"No. It's safer with me."

"Which is what he'll assume as well. Y chromosomes haven't changed that much in two hundred years. Give it to me. You just said anything I want."

"Is there ever going to be a point in the past, present, or future when you don't get your way?" He slipped the reverter in my pocket as he pulled me to stand. "I'll distract him. You—"

Finn didn't finish his thought.

I didn't blame him.

The other jogger had turned around.

It was another Wyck.

⊙

We stayed there for a few moments, all four of us, darting back and forth like we were dancing a complicated tango. It gave me the chance to look at the other Wyck, the Not-My Wyck. It was surreal—Wyck's body, but gaunt and emaciated. Wyck's hair, but scraggly and unwashed. His face, but the vicious sneer it wore was one I had never seen on another human before. And certainly not on my wisecracking friend.

Something terrible had happened to him. With a nauseating lurch of my stomach, I realized what it was. One of those Wycks was from the future. He must have used the IcePick to Shift here.

As I tried to decide what to do, one version of Wyck turned to the other and said something in a low voice I couldn't hear. I shook my head. This situation could get ridiculously confusing. Fast. So I decided to separate them in my mind as Real Wyck and Evil Wyck. Although, given the look of scorn on Real Wyck's face, he didn't look like he planned on snuggling kittens or herding unicorns anytime soon.

"We have to get out of here," I whispered to Finn.

He nodded.

"Okay. Now." I took off running east in the direction of the Capitol. Commuters would head in that direction and might be able to see us from the road. And if we were lucky, we'd lose the

Wycks in the blinding sunrise. Finn trailed close behind me. The Wycks kept pace across the Reflecting Pool.

When we reached the end of the water, I made for the outer edge of the World War II Memorial. One of the Wycks, Evil One, went the long way around and followed me. The other cut through the center of the pavilion. Finn ran toward Evil Wyck, but when it became apparent Real Wyck planned to ambush on far side Finn veered off and ran toward him, fists clenched.

There was a loud splash behind me. The smack of flesh hitting flesh. I glanced over my shoulder. Finn and Real Wyck had come to blows. As they wrestled each other in the memorial's shallow fountain, every bit of me ached to fly to Finn and help him. But Evil Wyck who still pursued me was gaining ground.

I ran down the path approaching the Washington Monument. I hadn't been up in the monument since my mom had dragged me kicking and screaming to the top at the age of nine.

It hadn't gotten any shorter.

Now it was draped in metal scaffold-like netting for renovation work. It was as if a hive of giant bees had built a honeycomb over the towering obelisk.

Evil Wyck gained a few more feet on me. A stitch caught in my side, and I wheezed. I'd already run so much the last hour. So much. The Mall stretched on and on. I couldn't go another step. And I didn't want Finn out of earshot.

Evil Wyck slowed, as if he sensed my exhaustion and was working out a way to use it to his advantage. I backed against the scaffold net. The frigid alloy stung my arms. Evil Wyck coughed up a coarse snarl of a laugh. I curled my fingers around the metal scaffolding. There was nowhere to run. I gulped and looked up the looming pillar.

Forget all the Rules of Shifting. First rule of classic horror movies: Every idiot who climbs one inch above normal human height is a goner.

Evil Wyck bared his teeth and prowled closer. I'd never beaten

Wyck in a single sparring match in Gym. And whatever had happened to him, he didn't look like he'd lost his fighting instinct. I looked up at the monument. I was going to have to be that idiot climber. I said a quick prayer and hiked my foot up on the net. There was no other choice but to take my chances with the beehive.

Noiselessly I climbed as the hardened version of Wyck circled beneath me, shaking the metal links when he passed them. I clenched my way higher and higher. From my perch I could see Real Wyck and Finn battle it out in the World War II fountain. Finn landed a heavy punch and in the pause turned and ran toward me.

"Come down, come down, wherever you are." The Wyck below me jostled the scaffolding. "I just want to talk."

One of my feet slipped behind the net. I had to hook my elbow around the links to yank the boot free with my other hand.

Oh, blark, I was almost thirty feet up. *Okay, stay calm.* Evil Wyck moved back toward the base of the monument for another shake. I grabbed the flashlight from my pocket and chucked it at his head. It ricocheted off the ground several feet from him, splintering one of the stones. His features changed from taunting to ticked.

"Shouldn't have done that," he said. "I never wanted to hurt you, Bree. Never."

"Then don't. Walk away."

He laughed. It was a hollow thing. "You Shifters think you're so high above the rest of us. You don't deserve that gene." His voice turned shrill and mocking: "*Can't you get me closer to the target, Wyck? Why did that fade hurt so much?* I haven't complained once. And all of you whine, whine, whine about your Buzz. The pain is a pittance."

He winced as he said it. Finn had crept silently up the path to the monument's base. I had to keep this demented Wyck distracted.

"Looks like more than a pittance to me," I said.

"They're working out the kinks."

"So you're one of their test subjects?" It made even more sense, why Bergin hadn't already gone to alter his own past. He wanted to make sure they took care of any unforeseen risks. And from the look of Wyck's future self, there were plenty of them. "I can't understand why you're doing this."

"That's because you can't see beyond that pastling," he spit, pointing back toward the arches of the World War II Memorial. At least he didn't realize Finn was behind us. "I can offer you a real life, a real future. Bree . . ." His voice trailed off and something softened in his eyes. But it passed as soon as it came. "He can't offer you anything on that pony-infested island of his in the past."

"How did you know he's from—?"

"I wanted to size up the competition." Evil Wyck put his foot on the first rung of the scaffolding.

"He's not your competition." *Wait.* "That comment Wyck made in the Launch Room . . . about the wild ponies . . ."

"Yeah. Heh, heh." He snickered, and for a flash it reminded me of *my* Wyck. "I told him to say that, to rattle Finn's cage."

Finn had been right before. He *had* seen Wyck in Chincoteague.

"So how much did you have to pay to use ICE's little contraption?" I asked, trying to buy time.

A fierce glint in Evil Wyck's eye made me wonder if the answer was his soul.

"Me? I got a freebie. In exchange for this errand." The scaffolding trembled as Wyck yanked on it. "So toss down that device and nobody gets hurt."

Finn had stealthed his way over to a few feet behind Evil Wyck, but I could see something neither of them could. The other Wyck who Finn had been fighting, Present Wyck, was headed up the path behind Finn, trembling in rage.

Couldn't get worse.

Second rule of horror movies: Oh, yes, it could.

chapter 32

"LOOK OUT!" yelled Real Wyck as he raced toward us.

Evil Wyck turned around and pushed a surprised Finn to the ground, then scrambled back to the scaffolding. His ascent was rapid. He made it up ten feet before I had time for any reaction at all. I threw the only other thing I had, my pocketknife, at him, but it only made him angrier. He quickened his pace. I climbed faster as well.

I zigzagged across the net trying to throw him off. Didn't work. For every move I made, he was three countermoves ahead. Like he'd done this before, I realized with a sinking sensation. I gave up on the zigzags and concentrated on putting as many inches between us as possible. But the higher I climbed, the fewer and fewer inches there were.

"You're snarling up the wrong tree," I said. "I don't have the reverter."

"You're a liar," he said in a cool, calm voice that was more disconcerting than if he'd kept yelling. "And don't forget: I'm from the future. I already know how this is going to end."

"Then why do you look so nervous?" I smirked. Bergin knew I'd get away. Then I remembered that was probably the reason Wyck was sent here. To change that.

But my words had their intended effect. Wyck looked like I'd slapped him. He paused mid-climb. There it was again, a brokenness.

"I don't remember everything," he said in a quiet, fearful voice. "There are holes. But also . . . extra memories."

"That means you've changed something in the past and it's been restored. Bergin's using you as a pawn. To line things up perfectly before he uses the Pick himself. He's going to let it drive you insane trying to get the reverter back while he stays safe behind his desk."

Wyck buried his face in his shirt. "I need your help."

"Wyck." My friend. He was still in there. That or he was faking. No, I *knew* him. There was no way he would do something like this if he were in his right mind. Maybe that mind could still be reached.

"Bree. Please." His shoulders shook.

"That memory gap—it's only going to get worse unless you stop Shifting. Stop trying to change things."

"I . . . I will. But I can't do it alone."

If there was any way I could help him, I had to try. "You're not alone, Wyck." I started to climb down to him.

When I was a few feet above him, he lifted his head. His shoulders were still shaking. In laughter. He clamped his hand around my ankle. I tried in vain to kick Evil Wyck off my leg. His sinewy fingers dug in deeper. I yelped in pain. He tugged me down, and I had to loop my arm over the metal netting to keep from falling.

"Oof." Evil Wyck's grip loosened. I kicked him in the head and clambered up a few more yards. From there, I could see Finn had crawled up next to Evil Wyck and hit him in the side. Real Wyck was a few yards below them.

"Finn, behind you," I said.

Evil Wyck growled and shot up the scaffolding after me. "What is it with you and that parasite?"

"Shut up!" I screamed. "You don't know anything about him."

"I know he's only good at holding on to you."

"That's nothing on his kissing." I lowered my head in a taunt.

Evil Wyck swore and called me a name that boiled my blood. There was nothing left to throw, except the reverter. But even if there had been, I wouldn't have thrown it for fear of hitting Finn instead.

"He's nothing!" yelled Wyck. "*Nothing!* Just a clueless prat who got tangled in your quantum tendrils."

"What are you talking about? Why would *my* tendrils have anything to do with him?"

"I suppose they wouldn't if your mother hadn't gone whoring in the past with your father. Conceived in one century, born in another—your tendrils don't seem to belong anywhere, now do they?"

Something akin to a howl came out of my mouth. I was going to kick his blarking head blarking *off*! I scooted down a rung, ready to deliver a boot to the face.

"Ignore him," Finn urged. "Climb."

Blindly I obeyed Finn and dodged Evil Wyck's outstretched hand. My mind tore through Wyck's explanation—it made sense. My tendrils were equally drawn to two different centuries, equally connected to both. But Wyck was wrong on one point. This quiet *pull* I'd felt all my life—it didn't mean that my tendrils didn't belong anywhere. It meant they belonged everywhere. My parents loved each other against all odds. That kind of love doesn't rip apart.

It knits together.

Finn's tendrils weren't clinging to the twenty-third century. They were clinging to mine.

I was temporal Velcro.

It wasn't like I'd ever known another Shifter born to parents of two different times who I could ask. I'd never even heard of—

"Aighh!"

Evil Wyck slammed his fist into my knee. Splinters of pain burst around the joint. When I tried to move, it cracked and stiffened.

"What are you doing?" yelled Real Wyck from below. "You said we weren't going to hurt her."

Evil Wyck scaled the last few feet and curled his fingers around my throat. "I lied."

"No!" The cry came in unison from Finn and Real Wyck, who had nearly caught up with us. When I glanced down, I realized how Real Wyck had made it up so fast. He had his gravbelt on and was merely grazing the metal links for support. Looking down was a bad idea. We were over a hundred feet high. I raised my eyes. They met Evil Wyck's savage stare and I regretted that, too.

Finn darted the rest of the way up and slammed his fist against Evil Wyck's jaw. But the ferocious grip on my throat didn't loosen. Everything spun around in dizzy loops. Holding on didn't seem as important as it had before. Air. Air was the only thing that mattered. I lifted one of my hands to pry his fingers off. Finn landed another blow, this time to Evil Wyck's gut. I managed to wrench his hand off my throat. Coughing and gasping, I fought back a rush of vomit.

Real Wyck had drifted his way up to the fray. He planted a hand on the back of his future self's shoulder to gain balance as he bobbed up and down.

"Just give me the device, Bree," said Real Wyck. "I don't want to hurt you."

Evil Wyck knocked Finn down a rung and kneed him in the head.

"Looks like you do." I tried to reach around Evil Wyck to steady Finn.

"He's not me. You understand that. You have to understand that." Wyck reached out to me. "This was the only way Bergin would let me Shift. I thought no one would get hurt."

"What about Mimi?" I asked. "Is she no one?"

"I didn't do that. *He* did." Wyck pointed at his future self. "It was supposed to be a warning to keep her mouth shut, only bruise her up a little. She saw him at the Institute yesterday on her way to breakfast, right before she found me with you when she came back to the room. It freaked her out. She thought he was a clone or something. But he didn't push her hard enough to put her in a coma. That was the ICE guys. You have to believe me."

"I do."

It didn't matter.

Finn doubled over as Evil Wyck drew his fist back from a blistering blow. Our attacker turned his attention back to me, snatched a clump of my hair, pulled. My already-tenuous hold on the net slipped. The left side of my body flew away from the scaffolding. I flapped like a flag in the wind, holding on by one arm and my injured leg.

"Stop!" roared Real Wyck. He catapulted himself at . . . himself.

With a harsh yelp, Evil Wyck leapt off the netting to meet Wyck midair. The gravbelt that now buoyed both of them sagged a few yards under the sudden addition of weight. They wrestled, but I could tell Real Wyck was holding back. Nothing like the fear of killing your future self.

Finn crawled up next to me. His right eye was swollen shut, and his nose looked broken. "We have to get off this thing," he whispered.

I winced when he brushed up against my hurt knee. I wished there was some way to know if all this had happened in the original time line. Or if Wyck was succeeding in changing it.

"Do you still have my grappling hook?" I asked.

He shook his head. "Left it on your desk. We'll take it slow."

We crept down at a snail's pace. My bum leg caught on a tool belt that workers had left on the net. It plummeted to the ground with a crash. The noise woke both Wycks from their brawl.

"We'll get the device another way." Real Wyck strained to hold his future self back from lunging onto the netting.

Evil Wyck pulled a QuantCom out of his pocket and tapped

it against Real Wyck. Instantly Real Wyck morphed into a floating statue, his eyes wide with terror. His future self turned to face Finn and me. Evil Wyck smirked. Using his stunned past self as some sort of bizarre hovercraft, he drifted toward us. He held up the QuantCom and fiddled with the controls.

"Do you like it?" He held it up as if I wanted to admire it. "I built it myself. A custom design. Had Wyck steal the parts for it from the Launch Room that first Family Night that Finn showed up. I've improved on the current models. The stunner conducts through metal. Funny how I knew that feature might come in handy right . . . about . . . now."

"Let us go. I'm begging you," I said.

Wyck ignored me.

"Do you have any idea how long I've waited for this?" He paused, and when Finn and I didn't answer he roared, "Do you?"

Prominent veins popped from his neck. He trembled head to toe.

Finn turned to me and dropped his voice to a hush: "You asked me to protect you. Now I know how."

"It's too late." I gulped. "He's going to change the story. He's going to win."

"Not this time." In Finn's whisper, the rest of the world disappeared. "Do you trust me?"

Yes.

I didn't get a chance to say it aloud. Evil Wyck thrust the stunner against the netting, his face more beast than human. But Finn had already wrapped his arms around me tighter than he ever had before.

And jumped.

chapter 33

I ONCE READ that people falling from tall heights die of a heart attack before hitting the ground.

Not true.

Apparently, they drown first.

There was a vague sense of a splash. My boots sank into gloppy sand. It sucked the soles down, trapping me underwater. I flailed and opened my mouth in a shriek. Salt water poured in. I kicked and kicked to escape the suction. The movement tore into my ripped-up knee.

I gritted my teeth to keep from gasping in pain. I had no idea how far away the surface was. I reached up, but there was only more water. I couldn't hold my breath any longer. I was going to drown. My arms thrashed around for a handhold in vain.

With one final kick, I shoved off in the direction that felt the most like up. My head broke the surface. I coughed out the briny seawater and gulped in a mouthful of air. I stretched the foot of my good leg down, but it was no use. I couldn't touch. Judging by the salt that stung my eyes, I was in the ocean. But I had no idea how.

The moon hung low on the endless horizon. Water everywhere.

Stay. Calm.

I must have Shifted somehow. It was the only explanation that made sense. It had been so fast, I'd barely felt it. And I had no idea how I'd done it. I swung my head around to get my bearings. Finn's lifeless body floated a few feet away.

"Finn!" I screamed.

No response.

I screamed again, for anyone this time, before the waves sucked me under. My cries were useless, and I knew it. I managed to pop up once more and drink in another lungful of precious oxygen. The spot where Finn had been was nothing but bubbles. My head whipped around. The last plunge had disoriented me. He was gone.

I took a deep breath and put my face under the surface, looking for him. It was no use. The salt battered my eyes, and I could barely keep my own body afloat as it was. My shoulders slumped in defeat, and the relaxation buoyed me for a moment before the panic set back in and I was pulled down again.

No. Not pulled down. Pulled forward.

Finn broke through the surface of the water. He shook his hair out like Triton returned from a refreshing midnight dip. He tugged me toward him, held me hard against his chest as he paddled through the water at the same time.

"I can't touch the bottom," I gasped. Water shot up my nose and choked me.

He stood to full height, his head above the water. "I know. But I can."

Land was visible. This would have calmed me if it weren't a hundred yards away.

I wrapped my legs around his waist to free up both his arms. "We're going to drown."

"We're not going to drown. But I am sorry." He dipped his now-free hand in the water and slicked his hair back. "I thought a beach landing would be romantic."

"Landing? What are you talking about?"

"We're home." He grinned. "Tide's low. I could navigate these sandbars in my sleep. Although it would be easier if you could, *ouch*"—he pried my frantic nails out of his chest and swung me around to his back—"*ahh, that's better.*"

"Home?" I paused to spit some oh-so-tasty flora from my mouth. "As in Chincoteague Island?"

"Yep." He paddled forward in lunges.

"You *Shifted* us here?"

He nodded.

"But you're not a Shifter. When we stuck you on the Launch-Pad, it had no effect on you, except the time when you were holding on to me."

"I didn't feel called anywhere at that particular moment." Finn shrugged. "And it wasn't like I have one of your microchip doohickeys to force it."

"You're really a Shifter?"

He nodded again.

"You knew that and didn't tell me?" *Unbelievable.*

"It started when I was staying at your house, but it took me a while to figure out what was going on. It was like bad déjà vu. I didn't want to bring it up in case it was nothing." His lips contorted into a guilty twist of a smile. "Then by the time I knew for sure what was happening, while I was staying in your, umm, in your closet, I didn't want to bring it up, period."

"That day I came back to the room early, you weren't talking to yourself. You were talking to *yourself*."

"You *did* hear us." He splashed the surface of the water. "I knew it."

"So you decided to wait until we were a hundred feet in the air and test yourself out with a *two-hundred-year Shift*? You could have gotten us killed!"

"Oh, I think Wyck was doing a pretty good job of that."

A sickle moon leered in the distance. On the one hand, I was so spitting mad. On the other, Finn *was* the only one who could protect me in that exact moment on the monument, a free Shifter who could pull us both to safety.

"And it wasn't a Shift," he said. "It was a synch. The pull's been getting stronger and stronger. But it wasn't an overwhelming urge until Wyck was about to kill us. In that moment, it was like everything disappeared but you. And I just . . . knew." He was quiet for a moment. "I never believed Dad when he said how hard it is to control his Shifting when emotions are high. But he's right."

Gradually, the water receded, as did my anger. When it reached Finn's knees, I hopped down and hobbled along beside him, clutching his arm to steady myself. In the distance the Mastersons' house glowed, but I didn't detect any movement inside. Dang if that boy didn't have some natural talent. A crab scuttled over my toes in the shallows, and when my feet touched dry sand I collapsed. The warm grains clung to me but couldn't quiet my shivers.

Even under my jeans, I could see my knee was puffed up to the size of a cantaloupe. The throbbing was so intense, I pinched the inside of my arm, the side of my neck, just to feel pain somewhere else.

Ha. Pain somewhere else. Yet no Buzz. I couldn't help but let out a tiny laugh.

"I really am sorry about the water," said Finn, lying down next to me. "And for not telling you about the Shifts. I didn't want to worry you."

"Worry me? Why would that have worried me?" I winced as I tugged off my boots and peeled down my socks. Water and grit poured out. "If I'd known you were able to Shift home on your own, it would have solved everything."

A wave rushed up and lapped our already-sopping legs. Finn ground the sole of my boot into the sand. "Right. Everything."

"Well, not *everything*," I said. "I mean, there are certified henchmen chasing me and, as far as I know, my headmaster is still bent on irreparably mucking up the space-time continuum. Oh, and let's not forget the angry smugglers. But I wouldn't have had to worry about what to do with you and—"

"We need to get going." Finn pushed himself up gruffly.

"Are you mad at me?"

"I'm not mad." Finn dug a trench on the beach with his heel. "I'm done."

"What do you mean, done?"

"What do you think I mean? I'm not an idiot! We don't have a future, Bree. I get that. Our future is in the past. All we have is the present—and that isn't looking real hopeful. I don't want to spend the rest of the time we have together fighting with you. And you won't let me fight *for* you. Here"—he lifted something shiny from his pocket—"I've been carrying this around, waiting for the perfect time to give it back to you. It doesn't look like that time's coming."

I reached out and touched the silver object. It was my heart. My sterling bracelet.

"Where did you find it?"

"In the grass outside the Pentagon. When I went back for the grappling hook." He dumped the locket in the sand next to me and backed away. "Leave the reverter here. I'll put it in our safe until I can figure out a better hiding spot."

"Finn, wait."

He turned around and ignored me.

"Wait."

Still ignored me.

"I said, *wait*." I lurched forward and grabbed him by his ankles. He face-planted into the sand next to me. "Don't do this. Please. I was wrong. I mean I will be wrong."

"Don't do what?" He spit sand out of his mouth.

"Don't leave. I've already lost my mom. And Mimi. I can't lose you, too. I don't want it to end like this." Then it hit me. I didn't want it to end. Ever. "I know Future Me told you to break my heart, but not now. Not like this."

Finn's expression softened, and he drew me close. "Shh . . . I'm not going anywhere." He rested his chin on top of my head and took deep, sure breaths that calmed me. His stubble tickled as I leaned my head back so I could look at him. But he was gazing out at the ocean.

"Penny for your thoughts," I said.

"You still have those in the future?"

"No. But my mom collects them."

He laughed. "I was just thinking, if you're asking me not to break your heart, wouldn't that mean"—he looked into my eyes and brushed his thumb down my cheek—"I have it already?"

Hmm. That was what it would mean.

"Ehh." I leaned away and brushed the sand from his chest. "You knew it was coming."

He pushed himself up and helped me stand. "Did not."

"Did so."

"Okay." He stood up to his full height in mock defiance. "When?"

"When what?"

"When did you fall for me?"

"Some point after the past but not quite the future." I scrunched my nose. "I think it was your love for talking frogs that did it."

Exultation flashed in Finn's eyes. He grabbed me around the waist and spun me in dizzy circles. His hands fit perfectly in the small of my back, like they were designed for that very purpose—to hold me. I stood on my tippy-toes as he lowered me to the ground. A few grains of sand clung to his cheek, and I brushed them off. Every last stone around my heart crumbled. He bent his mouth to my ear. I waited for a snarky comment, but instead he grazed his lower lip against my earlobe. A shiver slid down my spine that had nothing to do with my sopping clothes.

"I'm so sorry for how I treated you." I ran my hand along his jaw. "I—"

"No." He rested his forehead against mine. "I owe *you* an apology. I should have let you know about the Shifting before. When you dragged me to the Launch Room, I should have told you then. I knew I wasn't going anywhere. I was where I was meant to be. But now, I've brought you here and I thought I was protecting you, but what if . . . ?"

"Stop. This is where *I'm* meant to be. With you."

Finn ran his finger along my microchip scar. "They're going to know right where to look. Maybe I should try to Shift us somewhere else."

"Do you think you can?"

"I don't feel a pull." He closed his eyes so tight, it almost looked like he was praying, but he shook his head in frustration. "Nothing. Are you at least comfortable?"

"Not even the slightest Buzz." I tried to give him a reassuring smile even though I felt anything but. *Huh.* I thought back over the last week. Whenever Finn wasn't with me, I'd had a Buzz-like headache. But whenever he was . . . I didn't.

"I think I know why I don't have it here," I said. "Chip or no chip, I'm where I belong. With you."

Microchips didn't cure the Buzz, as we'd been lied to all these years. But I wasn't sure the chips caused it directly either. Maybe the Buzz was a result of not Shifting to where we were naturally called. That was why these nonShifters who had traveled to the past suffered so much with it. They weren't where they belonged. I thought of that picture with my mom, so happy and carefree with my dad. She was where she was supposed to be.

Well, I was right where I was supposed to be now.

I leaned forward. Finn's lips traced a path to the edge of mine. My lips parted. Each shallow, ragged breath invited contact. Every nerve in my body sparked. It was almost painful.

No, it *was* painful.

"Unhh." I groaned.

Finn flung himself away from me. "Is it your leg? Was I holding you too tight?"

I shook my head slowly. But shrapnels of pain pulsated down to my marrow with even so slight a movement. I swiped a smear of red from my nose.

"They found me." I doubled over as the pain grew. "And we don't have very long."

chapter 34

NO SOONER HAD THE WORDS "we don't have very long" come out of my mouth, Finn swooped me up and ran toward his house like the beach was on fire. There was no way my sprained knee could keep up with his pace. Heck, there was no way a cheetah could keep up with his pace.

"What are you doing?" I asked as he took the deck's steps two at a time.

"I've got to get to a phone." He laid me in a patio chair, then banged on the back door, rattled the windows, checking whether they were locked. The house was empty. "As long as that thing is in your head, they can keep dragging you back to the future. You won't be safe until it's out of you. We have to find my dad."

"And what's your dad going to do?"

"He's a surgeon. He'll . . . I don't know, cut it out."

"Finn." My voice cracked, as I realized what his idea of a microchip was. Something to find lost pets or track a runner's progress. "It's buried in the deepest section of my brain. Removal is an intricate surgery and so rarely done, even in my time. People have chips implanted. Not taken out.

"This is what we need to focus on with the time that we have." I held up the defunct reverter. "I have to get this working. They're going to suck me back to my time no matter what. This is the only thing that can fix the damage ICE is doing to the past. If I don't get this operational before Bergin goes back and saves his wife, I might forget everything. I might lose everything, all my memories and experiences leading me here. I might lose . . ."

I couldn't bring myself to say "you." But Finn wasn't listening to me anyway. He'd backed up to the edge of the deck and squared off his shoulders to make a run at the sliding glass door.

"Wait!" I stumbled up and limped over to block his path.

There was no stopping his determination to get in the house. Shifters learn early on to either get scars or get smarts on our missions. I'd chosen smarts after my first (and only) stint in a nineteenth-century jail for indecent public dressing. If I could pick the lock of the New York Macy's circa 1889, I could get into Finn's house.

There was no way John and Georgie managed to land in the house every time they got back from one of their Shifts. Charlotte would go bonks at the thought of them shivering outside in the night. She'd have hidden a key. Inconspicuous, yet accessible and . . .

A ring of dirt lined an oversized flowerpot next to the deck's top step. I dug my nails around the edge of the soil.

"Voilà." I held up a mud-caked key.

I scraped as much dirt off the key as I could, but it wouldn't turn in the lock. There was a scratching noise on the deck steps. I whirled around, but it was only Slug the dog. He came up and licked my hand. His pudge rolls swung from side to side in a full body wag.

"Good dog," I said, patting and pushing him away at the same time. "Now, go away."

I plucked the key from the lock and looked for something I could use to gouge more grunge out of it. The only thing I had was the reverter. It really did resemble a thick writing pen, a little wider in diameter than my pinky. I examined the triangle-shaped notch cut out of the end. It almost looked like it was missing a part. And then I remembered Bergin's comment about how it wasn't operational because it didn't have all the components.

Real brilliant there, Future Bree. Make me risk my life for a gadget that doesn't even work yet.

I scraped at the mud, as good as it was going to get. Slug came back and nudged his nose between my hand and the door.

"Get out of the way, Slug. I can't get the key in."

I leaned back toward the lock but dropped the key with a gasp.

"The key—Finn, we're missing the key!"

"It's right there." He pointed at the ground.

"No. For the reverter. There's a piece missing. It would fit here, in this notch. It must be some kind of key to operate it."

"What do you think it is?"

"I have no idea. Aigh." I doubled over. My pain had ramped to fork-rammed-in-my-eye-socket.

"Maybe—" Finn picked up the mud-covered house key and jammed it in the end of the reverter. Nothing happened. He ran down the deck stairs in a panic and started grabbing things at random, shells and rocks.

I stumbled down the stairs after him and placed my hand over his as he tried to jam a tiny fish bone in. "This isn't working."

"No." His voice broke. "I'm not going to fail."

Fail.

When all else fails, you have to break my heart.

My heart.

I grabbed the reverter from him. It could work.

"Finn, it will fit perfectly if we break it."

"What will?"

"My heart."

"Your . . . ?"

"My heart locket!"

Finn whipped me up in his arms and swung me around. When he put me down, he reached into his pocket at the same moment that I clasped my bare wrist.

That was also, of course, the moment that my head burst into a fireball. "Son of a—"

Finn threw me over his shoulder. "Beach."

chapter 35

THE COVE LOOKED LIKE we'd let a rabid mole loose on it. Piles pocked the sand in a haphazard pattern. No rhyme. No reason. We'd been at it for almost five minutes with no sign of the bracelet. Slug ran circles around us on the beach. Finn kept throwing rocks into the grass to get him out of the way, but he'd retrieve them, prancing back for more. He must have thought it was a game.

This game had no winner.

And I wasn't much help in our search. The pain of the forced fade had grown almost unbearable. Finn, ever positive, pointed out how thankful he was my nosebleed had stopped. I, however, was thankful that the dim moonlight hid the blood that had started trickling from my ears.

I kept a moderate distance from Finn as we continued the pointless hunt. I'd made up my mind the moment I realized I loved him. He belonged here, safe in his present with his family. Not hovering on the edge of disaster in mine.

But knowing Finn was out there somewhere, healthy and happy, that would be enough. That had to be enough.

"I've got it!" He lifted a silver object up in a triumphant fist, then lowered it. "No. Another bottle cap."

His third one.

"Finn." I broke my distance rule to walk over and rest my hand on his shoulder. He refused to abandon his sifting even for a moment. "Finn, there's something I need to say before . . . There's something I need to say now."

"No. It can wait until I find it. I'm not going to lose you."

With those words, both our lives spread before me. A depressing and dangerous game of tug-of-war neither of us could win. He would never have more than a too-short past with me. I would never have more than a too-short future with him. And when Bergin succeeded in yanking me back to my present, even that might be taken away from us.

"Finn, you will always have my heart." I lifted his face toward mine, but he refused to look into my eyes. "But we both know your great-grandchildren will be long dead before I'm so much as a glimmer in my father's eye. Actually, that's reversed, but that's my point. Look at my mom and dad. I don't want that for us. You have to let me go.

"They can do whatever they want up here." I pointed at my head. "They can never touch this." I moved his hand to my heart and took a step forward, lifting my lips to meet his. But as I did so, Slug jumped up on our clasped arms and sent both of us sprawling onto the beach.

"Seriously?" I let out a joyless laugh and stared up at the heavens. "I'm beginning to think God doesn't want this kiss to happen."

I rolled off of Finn. His red-rimmed eyes reflected a glimmer of moon. The time I had left with him could be measured in moments. I wanted to savor every one of them. I leaned over and kissed each of his eyelids, then his forehead, his right cheek, his left—

Slug jumped back on top of us, growling and dipping his head for Finn to throw the rock again.

"I swear." I reached into Slug's slobbery mouth for the rock so we could have some peace. "If you don't leave us alone, I'm going to—"

The rock wasn't a rock.

"Yeeeee!" I threw my arms around Slug. "Finn, look!"

I held out the locket for him to see. He grabbed my fist and kissed it.

The hinge was tight with age, but when I bent it back as far as it would go it snapped cleanly in two. The smaller piece fit perfectly into the end of the extractor. Like a key slipping into a lock. With the heart in place, the device whirred and glowed the same green hue as a Haven Beacon.

"Nice touch," said Finn.

We both stood there staring at it with goofy smiles on our faces. Mine was the first to disappear. The reverter stopped whirring. The light dimmed into an intermittent green blink.

"That's it?" I clicked the end in and out. Nothing.

This had all been pointless. There was no forever for us. Only this blip in time. And whatever stolen moments I could grab with his past. But now the thought of that depressed me, to go back and see him knowing we had no future.

If I even had that.

Agony tore through my body. I hunched over. All hope, all energy, evaporated. I had failed. At least here in Chincoteague, Finn would be immune to ICE's crazy-making changes. Bergin had said nonShifters could only change events within their own personal time line, which for me would be well after Finn's time. I clutched the reverter and ran my finger over the heart lodged in the end.

When all else fails, break my heart.

I sat up. I had *always* failed. Future Bree knew that and still chose this path, this heartbreak. Why?

I blinked at Finn. Here in Chincoteague, he was immune to the time-line changes. They couldn't steal the Truth from him like they could from me. This was never about my future. It was about his.

I could only see one way.

"You didn't break my heart," I whispered.

He'd been staring out at the ocean. He turned to face me. "What?"

"Future Bree told you, 'When all else fails, you have to break my heart.' That's what she said. But *I* was the one who broke the locket. *I* broke my heart."

"So?"

"Take this." I handed him the reverter. "Hide it or put it in your safe. Something. You have to get it to Quigley the next time she visits you. Explain everything to her if she doesn't already know by then."

"Aunt Lisa?"

"Or it may be some other Shifter from the future. Someone your dad meets. Someone he trusts." I didn't try to hide the defeat in my voice.

Finn shook his head and tried to give it back to me.

"You give it to her," he said. "You can hide it again. You're going to be okay."

I shook my head. "It was too easy, Finn."

"What?"

"Getting away from Bergin. Don't you see? He could have had a hundred of his henchmen waiting outside his office door to stop me. He could have sent Future Wyck back armed with a weapon beyond our worst imagining. You heard him." I held up the reverter. "This can't be destroyed until it has all its parts. He let us get away. Bergins *wants* this thing operational. You have to take it."

"No."

"It has to be this way."

"No. You're going to come back."

"Do it!" I screamed.

He clutched the reverter to his chest, looking as if I'd zapped him with the stunner again. He hung his head for a moment. When he looked up, his expression had turned to flint.

"Fight it." He pursed his lips.

And vanished.

"Finn?" I reached out to where he had stood. He was gone. He was really gone.

It was so fast.

Without even a good-bye. The selfish part of me wanted him to stay with me to the end, but he was right. It was better this way. Alone. I collapsed onto my side.

A fresh volley fired throughout my skull. I rolled into a ball. A tang of fresh blood gurgled into my throat. The sound of the pounding waves gave me something to concentrate on other than the pain. With each crash, the pull grew stronger and stronger. How easy it would be to give in to it. The pain percolated down to my teeth, gritted in agony. All the tension would release if I gave in to the pull. I'd land facedown somewhere on a soft lawn in the twenty-third century.

I drank in one last view of this little island I'd grown to love; then my eyesight dimmed. Would Bergin strip me of this memory as soon as I got home or would he let me keep it awhile? Torture me with it awhile?

The important thing was Finn and the reverter were out of ICE's reach now. He would hold on to the Truth even as it was stripped from me.

My body began to relax and surrender to the pull. Only a few more seconds and I'd be . . .

No.

I'd fight it. I'd promised Finn.

I'd fight *them.*

For as long as I could.

They might control where I went. They might control *when* I went. They'd never control who I was. But then the pain ratcheted up. I couldn't . . . I couldn't . . .

Everything faded.

chapter 36

COOL PINK LIGHT TRICKLED through the edges of my vision and tickled the backs of my eyelids. I didn't need to open them to know which century I was in. The jagged spasms of the forced fade had subsided. The all-too-familiar dull ache of the Buzz remained.

I had lost him.

I forced my eyes open. A ceiling fan paddled around in lazy circles, just fast enough so I couldn't tell if there were four or five blades. If I stared at the center too long, the fan appeared to go backward. But it was an optical illusion.

Going backward wasn't an option. They'd already found me. Only my own bleak future stretched out before me. I'd live a new fresh hell every time I snuck away to visit Finn—wondering if it would be the last time. That was if I managed even one visit before ICE changed something that stripped me of my memories.

Starched cotton sheets rustled against my still-achy bare leg as I turned to the side. The scent of fresh wisteria wafted in through an open window. At least my captors had sprung for a nice hospital room. I pushed myself up on my elbow to look for a call button.

"Don't let my mom see you do that. She'll have a conniption."

I flipped around so fast I bumped the glass of ice water balanced on the edge of the nightstand. It knocked over some action figures and splattered across the speaker's shirt. His glorious overpriced designer shirt.

"Finn?" I said. "How did you . . . ? Where did you . . . ? When did you . . . ?"

I had shimmied to the side of the bed, propelled by my stammered half questions, and was about to take a flying leap at him when he hopped up from the chair in which he'd been lounging. He pushed me back down on the pillows but curled next to me.

"No, really. If Mom catches you out of bed, she'll kill me."

"I'm at your house? They didn't force fade me back?"

"Nope. You blacked out. I was terrified I'd be too late. When you told me to leave, I wasn't going to. And then, I felt this Shift building up in me—calling to me—so I decided to trust you. It took me a few minutes to find him. Thank goodness he was in Afghanistan and nothing further back."

"What are you talking about? Find who?" But even before I finished asking, I knew. "Your dad."

"Fix 'em under fire," Finn said with a little grin. But dark circles of worry still hugged his eyes.

"I had no idea you were going to get him."

"I didn't either until I got there. Just following orders, ma'am," he said in a deep southern drawl, then switched to a more serious tone: "How are you feeling?"

"Good or, at least, okay. A little Buzzy, but . . . wait. *How* am I here?" Last I remembered, my quantum tendrils were being ripped in two. "Did your dad take out my chip somehow?"

Finn reached over to the nightstand and pulled the drawer open. He held up a case of half a dozen hypofuse syringes. One was empty.

"He didn't remove it. He injected you with this. Dad's theory is the serum disrupts the chip long enough for your brain to override it. Almost like a vaccine. Your body's natural defenses kicked in and switched it off. Course, he still had to know where to aim."

"Where did he get those?" The technology was way past Finn's time. Hypofusers were only on the verge of mine.

"You gave them to him a few months ago. Showed him how to use them. Then swore him to secrecy. Apparently, Future You and my parents"—he crossed his fingers—"like this."

He looked like he was about as happy at being kept in the dark as I was.

"Why did I bring him more than one?" I asked.

Finn shrugged. "Who knows? Your head will be sore a few days, but Dad thought it should be a pretty easy recovery. Still, he wants you to stick around here for a while."

"No."

"No?"

"I have to get back to my mom. She's safe at Resthaven for now, but ICE isn't going to be happy. And Leto could still get to her." And Mimi. And Quigley.

"You don't think he's in cahoots with ICE?"

I shook my head. The thought had occurred to me, but Leto was a sole proprietor. He wouldn't be anyone's lapdog.

"No. At least, not yet. But as soon as he finds out that IcePick exists and gets his hands on one, he'll have a heyday."

He'd no longer be constrained to any Shifters' scruples, to any of our Rules. ICE's technology obliterated the Rule Book.

Finn's mother bustled into the room laden with a stack of towels in one hand and a hamper of folded clothes in the other.

"Pumpkin, could you put these away?" Charlotte walked straight past without glancing at the bed. "Georgie's in a snit because she Shifted in the girls' bathroom at school and the vice principal accused her of climbing out the window. Got a week of in-school suspension. Now she's threatening to cling to Bree's synch. I don't think my nerves can handle another—"

Charlotte's mouth snapped shut. The corners curved up as she finally turned to face us. "Look who's awake."

I wiggled my wrist in a limp wave.

"How are you feeling, sweetie? Oh, Finn's room is in such a state." Charlotte tornadoed around, shoving socks and books and action figures in drawers. "I was going to put you in one of the guest rooms, but he insisted his bed is more comfortable. What kind of boy thinks his own mother puts guests on a hard mattress I don't even know. But he was having none of it with you down the hall. Can I get you a cold compress? Some lemonade? Or I could put the kettle on for tea. Do you need more pillows?"

"I'm fine." A little overwhelmed. "I *would* like some questions answered."

"Shoot," said Finn, kissing the top of my head.

"Okay. If I had the key to the reverter around my wrist all this time, why didn't Future Me just tell Quigley how to use it and about the locket?"

"If that had happened, would we have met?" Finn pulled me close to his side.

"Would you have trusted her?" asked Charlotte.

"Would you have trusted *yourself*?" asked Finn. "I think she wanted to keep those pieces separate until you were ready to find out what the Truth really is for yourself. Besides, Doctrine of Inevitability. It *didn't* happen."

"Yes, but . . . does the Doctrine of Inevitability even exist anymore?"

"The Truth still exists," said Finn, "the way things are supposed to be. The time line may be skewed, but it's still there, still fixable. With this."

He handed me the reverter.

"I guess you're right." I fiddled with the end of it, still clueless as to how the thing actually worked. I guess for now I just needed to trust that it did. "I suppose in hindsight—"

"Hindsight shmindsight." Charlotte waved her hands in the air. "It's pointless to you Shifters. The important thing is to keep your eyes open right where you are."

I sank back into the squishy pillows and pulled a blanket up to my chin. The deluge of overwhelming thoughts engulfed me once more.

"So it really was me all along. I came here because of that stupid Muffy van Sloot, whoever she is. But it was Future Me who got Finn all worked up when she came back to, umm, talk." I brushed past that part when Charlotte narrowed her eyes at her squirming son. "I was the one who told my mom about the enigmatic grin, which forced Quigley to erase any record of your family. Which, in turn, spurred *me* to come back. Good grief, watch me end up inventing that vaccine thingy in the first place."

"Actually," said Finn, "Future You's always whining about your Quantum Biology Specialization, but—"

"Are you blarking kidding me?" I kicked the covers off my legs until I remembered I wasn't wearing pants and yanked them back up. "Well, looks like it'll come in handy."

Chicken–egg. There was nothing I could do about it at the moment.

"All I know is that I can fix the changes ICE makes to the time line over and over and over, but that's only strapping butterflies to the *Hindenburg*. We're not safe until every trace of their technology is gone." I held up the reverter. "Including this."

The doorbell chimed downstairs, and Charlotte gave my foot a quick pat on the way out of the room. When Finn and I were alone again, I shimmied into my jeans under the covers, then swung my legs off the bed. Still achy, but that could be fixed soon enough in the twenty-third century.

"What are you doing?" asked Finn.

"I've gotta go." I lurched to the side dizzily as what I could only assume was an urge to synch hit me. This was going to take some getting used to.

Finn noticed my bobble and reached his hand out to steady me. I had a newfound respect for his ability to fight the pull for so long in my time.

"Bree." A trace of amused disbelief laced Finn's voice. "What's the hurry? You're a free time traveler now. You have nothing *but* time. Quigley took your mom to the safest place possible for the moment. Nurse Granderson can contact Mimi's parents to have her transferred to Resthaven. Who else . . . ?"

His voice trailed off and his smile faded.

I continued my clothes hunt, focusing my attention in every possible direction but Finn's.

He laid a gentle hand on my shoulder. "Repeat after me: 'I can't save everyone.'"

I bent down to feel under the bed for my boots. "I have to try."

A squeeze of Finn's hand stilled me. "You can't help him. Wyck made his choice."

"I *have* to try."

"I don't understand." Finn didn't bother to hide the hurt in his voice.

"I know you don't." And I prayed he never would. He'd never truly get it until he had to face down a decision his future self had made—one he hadn't planned on or approved of. One that changed everything. Wyck was still in there. I'd seen a glimpse of it on the monument, just a flash, but it was there. I needed to believe there was hope for him. I needed to believe ICE could be stopped. Somehow. And that everything could go back to the way it was. The way it was supposed to be.

Before I had a chance to finish explaining myself, though, shouting voices filled the whole house. Slug ran past the room barking. His claws click-a-clacked down the stairwell. Finn and I trailed close behind him to the source of the commotion in the living room.

"Oh, sakes," said Charlotte in a placating but still louder than usual tone, "I don't blame you for being upset, but this can all be explained if you'll—"

"Don't tell me to simmer down again." The angry shouting

started back up: "I want you to tell me where my daughter is and what your son has gotten her involved in!"

I rushed past Finn down the steps and froze near the bottom. "Mom?"

My mother paused and looked at us.

It was really her.

Really, truly *her*. Whole and healthy.

And, man, she looked ticked.

"Bree." She doubled over in relief, with her hands on her knees. She pushed her way around Charlotte and snatched me up in a bear hug. "Oh, sweetie. When they force faded you, I thought . . . Oh, I don't even know what I thought. But you're okay. That's the only thing that matters. I've been so worried for the last hour. Thank goodness these Masterson people are art collectors. I don't know if my boss would have approved the Shift otherwise."

Charlotte winked at me. I forced myself out of Mom's embrace.

"You came *here*." I shook my head in disbelief. This was my mom from six months ago. In her time, Finn and I had just left our house. "You came here for your final Shift."

The erased file. ICE must have destroyed it after they put my mom in the coma, to cover their tracks.

"Final Shift? What are you talking about, sugar booger?"

Just when I thought I was done with headaches.

⟲

I stood in the doorway of the Mastersons' guest bedroom and stared at the spot where, moments before, my mom had lain.

Bring back the tru-ants. Bring back the splintered knee. The almost drowning. The explosion in my head.

This was the hardest thing I'd ever done.

It had taken a while to explain everything to Mom, or at least everything that I understood. It had taken even longer to convince her to let John deactivate her chip. Now I knew why my future self had brought him more than one syringe. I thought it would make it easier, the knowledge that when she went back, to six months ago, she would actually be a free Shifter already. But it made it worse. Now I knew that when Mom landed on the Institute steps—right before ICE attacked her and drugged her into oblivion—she could have saved herself. She could have Shifted to safety. But she didn't.

The imprint from Mom's body was still smooshed into the fluffy duvet. I watched as it puffed up slowly, like she'd never been there. I hadn't had enough time with her, not that such a thing existed. The pull for her to synch had come too soon. She was still too weak from the vaccine to fight it. There was no point even if she'd wanted to. She had to go back. She knew now that she had to announce that Truth clue before Bergin came and silenced her.

But maybe in the end it was only in weakness that Mom could muster the strength to sacrifice herself. She knew what she was doing, giving up six months of her life, for me and for other Shifters, for the whole world that would never know. That knowledge should have made our final hug easier.

It didn't.

Finn wrapped his arms around me from behind. "Are you okay?"

A brave mask crept over my face, but I swept it aside. I was with Finn. No more walls. I turned around and clasped his hands in mine. I stood on my tippy-toes and brought my face toward his.

Finn took a half step back. "Are you sure? I was thinking that maybe . . . maybe it would be romantic for you to go back in time so we could share our first real kiss."

I pressed my thumb to my finger against his chest in a soft pinch. *This* was the real Finn. The Finn who stayed by my side when fading away would have been far easier. The Finn who disappeared when it was the hardest thing he ever had to do.

And this was the Finn who knew the real Bree.

I nodded and moved my lips to meet his.

This kiss wasn't the infatuation of a scared sixteen-year-old.

It wasn't the shock of a frantic hello from a stranger.

This kiss wasn't for anyone else.

This kiss was *real*. It was perfect. His strong hands pulled me close. Somehow, every caress comforted and thrilled in the same tender movement.

I closed my eyes and reached my hands out as far as I could. The past and the future tingled in my fingertips. When I opened my eyes, we were standing on the opposite side of Finn's room from where we just were, next to his desk. It was a mess.

"Are we in your past?" I asked.

Finn pointed to the key chain that had sunk with his Porsche. "Looks like it."

"Then I'm Future Bree, aren't I?"

"You're making my brain hurt."

"Chicken–egg." I spared him the mental torture. "But why are we here?"

"Privacy?" Finn shrugged and moved in for another kiss, but I spotted something on his desk. Something superthin and shiny and futuristic.

"Leto's delivery." I could give the flexiphone back to him. I pocketed it and started scribbling a note to Finn to explain its absence.

"No, you signed it: 'Love, Bree.'"

As I erased the last word and fixed my mistake, it gave me an idea. I wrote a set of instructions down for Finn and handed it to him. He read them.

"Why do you want me to—?"

"Don't worry about that. Can you spare it?"

"Sure." He looked down at his feet. "So what is this? Good-bye?"

"Of course not. It's . . . see you soon." I reached up and kissed him again. "Very soon."

"See *me* soon? Or Past Me soon?"

Oh, keeping up with this was going to kill me. But it was worth it.

"Both, I guess." I said. I couldn't imagine my tendrils would let me stay apart from him for long at all. "At least for a while. Until I fully catch up with my future self."

My extremities began to tingle once more, and I recognized it as the pull to synch. I reached up to give him a quick good-bye peck, but it turned into more.

"What are you thinking about?" asked Finn quietly when we finally pulled away from each other.

"Forever."

Finn tucked a flyaway wisp of hair behind my ear. The tingling moved to my heart. I circled my arms around his waist.

Forever could wait.

Epilogue
(aka Who the Heck Is Muffy van Sloot?)

I STOOD ON THE STEPS of the Institute in the chill of the wee morning, blowing on my hands to warm them. Leto had better show. It made me nervous standing out in the open like this. ICE hadn't approached me since I'd gotten home, and I sure as heck wasn't going to stroll into their headquarters. Yet.

But flashes of red still popped into my peripheral vision and disappeared just as quickly. They were watching.

I buried my hands in my sweater and was surprised to find a lump in the inner pocket. I hadn't worn it since I left Chincoteague yesterday afternoon. I pulled out a green velvet jewelry box. When I opened it, a note fell out.

For you. I know it had to be done, but I still felt bad about your broken bracelet. This one's not an antique like yours, and there was no time to have it professionally engraved, so I scratched our initials on it myself with a nail. But it's a really close match. Hope you like it. See you soon (at least for one of us). Love, Finn

I pulled a sterling heart locket from the box and clasped it around my wrist.

"It's perfect," I said to no one, light glinting off the bracelet as I held it up to the street lamp. It was exactly like mine. *Wait.* I squinted for a closer look. *No blarking way.* "It's *exactly* like mine."

Finn had given me *my* bracelet. But brand-new. The original etchings that had worn off were our initials. So somehow this one would end up in an antique shop and eventually my mom would buy it in my past, but really it would be the—

"What's exactly like yours?"

"Nothing." My shoulders tensed as Leto slithered up next to me out of the shadows. With zero prelude, I handed him the failed delivery. "Here."

"So you weren't lying? Well, thanks, kid. And no hard feelings. To prove it, I'll give you another shot. Double or nothin' on your next delivery."

How easy that would be as a free Shifter. But even if I were willing to sink to those depths again, I knew there was no way my tendrils would cooperate and pull me to the past for shady gain.

"You forget. I'm still Anchored."

"Right," he said with a look that was a bit too knowing. Nothing got past him in this town.

Which brought me to why I was here. I didn't like Leto. I certainly didn't trust him. But there was a very good chance that in the not-so-distant future I was going to need him.

I handed him a sheet of compufilm with nine digits on it.

"What is this?" he asked.

"A pile of money you can't even fathom. In exchange for your assistance from time to time."

His eyes widened, then narrowed to snake slits. "If this is a bank account, it's missing a number."

"And someone very precious to me is the only one who knows it. I don't even know it. If any harm should befall him, you'll lose your payout. If any harm should befall *me,* he won't tell you the last number. I suggest you get into the business of protecting life and not threatening it."

"How am I supposed to—?"

"You're a clever fella." My hand tapped his cheek with a *thwap.* "Figure it out."

Without another word, I turned on my heel and walked back into my school.

◯◯

"Well, looks like Charlie's been bored." My side of the room was completely flipped with Mimi's. This was my first time back to the Institute since returning. I'd spent last night with Mom at Resthaven (where both she and Mimi experienced miraculous recoveries from their comas), but Charlie must have gotten restless. Mimi was still sore from her injuries—he probably wanted her to be closer to the bathroom.

"Huh?" Mimi propped herself up on her pillow, groggy from sleep.

I pointed at my desk, a mirror of where it had been yesterday, in response.

"Oh, I know. I'm sorry. I tried to save her, but it was too long between feedings."

"Huh?" We were having two different conversations.

"Your fish." She pointed at the fishbowl on my desk, where I now noticed Franny Fishington was belly-up.

"I liked Fran." I frowned.

"Oh, I forgot to tell you. Fran kicked it a couple weeks ago, when you were on your History midterm. I replaced her for you. So you actually liked Muffy."

"What did you say?"

"I named her for you. Muffy—"

"Van Sloot," we said together.

"How did you know?" Mimi asked.

"Doesn't matter." I swirled the water, laughing. *Garden-variety colored pebbles. Just like the ones in my fish tank at home.* I really had taken care of every detail. Looked like Future Bree would be taking a few Shifts back to tie up some loose ends soon. What was that phrase? "There's no time like the past."

"I'll bury her on the beach," I said.

"What?" Mimi screwed up her nose.

A message popped into my in-box.

It was from Wyck. Another one. The same three words he kept sending me: "I'm not him." My heart hurt every time I thought about him. He *wasn't* Evil Wyck. But he was going to be. I wasn't ready to confront him yet, though.

I plopped down on my bed, which was now Mimi's, without thinking about it.

"Sorry," I said, jumping up. "I can't get used to the switch."

"What switch?"

"The room flip."

"What are you talking about?"

"Our stuff. It's flipp—" *Blark.* Charlie hadn't moved anything. There'd been a change to the time line. "Nothing."

I gripped the reverter in my pocket. It was whirring and glowing green. I guess I was supposed to click it, but I hesitated since I was standing in front of Mimi. But before I had a chance to excuse myself, it faded back to the intermittent blip. *Dang.* Maybe I had missed my chance. Finn had wanted to store the reverter in Chincoteague, but I insisted on keeping it with me until I figured out exactly how it worked. If I got in trouble, I could always Shift away. At least Bergin and ICE didn't seem to know that I was a free Shifter yet.

I glanced out the window. Hopefully, whatever had changed was small. The sky wasn't, like, purple now or anything. But the switched-bed thing confirmed my fears that every change had ripple effects further than intended. How many of these changes had I already experienced and not realized it as a chipped Shifter?

"Are you okay?" Mimi asked.

"I'm fine. I—" *No.* I couldn't tell her. I had debated whether to fill Mimi in about everything the moment I got back. There were still four more doses of that vaccine left. But she might not believe me. She might freak out. Or turn me in for the Madness because she was so worried for me.

If I was this terrified of my best friend's reaction, how on earth was I going to get the word out to other Shifters? They needed to know the truth. But the Truth was going to be almost impossible to accept. At least for now.

But this was the *oomph* I needed to face the one meeting I'd most dreaded since my return.

"I need to go do something. You go back to sleep. I'll see you later."

Bergin. We'd reached a stalemate in our chess match. He couldn't do anything to me while I held his queen, the reverter. But I also knew ICE still thought they could turn me into their pawn, just like him.

The door to his office was open, and I stepped inside, unsure of what I would find.

Bergin stood at the window, statue still. I glanced around to see if anything had changed, if there were any new photos. The room was stark. His possessions were arranged neatly in crates scattered about. I realized he was packing.

"I couldn't do it," he said.

"Couldn't do what?"

"I went back more times than I can count. Watched the accident from every conceivable angle. Watched my wife die from every conceivable angle." His voice was a husk of its normal boom.

"Why would you do that?" *The physical pain alone.*

"Her Pod crashed in front of a school. An emergency swerve to avoid plowing into a group of children. I measured each possible angle, timed each possible movement. And realized if I altered the events of that day—modified her Pod's trajectory or stopped her from leaving the house—an accident would have still occurred. Either her Pod or another would have crashed into those children. I couldn't change the events of that day knowing what it would cause."

"I'm . . . sorry." I didn't know what else to say. "I sensed a change in the time line, and I assumed it was—"

"Wasn't me." He smiled weakly and walked to his desk. "In fact, I've decided to destroy my IcePick. I'm going to advise ICE to do the same with their supply."

A deluge of relief flooded over me. He'd cooperate with my plans to get rid of the Picks. Without even a fight.

Bergin opened the secure compartment within his desk.

He frowned and felt around to the back of the drawer and clawed at the empty corners.

There was nothing there.

"Where is it?" I rushed to his side.

"I don't understand. I returned it here last night."

"You *lost* it? Who has it?" I grabbed his lapel. *"Who has it?"*

The possibilities were terrifying. One of those Red Scrubs. Leto. Someone worse. Before Bergin had a chance to answer me, though, my pocket began to shake violently and glow a burning emerald green. And suddenly my hands were clutching thin air. I was alone in the room, Bergin's possessions were back in their rightful place.

I pulled the reverter from my pocket. *Click.*

Time for the Truth.